'A beautifully paced quest, a novel that doles out its revelations slowly yet confidently. The characters are well-drawn and believable. There's more than enough here to suggest that British SF has a major new talent in its midst'

SFX

'The mutually dependent relationship between Kerin and the stranger is sensitively drawn, as is the depiction of a society kept in ignorance by a religious elite'

Guardian

'A potential star in the making'

SF Crowsnest

'[*Consorts of Heaven*] ... Takes the best of SF and blends it with a touch of fantasy'

Falcata Times

'I look forward very much to journeying once again into Fenn's universe'

Bookgeeks

Also by Jaine Fenn from Gollancz:

Principles of Angels
Consorts of Heaven

CONSORTS
OF HEAVEN

JAINE FENN

The right of Jaine Fenn to be identified as the author
of this work has been asserted by her in accordance with
the Copyright, Designs and Patents Act 1988.

First published in Great Britain in 2009 by Gollancz
An imprint of the Orion Publishing Group
Orion House, 5 Upper St Martin's Lane, London WC2H 9EA
An Hachette UK Company

This edition published in Great Britain in 2010 by Gollancz

1 3 5 7 9 10 8 6 4 2

A CIP catalogue record for this book
is available from the British Library

ISBN 978 0 575 08324 0

Typeset by Deltatype Ltd, Birkenhead, Merseyside

Printed in Great Britain by
CPI Mackays, Chatham, Kent

The Orion Publishing Group's policy is to use papers
that are natural, renewable and recyclable products and
made from wood grown in sustainable forests. The logging
and manufacturing processes are expected to conform to
the environmental regulations of the country of origin.

www.jainefenn.com
www.orionbooks.co.uk

For Emma. A good friend and an honest critic.

We get it right sometimes
We shine a light sometimes
We see the fish below the ice sometimes
Stand up and fight sometimes
We get the fright sometimes
How will we ever pay the price this time?

– 'Fish Below the Ice', Shriekback

The mind is not a vessel to be filled, but a fire to be ignited
– Plutarch

CHAPTER ONE

A storm was coming. Kerin scented it on the air, sharp yet heavy, as she walked down to the stream for the evening's water. By the time she got back to her hut, grey clouds were churning over the snow-capped mountains beyond the head of the valley. As she closed the door for the night, the first spits of rain hit the wood, growing heavier by the moment.

And there was no sign of Damaru.

Kerin tried not to worry. While the villagers valued her son because of his sky-touched nature, it made the job of caring for him all the harder. Let those who whispered that she should watch her only child more closely try to raise a boy whose wishes must be obeyed but whose mind was fixed on a world only he could see.

All too soon, he would be beyond her care for good. Until then, he would do as he pleased – even if that meant staying out late in a storm.

She stacked the fire, then filled her cooking pot with water and put it on the hearthstone to heat. A warming stew would use up meat she had dried for Damaru's journey, but she wanted to indulge him while she still could.

When she ran out of things to add to the stew, she covered the pot, then began to sort through her late husband's travelling gear. She was running her hands over his best shirt when she realised she was trying to occupy her mind to avoid the growing certainty that something bad had happened. She refolded the shirt, trying to calm her suddenly racing pulse.

Her boy was not dead. She knew that because the space in her heart that was his did not ache, not in the same way her heart had ached when Neithion had died on the drove; though her husband had been far away when he met his end, she had felt his passing. Though she was certain Damaru yet lived, he could have fallen and hurt himself; perhaps he was lying in a gully somewhere even now. She must go and look for him.

She changed out of her skirt into Neithion's old work breeches, then pulled on his travelling boots: her clogs would be worse than useless out on the moor. She put on a cloak, but did not bother with a hat – in this wind she would surely lose it. She took a stick, both for support and in case there were wilder-dogs about; any animal out scavenging on a night like this might be desperate enough to attack a person.

She wondered about enlisting help: if Damaru was in danger, the other men would put aside their feelings for her in the interests of saving the holy child. But he had stayed out late before in weather as bad as this, he knew the land around the village as well as she knew the inside of their hut, and he had senses she lacked. Right now she was going on nothing more than intuition, and given where that had got her mother, she knew better than to share unfounded worries. She would search alone.

As she ducked under the lintel, the wind cuffed her. She screwed up her eyes against the rain as she felt her way around the side of the hut; the quickest route would be up through the village, but she did not want to attract attention.

She skirted the huts, using the stick to support herself on the slippery ground, then struck out upslope. Damaru was most likely up at the mere. The constantly shifting landscape of water and vegetation fascinated him; Kerin suspected he understood that he would soon be leaving his home and was trying to soak up the essence of the place he loved most.

Water trickled down inside her cloak and seeped into her boots. She put her head down and curled over the stick until a brief lull in the weather enabled her to look up. She needed to head for a small dip between the higher peaks – an easy walk on a fine day, but in the dark and rain she would have to go carefully. Thank the

Mothers both moons were up and near full; their light combined with that from the stars to set the clouds aglow, bright enough to partially light her path.

Once, before Damaru had been born – perhaps the very night the seed of him had quickened in her – she and Neithion had climbed up here and lain together in the heather. In the breaks between their loving, they had looked up at the sky, which was clear for once. It had been a breathtaking sight, with each glance taking in more stars than could be counted by the tally-knots of every village in Creation, spread above them in patterns at once both random and filled with meaning. Neithion had pointed out the constellations the drovers used to help them navigate through the drylands. She knew most of them, but watching his finger outlined against the glowing sky with his arm protectively around her shoulders and her head nestled into the crook of his neck, she had let him explain them to her as though she knew nothing. Sometimes being right mattered less than being happy.

Tonight the beaten-down heather was a constant hazard underfoot. From the sound of it the rain had already swollen the stream to a torrent. The concentration necessary to keep on her feet and on course soon drove away both past recollections and future worries.

By the time she reached the top of the slope the rain had eased to a drizzle, though the wind still whipped and harried. There had been several previous spring squalls, coming in fast, driving hard and blowing out quickly – at least she was spared thunder and lightning this time.

Stands of bogwood grew here, their long dark leaves clacking in the wind. She spotted a pallid constellation of tiny yellow lights under one tree's aerial roots: boneweave flowers, their eerie glow visible even in the mossy darkness. She should remember this spot so she could return and harvest the tubers later in the year. Since Neithion's death she was the closest the village had to a healer. If some chose to mutter about bad blood and unseemly behaviour, and find their own cures, that was their problem.

The ground flattened out; ahead she saw the solid wall of reeds that edged the mere. Paths had been cut by villagers collecting material for roofing or matting, and she soon found an opening. She heard a faint sound on the wind – was that a night-hawk's cry, or the yelp of a dog? The rustling maze closed in on her and combined with the smell of rotting vegetation to tweak at her nerves. She began to call out, 'Damaru! Where are you?', but the wind whisked the words away and the reeds absorbed her voice. There was no reply.

At that moment the gale blew itself out, leaving a damp, eerie silence.

As the vegetation thinned she saw patches of light and dark ahead: pools of water, edged with stands of stunted reeds and the spiky balls of redthorn bushes. She slowed down, for the flat land between the pools was shifting and treacherous. According to the priests, in places such as this the land was no more than a thin skin over the formless chaos of the Abyss—

Suddenly she recalled, for the first time in years, what she had witnessed here, and what still lay, bound and weighted, beneath the silent mere.

She shuddered and drew a deep breath, trying to push the unwanted memory away. That was the past; this is now. Old nightmares mattered little when weighed against the fate of her child.

The clouds had begun to thin overhead and silvermoon showed as a bright smudge over the jagged peaks beyond the mere. She shouted Damaru's name again, listening hard for a response, but none came.

She glimpsed something over to the left, an odd-shaped patch at waist-height, bright as water under moonlight, yet subtly wrong. She started that way, testing the ground as she went, stopping to call out every few steps. Despite her caution, she soon found herself up to the ankles in stinking mud. She stopped as she spotted something else, lying by her feet. It looked like a shiny scrap of cloth. Steadying herself with her stick, she crouched down carefully to pick it up. It was indeed a piece of fabric, finer than any she had ever come across and with a shimmering sheen to it. She was amazed to find that no dirt adhered to it, and it felt merely damp to the touch. She tucked the strange fabric into her waistband and continued towards the bright patch. She saw now that it was more of the shining cloth, bigger than she had first thought, but further away, tangled up in a stand of redthorn.

Beyond the bushes she could make out a dark shape; it looked like something lying on the ground.

'Damaru!' she shouted, desperation making her voice break.

The shadow moved. 'Maman?'

Her shoulders sagged with relief. 'Damaru! Stay where you are. I am coming to you. Do you hear me, Damaru?'

He did not reply – but that was quite normal. She had his attention, and he sounded unhurt. Kerin resisted the urge to run; a false step now and the night could still end in disaster. She paused briefly as she passed the material caught in the bushes: though it looked thin, almost insubstantial, she could see no sign of any rip or tear from the thorns.

Then she looked at the prone figure, and stopped once more: she had assumed the shadow was Damaru – he could often be found lying flat on the ground at the oddest moments; it did not mean he was in trouble. Now she saw that there were two figures ahead, one stretched out, the other crouched beside it.

'Damaru?' she called. 'Look at me please, Damaru. Look towards my voice.'

The crouching figure turned. The one on the ground did not move.

What – who – had he found?

By the time Kerin was close enough to make out her son's features, Damaru had returned his attention to the body, which was, Kerin now saw, lying on its front, its head turned away. It appeared to be naked, and covered in mud. 'Damaru, are you all right?' she asked again as she came up to him. 'Are you hurt?'

'No.' He sounded perplexed that she thought he might be.

'What do you have there with you, Damaru?'

Damaru turned his head towards her and she saw his eyes glitter in the moonlight. 'Not part of the pattern,' he said, his voice a mixture of confusion and wonder: this was outside his experience.

It was outside Kerin's too. 'Let me see, please.' She crouched beside her son. The body was male, not someone from Dangwern, obviously, and if anyone had been missing from Carregogh or Penfrid she should have heard about it – unless, with the drove leaving soon, no one could be spared to carry the news. Yet he did not look like anyone she had ever seen: he was tall, and slightly built, and beneath the dirt his hair was fair and his skin pale and unblemished.

She looked at her son, who was still staring down at the body. 'Damaru? Did you find him here? This man, he was here, and you found him, is that right?'

'Aye.'

She did not bother to ask him when: Damaru's idea of time rarely matched anyone else's. Instead, she squelched around the body to get a look at the dead man's face. He had only a few days' growth of beard, and his short hair was neatly cut. She could see no sign of how he died … assuming he *was* dead. Maybe she should actually check.

She reached out to touch his cheek. It was warm.

She moved her hand to his neck, where she felt his pulse, beating faint and fast as a bird's. He might not be dead now, but if he stayed out here much longer he soon would be.

She looked at Damaru, then beyond him to the shining cloth. 'Damaru, I need you to help me,' she said firmly.

Darkness. Suffocating darkness – can't breathe – need to get free, find air. Throat closing – must get up, struggle up for air—

Yes! Alive!

But hurts so much – pain unbearable – want to go back – hide – safe in the dark.

Please, leave me alone.

Kerin had hoped, given it was the middle of the night and she lived on the very edge of the village, that they might return unseen, but the Mothers saw fit to choose another path for her.

It was the cloth that gave them away. She had retrieved it from the thorns at the cost of scratched hands, ripped clothes and soaking boots so she could use it as a sling. They rolled the unconscious man onto it, but when they tried to lift him, the sheer, soft fabric ran through their fingers. In the end they wrapped him up in it like a swaddled child and half-dragged, half-carried him back to the village. Both she and Damaru tripped several times on the treacherous slope, and each time they dropped their burden Kerin shuddered, afraid that her carelessness would end up killing the man whose life she was trying so hard to save.

But it was not to be so, thank the Mother of Mercy: when they got him into the hut and onto her bed, he actually appeared closer to consciousness: he moaned and twitched, and his eyes moved behind their closed lids. She piled the covers over him, then lit a rush and put it in the lamp over the bed. The two pieces of fabulous cloth she stuffed into an empty pot; when folded, the material was surprisingly compact. A quick examination of her patient showed the beginnings of a fever, thanks no doubt to his exposure to the elements. She must treat that.

First she and Damaru needed to eat after their exertions; she doled out the somewhat congealed stew and awakened Damaru, who had fallen asleep on top of his bedcovers. It wasn't the most appetising meal, but it was hot and filling. She finished hers quickly and cleaned the pot so she could put water on to boil.

She was sorting through her herbs when a boy's voice called from outside: 'Mistress Kerin?'

She pulled open the door to find Shim, Arthen's young bondsman. Behind him, the sky was pale grey; it was nearly dawn. She smiled and bade him good morning.

Shim peered wide-eyed into the hut and said, 'The chieftain says you are to come to the moot-hall.'

Kerin sighed. She was exhausted, and she did not want to leave the stranger untended – but Arthen demanded obedience, not reasons for disobeying him. Still, she would make him wait a little. 'Kindly tell him I will be there as soon as I have changed out of my wet clothes.'

Shim's expression said he had expected something like that. He turned and left.

Kerin sat on the low bench beside the hearth to remove her mud-spattered breeches. Instead of changing back into her everyday skirt she got down the embroidered one she had made for capel-best the autumn before Neithion died. It had become a keepsake: a reminder of her life with him; she remembered how this section had been woven while she listened to him pound herbs in the pestle, or how that piece of embroidery had been inspired by a tune he had been playing. Though she had held onto it for as long as she could, this year it would go with the drove, along with her second-best skirt and the new one she had yet to finish. She had nothing else left to trade.

Damaru, sitting on his bed and toying with the last of the stew, watched her as she put her sodden boots by the fire to dry. 'Will you watch over him?' she asked, pointing to the stranger in her bed. Damaru looked at the stranger, at her, then back at the stranger. She took that as assent.

She strapped on her clogs and clumped up the hill to the moot-hall.

The chieftain sat in his high-backed chair in front of the hearth. He was wrapped in his fur cloak. From the noises coming from the curtained alcoves around the edge of the hall she knew his household was already awake. As usual, Gwellys would eavesdrop on her son's business, and whatever was said here would be round the village by noon.

As she moved to stand in front of him Arthen said, 'Arlin's youngest has the flux again. She told my mother that she saw you and Damaru carrying something into your hut when they were coming back from the earth-closets. Did she see true?'

Kerin was exhausted, and now she was irritated. She decided to keep the existence of the rich cloth to herself. 'She did. We found a man at the mere. He is sick.'

'Who is he?'

'I do not know. He is sick, as I said, and if I do not tend him, he may not live long enough to awaken and tell us his tale.'

'Sick, or injured?'

Kerin looked around at the sound of the voice to see Fychan,

Arthen's younger son, lift the curtain and walk across the hall. This was all she needed. Arthen frowned at the intrusion, but Fychan appeared not to notice. He continued, 'Father, if he is injured, it could have been reivers, back this way. Or maybe this sais *is* a reiver.'

Kerin looked back at Arthen and said firmly, 'He has no injury. He is sick.' She could not resist adding, 'You are welcome to come and see for yourself.'

Fychan scowled, the expression pulling at his scar. Kerin suspected he would sooner put out his other eye than cross her threshold.

'No,' said Arthen, as much to curb his son, Kerin suspected, as in reply to her. 'Go. Tend your patient. Tell us what he has to say for himself when he wakes.'

Kerin nodded to Arthen and left the moot-hall.

CHAPTER TWO

Why are you doing this to me? Please, let me go – I want to go back to the darkness. I'm safe there, I can forget.

Patterns of melody catch and beguile, and the web of sound won't let go. It is something other than pain, something worth reaching for—

As she headed home across the square, Kerin heard the sound of a harp drifting up the slope. Skyfools had a natural affinity with music; Damaru had picked out a tune on his father's harp before he could walk and had often retreated into music when things confused or frustrated him. But since Neithion's death he had rarely played; when he did, it was usually slow, melancholy airs. This was different: wild music, conjuring music, cascades of notes chasing each other through the pre-dawn light. It was music fit to wake the dead.

She ran back down to the hut.

Inside, the single rush-light illuminated Damaru as he sat at the foot of her bed, his harp between his legs, his face twisted into an ecstasy of concentration. He continued to play as she stepped over his outstretched legs and bent to examine her patient.

The man's breath came hard and fast, like the panting of a dog, and his skin was burning hot. Kerin returned to the herbs she'd left strewn over the table, searching for a combination to bring down the fever and drive off the chill inside.

When the music slowed, Kerin looked up from her pestle. Damaru's expression had become pained, and he was biting his lip. She went over and knelt beside him. Damaru's lack of interest in music since his father's death had left his hands soft, and now blood was welling from the edges of his nails and smearing the harp strings.

Kerin felt tears spring to her eyes: her crazy, unearthly son, with no regard for himself. Whatever happened with this stranger would not change the fact that the drove would be leaving soon, and Damaru was now of age, and he would be leaving with it. She had begged Arthen to let her go too, just to have those last few weeks with her boy, but he had refused her.

She blinked to clear her eyes and murmured Damaru's name, repeating it over and over to get his attention. Finally he focused on her, though he kept playing. 'Damaru, stop now,' she said, but he ignored her.

When she tried again, he muttered, 'I want to keep him here.'

Kerin said gently, 'Damaru, I am making medicine to keep him here.'

Damaru shook his head, though he looked uncertain and the music faltered for a moment. Then he said, 'You only heal his body. His mind is broken too.'

Kerin was not sure what Damaru meant, so she said, 'Damaru, a mind can only grow well in a healthy body.' That had been one of Neithion's sayings – he had said it a lot when Damaru was younger, and he did everything he could to ensure his only surviving child's bodily health, hoping that one day his mind would develop as it should. That was back when they had believed him merely simple, not touched by the sky.

Hearing his father's words repeated must have got through to him, for Damaru stopped playing. Kerin lifted the harp from his lap and went back to the table as Damaru closed his eyes and rested his head against the end of the bed.

She selected herbs for fevers and chills, and counted out five of the precious berries her husband had bought on his final drove. His best friend, Huw, had passed them on to her, telling her the trader had charged a high price for them, for, he had claimed, they would cure anything from toothache to the falling fire. Huw's tone implied he thought Neithion had been duped, but with Neithion's death still a raw wound, Kerin had snapped at him for this harsh judgment. She had regretted her temper at once – Huw was a good man, one of the few who had never criticised Neithion for marrying her ...

She had not used the berries till now. No one in the village had deserved this last precious gift from her dead husband. When she crushed them they smelled sweet, more like food than medicine. While the mixture steeped, she took the remaining warm water and cleaned the man's head and chest. His skin felt sticky, even after she had got the mud off. It reminded her of Damaru after he had got at the honey-pot and smeared himself with the stuff when he was just a little lad.

She put the stranger's age at around the same as hers, perhaps a little younger. He had a handsome face, though there was an indefinable otherness about him. As she had thought, his skin was unmarked by scars or rashes, and when she examined his hands she saw no calluses, and the nails were clean and even. Where had this man come from, to have the skin of a child and the hands of an invalid?

She wondered if he too were sky-touched, and from a richer village, where he was honoured and given the best of everything. No, he was surely too old to be a skyfool: he would have gone to the Beloved by now. So maybe he was a noble from the lowlands. Neithion had told her how men down there had other men to tend their animals, grow their food, even to build their homes and bargain for their luxuries.

She found herself wanting to stroke the milky-white skin and soak up its fire. Seeing this exotic stranger in her bed was awakening feelings she had long suppressed – feelings she must continue to suppress ... She turned away and went back to the table to fetch her bowl.

When she returned, she piled blankets under his head, then dipped a clean linen square into the bowl and wrung out the cloth over his lips. The liquid dribbled down his face and onto the bedclothes. She tried again, and this time his lips parted and he swallowed a little. She repeated the exercise until the bowl was empty.

Kerin knew she was nowhere near as good as Neithion had been; she feared the stranger's illness would be beyond her meagre skill. Neithion had been so talented a healer that people had come from other villages to seek his help. He had trained her in the healing arts to indulge her, not because he had ever expected she would need to take on his role.

She returned the bowl to the table, then bent to shake her son awake. He blinked up at her. She held his hands up so he could see them. 'Your fingers are cut, Damaru. I am going to clean and bind them. It will sting a little.'

He nodded dumbly, still half-asleep, and bore her ministrations quietly. After she had finished she helped him to his bed.

She would have liked to sleep herself, but she needed to watch over her patient. She had not been able to do anything to save Neithion – she had not even been with him when he died. She composed a prayer to the Mother of Mercy, the first true prayer she had spoken for some days other than those small mutterings offered during the rituals of daily life. If the Skymothers willed it, and if it was in her power to do so, she would save this stranger.

The rush-light over the bed burned out as full daylight seeped in under the door. When she opened it, she found the night's storm had left them a fine day. She should take her loom outside to finish the final panel of her new skirt. And she was due to take her turn grinding oats this afternoon. Neither of these mattered as much as tending her patient.

She turned back inside. The man's fever was rising; she needed to get as much fluid as possible into him. She made a weaker infusion and set it to warm, then tidied away her herbs and put the last of the peat on the fire. When the drink was ready, she managed to get him to take a little more.

Once he had settled into an uneasy sleep she scraped the mud from her boots, then picked up her distaff and spun for a while, using the soft wool taken from the cattle's long belly-hair. Then she gave the stranger some more of the infusion, and drank the last of it herself. Damaru was snoring peacefully, but he would wake soon, and be thirsty. She needed more water, and fuel, and a trip to the earth-closets was in order too.

She might as well go out and get everything she needed for the rest of the day. If she could bring herself to make her apologies to Gwellys for not helping at the quern now she might just save herself a tongue-lashing later.

Free of the suffocating darkness, drawn by the memory of the music, he drifted slowly back towards consciousness.

He remembered: he had a mission, a purpose. Or he had, once. It had been taken from him. Taken, and replaced by—

Deep, dark eyes.

He recalled a violation so deep it had no name.

Silently, in the confines of his head, he screamed.

On such a fine day many of the women were washing clothes down at the stream. Kerin, having answered her most urgent need, nodded a greeting to the women at work downstream as she filled her water-jug. Arlin called back, 'Is it true I saw you carrying a naked man, and that he now sleeps in your bed?' Her remark had the others tittering.

Kerin weighed her answer carefully. Arlin was always friendly to Kerin's face, but she was also one of Gwellys's cronies. She would prefer to let her family suffer rather than seek out Kerin's skill as a healer.

More than once Kerin had responded thoughtlessly to Arlin's apparently easygoing comments, only to have her words turned against her by others. 'Your eyes did not deceive you,' replied Kerin carefully, 'though I pray he will soon be well enough to seek a more suitable place to lay his head.'

She decided to drop off the full water-jug and check on her patient before going to fetch fuel and see Gwellys. She had closed her door when she left, to discourage curious eyes; it was open now, and from inside she heard a low moan. She hurried in and saw the reason for the open door at once: Damaru had gone out. For a

14

moment she felt that guilty anger she knew so well. Why could the Mothers not have given her a normal child, one who gave as well as took, who would understand what needed to be done, and perhaps even help do it – one who would just remember to close the wretched door behind him sometimes, for Heaven's sake? But the anger blew out, as usual: with a normal boy she would never have known the wonder of loving one touched by the sky.

The stranger was shuddering, and thrashing about. His head lolled from side to side as he cried out: broken pleas for mercy or help, and once what sounded like a name, though not one she knew.

Damaru had implied that something had damaged the man's mind, which could be why he was now raving. If the damage was not physical, Arthen might send for a priest. Perhaps she should pray again, and maybe burn some incense, though she had thought to use what little she had to see Damaru safely on his way.

She leaned over the bed and started murmuring calming nonsense, as she did to Damaru when the nightmares took him. The stranger continued to toss and moan, as though pleading with unseen enemies. Damaru had said music helped, and she began to sing, though her voice was weak, another cause of shame in the village. Even so, she thought he strained to hear her. Still singing, she crossed the hut and filled a bowl from the water-jug, but when she tried to get him to drink, he turned his head. One hand flailed up to push the bowl away. Without thinking, Kerin caught the hand in hers. His fingers grasped hard. Her song faltered, but she did not pull away. When his hand fell back she kept hold of it. His touch was soft and hot, and reminded her of a child's: innocent, desperate, totally dependent on a parent. She drank the water herself and put the bowl down, keeping hold of his hand. Then she started to sing again, her eyes fixed on his face as though she could save him by will alone.

She went through every tune she knew – lullabies, hymns, story-songs, even the cheeky ditties the boys sang at star-season – and her voice grew hoarse, but if she stopped singing, she risked losing him.

Evening was approaching. The fire was down to embers. If it went out, she would have to go and ask for flame from the moot-hall.

It was dark by the time Damaru returned. She wondered whether she might persuade him to fetch some peat, knowing the thought futile even as it formed. But he could help in another way. She broke off from singing and said, 'Damaru, play. Play the harp for him again, please.'

He did not obey at once but came over and stared at the man, his expression hard to read. Kerin might have called it sympathy, had she thought her son capable of such an emotion. Then he got his harp down, sat on the floor and launched straight into a twirl-ing, urgent air.

In the dim light she saw the stranger's face change as it had when he first caught her hand. His movements became less fran-tic, his cries quieter. Kerin wished she could see him better, and, when the pressure on her hand eased for a moment, she pulled free. She stretched as she stood, then got an old basket down from the shelves and flung it onto the smouldering hearth.

She bent down to blow into the fire. For a moment she thought she had sacrificed the basket in vain. Then a flame caught. She sat back and looked over at her patient. He had raised his hand, reaching out to her.

She returned to his side and grasped his hand again. When she spared a glance for Damaru the flaring light from the fire revealed fresh stains on the harp strings. She almost told him to stop play-ing, then changed her mind. Fingers would heal; the stranger's mind might not.

She stroked the man's face. Lack of food and sleep was mak-ing her light-headed, and for a moment she thought it was her husband who was lying ill in their bed.

After a while Damaru's playing slowed, then stopped. He put the harp down and staggered over to the water-jug, cupping his hands to drink straight from it.

Her patient frowned in his delirium, then whimpered. Kerin shushed him and put a hand on his cheek. Her touch appeared to soothe him. She had planned to sleep on the floor, but after a moment's hesitation, she climbed onto the bed with him. Damaru crawled into his own bed.

Kerin lay down beside the man, stroking his head. He shifted against her until they touched, he inside the covers, she on top. She felt a strange mixture of emotions: guilt at such intimacy in her marriage bed, relief that the worst was past, and a less-than-healthy excitement.

But mainly, she felt exhausted.

CHAPTER THREE

Bad smell: acrid and harsh. Constriction. He was under a heavy, stiff covering. Weight pressed against his side. He was trapped. *Have to get free!* But—

He could hear something: a regular rasping sound. *Breathing?* Someone was breathing, very close by.

He forced his eyes open, gummy lids tearing apart. The momentary pain snapped him into full consciousness. But even with eyes open, he couldn't see. Was he blind too?

Not blind. Just in darkness. He lay somewhere dark and smelly and he couldn't move. *Oh, shit. This is bad.*

The thing pressing against him moved. He froze, his pulse thundering in his ears. The way it changed position – it was alive.

He was lying next to somebody. *This is really bad.*

He heard a 'mmmppfhh' noise beside his ear. His body felt too heavy to move but he managed to turn his head, and got a waft of foul breath. A vague shape resolved into a head. Right next to his.

He struggled harder and the rough cover slid off. His head pounded with the effort and his throat felt so dry that even breathing hurt.

The shape – *person* – twitched, gasped, then rolled away. The gasp sounded feminine. He edged backwards, flinching when his bare back came up against a cold, damp wall. The woman sat up, becoming a silhouette. She looked down at him.

'Hhhssh, sssshhh. Everything is all right.' Her voice was hoarse and oddly accented. He had no idea who she was.

18

'Wh—' he started breathlessly, disconcerted at the sound of his own voice. He tried again. 'Wh— What are you doing?'

''Tis all right,' she repeated, getting off the bed. 'Lie still.'

'Who— Who are you? Do I know you?'

'No, you do not—'

'Then what the fuck am I doing in bed with you? Where am I?'

'Please, you have been ill, you need to stay calm.'

'Ill? What do you mean?' He heard someone else moving. A shadowy shape loomed behind the woman. 'Who's that?' he squeaked.

'My son. You woke him.' She turned and spoke to the unidentifiable figure. ''Tis all right, Damaru. Go back to bed.'

'What's he doing in your bedroom? What am *I* doing in your bedroom?'

'You are confused. You should lie still, try to rest.'

'Rest? In your bed? Can we at least turn the lights on?' Maybe if he could see he could make some sense of all this.

'I— I will open the door. 'Tis nearly dawn, so that should give us some light,' the woman said. She moved off.

A scraping noise; greyish light oozed in from a rectangle beyond his feet. He started to make out his surroundings: a small circular room with a high roof and cluttered shelves around the whitewashed walls. It was completely unfamiliar. Should he know this place?

'I will get you some water,' she said, and crossed the room to a table; other than the shelves and beds it was the only furniture he could see. 'You must be thirsty.' Her voice had an emphatic lilt, pleasant, and oddly reassuring. She sounded efficient, concerned for his welfare. And she was right about him being thirsty.

She returned with a bowl and he realised that one of the nasty smells was her. Others included stale smoke, and the covers on the bed, which were a mixture of rough-woven blankets and what smelled like badly cured animal skins.

'Can you sit up?' asked the woman.

He was pressed against the wall, where he'd tried to get away from her. Now he tried to uncurl, though even small motions made his head spin. 'I'm not sure. My head hurts.'

19

She nodded. 'I think you may have banged it.'

'I thought you said I was ill?' She acted so caring, but he knew nothing about her, about how he came to be here— 'Are you lying to me? Is this some kind of trick?' His voice rose.

She put a hand out. 'No, no. There is no trick, master. I am trying to help you.'

Master? Why did she call him that? When he opened his mouth to ask, a cough caught him.

She held up the bowl, and said carefully, 'You need to drink. I will dip a cloth in this bowl, then squeeze it over your mouth.'

Given how grubby everything here looked he wasn't sure about that, but he was desperate for water. He eased himself back across the bed. She bundled the covers under his head to prop him up, then squeezed water into his mouth. Dirty it might be, but it tasted good. He finished the bowl and lay back, feeling better.

The light was brighter now; he could make out a steeply sloping ceiling above him ... no, not a ceiling: a roughly thatched roof, smoke-blackened. It was conical: he was in a round, windowless hut. Where the hut was, and how he came to be in it, he had no idea.

A male voice said peremptorily, 'Hungry!'

He started, then looked across to see a boy of about fifteen standing behind the woman, who was back at her table. He didn't recognise him either.

'I know, Damaru,' said the woman patiently, 'but I need to fetch fire to cook. You will have to wait.'

The boy gave a half-shrug, half-twitch and walked out without a word.

The woman called over, 'I am sorry, master. I cannot make food or medicine without fire. I will have to go and get some.'

Fire was something she needed to *go and get*? He understood her words, despite the odd accent, but they didn't make sense. He realised she was about to leave and said urgently, 'Wait, don't go – where am I?'

'To answer your first question,' she said, drawing herself up straighter, 'you are in the village of Dangwern.' She gave a short, barked laugh at his look of incomprehension. 'No, master, you would not know where that is. No one more than a day's walk from here does, and I know everyone who lives within a day's walk.'

'So this isn't my home.' That was good. Though he wasn't sure where he belonged, he hoped it wasn't in a filthy, stinking hovel like this one. 'How did I get here?'

'I do not know. We found you, up at the mere. Well, Damaru found you, and I found him.'

'The mere?'

'The boglands, up on the high moor. Some say it is an unholy place.'

He didn't like the sound of that. 'What did I have with me? Was I alone?'

'You were naked as a newborn.' She sounded embarrassed. Under the pungent bedclothes, he was still naked. She paused, then added, 'There was something with you, though.'

'What was with me? Where is it?' He needed clues, links to his life, anything that might explain this to him.

'I have it here.' She reached up to one of the packed shelves that covered the far wall, got down a clay pot and pulled out two pieces of silvery-white fabric, easily the brightest, cleanest items in the hut. She brought the larger one over to him.

He hugged the cloth to his chest. The fabric was soft, with a texture that seemed familiar, or at least comforting. 'You found this with me?'

'It was caught on a bush near where you lay, with a smaller piece in a pool nearby.'

'What is it?'

'I do not know.' She sounded confused at being asked. 'I have never seen cloth like this before, master.'

He wished she wouldn't call him *master*. Maybe she didn't know his name—

—*and neither did he*. His vision darkened. The fabric slipped through his fingers.

'What is it? Master, are you all right?'

He turned his head, anger and terror coursing through him. 'No, I'm fucking *not* all right! I've just woken up in a strange woman's bed, and I have no fucking idea who I am or how I got here!'

She recoiled from him and his anger evaporated. 'I'm sorry, I'm sorry – I shouldn't have shouted at you. You're only trying to help.' He started to sit up, only to fall back at the stabbing pain in his temples.

She stayed where she was and said firmly, 'You need medicine, and you need food. For that, I need fire. I will go and fetch it now. I will not be long.' Without waiting for a reply she took down something small from the shelf, stooped to pick up something else from the floor, and bustled out.

In the silence after she left he lay still, head throbbing, ashamed and afraid.

Kerin cursed herself for a fool. What did she think she was doing, bringing a stranger into her house? Did she expect him to wake up and shower her with gifts? She had already returned the only thing of value he had had with him. A cannier woman would have kept the larger piece of cloth as payment for the trouble he was putting her to. Then again, to have access to such fine material implied he was rich, perhaps a noble from a distant land. It was a shame, then, that he appeared to have no more idea of how he came to be here than she did.

There might be another explanation for his behaviour, she thought as she headed up to the moot-hall. Three summers back, Duffryn's lad had fallen from a roof he was rethatching and landed on his head; he had been a little like this, his moods changing fast as the sky before a storm, one moment afraid, then angry, then upset. The boy never really recovered, and he died the next winter.

She loaded her basket with peat from the lean-to beside the moot-hall, then walked round and went inside. The men might already be out. They were due to start bringing the cattle down from the high pastures today. If so, she would have to deal with Gwellys and put up with the inevitable tirade. Kerin wondered if this star-season Arthen might finally take a wife to replace the one who had died giving birth to Fychan, perhaps even one who would be strong enough to stand up to the chieftain's mother. She doubted it.

From the sounds coming from behind the curtains, it seemed the men were still here. Kerin smiled to herself, then walked up to the hearth, took a deep breath, and began to speak. 'In the name of the Mother of Hearth and Home I beg to take the gift of flame from—'

Gwellys burst out from behind a curtain, her face flushed. 'Vile witch-blood!' she shouted. 'How dare you show your face here?'

Arthen, following a few steps behind her, bellowed, 'Mother!'

Gwellys closed her mouth and for a moment the three of them stood there, staring at each other. Apparently Gwellys was annoyed about more than just Kerin's failure to help grind the oats yesterday.

Arthen said evenly, 'Kerin, how fares your patient?'

'He is awake, though confused.' Kerin was surprised at how firm her voice sounded. Dealing with a raving stranger put Gwellys's bitching into perspective.

Arthen said, 'What ails him?'

Kerin decided against telling Arthen that the man appeared to have lost his memory. 'A fever, from being out in the storm.'

'Just a fever?'

Gwellys was muttering, 'My eldest grandson has a fever too, and he cannot stand.'

Kerin said, 'If Sionyn is unwell perhaps I could help—'

'No!' screamed Gwellys. 'You are a curse on my family!'

Kerin looked at Arthen, who said, his own voice faltering, 'Even if I disregard my mother's wishes, there is little point in you examining my son. Prayer would be a better remedy.'

Kerin felt as though the ground had shifted beneath her. 'Wait, you think – is it the falling fire?'

'I believe so,' said Arthen.

Kerin circled her breast. 'Mothers preserve us,' she whispered. Though it had been many years since the winnowing times had last come to the village, she still remembered the smell of the pyres.

Gwellys pointed a trembling finger at Kerin. 'You have brought this upon us!'

Arthen said, 'That is not for you to say, Mother! Leave us, please.'

With a last venomous look, Gwellys turned and swept back to her alcove.

For a moment Kerin thought Arthen would send her away empty-handed. Then he gestured to the hearth and said, 'With the blessings of the Mothers, the gift of flame is mine to give, yours to take.'

She lifted her fire-pot.

In no immediate danger and feeling too drained to move, he calmed down. He looked up when the door opened, expecting to see the woman, but it was the boy. What had she called him? Damsomething—? Damaru, that was it. Trying to sound casual, he said, 'Hullo Damaru.'

The boy ignored him.

He tried again. 'Your mother tells me you're the one who found me.'

He said nothing, just reached into a jug by the door with a cupped hand.

The boy's indifference chilled him. Cold sweat prickled his skin. 'Damaru? Damaru, can you hear me?' *Am I really here?*

The boy finally looked up. He frowned and said, 'Sais.' Then he walked out of the hut again.

He was staring up at the tatty, smoke-stained thatch, trying to control his hammering heart, when the woman returned a few minutes later. She was carrying a basket of what looked like clods of earth, with a clay pot balanced on top. She nodded to him, then put down her burden and started to fuss with something on the floor in the centre of the hut.

With her return his fears eased. She might be shit-poor and smelly, but she wanted to help him. He took a long, slow breath, then asked as evenly as he could, 'What's your name?'

'I am called Kerin, master,' she said, still intent on whatever she was doing.

'Kerin, right,' he said. The name meant nothing to him. 'Damaru was here,' he added.

'Hoping for food. Well, he will have to wait till I have the fire going.'

'He called me "sais".'

'Oh.' Kerin stood, and he saw her clearly for the first time, caught in the harsh light from the open door. She wore a ragged brown shawl tied across a beige shirt, and a grey apron over a long, darker grey skirt. Her curly dark brown hair was pulled back by a strip of brown cloth. Her face was lined and filthy, though she had a delicate, slightly upturned nose, which on another woman might look vacuously pretty.

Her dark eyes met his and he remembered the eyes from his dream. Dread surfaced again for a moment. Then she looked down.

'Damaru was trying to make sense of you,' she said. 'I should have mentioned: my son is sky-touched.'

Sky-touched? Whatever that meant, it was something to be proud of, from the tone of her voice. He had nothing to lose, and she was being friendly. He had to trust her. 'Kerin, I'm confused. I still don't know why he called me sais.'

'It means outsider, stranger. Being a skyfool, he often names things literally.'

'That's – that's actually pretty accurate. You see, I can't recall my name just now. Until I remember it, I don't mind if you call me that. Or something else, if you prefer.'

She looked uncertain. 'Are you sure, master? *Sais* is not a proper name.'

'You have to call me something. Sais will do. Not master, all right?' Just until his name came back to him – which it would do, soon.

'All right,' she said carefully, then added, 'Sais.' She bent down again, and a few moments later, smoke billowed past the end of the bed, curling and twisting in the draught. His eyes watered and he smelled something rich and earthy burning.

He tried to take stock of his situation. He could name stuff around him, and the very squalor of the place was oddly reassuring: this wasn't his home, but neither was it part of the barely remembered, chaotic nightmare world that he'd awakened from. Something this mundanely grim had to be real. Yet some words and concepts – *skyfool*, *sais*, having to fetch fire – meant nothing to him. And he still had no idea who he was or how he came to be here.

Kerin interrupted his musings with a bowl of sweet-tasting medicine. Shortly after that Damaru came back. Sais – he'd call himself Sais for now, as he certainly felt like a stranger – watched the boy, searching for clues, looking for behaviour that identified him as 'sky-touched'. His mother fussed over him, muttering something about his fingers, and led him over to the table where she had some dried plants laid out. The boy endured her attention.

Afterwards she returned to the middle of the hut. Damaru followed her and sat down at her feet. The pounding in Sais's head had eased, and he lifted it to see what was going on. Damaru was sitting on a low bench, little more than a hewn log, staring intently into the fire burning in a shallow pit in the centre of the floor. Kerin crouched beside him, stirring a large earthenware pot that sat on a flat stone balanced half over the flames. She looked up and said, 'The porridge will be ready soon. I will help you sit up.'

'Porridge' turned out to be a tepid, lumpy goo, which under other circumstances would probably have tasted disgusting, but right now was the best food in the world. The woman's portion was half the size of his and Damaru's. Before she took her first spoonful she made a quick circling gesture over the food with her right forefinger. Damaru just tucked in.

After he'd eaten he felt another need, which he communicated to Kerin only after some embarrassment and misunderstanding. Kerin said he was not strong enough to stand and produced a shallow bowl. He felt his face redden. It continued to burn while she helped him use the bowl to relieve himself. She worked with impersonal efficiency. Despite her care, piss splashed onto his leg, but there was nothing he could do about that – nothing he could do about any of this, except try not to panic while he waited for his strength to return and his memory to come back to him.

Though the awkward intimacy of the situation was unpleasant, it dispelled any remaining distrust in Kerin. Any woman willing to help a man go to the toilet was unlikely to mean him harm.

After that he wanted to sleep. For a while he fought the urge, scared of returning to his nightmares. In the end, his body decided for him. He closed his eyes.

CHAPTER FOUR

Even asleep, the stranger's presence filled the hut – no, not 'the stranger', Sais. An odd choice of name, but she would respect it.

She found herself reacting to his needs as she did with Damaru, then catching herself when she remembered that this was not her sky-touched child but an adult stranger.

Though Sais had been confused and afraid when he had awakened, he obviously did not lack sense. He would be relying on her to help him get back the knowledge he had lost. Conversations with Damaru were often a fight to get meaning across, and everyone else spoke to her with the knowledge of her heritage behind their words. This man, though, knew only that she was happy to help him. She looked forward to answering his questions, and getting to know him better.

He woke from dark dreams of pursuit and pain, sweating into the rank covers. Fragments of half-remembered horrors receded when he blinked open his eyes.

For a moment he thought he wasn't in Kerin's hut any more: the place looked different. Then he saw that he was still in her bed, only now it was night. He expelled a relieved breath.

The lamps hanging from the roof-beams gave more light than the open door had. Other items hung from the beams too: bunches of leaves, cloth-wrapped bundles, skin pouches and woven bags. He saw several larger objects around the whitewashed walls, including a wooden frame with a triangle of dark cloth stretched over it. Stones hung from the bottom of the cloth.

Damaru sat on the floor, playing with carved wooden figures, lining them up and then moving them around like game pieces. It seemed an odd pastime for a boy in his mid-teens.

Kerin stood by the table, dangling a wooden object from a length of dark thread, teasing the thread through her fingers with firm, even strokes. She looked up and saw him watching her. 'How do you feel?' she asked.

'Much better, thanks.' He added, 'I'm sorry if I scared you when I first woke up.'

She blinked. 'Oh no, you did not frighten me. There is no need to apologise.' She wound the thread around her bit of wood, then put it on a shelf. 'I will make food.'

While she worked, he asked, 'Are you the village doctor?' That was the word that came to mind when he thought of being cared for in this way, though the concept didn't quite fit the primitive surroundings.

She gave him a puzzled look. 'I am sorry, Sais; I do not know that word.'

That made a change: he knew a word she didn't. 'All right, perhaps ... a healer?'

She looked embarrassed, then defiant. 'My husband, Neithion, was the healer. He taught me what he could.'

'Your husband?' He hadn't considered who, or where, Damaru's father was.

She drew a sharp breath and said, 'He died two years ago.' Then she went back to her preparations.

Sais shut up; he didn't want to accidentally offend or embarrass her.

Dinner was a meaty stew, rich-tasting, if rather chewy. After they'd eaten, Kerin whispered to Damaru and the boy got down a triangular bundle from a peg and unwrapped it to reveal a stringed instrument. He sat down on the floor and began to play. As the melody trickled out from the strings Sais found he could name the instrument: a *harp*. That was good: he could get back lost information when something triggered the memory. There was hope.

He listened while the boy played, soothed by the music, until Kerin came over and told her son to stop.

She smiled at Sais. 'I thought you would enjoy that, but his fingers are too tender to play for long.'

'I did enjoy it, thank you.' A fleeting thought chased through his consciousness and he pounced on it. 'Did Damaru play for me while I was out of it? I remember music.'

'Aye, he did.' She paused, then added, 'He said it would help.'

'I reckon he was right.' Perhaps skyfools weren't so foolish after all. 'Kerin, you're a healer: what do you think is wrong with me? You said something about a bang on the head. Is that what happened? Have I banged my head and forgotten stuff for the moment?'

She spread her hands. 'I cannot say. I found no injury, though these things do not always show themselves.'

'Was there … anything else? You said something about sickness, didn't you?'

She looked away for a moment, then said, 'You had a fever, from being outside in the rain. You were delirious. You were struggling, crying out.'

'What sort of things was I saying?'

'I think – you seemed to think you were being attacked, or perhaps imprisoned. I could not make much sense of your words, though you did call out what sounded like a name.'

'A name? What name?'

'It sounded like … Nu – Nual? Something like that.'

Nual? The name meant nothing to him; it had no more associations than 'sais' or 'skyfool' did. Why would he say a name in his delirium that meant nothing to him now?

'Sais,' said Kerin into his silence, 'you should rest.'

'You're probably right,' he agreed. Just sitting up to eat the meal had exhausted him all over again.

She blew out the lamps and settled at the foot of the bed.

He tried to relax, thinking of nothing. He listened to the wind in the thatch, the low crackle of the fire and Damaru's snuffling snores from the bed further round the wall. Eventually, he slept.

Kerin woke early, feeling stiff and cold. She got up, stretched until her joints popped, then went to stoke the fire. Her gaze kept returning to the man asleep in her bed.

Since Neithion's death, she had lived for Damaru. When the drove took her son, it would also take all hope and meaning for her. Even if her son was found worthy of Heaven, as she prayed he would be, she would not see him again. Her life would effectively be over.

But now the Mothers had sent this stranger to her. He was both a wonder and a responsibility, and the thought of him lightened her heart and sparked her imagination. As she threw oats into the pot for the morning meal, she entertained a dream in which, once he recovered his memory, he would ask her to come with him and they would leave the village together. They would rediscover his lost fortune and live happily in a big lowland home with many rooms and rich furnishings, and she would never have to cook porridge again.

Aye, and the cattle would grow wings and fly themselves to market.

Wonder he may be, but he was a mystery too. After his initial anger and frustration, his politeness and gratitude were disconcerting. How odd that a stranger – a *man* – should treat her better than her own people did.

'Good morning, Kerin.'

She jumped, and turned to see him watching her. 'I— You sound better this morning,' she said.

'I feel it. I'd like to try and get up today.'

'As you wish. But I must go to capel after we have eaten. I will find you some clothes when I get back.'

'Whatever you say.' He sounded uncertain.

Of course, he had no idea what day it was! 'I am so sorry, you would not know! Tis Sul today.'

'Sul?'

'Aye. The sevenday. The sabbath. So I must go to capel. You can come too, but I think you would do better to rest for now.'

'Right.'

He still sounded unsure. And he did not bless his food. Kerin wondered suddenly whether his injury had caused him to lose his knowledge of the Skymothers. It alarmed her that he should have such a vital part of life taken from him.

31

Though she usually washed, and changed her skirt, for capel, with a stranger in the hut she contented herself with putting on a clean shawl, dragging a comb through her hair and changing her plain headband for an embroidered one.

She went out into a bright and pleasant day. Damaru followed, heading off into the hills as usual.

A full day without rain had put a crust on the mud. Kerin smiled at the thought that the Mothers' tears were nearly spent, and soon the fertile fall of stars would rain their invisible bounty on the land, and all Creation would be warmed and coaxed into new life by the strengthening sun.

As she made her way up to the square, Shim came down through the huts to meet her. He looked uncomfortable.

'Good day to you,' said Kerin.

Shim bobbed his head. 'Mistress, Arthen says you are not to come to capel.'

'Why not?'

'Three more families have been touched by the sickness and people mutter that you and this stranger from the mere have brought the winnowing times upon us.' Into her stunned silence Shim continued, 'He says you and the sais are declared am-annwn.'

'Abyss-touched? No, he cannot do this! What am I saying? *He* did not do this, did he? Tis that bitch Gwellys, spreading her poison.' Shim looked distressed, and Kerin added, 'All right, Shim. Tis not your fault. Tell our chieftain that my patient and I will obey his command.' She stalked off.

Though she might despise her fellow villagers' close-minded views, that did not mean they were wrong. She had no doubt of the stranger's innocence in this matter – and of course it had been Damaru, the sky-touched one, who had found him. But what of her? What if it had been her impiety, her doubt, her selfishness, that had brought this curse upon them all?

She must not let fear cloud her judgment. Arthen was just being cautious. If she kept to the proscriptions of being ritually unclean – not touching or talking to anyone outside her own hearth, taking her water from the lower stream, not entering the capel – he would have no cause to take this any further. People would feel comforted that she was inconvenienced, and life would continue.

And if he insisted on excluding her from the weekly service, well then, she would commune with the Skymothers alone.

She walked to the side of the village that looked down the valley. She had sat on the dyke here as a child, dreaming of what might lie beyond the far hills, back before she realised that such dreams only made her yearn for what could never be. She found a relatively dry patch and knelt down. She traced the circle of the world on her breast, then opened her arms and raised her face to the sky. Faint chanting came from the capel and she joined in:

'Look over us, o owners of our souls, creators of our bodies, guardians of our minds.

'We give thanks to you for bringing us out of the chaos below into the bounty of your Creation.

'And for the future promise of everlasting joy above once we are purged of our sins.

'We vow to keep your wishes in our hearts, and to sing your praises at all times.

'We ask for your guidance and blessing on those still bound to the flesh and on those gone before, and for your protection from the forces of evil that wait below us.'

After speaking the familiar words, she offered up prayers to each of the Skymothers. She asked Turiach, the Mother of Mercy, that the coming plague should not take too many from the village, and that those who remained would be purified by the fire from Heaven. To speak thus of the falling fire made it suddenly, frighteningly, real, and she faltered. Why must it be this way? Why must parents be left sorrowing and children parentless? The promise of a possible reward later was surely not enough to justify the suffering. She opened her eyes, ashamed of the impious notion, surely a temptation straight from the Cursed One.

She sat, appalled at herself, unable to pray, until the damp seeped through her skirt and soaked her knees. Then she went back to the hut.

CHAPTER FIVE

Whatever else he did today, Sais was determined to go outside; hopefully that should trigger new memories and associations. He started by testing out his body, wriggling his toes under the covers, lifting his arms, bending his legs. Everything appeared to work. He sat up, bundling the blankets around himself to protect his bare back from the wall.

Kerin returned sooner than he expected, looking unhappy. Seeing him sitting up she said, 'You must be cold! I will find some clothes.' She produced a patched off-white shirt, baggy brown leggings and thick woollen socks from a basket. When he asked if he could get cleaned up before he dressed she looked flustered, until he assured her he was strong enough to manage the task by himself. She heated some water and found him a relatively clean cloth. Then she lifted the wooden frame he'd seen earlier and carried it outside, saying he should call if he needed anything.

He managed to get some of the dirt off, though even after he'd scrubbed every part he could reach, his skin still felt vile. He dressed lying on the bed. The clothes were softer than they looked, though the leggings were too short. He considered trying to get up by himself, then decided to ask for Kerin's help. The bed was high and rickety, and he still felt weak.

He called to her and she came back into the hut and helped him stand. This was the first time he had touched her, and her downcast eyes and hesitant manner implied such contact wasn't normal. She didn't smell as bad as he remembered; either that, or he was getting used to the general level of filth around here.

Kerin helped him to sit down by the fire, and brought over a cover from the bed to tuck round his legs. Now he was out of bed he didn't feel quite so eager to look outside. Kerin's hut might be primitive and dirty, but it was also familiar, and safe.

Kerin said, 'I will start on the food,' and began working at her table.

Aware that he posed more of an obstacle now he was out of bed, Sais asked, 'Am I all right here? I mean, is there anything I can do to help?'

'Help?' She sounded surprised. 'No, no, you stay there.'

Sais tried Damaru's pastime, watching the fire. What he knew of the world suggested there was something odd about burning lumps of earth, though his mind failed to provide any alternative. Still, he found himself content to watch the glowing caverns of red heat collapse and reform in plumes of sparks.

Kerin mixed more oatmeal into a beige paste, then made patties which she spread out on the flat stone set over one side of the fire. A few minutes later the nicest smell he'd yet experienced began to fill the air.

When he commented on this, Kerin said, 'Aye, tis oatcakes. For Sul.' From her tone this was something else she expected him to know.

Damaru returned in time for the food. The cakes didn't taste as good as they smelled; they were burnt on the bottom and barely cooked on top. However, Kerin served them with rich golden honey. Damaru stayed long enough to eat, then left, licking his fingers.

Strengthened by the meal, Sais asked if they could go out.

Kerin hesitated, then said, 'We can, but we should stay near the hut.'

'Why? What's wrong?'

She put a hand out to calm him. 'Please, there is no cause for worry. Tis just … some people do not welcome your coming to our village.'

If Kerin's lifestyle was typical, then of course they wouldn't; they probably didn't have resources to spare for visitors. And no one else seemed to be helping her care for him.

Kerin found him some carved wooden shoes she called clogs, and made him drape a blanket round his shoulders before she allowed him to leave the hut. The outside world was both a relief and a disappointment: a relief because he could recognise things – mountains, huts, muddy ground – and a disappointment because nothing he saw held any particular significance for him.

Kerin led him to a building whose function was obvious by the smell. On the way there he had a clog sucked off by the mud; by the time they returned he was splattered in mud to the knees – at least, he *hoped* it was only mud ...

Back at the hut, Kerin insisted on dragging the bench outside for him. The sun was warm, and Sais was happy to sit at her feet while she worked at her frame. As with the instrument the night before, after a while the name came to him. A *loom*. She worked the threads expertly, the quick tap-tap-tap of the stone weights overlaying the fainter noises of running water and the high whistle of the wind.

'What are you making?' he asked after a bit.

'A skirt, to go with the drove.'

'The drove?'

'The men drive the yearling cattle to market every year, and they also take crafts, like our fabrics. They trade for new stock and for items we do not have, such as salt and metal.'

'Where is this market?'

'Oh, many weeks' walk away.' And, from her tone, somewhere she'd never been.

'Are there any villages nearer than that?'

'Aye, in the valleys to either side of this one. Penfrid and Carregogh. They are smaller than Dangwern, though.'

Though her knowledge of the world beyond her village was limited, she was happy – eager, even – to share what she did know. He doubted she'd met anyone before who didn't already know all this. He listened politely, hoping she didn't expect him to remember all these names, relationships, histories and anecdotes. As the afternoon wore on, he got the impression she was uneasy, and was trying to cover it up with chatter.

When the sun began to set behind the mountains, she took the loom back inside. He carried the bench; he felt well enough, and he wanted to help, even if gratitude disconcerted her. Kerin went to fetch water and fuel again, leaving Sais sitting by the fire. Damaru was still out.

When Kerin returned she began to prepare the evening meal. She was just putting the pot on the fire when the door flew open. Sais looked up, expecting Damaru.

Instead, a youth holding a bronze-tipped spear ducked under the lintel. His hairy face and heavily muscled body filled the doorway, instantly transforming the hut from a sanctuary into a trap. An older man crowded in close behind him.

Sais looked at Kerin. From her expression she was as shocked as he was at the intrusion. He looked back at the men. They were ignoring him, their eyes fixed on a point over Kerin's head; they held themselves poised, ready for trouble.

The older man spoke. 'By command of our chieftain, you are both to come with us to the moot-hall.'

Before he or Kerin had a chance to respond the youth barked, 'Now!'

Sais felt his fragile grasp on the situation begin to unravel – *Need to run, get away!* – and with a wordless cry he launched himself at the man in front.

The youth recoiled, bumping against his companion. Sais's foot caught on something; he stumbled forward. In the cramped hut he fell into the youth, who gave a yelp of surprise. Even as Sais caught himself, he saw the boy recover and start to bring his spear round. The crazy fire that had propelled him forward cooled instantly into terror.

The spear caught on the thatch. The boy cursed.

Sais felt Kerin grab his arm. He let her drag him back, out of range of the men's weapons.

Kerin held out a hand to the men, addressing the older one. 'Master, please. We will come!'

Sais clung to her arm. She was real, she wasn't his enemy. She was his rock.

The youth looked at the older man and said, 'He attacked me!'

His companion said, 'Aye, he did. But he is quiet enough now.'

Who were these people? Did they even really exist? He couldn't be sure of anything any more. He realised he was swearing under his breath when Kerin shushed him gently. She spoke to the older man. 'You startled him. We will come, as commanded. But please allow us a moment.'

When the youth started to object, his companion spoke over him. 'We will wait outside. Do not be long.'

As they left, Kerin turned to Sais, her face full of concern. He tried to focus on her, to get control of himself again. She reached up and took hold of his shoulders. He looked down at her and forced himself to speak as though everything were all right, and the nightmare wasn't about to engulf him again.

'Those men – what do they want?'

'T'will be all right, do not fear. We just have to go see the chieftain.'

'The chieftain? Why?'

'I should perhaps have said, but I did not want to worry you—'

'Worry me?' Never mind worried, he felt as though everything he had managed to build up so far could be swept away at any moment. 'Should I be worried?'

She smiled, no doubt trying to reassure him. 'No, no. All will be well. I will not let anything happen to you. But we must obey Arthen's command.'

Of course, she was right. This was her village, her people. She knew best. He just needed to keep calm and trust her. She'd keep him safe.

She kept hold of his hand and led him to the door, pausing for a moment to grab a small pot from a shelf with her free hand, bundling it into her apron.

Once outside, the fear flared up again. He wasn't ready to face strangers. He needed more time to recover, to remember how the world worked. Even the night sky was wrong: there was full cloud cover, so surely it shouldn't be that bright?

The youth led the way, with the older man bringing up the

rear. They started to walk up into the heart of the village. The ground didn't swallow him up, though the mud sucked at his feet and the night air made him shiver. As he trudged up the slope, these ordinary discomforts began to reassure him. What he was experiencing might be unpleasant and unfamiliar, but it was real, and constant. After a little way he whispered to Kerin, 'I don't know what came over me just now. I – I was scared, and I felt trapped. I had to try and get out of there.'

'No harm has been done.'

'Why does the chieftain want to see us anyway?'

'Arthen wants us to defend ourselves before the council.'

That didn't sound good. 'Defend ourselves? Why?'

'They think your presence may have caused a return of the winnowing times.'

'The *what*?'

'It is the time when the falling fire rages. The disease comes as the Mothers will it.' They had reached a relatively open area, flanked by two big huts, one long and low, the other taller. Firelight spilled from the high-peaked porch of the taller hut.

'What's that got to do with me – with us?'

'Nothing.' She paused. 'But not everyone thinks that.'

He took a deep breath. 'Kerin, did you know something like this might happen if you helped me?'

'Aye,' she said bitterly.

'Then why didn't you just leave me where you found me?'

'Because you would have died.'

As they crossed the threshold of the big hut he murmured, 'Whatever happens, I just want to say … thank you.'

Kerin gave his hand a last squeeze, then let go.

CHAPTER SIX

Arthen sat in his usual chair before the hearth, his face in shadow. All ten of the stools ranged to either side of him were occupied. Kerin was dismayed, though unsurprised, to see the position at the chieftain's right occupied by Fychan, taking the place of his sick brother. Sending his crony Adris with Gwilym, the village's bravest warrior, to fetch them showed that Arthen's younger son was already making his voice heard amongst the men.

After Adris led them to stand before the half-circle of councillors he scurried across and whispered in Fychan's ear, until a look from Arthen sent him back to wait with the men who watched from outside the circle. The other council members, none of them quite looking at her and Sais, wore expressions ranging from unease to open hostility. Gwilym remained behind them, his spear at the ready.

Arthen stood with a cracking of joints and drew out his skymetal disc, holding it flat in his palm for all to see. 'We are convened,' he said gravely. 'What is decided here tonight is law.' He turned to Kerin. 'Kerin, I release you from am-annwn while you stand before this council. Your companion remains bound by its strictures.'

She had expected that: for all the council knew Sais was a creature of the Abyss, a servant of the Cursed One. She bobbed her head to acknowledge Arthen's ruling. Sais looked terrified, though he stood straight and tall.

Arthen continued, 'Kerin: the charge is brought that you have drawn a fell influence into this village, leading to a return of the winnowing times.' Several councillors nodded, as though Arthen speaking their fears made them valid. He sat down again, looked directly at Kerin and said, 'What say you to this, woman?'

For a moment, Kerin's voice deserted her. Years of shame and distrust had finally come to a head: they had found an excuse to call her to account. But this was not just about her. Knowing Sais's life also hung in the balance freed her tongue, and all at once a response sprang to her lips. 'I believe, masters, that the Traditions speak of the realm below as a place of chaos and horror, where damned spirits are trapped in a pit of turmoil and degradation, and the Cursed One and its servants impotently rage against the light and order above.'

Men shifted in their seats, unsure what to make of what sounded more like a bard's tale than the defence of an accused man. With thoughts of Kerin's mother no doubt at the front of their minds, her words would cut deep. Before she lost her nerve she continued, 'The man who stands before you is no unquiet spirit denied the grace of the Mothers, nor is he a servant of Melltith. Masters, he is a man of flesh and blood! Any of you who doubt this should touch him – or else ask Adris, who knows him to be a normal man.'

Arthen gestured. 'Adris? Stand forward and tell us what you have witnessed.'

The lad reluctantly walked into the circle, avoiding both Kerin and Sais. 'He attacked me!' he said, pointing at Sais's feet, which rather ruined the impact of his accusation. 'When we told him he was to come before you he turned on me!'

'Attacked you how?' asked Arthen.

'He tried to strangle me.'

Kerin looked at the boy sharply. Constrained by the rules of council, she could not speak up to correct him.

Arthen said, 'And did Gwilym see this attack as well?'

'I did,' said Gwilym from behind them.

'Does Adris speak true?'

'I would not have put it quite like that. The stranger did not strangle Adris so much as fall against him.'

Someone laughed. Fychan looked annoyed and raised his hand.

When his father nodded permission to speak he said, 'But he still attacked you, did he not?'

'Aye, he did!'

'So he means us ill!' said Fychan.

This got heads nodding, and several hands went up.

The first councillor Arthen gave leave to speak, Bodfan, was always quick to pass all blame or responsibility on to unseen forces. 'Our course is obvious,' he said. 'This creature must be cast out – or better yet, put to death.'

Beside her, Sais gasped.

Arthen pointed to a second speaker. Cadmael's status as a bard gave him some leeway and his views sometimes went against the common wisdom. 'I know nothing of this individual's intent, but I wonder about the nature of his attack. Surely a creature of the Abyss would befuddle Adris's sight, or fill his soul with despair.'

Arthen said, 'An interesting point.' Then, seeing Bodfan still eager to have his say, he indicated he could speak again.

'Even if he is not unholy, he has brought the falling fire! Better rid ourselves of him and not take the risk.'

'Wait.' Sais was listening in horrified disbelief, his arms clamped over his chest, as if to ward off a blow. 'Please – you can't mean that. I don't even know what the falling fire is!'

Aghast faces turned to him. Sais could not speak up like this! He was doubly bound to silence, by am-annwn and by the rules of council. But of course he did not know that. Kerin put a hand out to him and whispered, 'You cannot—'

He shook her off. 'Listen, please! You have to understand, I don't mean you any harm. I don't even know how I came to be here!'

His words were drowned out as chaos erupted. Bodfan, pointing at Sais, though still without looking directly at him, started to shout, 'Am-annwn! Am-annwn!' Fychan was haranguing Arthen, and several others, both councillors and observers, had turned to their neighbours in shock and dismay. Many made gestures to ward off ill luck. Old Lorar got up, knocking his stool over, and began to back off unsteadily.

Sais turned to flee, but found his way blocked by Gwilym and his spear.

'*I will have silence!*' Arthen rarely raised his voice, but when he did, people listened. He backed up his words by holding up his skymetal disc.

The hubbub fell away at once, and Arthen addressed Sais directly. 'Stranger, you are talking yourself into your own death. If you have any sense you will remain silent.'

Sais gave a tiny, sharp nod, and swallowed convulsively.

Arthen sighed and looked at his council. 'If this man were a demon of the Abyss or some unquiet spirit sent to beguile us, I put it to you that he would use cannier tricks than fighting like an inexperienced boy and then feigning terror. I believe he is merely a mortal man.'

Howen, always a stickler for detail, raised a hand cautiously. When Arthen nodded permission, he said, 'Yet was he not found at the mere, the place where the horrors of the Abyss come closest to the Skymothers' Creation?'

More agreement, though muted; the men knew they had already made fools of themselves.

Kerin held up a hand and Arthen gave her leave to speak. Though fear still thrummed through her, it brought with it a strange exhilaration, and her voice did not quaver. 'It is true he was found at the mere. But I did not find him. Damaru did.' From the expressions on the faces of some of the men, that news made them reconsider. For the benefit of the slower-witted councillors and watchers she added, 'I humbly suggest that it would be strange indeed if one blessed by the sky were to have dealings with a creature of the Abyss.'

Though most of the councillors obviously agreed, Bodfan still sought leave to speak. 'Flesh and blood the stranger may be, but he attacked one of our own.'

'I suspect,' said Arthen, 'that he acted in fear.'

'Yet it cannot be denied that within a day of his arrival, the falling fire was among us. Can that be mere chance?' Bodfan looked around the circle for support.

Arthen said, 'If I am not mistaken, the return of the winnowing times should not be so great a surprise.' He turned to the council's oldest member. 'Lorar, how many years is it since the falling fire was last amongst us?'

Lorar was still settling himself back on his stool and the question had to be repeated before he responded. 'Oh, tis true,' he rasped, 'we are due the judgment of Heaven.'

Fychan raised his hand. 'Yet as Bodfan says, to have this man arrive the day before my brother is struck down surely cannot be chance!'

'I do not think any of us can presume to know the will of Heaven,' said Arthen.

This comment got several nods, though other hands were going up. Kerin raised hers. Somewhat to her surprise Arthen turned to her first. 'Did you wish to add something, Kerin?'

'Masters,' she said, 'I believe the Traditions say that the winnowing times come to the whole land at once. Could this one man truly be the cause of the falling fire appearing everywhere throughout Creation? Is it not more likely that his appearance is a matter of chance?'

Kerin was pleased to see that this satisfied some of the dissenters.

Fychan raised his hand again. 'Even if this is so, might this man not be a reiver, and therefore an enemy?'

'It is possible,' conceded Arthen, 'though I would have thought a reiver unlikely to throw himself on our mercy as this stranger has.'

Howen, never known for his generosity, said, 'Even if he is not a criminal or outcast, this is no time to entertain guests! We do not want strangers here. We should do as Bodfan suggested and send him back up into the mountains.'

Cadmael spoke up. 'That would be as good as a death sentence, even more so in the winnowing times.'

'If that is what the Mothers will,' said Howen piously.

Sais stood still as a tree, his face stricken. Kerin got the impression that any move, any gesture, would lead to total collapse. Though he might not be a creature of evil, nor the cause of their afflictions, he was still a threat to the usual order, and they wanted him gone. They would not let reason or compassion get in the way. And in the end, Arthen would do what was best for the village.

The silence stretched. Finally Arthen said, 'I do not wish to have this man's death on my conscience.' He looked round the council. 'And neither should you.'

Kerin began to let go a slow, relieved breath.

Arthen turned to Sais. 'Stranger, you have leave to speak. Tell us how you came to be here.'

The breath caught in Kerin's throat.

She wondered if Sais had not heard the question. Then he said, in a small, uncertain voice, 'I don't know. Honestly, I can't remember anything before I woke up in Kerin's hut. I don't even know my name. I'm sorry.'

People looked surprised and confused. He spoke with an accent none had heard before, establishing him as a man from afar: they had anticipated a tale of interest, not a denial of knowledge.

Fychan had his hand up again. 'Why should we believe this? Is this memory loss not a convenience that one of ill intent might affect?' he asked.

Arthen frowned, perhaps tiring of his son's troublemaking. When no one else spoke up, Kerin raised her hand. Arthen nodded to her, and she said, 'Masters, I believe I know who he is.'

Out of the corner of her eye Kerin saw Sais's head whip round. She kept her gaze on Arthen. 'Not his name. But I believe he is a noble from the lowlands.'

'Why do you say that when your knowledge of such places comes only from others?' asked Arthen mildly.

'My husband told me that the rich men in the lowlands live very different lives to us, and many do not have beards. My guest has had a life with little hard work, he has no beard and his ways are strange to us. And then—' she fumbled in her apron for the pot she had taken from her hut, and stuck her hand inside it '—then there is this!'

She had intended to produce the fabric with a flourish, but

ended up dropping the pot. The appearance of the shining cloth still had the desired effect.

Into the rapt silence Kerin said, 'I found this with him. A man who can afford such cloth will have been missed. His people would be grateful for his return.'

She passed the cloth to Arthen. He felt the weave, then gave it into Fychan's eager hands. The etiquette of the meeting temporarily forgotten, Fychan said, 'Was there more of this stuff?'

Kerin felt a weight lift from her shoulders. Greed would overrule suspicion. She kept her voice uncertain. 'I found a smaller piece as well, so there may well be more. I have been too busy tending my patient to look.'

When it had gone around everyone, Arthen nodded to show that the fabric should be returned to Kerin. Then he said, 'We can search the mere later. This is proof he is not from the uplands. The obvious solution would be for him to travel to the lowlands with the drove.'

No one spoke up against the suggestion. Kerin pressed her lips together, fighting the urge to laugh out loud.

Arthen added, 'Assuming he is fit to travel. Kerin?'

Her head felt light as thistledown. Possible disaster had become salvation: the drove would return Sais to his home. And it had been due, in part, to her! It suddenly struck Kerin that if she kept her wits about her, here was also her one chance to escape a life of unspoken secrets, small unkindnesses and constant drudgery.

'He is recovering from a fever caught at the mere, master,' she said to Arthen, 'and his missing knowledge still causes him problems. I would say that though he can travel, it would go easier for him, and for the drovers, if he had someone to care for him.' She paused, a tiny shiver going through her at her own temerity, then added, 'Therefore I suggest that I be allowed to accompany the drove.'

'What?' said Lorar.

Howen muttered, 'A woman on the drove? Ridiculous!'

Though unease rippled through the council, Arthen was still looking at her, indicating she retained the right to speak. She continued in a rush, 'As well as caring for my patient, I would tend to my son's needs. Damaru carries our hopes with him on his journey; I am sure that you would not wish his chance of success to be hurt by having suffered unduly from the rigours of the road. For myself, I would not be a burden on the men, nor would I ask that any concession be made for my sex.'

Several men had their hands up, and most had expressions of indignation and disbelief on their faces.

Arthen ignored the raised hands and addressed Cadmael. 'What does your knowledge of the Traditions tell you? As I recall, a woman may travel if there is a good enough reason.'

'Aye,' said Cadmael, 'that is my recollection too.'

Kerin had given him a reason, and she suspected that, despite refusing her initial request to accompany Damaru, he would prefer her gone. It would be easier to face the winnowing times without her around. But was the reason good enough to convince his council? In the end, they were as easily led as their own herds.

Bodfan's attempts to gain the floor were almost comical. 'Surely,' he said when Arthen gave him leave to speak, 'the last thing we should do in these troubled times is risk the displeasure of the Mothers? A woman *asking* to go on the drove is hardly a good reason.'

Fychan put his hand up, and Kerin's heart sank. 'I agree that a woman's word should not hold weight in council,' he said. 'But in this case her reasons have some merit. It is a woman's place to care, and the drove will now carry two who require that care.'

Kerin's eyes widened in surprise at Fychan's unexpected support. But he was in a minority. Lorar was shaking his head and muttering loudly, Bodfan looked like he had more to say against her, and none appeared to be willing to speak up for her.

Though Arthen had now lent back so his face was in shadow, she knew he was watching her. Her mind raced, trying to find another argument the men might listen to. He had opened the way, but in the end he would not directly oppose the will of the majority.

Next to her Sais swayed on his feet, his lips pressed into a thin line.

When the mood of the hall changed, at first Kerin could not see the reason. Men became still and attention focused behind her. She turned.

Damaru was wandering towards her, his expression unhappy. He must have come home to find the hut empty and wondered at the lack of his mother – and his dinner. She reached out to him. He let her hold him and rested his head on her shoulder with a sigh.

Arthen stood. 'I think,' he said, relief evident in his tone, 'that the Skymothers have just indicated the course they wish us to take.' He put his palm out to show the skymetal disc. 'All voices have been heard, and a decision reached: Kerin and the stranger are no longer considered cursed. And they will travel with the drove – both of them.'

CHAPTER SEVEN

Walking back down the slope to Kerin's hut, the village council began to assume an air of unreality, as though the men were manifestations of his fears, from the mouthy boy with the scarf round his head to the old fart whose opinion was probably only valid because he'd been too stubborn to keel over yet. The danger they'd posed already seemed like no more than another nightmare. But it had been real, and Sais had acted stupidly. As they ducked into the hut he said, 'Kerin, I'm sorry.'

'What for?'

'For making an idiot of myself like that.'

'Fear makes fools of all of us. All that matters is that it turned out for the best.'

Damaru sat down by the fire. Sais sat on the other end of the bench, facing Kerin. As she got to work on the evening meal, he asked, 'This falling fire that the council are worried about, does it happen every year?' He'd have expected to remember something as regular as that.

She shot him that perplexed expression he'd come to associate with answers that were obvious to her. 'The winnowing times return every generation.'

'And it just turns up out of the blue?' *Like me*, he didn't say.

'Aye, in the weeks before star-season. So its appearance now should not be such a surprise.'

Whenever *star-season* was – soon, presumably. 'How serious is it?' he asked.

'Every family will be touched by it, and most who fall will not recover. Those who do will be left barren,' she said grimly.

Pretty serious then. 'How do the winnowing times end?'

'With the red rain.' At his quizzical look she continued, 'The falling fire is no ordinary ailment. It comes when the weight of our sin has tainted us, and we must be cleansed. It cannot be cured or treated, only endured. But soon after the festival of Sul Esgyniad the rains are stained with red. Tis the blood of Consorts, shed willingly to heal and renew Creation, just as the brighter rain of star-season is their' – she coloured, and completed her sentence – 'just as the rain of stars brings fertility. It is all part of the Skymothers' plan for their children.'

He'd have to take her word for that, given how little what she was saying meant to him. But the fact they considered this disease a heaven-sent curse did explain why the council were willing to send away their only healer. Then again, they obviously didn't think much of Kerin. He was just glad he was going with her. 'When do we leave?'

'On the drove? In four days.' Her brow furrowed. 'There is much to do now we are all going.'

'And did I hear right? Damaru's going too?' Sais found himself happy to talk about Damaru as though the boy wasn't there. Perhaps, in some indefinable way, he wasn't.

'Aye, he goes to stand before the Cariad, the Beloved Daughter of Heaven. He will be tested to find whether he is worthy to become a Consort of the Skymothers.' She spoke with an odd mixture of pride and sorrow. 'Damaru is the first skyfool to be born in our village for many generations, and those few who have come before have not been found worthy. When a skyfool becomes a Consort then tis a wondrous thing for all who know him. For just as he has the sky in him while in the realm of earthly Creation, so he retains part of his earthly life when he ascends to Heaven. The Skymothers will favour the prayers of those who were known to their Consorts while they lived below.'

Damaru chose that moment to spring to his feet and make a grab for some morsel on the table. Kerin batted at his hand. He yelped, then scooted away and jumped onto his bed, where he sat and sulked.

'Are skyfool girls this badly behaved?' asked Sais, caught between amusement and irritation. However divine and glorious Damaru's future might be, right now he was quite a handful.

Kerin said slowly, 'I am not sure what you mean.'

Sais sensed he was on dangerous ground, but he needed to know what was what. 'Sky-touched girls? Or are skyfools always boys?'

Kerin stood rigid, her expression pained. 'For a girl to be touched by the sky is not a blessing. It is a curse.' She turned away.

Though Sais had plenty more questions, now was obviously not the time to ask them.

Suspended, weightless—

He could lie here forever, except for the voice, the woman calling to him. She needs his help.

But he can't help. He can't even move.

He's trapped – trapped, and sinking.

He opens his eyes, but the darkness remains unchanged. He wonders if it would help to panic, then decides not.

The thick, viscous liquid begins to ooze over his limbs, dragging him down. He feels the leading edge of it creep up his flank, over his belly.

Still he doesn't react.

When it reaches his ears he can hear it as well as feel it, a slow tidal surge. He shudders as it flows into his ears, intimate, vile. He can't hear anything now, not even the woman.

The liquid touches the corners of his mouth. Fear finally overcomes his numbness. He exerts his will to move, just a muscle, anything to escape his inevitable fate.

He can't. He's dead flesh. And any moment now the liquid will reach his nose, flow down into his lungs. He'll drown from the inside out—

The crash is deafening.

*

51

Sais opened his eyes.

The darkness was filled with a vortex of sparks, blotted out by a dark figure rising in front of him. He cried out in terror.

'Tis all right!' Kerin's whisper cut through his fear. She put out a hand to calm him, and everything dropped into place. He was in her hut, safe. 'Your nightmare set Damaru off,' she continued, moving away. 'He broke a pot. I will calm him and clear up. Do not concern yourself.'

Even as he wondered what she was talking about, he found himself slipping back towards sleep.

He woke to the sound of rain and the smell of porridge, a meal he was already getting sick of. Kerin didn't mention the incident in the night, and he wondered if it had been part of his dream.

After they'd eaten Kerin said, 'I must see if I can find us more travelling gear.' She put on a broad-brimmed hat and stiff cloak woven from the same stuff as the mats that covered the beaten earth floor, then went out.

Damaru settled down on the floor near the fire, and began to play with his little carved figures of men and animals. He lined them up, moved them round, then lined them up again, and again.

Sais spent the morning sitting on the bench. For a while he faced out, watching the ragged wet curtain of rain dribble down over the doorway. When his backside went numb and his legs started to stiffen, he turned round and stared into the fire.

He tried to order his thoughts and plan, as far as he could, for the future. He was still fragile and obviously prey to nightmares. He also needed to avoid antagonising his hostess, or upsetting the other villagers. At the same time he had to be open to anything that might help him regain his past. All in all, it was a bit of a tall order.

Kerin returned with a pair of boots and a blanket, which didn't look like much for a morning's work – not that Sais said anything.

After a meal of soggy left-over oatcakes and slivers of hard, sour cheese, Damaru went out again, wearing the cumbersome wet-weather gear Kerin had persuaded him, not without difficulty, to put on.

There was only so much staring and thinking a man could do and, left alone again that afternoon, Sais turned his attention to the contents of the shelves. They held everything two people needed to live, albeit in what he would consider poverty. When he came across the fabric Kerin had found with him, he got it down and felt it, then held it up to the light. He even smelt it. Despite the sense of familiarity when Kerin had first showed it to him, the cloth held no new insights.

When Kerin returned, this time with her arms full, she found him gazing into the fire, running the cloth through his hands. He saw her look at the cloth and said, on impulse, 'I think you should have this. For all you've done for me. Maybe we can even find you some more, once I've got my life back.' She deserved it: she could easily have lied about finding the fabric and kept it for herself. Besides, it was no use to him.

'Thank you,' she said quietly.

That evening she cooked pottage, which tasted like the vegetable equivalent of porridge. Sais guessed meat and honey were luxuries here.

After they'd eaten, Kerin asked Sais if he remembered how to play gem. When he shook his head she offered to remind him and got down a small roll of tanned leather from a high shelf. She spread it out on the wooden slab she chopped her herbs on. A six-sided web of red, brown and black lines and points covered the surface, and the playing pieces were slices of bone, also stained red, black or brown. The rules, involving limited movement and taking the other player's pieces, were deceptively simple; the strategies were complex. He wondered how long it was since she'd had someone to play with.

That night he offered her the use of her bed back. She gave him a sharp look and he wondered if she'd misunderstood. She murmured that he was the guest and must have the bed, then went back to her place on the floor.

The following morning Kerin brought back the last of the gear for the drove. He asked if he could help at all.

Kerin, busy rubbing something pungent into a pair of boots, looked up and said, 'Are you sure? Most of this is women's work.'

'That's all right. I won't tell the men I'm doing it.'

She smiled and said, 'These boots are for you, but they have not been used for some time. You need to rub the fat into the leather.'

It was smelly, messy work. The next task was to repair a rain-hat with dried rushes. His work was uneven, and his fingertips were soon pricked with tiny cuts. If this was women's work, they were tougher creatures than him. He kept at it, both because he'd promised Kerin he would, and because he had nothing better to do.

The rain eased off in the afternoon, and he went outside, wearing his newly greased boots. Kerin got him to strap low wooden blocks under the boots to keep the worst of the mud off.

Dangwern consisted of forty or so huts, ringed about with a shallow ditch and a waist-high bank. The settlement was perched on a small mound halfway up the slope, near the head of a valley. It was surrounded by low mountains, and though Sais could identify the white covering on the taller peaks as snow, he had no idea what the green, russet and purple vegetation on the mountainsides was.

The valley curved, so he couldn't see the end. Beside the village itself, the only evidence of human influence on the landscape were the fields and animal pens on the valley floor. He watched some men driving dark, shaggy cattle into the pens with the help of low-slung brown and white dogs.

When that excitement was over, he walked up towards the centre of the village. He passed several women and children, all with Kerin's dark hair, ingrained dirt and drab, worn clothes. They were a sad lot. One woman had a withered arm, and he saw a child with scabbed and crusted eyes, obviously blind. No one spoke to him, though most stopped to watch him pass.

The moot-hall looked smaller in daylight, despite the lean-tos and animal pens crowded around the outside. Sais was pleased to find he could identify most of the animals: pigs, goats, chickens, geese, even the small, dark creature that darted up into the thatch, which he recognised as a rat. Every new fragment of knowledge was a small victory; he just wished it would come together.

The low building opposite the moot-hall turned out to be a large roofless compound. The rough whitewashed walls were covered in stylised pictures painted in bright colours: female figures amongst stars and moons and plants and animals. One woman was unfeasibly curvaceous with red lips, golden hair and a harp in her hand; another held a set of scales; a third, with a blue apron, had a child cradled in one arm and a tool like the one Kerin used to make her thread in the other hand.

Within the walls the ground had been covered with layers of rush matting. The inside walls were also decorated, though the far wall showed only one image, a circle bisected by a horizontal line. Below it he could make out a great table loaded and festooned with various items, including flowers, figures carved from wood or bone, bunches of leaves, pottery bowls, woven braid, even flat loaves of bread. The wind shifted and he caught a whiff of something sweet and smoky.

This place was vital to the village, yet it meant nothing to him.

When Sais walked back into the cramped, dark hut, the smell of stale sweat and old smoke made his eyes sting. Damaru was already home, and he commented that her son wasn't such a fool, given he never missed meals.

Kerin said lightly, 'Or perhaps tis a skyfool ability not generally known about.'

He decided that the time had come to get to grips with spiritual matters – better to bemuse Kerin now, before they left, than screw up in front of unsympathetic villagers later. Damaru's strange affliction – or blessing – seemed a good place to start.

'Actually, Kerin, I can't quite remember what being sky-touched involves,' he admitted.

She looked at him for a moment, then said, 'Skyfools do not see things as we do. They sense the underlying pattern of the world, and sometimes they influence it.'

'Influence it? How?'

'Why, you have experienced that for yourself! Two nights back, when Damaru picked up on your nightmare. Perhaps you do not remember—?'

'I remember waking up, and you said something about a broken pot.'

'Aye. Damaru broke it. He was disturbed and reached out in his panic. He stirred the fire up and broke the pot that held the shining fabric.'

'I still don't understand. I saw you get up, but I didn't see any sign of Damaru.'

'No, he was in bed.'

'Then how did he break the pot?'

'By moving the pattern.'

Which left Sais none the wiser. 'And is this the ability that's tested by the – the Cariad?'

'I am not sure. I do know that if he fails before the Beloved Daughter of Heaven, he will forfeit his life. So say the Traditions.'

Poor cow: one way or another she would lose her son. 'The Traditions? The council talked about those. Is there a book somewhere with all this stuff in?'

'A book? Now there is proof you come from the lowlands!'

'So there's no book here I can read, to help me remember?'

'If you can read, Sais, then you are not a noble, but a priest!'

'I don't know if I can read,' he said hurriedly, 'but I do remember books. They have them in the lowlands then, do they? For priests, of course.'

'I have heard that the Reeve of Plas Aethnen has a written copy of the Traditions, and his Rhethor reads directly from it to settle matters of law.'

Presumably Reeves were rulers, and Rhethors some sort of priestly judges. 'And where's Plas Aethnen?'

'Tis where the cattle market is at star-season.'

'Is this Cariad there too?'

'No, she dwells at Dinas Emrys, the City of Light. That is further on again.'

'Presumably the drove's not going that far?'

'Damaru's guardian will accompany him for the final part of the journey.'

'Are you his guardian? I thought you weren't going on the drove until I came along.'

'No,' she said curtly, 'it must be a man.'

Sais was pretty sure that where he came from, women had more status.

The next day was sunny. Kerin went out to wash some clothes.

Despite the improved weather, Damaru stayed in, sitting on the floor at the foot of his bed with his knees drawn up, his chin resting on them. Sais suspected the disruption had finally got through to him.

He bent down until he was in his eye-line. 'Damaru?'

That got a grimace and a frown. He tried again. 'Damaru, I need your help. Please.'

Damaru twitched his shoulders and raised his head. Sais decided to carry on. 'I'd like you to show me where you found me. Can you do that?'

'No.' Damaru sounded incredulous at being asked.

'Why not, Damaru?'

'Because you are here now.'

'Yes I am, that's true. But when you first found me I wasn't, was I?'

Damaru thought for a while, then said, 'No.' He put his head back on his knees.

Sais wasn't sure if he was agreeing with him, claiming he had no knowledge of having ever found him or just refusing to help. He tried a different approach. 'Do you remember before, when you found me? Can you remember that?'

'Yes,' sighed the boy. 'I remember.'

'That's good. So what can you tell me about how you found me?'

'I go out to see the pattern. You are not part of the pattern, so I stay and watch you, to see how you change the pattern.'

'Can you remember where you found me? Where the pattern was ... wrong.'

He shook his head. 'Not wrong. *Different*.'

'All right, different. Do you know where that was? Could you go there, now?'

'Why?'

Good question. Sais thought for a moment, then said, 'Because I want to find the parts of the pattern I've lost.'

Damaru nodded, as though this made perfect sense, then got up and left. Sais followed.

Damaru led him out of the village towards the valley's head. When they passed the stream where Kerin was spreading wet clothes on bushes to dry, she called out, 'Where are you going?'

'To where Damaru found me.'

'The mere? Take care. Make sure you follow Damaru closely and stay away from dark green patches of floating moss or anywhere you see the white tufts of bog-cotton.'

'Will Damaru be all right?'

'Aye. He will know where to tread.'

Damaru led him up the side of one of the smaller mountains. The climb left him breathless and sore-footed. Despite his efforts with the grease, his boots were soon damp, and they rubbed his heels.

He paused at the top to gaze down at the village. The smoke seeping up through the roofs stained the clear blue sky, and the cattle looked like specks of soot on the valley floor.

Damaru disappeared into a small copse of odd-looking trees. Sais followed him, and they came out into reeds. The path had been well-trodden, presumably by villagers up here searching for more of his cloth. On the far side of the reeds, Damaru started striding across the boggy ground with a disconcerting certainty. Sais called out for him to slow down, and he did, grudgingly. They went on like this for a while: Damaru getting ahead, then reluctantly waiting while Sais struggled to catch up. Finally the boy stopped and crouched down, one hand on the earth. Sais took this to mean that they'd reached the place. The ground looked disturbed, but any tracks had been swallowed by the bog. There was no sign of more cloth, or any other clue as to what had happened here. He stood still for some time, while the smell of rotting plants filled his nostrils and his feet slowly sank into the mud. He waited to tune into his lost memories of how he had come to be here.

Nothing came.

Eventually he turned around and started back down.

CHAPTER EIGHT

Kerin's joy at the chance to escape Dangwern soon faded in the face of the practicalities. She would need to find more dried food, two extra sets of travelling kit, and another pack; Damaru would not wear a pack – at least not for long – so his gear would go on the sled with her trade-goods.

The day after the council had summoned them, she went from hut to hut, visiting those who had shown her kindness in the past. In each household she requested the hospitality of the hearth, though to have to abase herself so left a bad taste in her mouth.

She started at Huw's, and after the formalities had been observed his wife said grudgingly, 'For the friendship my husband bore your husband, Huw will take extra food that you and the stranger may share.'

From the second household she received the traditional cup of water and a seat by the fire, but with a child sick and the head of the household going off with the drove, nothing could be spared.

The third household she visited was Arlin's. Arlin insisted on a blow-by-blow account of Sais's recovery and gave Kerin a blanket for her pains, though she later found it was torn.

Finally she visited old Macha. Macha had lost her husband too, and had no son to care for her, only a daughter, who had married a man from Penfrid. Though their shared situation gave Macha and Kerin understanding, it had also led to an unspoken rivalry, as the village's means were overstretched, having to care for two useless widows. Kerin was surprised when Macha offered her husband's boots, which were old, but had plenty of wear left in them. 'When your son ascends,' said Macha as she handed them over, 'I pray that the shame of his family's past may finally be put to rest.' There was no accusation in her voice, only weariness, and Kerin felt her eyes fill with tears.

When she returned to the hut, Sais's gift of the fabric, and his promise to find her more, nearly had her crying again.

But she needed more than a pair of old boots, a damaged blanket and a length of fine cloth for the drove. As a woman she could not till the fields or tend livestock, for fear her own fertility might sour the growing grain or make the animals barren. Her hearth, however, was hers to give. The implications of this did not shock her: she already knew in her heart that she would not be returning to Dangwern after the drove.

So she visited households where a recent baby or new marriage had resulted in too many mouths at the same hearth – the falling fire would solve many such problems in its own brutal way, but people cared more about current discomfort than future pain. She offered her hut, and those possessions she would not be taking on the drove, in return for the remaining items she needed for the journey. Suddenly her welcome was far warmer. People hurried from hut to hut in her wake as those families who needed space to expand, or a spare loom, or new pots, began to trade with each other, trying to work out a deal by which everyone got what they wanted.

By the time night fell, she had a new pack, bedrolls for all of them, a large water-skin, even some spare clothes – all she needed for the future – because now she *had* a future: one that included Sais, perhaps. Though she would always love Neithion, she had made a virtue of loneliness for too long. Despite Sais's peculiar ways – offering to help around the hut, professing ignorance of the oddest things – he had a good heart. Perhaps her dream of sharing his life was not so impossible.

For the final couple of days before the drove left, Kerin lost herself in preparations, though her mood soured when she went to collect her clothes from the bushes beside the stream: whilst Damaru's spare shirts and breeches were clean and dry, her own skirts and shirts had muddy footprints over them. She washed the worst of the mud off and took the clothes back to dry on the shelves in her hut.

When she heard that Sionyn's condition had worsened, and Fychan was to take his brother's place as drove leader, dread settled on her, not just for whatever foolish choices the lad might make for the drove, but because he would be called to act as Damaru's guardian. That was why Fychan had not spoken up against her in the council: he wanted her on the drove to control her son, a task that would otherwise fall to him.

She stayed away from the drovers' farewell feast, and advised Sais to do the same, advice he was happy to heed. They heard raised voices outside, and at one point something soft thudded into the hut door.

Damaru left for an evening walk shortly afterwards. Sais asked, 'Will he be all right? It sounds like people are getting a bit restless out there.'

'They would not hurt him. He is a skyfool, remember?' She wished he would not keep coming out with these odd statements, but his next words chilled her to the core.

'Kerin, I still can't remember anything about the Skymothers. Would you remind me, please?'

She would have been less upset had he said he no longer knew how to use a spoon, or how to dress himself. What if he *was* Abyss-touched, and her growing attachment to him had blinded her to his true nature?

'Kerin? Are you all right? I mean, if you'd rather not tell me—'

'No,' Kerin swallowed. 'I mean, aye, I will tell you. T'would be a sin not to.' Where to start though, when such knowledge was absorbed with a mother's milk? 'Everything you see around us is the Creation of the Skymothers, pulled from the chaos of the Abyss by their will.'

'And the Abyss is ... below us?'

'Tis a place of chaos, ruled over by the Cursed One, Melltith, a creature of unimaginable vileness that opposes all that the

62

Skymothers are. But for their grace we would fall into its foulness, and become nothing ourselves.'

He nodded. 'Right. And the Skymothers live in Heaven, above us?'

'Aye. As we could see, if the sky were clear.'

'You can see them?'

'We see the lights that represent their grace, aye. Heaven itself is not something our petty souls can encompass. But each of the Five has a light to focus our prayers upon.'

'So there're five of them? What are their names?'

Such innocently asked questions, as though a man could live without knowing the answers! She fought to keep her voice even, 'Frythil is the sower, the Seed Mother, and keeper of hidden knowledge; her time is dawn, her colour green. Medelwyr is the Weaver and the Reaper, Harvest Mother, ruler of dusk, and her colour is the orange of sunset; Turiach is the Mother of Mercy, who heals and watches over the home and hearth; she rules the morning and her colour is blue. Mantoliawn is the Mother of Justice and the guardian of travellers, who we must ask to bless us when we leave tomorrow; her colour is yellow and her time is the afternoon. Carunwyd is the night's touch, Mother of Passion, mistress of chance and luck, and bringer of poetry and song; her colour is red.'

'Thank you. I understand better now.' Kerin had the worrying notion that he was trying to commit what she had said to memory, rather than reclaiming old knowledge. 'And what's that gesture you keep making?'

'Gesture?'

'You draw a circle in the air over your chest whenever you mention the names. I saw you do it before eating too.'

'The circle of the world. Tis like … a small unspoken prayer.'

'How does it go?'

She showed him, tracing the circle that showed Heaven and the Abyss with her right forefinger – perfection and corruption in one – then drawing her middle finger across to show the place between, the realm created by the Mothers for their children.

Though he asked no more that evening, perhaps sensing her

unease, he practised drawing the sigil as though it were some sleight-of-hand trick.

It rained in the night, but the day of departure dawned fresh and clear. Kerin rose early and went to bid farewell to those few villagers she considered friends. Then she prepared their last meal, and made ready to leave. Sais tried to help in his inept way. Damaru was flustered and upset, constantly getting underfoot.

When they were ready, Kerin gestured for the others to go first. She paused on the threshold, taking a last look at her hut, already looking abandoned in the early light. The yearly departure of the drove had always been a bit of welcome excitement in Kerin's life. This year, she was the one leaving, and she had been so busy planning her departure that she had spared little thought for what she might be heading into. At that moment she would have given anything to be able to live out a quiet, ordinary life in the only home she knew. If only the Weaver had not seen fit to make the cloth of her life so, born of violence and a cursed mother and losing her loving husband too soon. She shook her head: such thoughts achieved nothing.

She spoke a prayer to the Mother of Mercy that this hearth might be re-awakened to provide warmth and shelter for the family who would make their home here next. Then she picked up the water-jug and threw the contents into the flames, pulling the door shut on the hissing, steaming fire-pit.

As they walked down from the village to the milling mass of people and animals on the valley floor Kerin heard a high keening from the moot-hall. Sionyn was dead. She found herself glancing over her shoulder, half-expecting Gwellys to come running out to attack her.

No one appeared, and soon the familiar smoke-and-ordure reek of the village was replaced by the subtler smells of the moor: damp grass, bruised heather and the occasional sweet whiff of cloudberry flowers, their scent released by the night's rain. The sounds of mourning were drowned out by the cries of the animals and the terse shouted orders of the drovers.

Kerin led them to the back of the drove, behind the sled. As they approached she counted nineteen men; in a normal year thirty or more would go. Fychan was at the front with two other council members: Cadmael, who had no family and who she expected to see; and Howen, whose presence was an unwelcome surprise.

The men near the back nodded to acknowledge them, though her decision to travel in her husband's drove gear garnered her some odd looks. Still, she had no intention of walking to market in a skirt and clogs; whatever concern she might once have had for what others thought of her was disappearing like dew under the morning sun.

Arthen stood in front of the crowd of villagers who were staying behind. When the drovers had got themselves into some sort of order he called out in a voice loud and confident enough to carry over the sounds of the animals:

'Bad times may be upon us, but they have come before, and will again. We will endure, as we always have. This year we are also blessed. We must all pray that the sky-touched child finds favour with the Cariad, and so may bring us closer to Heaven. Now, travel safely, trade well, and be an example to others as to the merits of our folk.'

He traced the circle of the world, and everyone – including Sais, Kerin was pleased to note – echoed him.

At the front of the drove, Fychan gave a high repetitive cry – *hi-hi-hi* – and with lows of protest from the cattle and yips and barks from the dogs, the drove lurched into motion. Everyone, drovers and villagers alike, sang the Drovers' Hymn as they moved off. After their initial complaints the animals fell silent, heads down, fly-brush tails swishing as they plodded along. Despite herself, Kerin kept looking back as the village slowly receded.

Damaru capered ahead, taking no notice of the drove while managing to more-or-less keep pace with it. Sais trudged determinedly by her side, his face grey.

'Are you all right?' she asked after a while.

'I – I think I'm going to find this hard work.'

'The men say you get used to it after a few days.'

'I hope so. Kerin, I was wondering ... isn't that boy with the scarf around his head a bit young to be in charge?'

'Fychan? Oh aye, that he is,' she said bitterly. Of course, she knew about everyone here, but they were all strangers to Sais. 'He is Arthen's son. Before, his elder brother has gone, but now Sionyn is – Sionyn caught the falling fire, so Fychan goes in his stead.' Sais needed to know about their travelling companions, and so she quietly filled him in on names and trades and talents. Talking of such familiar matters gave her some comfort against the coming uncertainty.

Shortly after they lost sight of the village they passed the slight dip in the side of the valley that marked the narrow trail to Penfrid. She had walked that path just last year, when it was Penfrid's turn to host the star-season celebrations.

This must have been the signal to stop for lunch as the sled-men stumbled to a halt. One of the dog-handlers gave a series of short whistles and the dogs wheeled round to the front of the herd. The cattle stalled, milled back on themselves and put their heads down to start foraging for grass.

Damaru showed no sign of stopping. Kerin shucked her pack and sprinted after him, calling his name. She suspected he saw only the pattern of the Skymothers' Creation laid out and expanded before him. When she waved a water-skin under his nose he stopped to drink, then sat down on a hummock. She looked back to see Sais talking to Huw. As she watched, both men laughed.

Huw had returned to the sled, leaving food enough for the three of them, by the time she persuaded Damaru to come back with her.

'Did he introduce himself?' asked Kerin.

'Huw? Yes. He's – He was Neithion's friend, wasn't he?'

'Aye. They were born but weeks apart, and had similar temperaments.' Like Neithion, Huw was one of the few men in Dangwern who did not hold the past against her. 'What were you laughing about?' she added.

'He said that calling myself Sais proved I'd lost my memory.

I said I know it's an odd name, so perhaps if people call me it enough I'll be encouraged to remember my real one.'

Kerin smiled at that.

They started off again, passing the path to Carregogh, even steeper and narrower than the one to Penfrid. This was as far as Kerin had ever been from Dangwern. Every step now took her further into the unknown.

CHAPTER NINE

By the first evening Sais was already looking back fondly on the tedium and foetid darkness of Kerin's hut. If one day on the road left him this exhausted and footsore then it seemed highly unlikely he had walked to Dangwern, though he couldn't imagine how else he'd arrived. At least his presumed status as a noble meant that the villagers didn't expect him to take a turn carrying the sled.

It would take them a little over two weeks to reach Piper's Steps, where they would meet up with drovers from the other mountain villages; then they had another five weeks' travelling to reach the market in the lowlands. Seven weeks of hard walking: Sais knew he'd never survive.

Finally the sun sank below the mountains and the cry to halt went up.

Once again, Damaru didn't stop. Kerin ran after him. He ignored her calls and when she tried to touch him, he shook her off. She tripped and fell. Despite his exhaustion, Sais hurried over to help. Kerin was already on her feet by the time he reached her, and they set off after Damaru together. Sais hoped they wouldn't have to physically carry the boy back to the camp – he'd never manage it.

'Damaru!' said Kerin, when they caught up with him. 'Please, you have to stop and rest for the night. Time to sleep, Damaru.'

He shook his head fiercely. 'No ... wrong wrong *wrong*. This is not where I sleep.'

'That is right. But you cannot just keep walking, Damaru. You must rest.'

He paused long enough to look at her, then shook his head. 'Wrong,' he said emphatically. 'Your pattern is *home*. Not *here*. Here I am. Just me.'

'Damaru, I know this is strange, but—'

'Not strange. *Wrong*. You are wrong. Maman is hut is food is ... not here.'

On impulse, Sais stepped forward. 'How about me?' he said. 'What am I?'

Damaru stopped, looking confused. 'Different pattern,' he muttered.

'That's right!' said Sais, hoping he'd understood – as far as anyone could – what was going on in the boy's head. 'I was outside the pattern, then I— I came in. And now – now your Maman, Kerin, has come out of the pattern she was in. Into your world. I'm here, she's here, you're here. Together, outside the hut and the village. And she's still your Maman, Damaru. She still loves you, still wants to help you. Do you understand?'

Damaru turned to Kerin, looking uncertain. Then he said, 'You are wearing Da's clothes.'

'Aye,' said Kerin, 'I am. Because that is what I need to do to be your Maman outside the hut. I know it is hard, and everything we have known is gone, but you are still my beautiful boy, and I am still your loving Maman.'

He thought for a moment, then said, 'All right.' When Kerin reached out to take his hand Damaru let her lead him back towards the drovers.

As they passed Fychan, he called out, 'Kerin! Control your son!'

'He is just tired,' she replied.

The word 'arsehole' came unbidden into Sais's mind – though perhaps the boy had a point. He asked Kerin if she thought Damaru would be this much trouble the whole way. She shook her head. 'He just needs to adjust. Besides,' she added, 'I have a supply of powdered bogwood bark. It will relax him, make him more compliant. If I were not here they would probably be giving it to him with most meals. I would prefer to save it until we need it.'

They watched as the drovers pulled out the sled's two carrying poles, each made of bundles of thinner poles lashed together, and untied the ropes securing the waxed fabric covering the sled. They extended the fabric out on either side, supporting it with the poles and ropes. The resulting pair of shelters were large enough for everyone to sleep with heads and chests under cover, though they'd have to rely on the greased leather of their bedrolls to keep their lower body and legs dry.

Sais had hoped for a fire, both for warmth and for comfort. The idea of sleeping outside made him feel exposed and vulnerable. He asked Kerin, 'Are we safe out here at night?'

'There might be wilder-dogs: someone will stay awake to watch for them,' she said.

'Wilder-dogs? I don't know what those are.'

'They are scavengers. They are too small to take a bullock, and rarely bother people. We should be fine.'

'So the ditch around the village wasn't to keep these dogs out?' It hadn't looked like much of a deterrent.

'No, that is to defend against reivers.'

'And they're what? Outlaws?'

'Aye. But they have not troubled us for many years.' Kerin didn't sound convinced, but before he could ask more, Huw called them over to eat – he appeared to have appointed himself their guide. Sais tried hard not to stare when Huw picked at the scabby rash on his neck and ear.

Bedrolls were unrolled and food was passed around. Without a fire to sit round, the men formed little groups. Sais nodded to the two men sitting with Huw when he took his place. He was careful to mutter under his breath and make the 'circle of the world' gesture over his food before he ate.

After the food was finished, a water-skin went around. Sais took a gulp and spluttered: it wasn't water but a sour yeasty drink that foamed up his nose.

Huw and his companions laughed. 'Ha,' said one, 'looks like our upland ale is too strong for delicate lowland tastes.' Sais toasted him with the skin and took another, more careful swig.

Sais had hoped to see the night sky, but as darkness fell, clouds crowded in. He steeled himself to pull his boots off. By the end of the day's walking his feet had become mercifully numb, but when he'd taken the weight off them they had started to throb and now he could feel the blisters as well. He kept the socks on, despite the smell.

His sleep was fitful. He found himself waking up every few minutes, because he was cold or stiff or damp, or all three. At least there were no nightmares.

The next morning his feet felt like they'd been boiled. He forced them into his boots, biting his lip. Every step hurt. He tried walking in slightly different ways, putting his foot down at an angle, taking longer strides, walking on the sides of his feet. Some ploys worked for a while, until something else hurt – a calf muscle, his knees, his toes. When Kerin asked if he was all right, he snapped at her. He didn't apologise, because that would have meant opening his mouth, and if he did that he might just start crying from the pain.

The valley opened out onto a plain of tawny grass. Distant mountains lurked like earthbound clouds under the overcast sky. They ate their lunch beside the stream they'd been following, then filled their water-skins before striking out across the plain. Damaru stuck close, apparently disconcerted by the open terrain. From the pointing fingers at the front of the party, Sais guessed they were aiming for a particular feature in the far mountains. During the afternoon they also passed several waymarkers, chest-high posts painted white, with a deep groove cut in the top. The ground was relatively even, allowing the sled to be towed rather than carried.

Huw spent most of the day walking with them, chatting with Kerin. At one point he darted away and returned with a handful of pale green leaves, which he waved under Sais's nose. Sais, sunk in misery, was tempted to tell him where he could shove his leaves, but Huw said, 'Put these on the blisters tonight. T'will sting like a scold's tongue, then the blisters will go numb. The next day you will feel as though you have grown a second skin just for walking on.'

Sais made himself grunt a thank you.

That evening, Damaru again refused to stop. Sais was in no state to help, but he watched, concerned, as Kerin physically wrangled her son back to the drove. Fychan stared belligerently at them, but said nothing this time.

While the drovers made camp Sais addressed himself to his feet. He took a deep breath and pulled one sock off, wincing as the skin tore. He felt compelled to count the blisters – just *six*, so why did his whole foot hurt? He applied one of Huw's leaves to the largest blister on his heel and gasped in shock – even though he'd been expecting pain, this felt like acid being dropped onto raw skin. He fought the urge to rip the leaf off, and after a few moments, glorious numbness spread. He gritted his teeth and applied the rest, then eased the sock back on to keep the leaves in place. The other foot hurt just as much.

He was colder than ever that night, and more than once he awakened thinking he could hear howls in the darkness.

Once they got going the next morning he felt better. Huw's herb had reduced his blisters from agonising to merely sore, and his body had started to get used to walking. The journey was giving him a chance to think, though the conclusions he was reaching weren't comforting: his memory wasn't returning by itself, and though he was getting by, some things, like the Skymothers, or his own past, remained complete blanks. When Huw went off to take a turn on the sleds he mentioned his concerns to Kerin. 'It is possible you have a malady of the spirit,' she said.

'I'm not sure what you mean.'

'I am not sure myself. Perhaps you need a priest.' Kerin didn't sound enthusiastic.

'Are we likely to meet one out here?'

'There will be one waiting for us at Piper's Steps, to accompany the drove to Plas Aethnen. And we can ask the men from the other villages who will meet us at the Steps if they know anything about you.'

In the afternoon sleet like chunks of freezing cloud began to fall. Though Sais's rain gear was well-greased, the wind drove the sleet inside the stiff woven cloak and the damp seeped through the hat to chill his head.

When he saw an orange glow ahead he wondered if the bone-biting cold and constant discomfort was making him hallucinate.

Around him, the drovers sped up: they must have seen it too.

Huw, walking with them again, said, 'Ah, we have not made such bad time; we should be there long before nightfall.'

'Is that the meeting point?' asked Kerin. When Huw nodded, she explained to Sais, 'This is where we meet the drovers from Penfrid and Carregogh. The fire is lit by the first of the three villages to arrive.'

A fire sounded like a great idea, though Sais hadn't seen any trees since they left the village. 'What do they burn?' he asked.

Kerin replied, 'When a boy becomes a man, he walks out here with a pack full of supplies – much more than he needs for his journey. He spends the night out here, making any repairs that are needed to the storage hut. Older men do it too, as a way of being alone with their thoughts and the grace of the Mothers. They leave most of what they bring for the drove. I expect you have similar customs in the lowlands.'

'I'm sure we do,' he said. Everyone assumed he was a lowlander, but he had his doubts, though he said nothing.

CHAPTER TEN

Just by dint of travelling with the drove without complaint or fuss, Kerin found she and Sais were becoming accepted. When they met up with the drovers from Penfrid and Carregogh, most of the Dangwern men were happy to explain the presence of a stranger and a woman; only Fychan and Howen scowled and changed the subject when asked.

They made merry that evening, passing around a skin of heather ale, singing, and telling tales of old droves. Kerin enjoyed being included in the fireside circle, and even Damaru came into the light for a while, leaning up against Kerin as he watched the flames. Sais, sitting on her other side, politely declined requests for a song or story.

The next morning, there was dissent. By tradition, the drove leader from Dangwern took charge, but the councillors from Penfrid and Carregogh would not accept the leadership of a boy on his first drove. In the end, Howen took over.

The argument was loud and public, and watching it Sais whispered, 'Did Arthen really think the others would accept Fychan? He's such – he's so inexperienced.'

'Arthen does not make his decisions lightly,' Kerin replied. 'He may have suspected Howen would take charge, but he must believe Fychan will make his peace with Damaru.'

'I didn't know Fychan had a problem with your boy – well, no more than he appears to have with anyone else.'

'Back when people thought Damaru merely simple, some of the village lads used to tease him. One day he fought back, and moved the pattern so the leader's stick went into his eye. That was the first time his true nature became apparent.'

'Shit, Kerin! So the reason Fychan wears a scarf round his head is because Damaru *put his eye out*?'

'It was not so bad at the time. I tried to help, but Gwellys would not let me. Then the cut went bad, and he lost his sight.'

'We'd better hope he doesn't bear a grudge, though I'd say he's just the type.'

Once the new order of the drove was settled they set off: the councillors at the front, then the common men, then the three sleds, with the cattle bringing up the rear. Fychan walked a little apart from the other leaders, talking to Cadmael but ignoring everyone else.

The next day they woke to fog. They could see but a short distance and the plod and plash of the animals' hooves on the damp ground was swallowed by the mist. Kerin found herself more alert then ever to Damaru's position, concerned he would wander out of sight. Sais made little attempt at conversation.

That evening another row broke out amongst the leaders, conducted in harsh, angry whispers to avoid eavesdroppers. Fychan was not the focus this time; he stood off to one side and glared.

Despite their leaders' attempts at secrecy, the rumour soon went round: they had missed a way-marker. They were lost.

'Can't we just wait until the fog lifts and retrace our steps?' asked Sais.

'Aye,' said Huw, 'we can. But if we do not reach Piper's Steps in time to meet the ox-carts, we will have to carry the sleds the whole way. That will be hard work, especially in the drylands, and we will most likely not arrive in Plas Aethnen in time for the market.'

The fog persisted the next day. Kerin asked Damaru if he could find their path, but he just gave her a look she knew well, the one that said her question had no meaning for him.

In the evening Kerin heard howls in the darkness: the wilder-dogs shadowing the herd were awaiting their moment. Those on watch that night kept their weapons close to hand.

The fog lifted the following afternoon, and the sun set in a froth of red cloud. The next day broke clear, and the dawn was greeted with smiles and prayers of thanks. The joy was short-lived: those who knew the route took their bearings on the mountains at the edge of the plain and soon confirmed that they were a long way off-course.

The following day they set off before dawn and travelled until after dark. By the time they stopped Sais looked fit to drop, and even Damaru was flagging. The day after that they started out early again. Huw had overheard the leaders talking the night before when he went to relieve himself. 'We will reach Maen Bulch today – they plan to carry on through, rather than risk stopping,' he told Kerin and Sais.

'What's wrong with stopping there?' asked Sais tetchily.

'Tis just' – Huw made a dismissive gesture with his hand – 'tis not a very comfortable place to sleep, is all. Do not mind me, I fuss like a girl.' He walked off.

'Kerin, is there a problem?' Sais asked once Huw was out of earshot.

'I did not want to say, in case it worried you. The last time the drove encountered reivers, it was in Maen Bulch.'

'Great,' he said.

The land rose gently for the first part of the morning, and soon slabs of rock showed through the grass.

They reached a cleft in the hills at midmorning. Howen called for the drove to halt and a contingent of armed men, including Gwilym and Fychan, moved to the rear.

As they headed into the valley grass gave way to rocks. The overhanging crags combined with the low cloud to give the impression that the land and sky had sealed them in. The valley floor was strewn with boulders spattered with growths in hues of green and orange and yellow. Sometimes the way was barely wide enough to allow three to walk abreast, and the sleds had to be carried all the time. They kept crossing and re-crossing the stream that tumbled down the centre of the valley, and Kerin soon had splashes up her legs and grazes on her hands from scrambling amongst the rocks and pools. The cattle managed better, as they were well suited to rocky terrain, and they did not mind getting wet.

At first Damaru clambered over rocks and peered into crevices; Kerin kept an eye on him, but was not too concerned. When he started to climb up the valley walls, his eyes fixed on the distant skyline, she panicked, and almost screamed at him to come down, drawing sharp looks from the men. After that he stayed close.

Those men not carrying the sleds unwound slings from their belts and picked up stones as they went along. Kerin jumped at every slight movement among the rocks, real or imagined.

Lunch was grabbed while they changed shifts on the sleds. By the afternoon Kerin felt calmer, even smiling to herself when she spotted a dipper bobbing its tail before flying low over the bubbling stream.

A while later, a shout came from behind for the drove to halt. Sais scanned the rocks nervously. Kerin turned when she heard someone calling, 'Mistress Kerin, your services are required!'

She ran back to find several men standing over a small bundle of fur. A steer had kicked one of the dogs into the stream. His master had rescued it and now it lay on the bank, wide-eyed and trembling. Though there was no mark save a small cut on its side, Kerin saw in the animal's eyes that it was doomed. When she felt its flank, bone ground under her hand. The animal gave a sharp yelp and feebly tried to bite her. She looked up at the dog's master and shook her head. 'I am sorry,' she said. The man *hurrumphed* and turned away. One of the men murmured that he would take care of it.

Walking back, Kerin's sympathy for the dog was tempered with the small satisfaction that they had been willing to call on her skills as a healer.

The delay cost them precious time. As the sun sank behind them and darkness crept up the valley, several drovers began to pray under their breath.

They would have to stop soon, or risk injuring themselves on the treacherous terrain. Before the light went completely, Cadmael came along the line, organising watches for the night. Kerin offered to take the first watch by the Dangwern sled with Sais; with the drove strung out along the valley floor, they needed every pair of eyes. There was no room to unfurl the awnings, so the men slept wherever they could find space to stretch out.

She and Sais sat next to each other against the sled, not quite touching, facing up the side of the valley. They could see very little: clouds hid the sky, and the moons were both on the wane. Kerin made out the faint glint of the stream, and the dark shapes of the larger rocks, but little else. She would have enjoyed the comfort of conversation, but they found themselves listening hard for any sound not made by the stream or the restless cattle.

Eventually she felt Sais sag beside her and then give a gentle snore. Exhaustion had won out over fear. Despite the tension and discomfort, her own eyes were getting heavy, and her legs had gone numb. She got up and stretched, careful not to disturb Sais.

One of the nearby rocks was gone.

That had not been a rock; that was where Damaru had been sleeping. He must have got up. It could be disastrous for him to wander off now: many of the men on guard had spears and knives, which they would eagerly employ against any apparent intruder who did not immediately identify themselves.

She heard the scrape of a boot on rock. Without thinking she called out, 'Damaru, is that you?' The night swallowed her voice.

Whoever it was stopped moving.

'Damaru, answer me!' she hissed, taking a step forward.

Silence.

All she could think of was finding her son. She must wake Sais—

She turned around. *There!* Was that movement? A moment later someone grabbed for her, but her attacker must have assumed she was facing the other way. He brushed past, and missed.

Stark terror coursed through her. She stumbled and fell, then began to crawl away hurriedly, her limbs at once weak with fear and suffused with energy. Her heart thundered in her ears.

She stubbed her finger on a rock, and the pain brought her back to herself. She must warn the drovers that something was amiss! Yet if she drew attention to herself, she was doomed. Indecision froze her voice and limbs, even as one grasping hand found a loose stone.

From the far side of the sled she heard a scuffle and a groan, then the sound of a body falling to the ground.

The worst had happened. Reivers were overrunning the camp.

She sat down, her back against the rock she had bruised her finger on. Shapes moved silently through the darkness. The nearest, she knew, was looking for her. She raised her arm so she could thump him with the stone when he found her and drew a deep, ragged breath, ready to scream—

Someone grabbed her wrist. For a brief but wonderful moment she thought it was Sais, or Gwilym, or even Fychan, and that this was all a mistake, and they were not under attack after all. Then she felt something cold across her neck, and a voice she had never heard before said in her ear, 'Make a noise, and you die.' The rough hand on her wrist moved up to fold itself over her upraised hand. 'Let go of the stone, boy.' She did. It fell to the ground. He kept hold of her hand and whispered, 'Cover his mouth.' Another man scuttled round to crouch in front of her.

Over the man's shoulder, Kerin saw sudden movement. Sais – it had to be him – exploded to his feet and hurtled into the reiver nearest the sled. Both men flew back. She heard a splash.

The man in front reached out towards her. His hand brushed her neck, and she pressed herself into the rock. The man paused, and felt lower. He gave a brief huff of surprise. 'Tis the woman we heard!' he whispered to his companion.

The man behind her said, 'Then this one we'll keep.'

In that moment, Kerin weighed up the two paths her life had suddenly been reduced to: to die here tonight, or to spend the rest of her life as a reivers' whore.

She kicked out and up as hard as she could.

Her foot connected, though not where she had hoped; she had caught his leg. She heard the hiss of indrawn breath and the reiver teetered, then caught himself. 'She is not worth the trouble,' he muttered. 'Kill her!'

The man behind her let go of her arm and grabbed her hair, dragging her head back against the rock. She felt the blade move away from her neck by a hair's breadth. She could do nothing to fight him; as though accepting death, her body had already begun to go limp.

As the reiver drew the weapon across her neck and she felt it bite into her flesh, she found time for one last clear thought: *At least I'll not suffer as you did, Maman.*

Then everything stopped.

CHAPTER ELEVEN

If he'd had any sense, Sais would have waited to see what was going on before charging in blindly. He wasn't thinking straight: half-asleep, aware Kerin was gone and sure the people he'd seen moving around in the dark weren't drovers, he reacted instinctively, throwing himself at the silhouette in front of him. In the dark he misjudged the distance and the man dodged to the side.

Sais tried to catch himself. No chance!

He sprawled forward into the stream. His head went under and hit something. A rush of stars exploded across the inside of his eyelids. He pushed himself back up and broke the surface, spluttering.

Hands grabbed his shoulders and started to haul him out the water: he in turn reached up to grab the man's arms and pulled him forward. His attacker gave a surprised grunt and tried to pull away, but he was already off-balance and tumbled forward. Sais, too stunned to dodge, partially broke the reiver's fall, getting winded in the process. He still heard the stomach-churning thud of a skull hitting rock. The reiver went limp.

Was the man dead? Had he killed him? He obviously knew how to fight, and to fight dirty at that – had he killed before?

Movement in the dark: another man heading his way. Something glinted in the man's hand.

Sais started to push the reiver's body off him. His arms felt like putty and he was shivering hard.

The reiver closed, swung his arm back—

Reality *lurched*.

Suddenly nothing made sense.

Except …

Something about this state hit him in the hindbrain. If only he could think straight, remember—?

Then he was back in the moment, sitting in a freezing stream in the dark with a dead reiver on his legs. There was no sign of the man with the knife.

He heard screams from overhead. Against the faintly glowing clouds he could make out the silhouettes of half-a-dozen figures floating, or rather, flailing, in the air.

Shouts were erupting along the line.

A knife landed in the stream next to him with a splash. Sais reached out to pick it up. His hand had just closed on the hilt when the weirdness happened again, this time over before he could register it. The figures in the sky were whisked away, as though by a sudden wind.

He didn't see where they landed, but he heard the noise they made: a sound somewhere between snapping branches and a load of water-skins being stamped on.

Sais stood, shaking his head to clear it. He looked around and saw movement up-slope. A piercing double whistle sounded, and the movement sped up: people running away.

Someone was crying, back at the sled.

He staggered over. As he approached, a figure stood up, a hand pressed against its neck. 'Who's there?' he asked, wielding the reiver's knife drunkenly.

'Sais, is that you?'

'Kerin? Are you all right?'

'I am cut … I will live. Damaru— I—' She stumbled forward to the source of the crying. Sais saw the shadowy figure of Damaru sitting on the grass, hugging his knees and rocking, sobbing gently to himself. The shadow that was Kerin went over and embraced him. Kerin began saying something over and over to her son. It sounded like, 'I'm so proud. So proud of you.'

'Kerin,' said Sais urgently, 'what just happened?'

'Damaru saved us all.'

'What did he do?'

'He moved the pattern.'

'Fuck me.' Sais sat down heavily. He needed to work out how he knew the sensation of whatever it was that Damaru had just done. He had no conscious recollection of it, but his body remembered the feeling. It must have happened in the hut when Damaru broke the pot, but Sais had been asleep then. Besides, it was *so* familiar. Some time in the past, the past he'd lost, he had experienced this effect, and more than once.

Drovers came up to them, asking if they were hurt. Someone got a small fire going. Kerin had them bring her pack over; Damaru was uninjured, but she had a shallow gash on her neck, which she got Sais to dress. Sais had minor cuts and the promise of some impressive bruises to come, not to mention a nasty headache, but nothing serious. He offered to look after Damaru while Kerin went off to deal with the other casualties. He knew better than to ask the boy about what had happened and already the strange mix of confusion and familiarity was fading to a vague niggling disquiet.

Three men had nasty cuts, one across his back, the other two on their arms. Two men had been killed. The drovers dealt with this turn of events with quiet stoicism.

Sais didn't expect to be able to sleep, but exhaustion and shock took their toll. He fell asleep listening to a whispered argument between Fychan and Howen about how they should honour the dead.

He awoke at dawn, stiff, sore and with an aching head, to find most people already up. The two dead men were lying side by side by the stream. Something smouldered in a shallow pottery bowl on the ground between them; after a moment Sais remembered the smell from the capel in the village. Kerin was sitting next to Damaru, who was still asleep. She nodded at the two bodies. 'I was saving the incense to burn for Damaru, but we have no pyre to free their spirits. It was the least I could do.' She gave a tired laugh. 'Fychan actually thanked me. Whatever else he may be, the boy is devout.'

Howen led prayers for the dead men's souls before the drove set off.

The reivers who'd been subjected to the demonstration of Damaru's power received no such respect. From the look of the mess on the rocks further up the slope, there wasn't much left of them anyway.

That day the overhanging craggy cliffs of Maen Bulch opened out to rocky slopes. Thin streams cascaded down deep-cut rills and the valley floor widened until the drove could move freely again.

Cadmael told Kerin and Sais that Damaru's miracle would make a fine tale.

The next day, the drove stopped suddenly halfway through the afternoon. When a shout went up for Kerin, Sais assumed that one of the wounded men needed her attention. Kerin went forward with her pack.

When she returned, Sais took one look at her face and asked, 'What is it? What's happened?'

'Tis Manawn, one of the Penfrid drovers,' she said dully. 'He has the falling fire.'

'Shit.' Distracted by the rigours of the drove, Sais had almost forgotten about that. 'What'll they do? They could probably fit him on one of the sleds now we're on even ground.'

'No,' said Kerin, 'the men will leave him.'

'Leave him? *Out here?* He'll die.'

Looking at her feet, Kerin whispered, 'If the Mothers will it.'

After a brief discussion the leaders called everyone up to the front. People offered up prayers for the sick man, who lay beside the track, staring wide-eyed at the sky. They left him a water-skin and some food, in case, Huw said, the Mothers showed their mercy.

Then they carried on. No one looked back.

Two days later they came to a large village in the centre of a wide, fertile valley.

'If the drovers knew we were passing this place, why didn't they bring Manawn here to be looked after?' Sais asked Kerin.

Kerin pointed to a line of dark smoke curling up from behind the cluster of huts. 'That is a pyre; the winnowing times are upon us, and each must look to their own and not presume upon others.'

Sais hung back while the drovers went up to trade rush mats and capes for fresh food. Damaru was greeted with awe. People made the circle sign whenever they looked his way and several of them darted up to touch him. He shied away and flapped his hands at them. Sais was surprised Kerin didn't intervene.

Huw asked the villagers if anyone recognised Sais, as he would have come this way to get to Dangwern from the lowlands, but no one had.

When they left Sais asked Kerin why she'd let the villagers paw at Damaru.

'They wish the blessing of a sky-touched child against the winnowing times. I cannot deny them that.'

'Aren't you worried they might infect him?'

'Infect him? The falling fire is not something you *catch*. It is the judgment of Heaven. Besides, he is a *skyfool*. He can no more succumb to the falling fire than a priest could.'

That night, for the first time, the sky was clear. As twilight faded into darkness, stars began to emerge. Sais sat on his bedroll watching the turquoise sky come alive with light. It was spectacular, and totally unfamiliar.

After a while he realised Kerin was standing near him. He said, 'I don't know how I can have forgotten this.' Unless he'd never known it, of course.

'I am glad you have finally seen it.' Then she added tentatively, 'May I sit with you?'

'Of course.' He moved over.

'Do you understand a little of what Heaven must be now?'

'Perhaps I do. It's beautiful. So bright, so … big.'

'Aye.' He could tell by her voice that she was smiling.

After a while he said, 'Why are there so many stars above us, and almost none round the edge of the sky?'

'Because that is Heaven! The stars are the light of Heaven that we are given to see, so the further from Creation – and from the Abyss that lurks below us – the more light there is.'

'How about the Skymothers?'

'They are nearer their Creation because they watch over it.'

He pointed to a reddish star near the horizon. 'So is that one?'

She pulled his arm down and said quickly, 'Do not point! Not towards a Skymother!'

'Sorry. I forgot.'

'No, I should not have reacted like that. But that is a Skymother, aye. Medelwyr, our lady of the dusk.'

'And is another one coming up over there, where the horizon's glowing?'

'No, that is silvermoon rising, or perhaps cloudmoon.'

'I've forgotten about the moons too. Can you remind me?'

'The two moons and the sun that light the day are places of spirit and fire. When we die, our soul goes to one of those places – men to the sun, women to cloudmoon, children to silvermoon – where it is purged and judged. Most times, it will be found wanting, and returned to be clothed in flesh again. After all lessons have been learned, all suffering endured and all temptations overcome, a spirit may break free and ascend. Or, if it has fallen under the influence of the Cursed One it may be lost, banished forever to the Abyss.'

'Right, I see.' Sais started as a trace of white light, gone in an eye-blink, streaked across the sky. 'What was that?'

'Ah – I missed it! That was an early one.'

'An early what?'

'A falling star. We call them that but they are not stars, as the sky remains unchanged, no matter how many fall. They are a gift from the Consorts, for star-season: their bounty raining down.'

'I think you mentioned that. You were talking about the red rain and this silver one.' He remembered what she'd said now. 'So these falling stars bring fertility?'

'Aye. The land would not produce life save for this grace. And they bring skymetal too, sometimes.'

'Skymetal?'

'Aye, tis far stronger and brighter than ordinary metal. But only servants of the Skymothers may wield it. Arthen acts as priest for the village, so he has a disc of it.'

'The thing he held up in the council?' Besides a few bronze knives and spear-tips, Arthen's disc was the only metal he'd seen here, which seemed odd to him. 'And star-season is when this – ah – bounty, and skymetal, come to earth?'

'In truth it happens for some weeks. The week when the fall is greatest is star-season. The end of spring and the start of summer.' She laughed a little nervously. 'I am surprised you have forgotten star-season. Status is put aside, the Traditions disregarded. No work is done, and people are free to do what they will.'

'Sounds fun,' he said.

'Sometimes,' she said, then added, 'Neithion died at star-season, in a fight. I doubt he started it – most likely he tried to intervene.'

'I'm sorry.'

'It was the will of the Mothers.'

They were two weeks in now – nearly a third of the way to the market – and Sais was adjusting to the bustle and slog of the drove. He accepted going to sleep each night with his nostrils full of the reek of damp wool, rancid fat and sweaty feet, then waking up feeling as though he'd hardly had any rest, to eat an inadequate meal of unidentifiable dried fruit or a jerky indistinguishable in texture – and probably taste – from the straps on his pack.

Whenever the exhaustion and the cold and the filth and the hunger got too much, he reminded himself that he had no choice other than to go with these people. Eventually he would eat hot meals and sleep in a bed again, if he just *kept walking*.

Though the first few nights on the road had been free of dreams, after the incident with the reivers, the nightmares returned with a vengeance. Every night he was chased through bright corridors, pursued down dark passages, or mired and paralysed, waiting for a terrible fate. Often the dark eyes were there, watching him, boring into his soul. Sometimes the unknown woman called to him, entreating, or encouraging, or even cursing him.

It wouldn't have been so bad if the nightmares had led to him regaining any of his lost memories, but the details fled as soon as he woke up.

Kerin and Damaru took to sleeping away from him, in case his bad dreams triggered Damaru's skyfool abilities. Whilst Sais would have happily revisited the sensation Damaru had caused if there was any chance it might help him connect with his past, given the violent way Damaru's skyfool powers had manifested so far, he decided Kerin was wise to be cautious.

The valley they'd been following fed into one steeper and more dramatic, edged by the highest mountains he'd yet seen. Their tops were lost in cloud, and scree from their slopes swept down the valley sides in great grey fans. The stream from Maen Bulch, now a river, ran down the gentle creased slope to the valley bottom where it met a larger river called the Glaslyn.

They forded the Glaslyn at the bottom of the valley, rigging up ropes to guide the sleds across. From the caution they displayed, the drovers were terrified of falling in. Sais felt less concerned – he had an idea he could swim, though he didn't much fancy testing this assumption in a fast-running, ice-cold mountain river.

The valley bottom supported stands of trees; they took advantage to shelter from the frequent showers and to light campfires at night. On those nights when it didn't rain it was almost cosy sitting next to Kerin while she sewed, listening to the men sing and tell tales. Wild goats wandered the woods, and a couple of days out from Piper's Steps, Gwilym managed to bring down a youngster with a well-aimed slingshot to the head. Kerin roasted the choicest cuts on a lattice of green twigs, a meal which Sais found unbelievably delicious.

He was less enthusiastic about the fresh meat the next morning, having spent much of the night crouched in a bush trying to get rid of it. He made more unscheduled stops that morning, and by the afternoon felt weak and feverish. Kerin said she would make him an infusion to calm his stomach when they stopped that evening.

Then, near the end of the day, Huw ran back and said, 'The councillors have decided we need to press on through the night if we are to reach the Steps in time.'

Sais stared at him. 'You're joking.'

Unfortunately, he wasn't.

CHAPTER TWELVE

'They are here!'

Einon opened his eyes to the grey dawn light, confused for a moment to see grubby canvas, not smooth rock, over his head. Then he remembered: he was not in his room in the Tyr any more, he was in a tent halfway up a mountain with a bunch of hairy, ignorant uplanders.

'What?' he snapped at the man looking in through the flap.

'I am sorry, Gwas, I did not realise you still slept. Tis the drovers from beyond the grass plain. They are coming along the valley now.'

Einon sighed, 'Ah, give me a moment—' as the man withdrew. He had rather hoped these last three villages would not make it in time. He already had eleven sets of bickering clansmen expecting him to act as arbiter in their interminable disputes over cattle and precedence and ancient, half-remembered feuds.

Perhaps Einon's mentor had shown the wisdom of his rank when he dispatched Einon to this skyforsaken wilderness. Perhaps, as the terse letter that had ordered him out of the City of Light had stated, it *would* do Einon good to leave the confines of the Tyr and see new places for himself. More likely, there were hidden reasons for Urien, Escori of Frythil and the man Einon loved and trusted above all others, to send him out on a job better suited to a Rhethor from the estates. It probably came down to politics, something his mentor excelled in, but from which Einon had tried – and apparently failed – to remain aloof.

Yawning and shivering, he splashed water on his face, pulled his cloak around him and staggered into the morning twilight. The cattle were low shapes in the half-light, as still as the hills themselves. As the messenger led him past the fire the men sitting round it stood up and traced the circle. Einon nodded an acknowledgement.

By the time he reached the spot where he would greet this last group of drovers he could see an amorphous mass lumbering along the valley side. It began to resolve into individual figures as they closed the distance. His eye was caught by a lone figure walking a little apart. It loped along, then stopped abruptly to bend down, as if looking at some item of interest. Einon heard a faint, high-pitched shout and the figure appeared to hesitate, then came back towards the rest of the drove. The one who had called out went a little way up the slope and together they walked over to the sleds where they joined a much taller man. Even at this distance Einon could see he was different from the clansmen who surrounded them.

As they approached, Einon realised why the shout he had heard sounded so odd. It came from a woman. What in the name of the Mother of Secrets was a *woman* doing here?

As soon as the drove leaders were close enough to hail he called out, 'Well met, brothers. Be welcome in the name of the Five and take your rest.' Not that they would get much rest: the main body of the drove was already preparing to ascend the Steps.

The men at the front traced the circle, and one of them stepped forward and gave the ritual response: 'We seek to join those under your protection, and submit ourselves to the will of the Mothers, as given through your words.' Everyone traced the circle again, and the man added, 'I am Howen am Dangwern, and I lead the drovers from beyond the grass plain.'

'You have time for some food and to water your animals, Clansman, but we cannot delay much longer,' Einon said a little apologetically. 'We must climb the Steps today.'

A straggly-bearded youth with a scrap of cloth tied over one eye stepped forward and said, 'Gwas, I beg your indulgence.'

The older man glared at him, but the boy ignored him. He

made the circle and continued, 'I come before you as guardian to a skyfool.'

So that was the strange figure who had broken away from the others! But surely this youth could not be his father, notwithstanding the rumours of sexual improprieties amongst uplanders. 'Really, Chilwar?'

'Aye, Gwas. He is from Dangwern. My name is Fychan am Dangwern.'

'Kindly show me this, ah, skyfool,' Einon asked. 'The rest of you should make your way to the marshalling stations.'

As the drove started up again with whistles and cries, Fychan led him back towards the three figures he had spotted earlier. The skyfool paid the approaching pair no mind. He was trying to shake the woman off; he was on the verge of tears, she on the verge of exasperation.

The pale stranger sat on a rock, head in hands. He looked up as Einon approached, and Einon thought what a striking man he was, with a nobility entirely lacking in these uplanders. Fychan did not bother to introduce him, but Einon stopped anyway.

The man stared at him uncertainly and said, 'Are you a priest?' – as though, with his shaved and tattooed head, Einon could be anything else. His accent was odd; Einon had met people from the four corners of Creation in the City of Light, but he had never heard an accent quite like that.

'Aye, Chilwar, I am a priest,' he said. 'Do you, ah, do you have need of my services?'

'I'm not sure, perhaps … I think I may need to talk to you later.'

'Gwas!'

Einon looked up at Fychan's call. Fychan had the candidate skyfool by one wrist; the boy wriggled and squirmed. The woman next to him had a face as dark as thunder.

'Gwas, I present to you Damaru am Dangwern, who is of my blood and of my village, and who petitions to come before the Cariad and be tested,' Fychan said hurriedly.

Einon looked at the boy. He had seen candidates before, at the presentations and public testings, though never this close. This Damaru certainly had the ever-shifting gaze and gawky yet oddly graceful movements of a skyfool. This could change everything.

'I will hear your petition, Chilwar. Give me, ah, a little while to prepare, then bring him to the capel.'

'Aye, Gwas. Er, where is the capel, please?'

Einon pointed up the slope to the stone enclosure at the base of the Steps. 'There. Do not take too long. The drove must leave soon.'

As soon as the priest was out of earshot Kerin said, 'Fychan, kindly let go of my son!'

Fychan released Damaru's arm and the boy walked off, shook himself, then turned and came back and sat at Kerin's feet in a flurry of limbs. She put her hand on his head and stroked his hair to calm him.

Fychan began, 'He must be told to—'

'Fychan, what do you think you are doing?' Kerin interrupted. She had curbed her anger for too long. 'We have walked all night, Damaru is exhausted and confused, and now he must be *tested* – here, now? Why in the name of the Abyss did you not tell me this?'

'Do not interrupt me, woman!' Fychan shouted, going white with rage. 'I am his guardian! His affirmation is *my* responsibility – and it is *not* a test. Tis merely the first stage, when I come before a priest and swear to his worthiness!'

Kerin got herself under control and asked, more equably, 'Must Damaru go himself? Can you not speak for him?'

'My father said that the Traditions demand he be examined by a priest before he can continue any further.'

'Then we had best not keep the priest waiting, had we?' she said, her voice conciliatory.

'No! Arthen appointed *me* as his guardian,' Fychan said. 'You stay here – tend Sais, he looks unwell.'

Fychan was not wrong in that, but Kerin was not about to back down. She straightened and looked Fychan in the eye. 'If you believe you can convince my son to come with you without my help, then go right ahead. But consider this: if you hurt him, or distress him, not only might *I* never forgive you, but you may not live long enough to ask for that forgiveness. Or have you forgotten what happened to the reivers?' She strode off a few paces.

Damaru watched her, puzzled.

Into the tense silence Sais called, 'Listen, I don't want to interrupt, but I just wondered what'll happen if you don't do this affirmation thing now.'

Fychan lowered his head. 'If Damaru does not come before the priest, or if he is not found worthy – which he will be – then he and I must return to the village in shame.'

Kerin felt her cheeks reddening. This should not be about her dislike of Fychan, but about Damaru. 'Fychan,' she said evenly, 'will you permit me to lead my son to the capel? I will explain to him that when we get there he must go with you, and you can take him inside.'

Fychan's mouth twisted. Then he nodded. 'All right.'

Kerin looked at Sais.

'I'm just tired,' he said. 'I'll sit here and do nothing for a bit while you take Damaru to the priest.'

She nodded and went over to Damaru. After some whining on his part, she managed to get him to go with her.

Like the huts in the village they had passed through a few days earlier, the capel was square and built of stone. Two men lay in bedrolls on either side of the entrance. One, his clawed hands clasped on his chest, slept fitfully; the other, who had incense burning in a bowl next to him, was awake, moaning to himself. More victims of the falling fire, left to the mercy of the Mothers.

She told Damaru that he must go with Fychan, but he was unwilling to leave her at the threshold of the capel. Fychan tutted, and grudgingly indicated that she had better come inside too.

The priest, who had been kneeling before the crammed offering table, stood up and turned around. He had his ceremonial stole on: he now spoke as the voice of the Skymothers. As she made the circle, Kerin noted that this priest's stole was brightly woven and encrusted with polished metal, far richer than those of the travelling lay-priests who visited Dangwern. It also had a lot of green in it, rather than an even mix of all five colours.

The priest's eyes flicked over her dismissively, then he gestured to Fychan. 'Approach, Fychan am Dangwern.'

Kerin looked to Fychan, who said, a little sulkily, 'Gwas, Damaru is tired by his journey, and will not be parted from his mother.'

The priest raised his eyebrows, then cleared his throat. 'So be it. Tell her she may enter, but she must not intervene.'

Presumably the priest felt it below his dignity to speak to her himself, Kerin thought. To Fychan, she whispered, 'I will remain where Damaru can see me. Do not worry; I will not get in the way.'

Fychan led Damaru up to stand before the priest. Kerin shadowed them, making sure Damaru could see her out of the corner of his eye.

The priest raised his hands and eyes to Heaven and was silent for a moment. Then he looked at Fychan and intoned, 'Fychan am Dangwern, do you swear on the names of the Five that the boy who stands before me is, as far as you know and believe, touched by the sky?'

'Aye, I do,' Fychan said, his voice shaking a little.

'Damaru?' said the priest tentatively. Damaru had been looking towards Kerin and did not show any sign of having heard the priest. Einon moved in front of him and called his name again. When she saw Damaru frown, Kerin tensed, ready to call out a reassurance. Then Damaru looked at the priest; something about the man caught his attention and Damaru kept watching him, an expression of interest on his face. They stood like that for a while, the priest staring Damaru in the eyes, Damaru standing perfectly still, while Kerin and Fychan looked on.

Finally the priest stepped back. Damaru twitched his shoulders and looked around. He saw Kerin, focused on her briefly, then began to wander towards the capel entrance.

The priest spoke to Fychan. 'The candidate's petition is accepted.

Will you stand guardian for him in the coming journey and at his presentation and testing in the City of Light?'

'Aye,' Fychan said, then remembered his words and added, 'I so agree.'

'Then I recognise your role on behalf of the Skymothers. You will journey with this boy to Tyr Aryir, the Tower of the Sky, and there stand before the Cariad, the Beloved Daughter of Heaven herself. Go in peace under the sight of Heaven.'

Fychan made the circle. Kerin hastily did the same and followed Damaru out.

Sais was where she had left him. While they waited to be called to take their places for the ascent of the Steps, Kerin found the three of them some food. After Damaru had eaten he curled up on the ground and fell asleep.

'Will you be able to manage the climb?' she asked Sais quietly. 'Neithion said it was hard.'

'There's not much alternative.' He sounded awful.

On impulse she said, 'I know something that may help. Something Neithion showed me.'

'I'm open to suggestions,' he said.

'You will need to sit in front of me while I kneel up behind you.' She blushed, but he did not appear to notice any impropriety in her suggestion. As he settled himself, she began to massage his shoulders. He grunted as the knots in his muscles popped under her fingers, then relaxed, leaning back against her. 'That's really good,' he murmured. She questioned whether this intimacy dishonoured her dead husband's memory, then decided not: Neithion was at his rest, and she had to live for the future now, not the past. She kept her hands on Sais's shoulders for a while after she had finished. He did not tell her to remove them.

The call went up to move, and they joined the now far larger group of villagers who travelled with the sleds behind the councillors and the priest. The great mass of beasts, and the men and dogs herding them, brought up the rear. Kerin had never seen so many living beings in one place.

On the relatively gentle lower slopes great stone slabs had been laid, wide enough for ten men to walk abreast. Each stone tilted gently upwards and formed a shallow step. Damaru kept to the path most of the time, making occasional short forays up or down the hillside. As they walked, Sais asked her how the Steps got their name.

'It is said that long ago a Consort from the uplands played the slabs of rock into place with his bogwood pipes,' she replied. 'He did it to give his people a way over the mountains to the market without having to take the treacherous route along the Glaslyn Gorge.'

'This is the *easy* route? I'd hate to try the hard one!'

Kerin thought about her own words. There was something unreal about recalling this tale at the Steps themselves. And she was here in the company of a boy who might, Mothers willing, become a Consort himself. She had never questioned the underlying truth of such stories. Yet the Steps were obviously the work of men, and the skyfool was her own son.

After lunch, the mountain grew steeper and the Steps narrowed to become long sweeping switchbacks. Kerin looked back down the slope to see the line of men and animals strung out below her, the last of the herd still on the flatter, lower section. Above them, the path disappeared into cloud. Damaru stayed close now, as to leave the path risked slipping and falling.

The path narrowed further, and they moved into single file. Wet snow began to fall in great soggy flakes. They pressed on despite the cold and the poor visibility until the snow hardened to hail and the drove straggled to a halt. The men pressed themselves back into the hillside, hunching down in their cloaks until the hail had passed, leaving the air bitter. When Sais looked back at Kerin his face was pale as whey. She offered up a prayer to Turiach to give him strength; there was nothing else she could do for him right now.

A little later, they entered the clouds. The air grew misty, and droplets of water condensed on hair and clothes and soon froze. The view back down the mountain was swallowed up in featureless grey. Kerin found it odd that clouds looked like solid objects far up in the sky, but once you were inside them they were really nothing more than floating fogbanks.

The path was cut into the near-vertical rock face now, and Kerin found herself grateful that the mist hid the lethal drop off to the side. The endless climb through the chill grey twilight made her feel as though she were in a featureless nowhereland, on the way out of her old life into her new one. The thought did not worry her as much as she might have expected.

Sais was almost crawling now, leaning forward to feel his way along, his breath coming in harsh gasps. As the drovers in front of them began to pull away, a muffled cry came from up ahead.

Kerin, freezing and exhausted, assumed something bad had happened. She turned to look at Huw, who was following behind Damaru, to ask if she should go forward, but he was grinning.

'Do not fear,' he called back. ''Tis the men who go before us giving thanks for having safely reached the top.'

There is only so much that willpower can do, Sais concluded during the climb up Piper's Steps. Regardless of the will driving it, a body can take only so much punishment before it gives up.

The rest at the bottom of the Steps and Kerin's massage had helped a little, but all too soon they were off again, when all he wanted to do was lie down and never get up. Dizzy spells began to come in waves, along with weird visual effects. Despite the bone-numbing cold, the view shimmered as though in a heat-haze, and he kept glimpsing patches of darkness at the edges of his vision.

As his body climbed, his mind chased shadowy thoughts and he wondered – a faint hope – if in his delirium he might access those missing memories. At least if he were lost in his head, then his body might get on without him. It was a stupid thing to consider on a mountain, but he couldn't summon up the energy to be afraid.

He was already shivering by the time it began to snow, and after that his teeth chattered so hard he began to worry that he'd bite off his tongue and lose the ability to speak. This possibility terrified him, in a way the risk of falling hadn't, and he felt himself sliding back into the nightmare of evil, mesmerising eyes waiting to strip his soul. Only now he wasn't asleep; this time he wouldn't wake up—

A shout jolted him out of his reverie and he looked around, finding the world had been eaten by grey nothingness. His surprise turned to shock as his left foot slipped on a rock. Instinct took over: his right knee tensed to take the load and his arms went out for balance. His consciousness shot fully back into the moment and in his first clear thought for some time, he realised:

He was screwed.

His body was trying to compensate for the inevitability of gravity – arms flailing, the beginning of a shout coming up his throat – but he knew it was pointless. The formless void yawned seductively on his right and he was powerless against it. His knee buckled, but even as his mind welcomed the inevitability of the fall, he was vaguely annoyed to find that his body hadn't got the message yet and his hands grabbed at air.

He hoped the end would be quick, and not too painful.

CHAPTER THIRTEEN

Kerin knew what was about to happen a moment before it did; something – intuition, a sound, a movement out the corner of her eye – tipped her off—

But before she could react, her breath, her heart, her very being, was *frozen*—

—then freed again.

She staggered to her left, into the mountainside, hands splayed to catch herself, and while she teetered for a moment, her fear of the sheer drop was overlaid with the memory of this sensation ...

She took a deep breath, then another, until she was sure of herself again. Then she looked around. Sais was lying face down on the path, one arm dangling over the edge. Behind her, Damaru was sitting on the ground, whimpering to himself. Huw stood beyond Damaru, looking astonished.

'Did you see what happened?' asked Kerin.

'Sais slipped and fell,' said Huw, 'and Damaru snatched him from the air.' He circled his breast, then, coming to himself, called back down the line, 'We have a fallen man here! Everyone halt!'

Kerin bent to check on Damaru, who was upset, but unhurt. She murmured a quick reassurance to him and made her way further up the path to Sais. 'Can you hear me?' she whispered urgently. 'Sais, can you hear me? Are you all right?' He didn't react to her voice at all.

'How far to the top?' she called back to Huw.

'Not far. Is he hurt?'

'I do not believe so, though I cannot rouse him.'

'I will come forward,' he said, making his way carefully past Damaru. 'We will have to carry him.'

He and Kerin were trying to work out how to lift Sais safely when a couple of drovers appeared; they had come back down from the top to find out what was going on. One man took Sais's and Huw's packs; the other helped Huw carry Sais, leaving Kerin free to lead Damaru to safety.

Huw had been right: it wasn't long before the rocky steps became a wide, shallow path once again, and they soon found themselves on flat, open ground. The mist was thinner up here, though darkness was beginning to fall. They laid Sais down on one side of the path and Damaru plopped himself down beside him, all gangly limbs, like a basket of dropped sticks. He leaned forward on his elbows and stared moodily at the ground in front of his nose.

Huw and the drovers waved Kerin's grateful thanks away. 'The drove will camp here tonight,' said Huw, 'and that should give everyone time to get over the climb.' He patted her awkwardly on the shoulder and left her to look to her charges.

Damaru was already recovering – presumably it had taken less out of him to save Sais from falling than it had to kill the reivers.

Sais, however, showed no sign of awakening. She pulled up the lids of his eyes but in the dim grey light she could not see if the whites were discoloured. He was already unconscious, so there was no way of checking the other sign that everyone recognised: the inability to stand up. Perhaps it was just a fever brought on by exhaustion and shock.

That night Kerin prayed hard. Despite her exhaustion, she slept little.

The next morning, she awakened to find Sais clawing the air. When she checked his eyes, she saw the tell-tale orange tinge.

The mist had rolled back with the dawn to reveal a strange, barren land of low brown hills under a cloud-raked sky of deepest blue. Men were transferring the contents of the sleds onto carts, great sleds on wheels pulled by muscular oxen twice the size of their cattle. Kerin had seen such things only as toys Neithion had brought home for Damaru from previous droves; had she the energy to spare for wonder, she would have been amazed.

She was trying to get Sais to drink some water when Huw came over to check on them. 'Is he no better?'

'No,' Kerin said shortly.

'Then is it—?'

'Aye, I fear it is.'

He paused for a moment, then said, 'I will get the priest.'

Kerin nodded reluctantly, and Huw left.

The priest arrived with Fychan in tow, as she had expected. Fychan wanted to be in on this matter of interest, and for the first time in her life Kerin was glad to see Arthen's son. Though the priest would pray for Sais, in the end he would want to leave him behind. Her only hope of preventing this depended on Fychan.

As she stood to trace the circle she looked at the priest properly for the first time. He was older than her, and a little overweight. His heavily cleft chin and large ears were made more prominent by his hairless, blue-tattooed head. He regarded her and Sais with an odd mixture of confusion and compassion. 'Chilwar,' he said, surprisingly gently, 'your, ah, mercy does you credit.'

'Thank you, Gwas,' she said.

'Kindly arrange to leave what supplies you can spare in case the Mothers see fit to allow him to live through the fire's purge. I, ah, I will pray over him until it is time to go.'

Kerin took a deep breath. 'Gwas, I will not leave him.'

'What?' For the first time in her life, Kerin saw a priest looking confounded. After a few moments he said, 'Chilwar, you cannot stay here.'

'I will not leave this man. If he cannot go with the drove, I will remain with him.'

'You do realise,' said the priest, 'that most likely he will die, and you with him?'

'If you do not permit us to travel with the drove, then that may well be our fate. It is my choice.' Or rather, it was a gambit such as she made when playing gem, putting forward a brown to sacrifice in order to draw out an opponent's red.

'Then,' the priest said, looking perplexed, 'so be it. He must stay, and if you, ah, choose to stay with him, then I will pray for you too.' From the tone of his voice Kerin suspected he had only just avoided adding, *you stupid woman*.

'Gwas,' said Fychan, 'please permit me to talk to her.'

Kerin kept her eyes downcast, her expression fixed.

'If you think it will help,' said the priest. 'I will wait with the skyfool.' He walked off to where Damaru was pacing, staring alternately up at the sky and back at Kerin. Damaru ignored him.

'What in the name of the Abyss do you think you are doing?' squeaked Fychan as soon as the priest was out of earshot.

Kerin found it easy to be calm in the face of the boy's barely concealed panic. 'It is as I have said. I will not leave Sais.'

'What about Damaru?'

'He will do as he wishes, of course.'

'Which might be to stay with you!' Fychan slashed at the air with his hand.

'It may well be, aye.'

'You – then you must give me the bogwood bark. Now! Make a drink to calm him, and—'

'No, I will not drug my son to make your life easier. He will do as he chooses.'

Fychan started to raise his hand, and for a moment Kerin thought he might strike her. Then he dropped it again. 'I order you to give me the bogwood bark!' he shouted, and when Kerin shook her head, he screamed, 'You stupid old hag!'

Kerin said nothing. Gwellys had called her far worse.

Fychan said, 'You might not respect my authority, woman, but you would not refuse a priest's command!'

'So you are going to ask the priest to tell me to give you the means to drug my son?' asked Kerin innocently.

Fychan stared at her.

One of the many things Kerin had considered on this journey was why Fychan was so unpleasant. She had decided it came from living his life in the shadow of his father and older brother, with the fearful spectre of his dead grandfather in the background. He had never known his mother, and his grandmother alternately bullied and cosseted him. Now his father had finally given him a chance to prove himself – and Kerin was putting him in a position where he would have to expose his inadequacies to a priest, of all people, by admitting he could not control one wayward woman.

When she continued to silently meet his gaze, Fychan's shoulders sagged. 'No. I will not ask that,' he said.

Kerin said gently, 'Perhaps if you tell the gwas the nature of our companion, he might allow Sais to ride on one of the carts. I will take full responsibility for him, of course.'

'You had better,' said Fychan, and stalked off.

Kerin had won the first battle.

While Fychan spoke to the priest, Kerin murmured a prayer to the Weaver that fate continue to smile on her. She was relying on the priest not wanting to let a skyfool – who mattered far more than any number of disobedient widows – remain behind ... and that assumed Damaru would stay, and not let his desire to experience the pattern of the world overcome his sometimes vague and inconstant love for her. If that happened, she would be faced with a terrible choice: to see her son walk away, leaving her alone with Sais in this bleak, lifeless place, or to abandon Sais and crawl back to Fychan with a grovelling apology. But in the end nothing in Creation would stop Damaru going to his fate; Sais, if he lived, might stay with her.

Fychan and the priest conferred for some time. Damaru wandered off and Kerin found herself watching him, swallowing hard every few moments.

When Fychan came back he did not look happy, but he said, 'Gwas Einon agrees; he will speak to the carter who carries Dangwern's trade gear. But Sais's care is your problem!' Then he strode away.

Kerin let go a long hard breath and looked around. The priest – Einon – was walking across to the carts. She went to find Huw to help carry Sais.

The carter carrying the trade goods from the three villages was unenthusiastic about the arrangements, but he insisted on re-arranging his load himself to make space for Sais to lie down. Kerin dismantled Sais's pack to form a pillow and spread out his bedroll over him.

The drove continued to head steadily upwards. Though the path was not hard, Kerin's head felt as though she wore a band of metal around her temples, and her chest heaved at the slightest exertion.

Damaru was alternately entranced and perplexed by the novelty of this spare, unformed land. He would lope off, then stop and stare up at the sky, breathing hard, while the drovers filed past him.

Yet there was life here too. Kerin spotted grey-green rosettes no larger than the palm of her hand, the fat, fleshy leaves covered in fine white hairs. Tiny black beetles nestled in the stunted plants, hunted by lizards the size of a little finger, their colour exactly matched to their surroundings, so she saw them only when they pounced on their prey.

Sais was burning up, with high spots of colour on his ashen cheeks and his hands grasping and clawing over his chest. She managed, with some difficulty, to get him to suck some water from a wet cloth.

When they stopped in the evening Damaru carried on. Kerin ran after him, feeling as though she was running through mud. Ahead, Fychan also started to run. For a moment her heart skipped, as she half-expected him to try and grab for Damaru. Instead he drew level with the boy and called out to him. Damaru, distracted by the interruption, slowed, giving Kerin the chance to catch up a few moments later. By the time she had caught her breath and persuaded Damaru to return to the camp, Fychan had gone.

The carts had left caches of water and wood on their way up, and brought fresh food with them from the lowlands – barley-bread and herbed cheese, and succulent part-dried brown fruits Kerin had not tasted before. They lit a fire and ate well that night. After the meal Cadmael passed around a small flask of cloudberry liqueur against the night's chill. Were it not for her anxiety over

Sais and the relentless cold, the camp might have been the most pleasant yet. As the songs started, Kerin came up behind Fychan and asked if she could talk to him. After a moment's hesitation and a quick look around to check no one was looking their way he agreed. They left the circle of firelight and walked away into the freezing night. 'I wanted to thank you,' said Kerin, 'for showing mercy this morning, and also for earlier this evening, when you helped me with Damaru.'

He shrugged, a surprisingly shy gesture.

'And I wondered,' she continued, keeping her eyes down and her voice deferential, 'whether you would be willing to try and help look after Damaru while I am tending Sais?'

'I will keep an eye on him,' Fychan said, his voice a little husky. 'It is my duty as his guardian.'

She pressed a small packet into his hand. 'If he becomes too difficult and I am busy with Sais, mix a pinch with water; you will need to get him to eat something too, to disguise the taste.'

'You give me this now?' Between the firelight and the bright-blazing sky Kerin clearly saw Fychan's expression of irritated disbelief. 'Mothers give me strength!' he said, and walked off.

Kerin asked Huw to accompany her on a visit to the other campfires, where she asked people about their experiences of the falling fire. One man said his sister had recovered fully after five days; another told her how his cousin had hung on for ten full days, then appeared to rally before dying in the night. None of them had any advice on how to help, save to pray.

When Kerin came back to the cart where she had left Sais nestled under his bedding, she found this remedy already being given: Einon knelt by the cart, arms outstretched and face upturned; by his feet was a strangely wrought lantern that shone with a clear white light. Kerin knelt herself, a little way off, though she did not spread her arms; hugging herself was the only way to stop herself shivering.

Einon finished his prayers, picked up his lantern and left.

She made the circle as he passed and murmured, 'Thank you, Gwas.' He acknowledged her with a nod.

Sais remained much the same the next day, and the one after that: fevered, quietly moaning, with bouts of hand spasms followed by periods of deep unconsciousness. Einon prayed over him nightly, as did Kerin. The sky was always clear up here, and with the moons down to a sliver and nothing, the stars shone brighter than ever. This was as it should be, given they were closer to Heaven, yet the wondrous sky looked cold and unfeeling to her eyes, and her prayers sounded weak in the thin, chill air.

Damaru grew fractious, becoming withdrawn, grizzling and fussing if he was disturbed. Fychan did as Kerin had asked and shadowed him. When Damaru became distressed, Fychan came to find Kerin and she left Sais's side to comfort and cajole her son. Sais had been wrong to suggest that Fychan held a grudge against Damaru: to Fychan, Damaru was an unpredictable and dangerous force of nature, like fire or lightning – not a cause for hatred, only caution.

Around midmorning of the fourth day in the drylands, the wind rose, gusting up dust eddies like conjured spirits. Soon Kerin found herself blinking grit out of her eyes, barely able to see the cart ahead. What had started as a gentle sigh grew, with fearsome speed, to a deep moan.

The cart slowed, then stopped. People were shouting and animals bellowing, unseen beyond the whirling dust. The carter came up and shouted, 'Get under the cart, woman!' Kerin shook her head, pulled her shawl up around her face and struck out to where she had last seen Damaru. She found him crouched on his heels, his hands brushing ineffectually at the dust flying round his head. By the time she got him to his feet and led him to shelter, the dust was coming at them like knives in the wind.

She installed Damaru under the cart, then looked across to where Sais lay in his makeshift bed. He rested in a hollow in the centre of the luggage. Though he was in the lee of the wind, the bedding heaped on him was not, and as she watched, the end of his bedroll flapped free. She grabbed for it, and, stretching out over the rocking cart, caught an edge. As she grasped the bedding more firmly she climbed up the spokes of the wheels. She felt that if she let the wind get under her now, it might whisk her away into the wild sky, flensing the flesh from her bones. She pressed herself into the bundles, slithering over them until, half-falling, half-rolling, she fell into Sais's nest and rested beside him while the wind screamed overhead.

When she had got her breath back she checked Sais over. Dust crusted his nostrils and his breath wheezed and whistled. Left unprotected, he could suffocate. Kerin pulled her shawl up and held it out on her outstretched arm, forming a makeshift windbreak to protect his face.

Then she began to pray.

She reached the end of every formal prayer for deliverance she knew, and made up several more, yet still the storm raged. Her arm ached and threatened to collapse. Beside her, Sais burned hotter than ever.

Now out of prayers, she began to talk – or rather shout – against the wind, against the fear. 'Do not die, Sais! You must live, do you hear me? *Live!*' She paused, knowing no one would hear her, and wanting to say the words because she would not die without uttering them. 'You have to live. We must both live because I love you.'

As though it heard her, the wind dropped for a moment. It picked up again almost at once, and she felt suddenly foolish. When had that happened? When had she given this stranger her heart? And why? For all she knew, he had a wife waiting for him in the lowlands!

She put her head down, pressing it into the bundles, smelling coarse fabric, leather and dry dust. She had never felt so exposed, so alone, in her life.

Eventually, the storm blew itself out. As it abated, Kerin uncovered their faces and tried to massage some life back into her arm. Grit trickled over them and settled into every nook and cranny.

Sais's pulse was running weak and slow. The danger from the storm was past, but the falling fire had him deep in its grip. Around her she could see people standing up, brushing themselves off. She sent more dust cascading over them as she climbed down to check on Damaru, but he had already crawled out from under the cart.

He ignored her queries, which she took to mean he was unharmed, but indicating Sais with a nod of his head he said, 'Fading.'

'Aye, he is, Damaru,' she admitted sadly.

'Do you make medicine?'

'I would if I thought—' She stopped. If she *thought* indeed – this terrible place had driven all the sense from her. Perhaps she did have the means to save him!

CHAPTER FOURTEEN

As he huddled under the cart with the wind howling overhead, Einon wondered what in the name of Heaven he had done to deserve such suffering. Most likely he was a victim of others' schemes; much as he might wish the Tyr to be purely a seat of learning, it was the heart of power too, and politicking between the Escorai was ever apt to disrupt the lives of those serving them.

Yet that earthly explanation might merely be the means, not the cause. Could this punishment be a Heavenly judgment? He had been worried about his discovery, concerned that the Mothers had deliberately not granted their children the knowledge he had found, and so he had shown his researches to his Escori.

Urien had reassured him that his theories did not contravene the will of the Mothers – yet only a week later the Escori of Carunwyd had disappeared, and shortly after that, Einon had received the letter banishing him to these uncivilised western wastes. There *had* to be a connection. He prayed he would live long enough to uncover it.

The wind eased off, and with the danger passing, his fears of divine retribution felt rather foolish. If the Mothers had wished to show their displeasure he would never have survived the journey out here to meet the drove.

Nor would he have been blessed by the discovery of a skyfool. Damaru's rout of the reivers was the talk of every campfire, with the bard from his village called upon to recount it nightly in his quaint upland style of musical storytelling. Einon's own examination of the boy backed up the drovers' conviction: most souls

Einon sensed showed up as a tangled mess, with flashes of guilt or greed or love or other small, difficult emotions. He had felt a strange emptiness in Damaru, as though the boy were a blank piece of paper waiting for words to fill him, but at the same time the immensity of that emptiness had been frightening. It was like looking through a window, expecting to see a closed courtyard, and instead glimpsing the glory of Heaven.

A candidate that promising needed a priest to accompany him to his meeting with the Beloved Daughter of Heaven, and it was Einon's duty to take on that task. The Mothers had given him a reason to return to the City of Light.

The boy's mother might be a problem. He had still not discovered how the woman – Fychan said her name was Kerin – had managed to inveigle her way onto the drove, and he was already regretting his decision to let her bring the sick man with them. Two more cases of the falling fire had developed in the drylands, and they had been left by the side of the trail, as this man should have been. It did nothing for Einon's standing amongst the drovers that he should give in to a woman, then deny the wishes of men.

When he was sure the storm had blown over, Einon got up and brushed himself off. What he would not give for a hot bath – but no chance of that until they reached Plas Aethnen and he could call upon the hospitality of the Reeve. For now he must check that everyone had survived the storm.

No one had been hurt, though a steer had fallen and broken a leg. Einon showed the required regret, whilst secretly looking forward to a meal of fresh meat.

When he approached the invalid's cart, ready to perform his evening prayers, he smelled not just the aroma of roasting beef now drifting over the camp, but a different scent, not one he would have expected to encounter out here.

Kerin, leaning over her patient and squeezing a cloth into his mouth, did not see Einon approach, and she jumped as he asked her, 'Where did you get the Byth Melys berries, Chilwar?'

She made the circle, the cloth still in her hand, and said, 'Is that what they are? My husband traded for them on his last drove. I hoped they might help.'

'That is unlikely, Chilwar.'

'Why not?' she asked boldly. 'Are they not medicine?'

'Heavens, no! They are, ah, a delicacy in the City, well flavoured and keeping their taste for many years – but medicine? Only, perhaps, for the spirit in their toothsome and sweet flavour.' How uneducated these uplanders were!

Kerin flinched as though she had been slapped, dropped the cloth back into her bowl and glared at him.

Einon relented and added, 'I suppose your husband could not, ah, be expected to know that, and if some unscrupulous trader told him so—'

When she continued to stare at him in silence he felt his anger rise. It was almost as if this obstreperous, ignorant woman were somehow blaming him for her patient's condition. 'I have no time for this! My prayers will do far more for this man than giving him children's treats, so kindly remove yourself and allow me to petition the Mothers on his behalf.'

She turned on her heel and left without tracing the circle.

Einon sought out Fychan later that evening. 'The woman, Kerin,' he asked. 'Is her husband dead?'

'Aye, Gwas.'

It was as he had suspected, both because the husband was not here standing guardian to his son, and from her own unruly ways. What was less obvious was why she was going out of her way to help the sick man. 'And this Sais,' asked Einon, 'what, ah, what is he to her?'

'I do not know,' said Fychan, and Einon sensed the truth of his words.

'Tell me what you know of Sais,' commanded the priest.

When Fychan spoke of the man's lost past, Einon's interest was piqued. Here, at last, was a mystery worthy of a servant of the Mother of Secrets – always assuming the man lived, of course.

Perhaps the Weaver had set him on this path for a good reason after all.

*

Those tears of anger and frustration that escaped before Kerin could stop them dried quickly, leaving chill, taut trails on her cheeks. She hoped her ignorance had amused the priest.

She went back to the campfire to do some sewing. She had finished assembling the skirt; embroidering it would increase its value. Whilst looking for her threads she found the folded square of Sais's fabric. She pulled it out and ran it through her fingers: she would make a shirt out of it, for him to wear when he recovered – for he *would* recover; she had decided that. She set to her task at once, though she found the cloth surprisingly hard to cut.

The next day they came up onto a high plateau where pockets of frost lay in the hollows and everyone's breath steamed. They camped by a brackish lake edged with fragile fans of ice. When the animals approached to drink, swarms of black flies rose from the water. Though they did not bite, the flies investigated every crack and crevice, and Kerin wrapped Sais's head in her shawl for protection.

As she lay down by the cart to sleep that night, Kerin wondered if the priest had been to Dinas Emrys – he had mentioned the City, after all. Perhaps he had even witnessed a skyfool's testing. Getting him to tell her about it would be another matter.

The next day the land began to slope downwards. They followed the stream that issued from the lake. The ground started to support scrubby bushes and patches of wind-blown grass.

Kerin found herself increasingly glad of Fychan's watchfulness. As Damaru's irritation with this tedious place grew, so he took to misbehaving more than usual, deciding to lie down and stare at the sky in the middle of the day, or hiding amongst strangers, as though the other drovers were the most interesting thing he could find up here. Kerin was constantly being called over, and began to wonder about giving him the bogwood bark herself.

That night she took Damaru aside and asked him to play the harp, partly to divert him, partly because she had run out of ways to help Sais. She knew the falling fire was nothing like the malady that had first afflicted him, but her powerlessness in the face of his continuing illness twisted in her guts. But the harp strings went out of tune quickly in the high, dry air and Damaru gave up in disgust.

Sais remained unchanged: barely conscious, hot as the sun at noon, his body periodically afflicted with cramps and contortions.

The following afternoon they spotted the end of the drylands. At first Kerin could not make sense of what she saw: it looked as though the land fell away into white nothingness. Then she realised she was looking down onto the tops of clouds. They camped in a wide saddle at the head of the slope, where the sigh of the wind competed with the crash of the stream tumbling over the edge.

The next morning the carters had the strongest men from each village surround the carts to stop them running away during the descent.

Kerin was treated to the sight of the sun rising over a fluffy rose-gold landscape of mist and light. Damaru stared at the view, an absent smile on his face, until she dragged him away. The descent was nothing like as steep or narrow as Piper's Steps, though they had to zig and zag their way down meandering switchbacks. The stream took a more direct route, down a deep channel; the only sign of it was the roar of falling water and the occasional puff of spray.

As the morning warmed, the clouds dispersed and a rolling, fertile landscape appeared out of the mist below. Kerin was filled with joy to look upon green growing things after days of parched brown.

The wind dropped when they grew level with the remaining wisps of cloud and the air became thick and moist. The lower slopes supported stunted trees, their trunks covered in dripping moss, and the ground between them was carpeted with ferns, forming a miraculous land of soft, damp green.

That night they camped in the thick forest on the lower slopes, amongst more trees than Kerin thought could exist in the whole of Creation.

The next morning Kerin woke to music: a melodious twittering that filled the air. *Birdsong.* Back in Dangwern she had heard the

113

harsh cries of ravens and hawks, and occasionally the high trill of a moorlark. Neithion had told her that birds were everywhere in the lowlands, and how they sang to greet the dawn. She thought it the most beautiful sound she had ever heard.

Standing up after relieving herself behind a tree she came face to face with a small red-furred creature, somewhat larger than a vole, and with a twitching, bushy tail. It clung, head down, to the tree, regarding her with beady black eyes. When she put a hand out towards it, it turned on the spot and shot back up the trunk.

'Kerin!'

She recognised the panic in Huw's voice and rushed back towards the camp. Was Damaru in trouble? But as she came out of the trees she saw Huw standing by the cart where Sais lay, and her heart dropped like a stone. After all she had done, if the Mothers had taken him while her back was turned, if he had died alone—

She ran to Sais, who was drawing deep heaving breaths, his back arching. Huw looked at her as if she should know what to do; she wished she did. Suddenly Sais took a great gulp of air and fell back.

Kerin's own breath filled her body, fit to burst, to scream, to pray—

Sais gave a feeble cough, and opened his eyes. The whites were unstained. Kerin leaned over him, smiling so hard her chapped lips cracked. He blinked, and looked up at her.

He would live.

CHAPTER FIFTEEN

When he'd first awakened in Kerin's hut he'd clawed his way up from darkness into an unknown and frightening world. This time, there had been a merciful lack of nightmares, though he retained odd flashes of awareness from his illness – paralysing cold, Kerin's face blotting out the starlight, the feel of her body against his while dust pattered down on his face. This time, when he woke up, he knew he was with Kerin and the drovers.

He was surprised to see trees above him, and shocked when Kerin said he'd been unconscious for nine days, the whole journey through the drylands. 'You did not miss much,' she said. 'I would not have minded sleeping through that myself.'

He remained weak, and continued to ride on the cart for the next two days, walking for brief periods to get his strength back. It rained almost constantly, and he soon decided that the one thing worse than walking all day through rain was spending all day sitting on a damp cart being rained on.

On the third day, the rain finally stopped. Sais, still too weak to be much help, went for a walk while the men made camp. As darkness fell, he looked up through the tree branches to see a pair of moons emerging from tattered clouds, one a bright crescent, thin as a wire, the other just under a quarter full, pale grey in colour. He guessed the thin bright one was silvermoon, the other cloudmoon.

Staring at the moons he realised that everything he came across fell into one of three categories: things he knew about without being told, like clothes and eating utensils; things like the moons, that he didn't know about, but which made sense to him, or which he could work out with a little help; and finally, abstract concepts like the Skymothers and their Traditions, which meant nothing at all to him.

He looked down to see what appeared to be a small patch of brighter moonlight coming through the trees. He stood hurriedly.

The light was a lantern, carried by a portly man wearing robes. His bald head was tattooed with dark swirling lines that looked like stylised writing. Even as Sais remembered the priest he had met at the bottom of Piper's Steps his gaze was drawn to the cold, white light in the man's hand. He knew he'd seen lights like that before.

'Good evening, Chilwar,' said the priest as he approached.

Sais had no idea what *Chilwar* meant. 'Good evening,' he said.

After a moment's silence the priest said, 'Ah, tis true then.'

'What is?' asked Sais carefully.

'The drovers told me you have lost your memory. That you did not greet me correctly confirms this.'

Sais tried not to let his dismay at having screwed up in front of a priest show. Fortunately the man sounded more intrigued than offended. 'They're not wrong,' he admitted.

'So that was why you wished to call on my services?'

Sais tried to remember their brief conversation back before his illness and decided it was best just to agree.

'Ah, good,' the priest said, smiling. 'I may be able to help you.' He took a step closer. 'I have received some training in a technique that can, ah, uncover the hidden corners of a man's mind.'

Whilst that sounded like what Sais needed, he wasn't sure he needed it from a priest he hardly knew. And if the dreams that had been haunting him were anything to go by, the hidden corners of his mind might contain some scary stuff. 'Sounds interesting,' he said evenly.

The priest nodded. 'Aye, so it is. The technique, and the state you enter, is known as Cof Hlesmair. It is used by priests of my order to uncover memories thought lost. I wonder if you might permit me to, ah, to practise it upon you, to aid your recollection.'

'What does it involve?'

'I put you into a trance, and guide your memory back to the places it would not normally be able to go.'

Perhaps to places it didn't want to go – with good reason. But what was the alternative? His memory wasn't coming back by itself. 'I— Let me think about it.'

'As you wish.' The priest sounded disappointed. 'Perhaps when you are stronger?'

'Maybe. Thank you for the offer.' Then he added, 'That is a very fine lantern you have.'

'Aye, Chilwar. Such devices are given to priests of the Tyr to light our path when we are abroad from Dinas Emrys.' His tone implied that stuff like this wasn't meant for ordinary men. Sais filed the information away for later consideration.

As he headed back towards the camp he met Kerin coming out to find him.

'Are you all right?' she asked.

'I've just been talking to the priest. He kept calling me *Chilwar* but I wasn't sure what he meant.'

'Chilwar means penitent, or seeker. And you must call him Gwas, though his name is Einon.' Then she added, 'He has heard Damaru's affirmation and says he will accompany him all the way to the City of Light.' She didn't sound enthusiastic at the prospect.

'Instead of Fychan?' Fychan was no longer avoiding Damaru – that afternoon he had helped Kerin coax the boy down from a tree he had taken it into his head to climb.

'Oh no, Fychan is his appointed guardian and must accompany Damaru to his testing.'

'Kerin, I'm confused,' Sais admitted. 'I assumed that when Howen took over as leader for the three villages, that made him Dangwern drove leader, and also Damaru's guardian.'

'The guardianship has nothing to do with being drove leader.' Kerin sounded uncomfortable.

'Then what is it to do with?'

'I ...' She hesitated. ''Tis something that is never spoken of in Dangwern.' She sighed. 'Sais, everyone I have ever met knows everything about me … About my family. People never speak of it, but it waits like a blade dropped in the mud.'

'You don't have to talk about it if you don't want to.'

'No, this wound has festered long enough. We are no longer in Dangwern, and it is something you should know. May we sit down?'

'Of course. Pull up a tree.' He sat down on a knot of exposed tree-roots, glad to get off his feet.

Kerin hunkered down, leaning back against the tree opposite him. She started to speak, her voice a low whisper coming out of the shadows. 'My mother's father was a lay-priest. He was one of the gwas who wander between the villages preaching sermons and giving blessings in return for charity. My mother's mother was unmarried, and he claimed the right of Gras Cenadol – the fleshly grace – from her. He never returned to Dangwern, and my grandmother died giving birth to my mother.

'No one in the village had room for an orphan girl of low birth, so my mother was bonded to Loctar, the old chieftain. He had his pleasure of her even before she was old enough to bleed, and thereafter whenever he wished. Though Gwellys knew whose fault it was, when she saw that my mother was with child she beat her half to death. My mother ran away. I was born in the wilds, then left at the edge of the village.'

'Wait a minute – you're Arthen's *sister*?'

'Aye, half-sister anyway.'

'Shit! But the way they treated you in the village—'

''Tis shame. People are ashamed. Loctar was the chieftain. His crime could never be punished, or even spoken of, but to let me die would compound it, so I was fostered with a family who had lost their own baby.'

Though he couldn't see Kerin's expression, Sais could hear in her voice how hard she found it to talk about this. 'So Fychan is Damaru's cousin?'

'Aye. And the Traditions have it that if a candidate's father is dead, it must be another close blood-relative who stands guardian.'

Sais almost said, *You're his mother: how much closer a relative do they want?* but he already knew his views about sexual equality didn't match up to reality.

'So,' said Kerin, 'now you know.'

He wanted to go over and give her a hug, and tell her that one person in the world did care that she'd had to pay the price for her mother's rape, but she had stood up already and he could hear her moving off through the trees.

'We should get back,' she said softly.

Sais stood and followed her back to the camp.

The next morning the woodland gave way to rounded hills, a mixture of moorland and stony grassland, grazed by sheep. Around noon they came to a village surrounded by a stockade built of stone and wood. Huw told them the carters came from this village; the stockade was protection against outlaw bands, though they wouldn't bother the drove, given it now numbered more than two hundred men.

'It's a veritable army,' joked Sais – but Huw didn't know the word.

Sais decided not to visit the village. Though he felt strong enough, he was uneasy about making social mistakes. But he accepted Huw's offer to ask if anyone had seen him come this way.

He waited with Damaru while the others went into the village. People leaving the village to fetch water from the stream or work in the fields went out of their way to pass the dry-stone wall where Damaru squatted, obliviously tracing the lines of the stones with his fingers, but with Sais sitting next to him, no one approached too close. The dalesmen had the same wiry build as the uplanders, though they looked better fed. They were fairer in colouring, and instead of the drab browns and greys of Dangwern, their clothes were forest green or saffron yellow or ochre, and the women covered their hair with bleached white scarves.

Huw's enquiries didn't result in any useful information. If Sais *had* come this way, no one had seen him.

That night, camped outside the village, he asked Einon if this route was the only way up to the highlands. The priest said it wasn't, but that the others – via the rocky Glaslyn Gorge or the chill northern reaches – were far harder paths.

Sais asked if he could have come from the far side of the uplands, but Einon shook his head. 'Ah, no, Chilwar. There is nothing there.' Then he added, 'Wait here, I can show you.'

He went to his pack and brought back a hand-drawn map on a piece of thick off-white paper. Seeing how Einon handled the paper with careful reverence, Sais had a sudden moment of vertigo. Where he came from, such items weren't ways of storing valuable knowledge, they were *art*. Information wasn't shared using scraps of paper, but via books, which were sleek, clean boxes that displayed words – nothing like anything he'd seen here.

Einon, apparently oblivious of the effect his map was having on Sais, pointed out the mountains, symbolised by little upturned cones along the top and down the left-hand side; to the right, broken lines represented what he called the Great Waste, and along the bottom wavy lines showed fenlands. A stylised house marked Plas Aethnen. There were a few dozen such symbols on the map.

'Is that the City of Light?' asked Sais, pointing to a symbol like a spire with a cluster of tiny houses around its base. It was near the fenlands, to the south-east of Plas Aethnen.

'Aye, Chilwar, it is.'

Though the map made sense once Einon had explained it, nothing on it looked remotely familiar to Sais.

For the next week the weather remained wet and evenings were spent huddling miserably under the awnings. They stopped briefly at each of the few villages they passed.

The land became softer, the valleys covered in a patchwork of fields, the heathland relegated to the tops of the hills. They took to stopping over at farms with large animal pens, presumably built to house the drove. Some of the farms let the drove leaders sleep in their barns, an invitation Einon extended to Sais – the priest subscribed to the view that Sais was a lowland noble who'd somehow found his way into the mountains. Kerin, whom the priest generally ignored, was not invited. Sais accepted on rainy nights; otherwise he stayed with the drove.

Sais began to enjoy talking to Einon: the priest was intelligent, curious, and eager for knowledge. Sais was also hoping for more moments like those he'd experienced with the priest's light, and the map – flashes of insight that might point him back to his lost life. Unfortunately, nothing new got shaken loose.

When Einon repeated his offer of the trance-therapy Sais gave it more thought. The enquiries Huw had made had all drawn a blank, while there was definitely something about the priest – or at least his possessions – that linked in with Sais's past. He'd be running the risk of dredging up the nastiness from his dreams, but he'd had only a couple of bad nights since his recovery from the falling fire – perhaps the disease had burned the nightmares out of him. He decided to give it a go.

At the next farm Einon arranged to use the farmer's parlour, where they wouldn't be disturbed. Sais, still with misgivings, asked the farmer for a mug of beer to relax him. The farmer was happy to oblige the strange nobleman and one beer turned to several …

Sais sat across from Einon with an oil-lamp on the table between them. The priest produced a small, square-bladed knife to which he had attached a thread. 'My razor, which I will use to catch the light.'

'Your razor?' Sais had been wondering how the priest managed to keep his face and head hair-free. 'I don't suppose I could borrow that?'

Einon frowned. 'Ah, no, you may not! Tis made of skymetal – that is why it shines so.'

The beer was making him careless. 'Sorry. Of course it is.'

'Now, Chilwar, get yourself comfortable.'

Sais did his best, perched on a wooden stool. He could already feel the beer working its way to his bladder, and he wasn't convinced he wanted to do this at all—

'Relax, Chilwar,' Einon interrupted his musings. 'The mind can be seen as a great house with many rooms. Some are above ground, in the light. Others are below, in the cellar. In a case like yours, most of the rooms are in the darkness below. We need to, ah, explore this cellar together, to bring the memories into the light. You are with me so far?'

'Makes sense to me.' Sais wondered if Einon knew how patronising he sounded.

'As you have some knowledge of the world and the ability to make sense of new experiences, we can assume that the time of your life when you acquired such knowledge and skills is accessible. Therefore, we will, ah, we will start with something from long ago. We are going to find the door that leads to your earliest memory of being safe and happy and look inside. I will lead you down into the place where this memory is, and ask you what you find. When we have had a look around I will bring you back to the present where you will, ah, you will now have that memory to add to the manor house of your thinking mind. Do you understand?'

'Let's give a go.'

Einon twisted the razor over the flame. 'Watch the light on the blade. Do not think of anything else, do not worry, just relax. In a while I will count to ten very slowly, and each time I count, imagine yourself going down a step into this cellar. You should find your eyes closing: let them. You will be safe; I will be with you. We will find the lost memories together.'

'One …'

The uneven play of light on the blade made Sais blink.

'Two …' This would be easier if he wasn't having to hold himself straight on the stool, and he didn't need to pee.

'Three …' Einon had a very persuasive voice, but Sais knew very little about him, or about this technique.

'Four …' How far would this put him in the priest's power anyway?

'Five …' No, he needed to relax. His eyes were getting tired, so that was good.

'Six …' He began to sag on the seat; worried about falling, he pulled himself upright.

'Seven …' Get comfortable, close the eyes. Come on.

'Eight …' Einon had talked about steps, and he should have been using that to focus. He visualised a step.

'Nine …' Visualised stepping off it.

'Ten …' Into darkness.

Darkness was bad, the place were the pain was, he mustn't go there—

He opened his eyes. Einon was staring intently at him, still holding the blade over the flame.

Sais said, 'I don't think that worked.'

Einon lowered the blade and sighed. 'Apparently not. We can try again.'

'I think … Actually I think I need to get rid of this beer first.'

'Ah. The technique works best on an unclouded mind,' Einon's voice was tinged with disapproval. Then, seeing Sais's expression he added, 'But we should not give up. Perhaps another night?'

'Perhaps.'

CHAPTER SIXTEEN

Kerin found herself soaking up the new experiences as woollen cloth soaks up water: the gentle, sweeping hills with their towering forests, the light-haired dalespeople and their bright clothes; big, square houses with windows – she had not even known the word 'window' until Huw told her! – and countless new varieties of plants and animals.

Damaru was happy to be somewhere interesting again, though being amongst people brought its own problems. At one farm, Einon held a sevenday service in front of the small shrine that served as the farm's capel. Afterwards Kerin could not find Damaru anywhere until a shriek came from the stone farmhouse and a few moments later Damaru pelted out, followed by an irate woman: the farmer's wife had found him eating the bread she had left out to cool, and not knowing him to be a skyfool, she had grabbed her broom and chased him off.

After this, Einon said it was time to show Damaru's status by drawing the circle of the world on his forehead, as candidates in the City were so marked. Kerin saved a piece of charcoal from the night's fire and re-drew the circle each morning. Damaru treated the process with an air of bemused tolerance, soon coming to accept it as part of his routine.

Kerin was surprised the farms let them stay, given the fuss and mess the drove made; she had not even seen them leave any animals as payment for this service. Huw explained that they used money down here; she had Neithion's string threaded with a handful of thin metal discs – *coins* – but they would not buy much

124

in the City, Huw said. She must hope her skirts fetched a good price.

Money was on Howen's mind too: he complained loudly of the drain Sais was putting on the drove's resources, and wondered when they would get the promised reward for saving him. Fychan, who had seen Kerin making the shirt from Sais's fabric, suggested she should sell it and give the profits to the village. Kerin refused.

Kerin had achieved a strange sort of status amongst the drovers: mother of the miraculous sky-touched child and nurse to the mysterious stranger who survived the falling fire. Sais's presence was seen as part of this peculiar blessing, particularly as there had been just one new case of the falling fire since his recovery. Though the drovers chose to get their injuries and ailments treated by one of the male healers now travelling with them, several had Kerin look over them afterwards, as though her touch would aid healing. Even Huw, troubled by an infected tooth he would have to get pulled at the star-season fair, asked for her blessing.

Sais's company brought joy to Kerin. He showed her tenderness and respect such as no man save Neithion ever had, and she dared hope he might return her feelings for him. She began to wonder if the Weaver, who had laid the cloth of her life so rough and uneven until now, had finally seen fit to release the tension on the threads. She looked forward to star-season, when, if the Mothers willed, she and Sais might become more than friends.

But before they grew any closer, she must tell him her full history, not just the circumstances of her birth. She had to know he could accept her tainted heritage completely ...

The chance came on the evening that Sais tried Einon's trance healing. When he returned to the drovers, she asked him whether the priest's ministrations had helped.

'Unfortunately, no; it didn't work,' said Sais. 'I don't think I was relaxed enough.'

'Were you worried about touching on the matters that disturb your sleep so?'

'That was the main thing, yes. Perhaps I should have told Einon about my dreams, but it's pretty private stuff.'

So Sais did not trust the priest completely. Kerin tried not to let her relief show. 'As long as you do not directly lie to him ...'

'What do you mean?'

'Priests have the ability to smell out untruths.'

'Shit, I didn't know that! I'll have to be careful.' Then he added, 'I hope you don't mind me saying this, but you don't seem to like Einon much. Did something happen while I was ill?'

Kerin said, 'Not really.' Then, before she could lose her nerve she added, 'Tis not Einon as such I dislike. I ... I have a problem with priests.'

'Because of your grandfather? I got the impression that was quite normal; being able to have their way with any woman they take a fancy to seems to be one of the perks of the job.'

'Aye, so it is. No, tis not that. Can we – can we go somewhere quieter?' She led him away from the farm buildings and they sat by one of the animal pens, leaning against the hurdles. Behind them the animals shifted, lowing and stamping.

'Tis about my past,' Kerin began, 'about what happened when I was a child.' She paused, and took her courage in hand. Sais had to know it all. 'The family who fostered me treated me well, though no one would speak of my birth, save to say it was a matter of shame. In my fifth year my mother returned. She must have been watching a while, as she came to me in the oat-fields at harvest-time. She told me who she was, and said not a day had gone by that she did not think of me. At first I did not believe her. Then I became angry – she had abandoned me! Then she told me how she had come to be with child, and been cast out for it, and how by the time I was born she was half dead and had no milk to feed me. By leaving me she gave me at least the chance of life.'

'How did she survive?'

'Reivers caught her. They have few women and it suited them to keep her alive.'

'Poor woman. How did she escape?'

'She did not. The reivers let her go. Two men had fought over her, and after both died of their wounds the reivers abandoned her and moved on.'

'She was lucky they didn't kill her.'

'T'was not luck. My mother was sky-cursed.'

'Oh.' He looked concerned, and added, 'I'm afraid I don't really know what that means.'

'A sky-cursed woman will charm and control those around her, and they will not even know they are under her influence. As with a skyfool, the change comes as the child enters adulthood, and is slow to flower. My mother was a young girl when she fled; she did not fall to the depths of her curse until she was amongst the reivers.

'She did not tell me she was a witch, of course. I found that out later.

'She took my hand and led me from the field into the village. I trembled like a reed, but she strode into the moot-hall to confront the man who had wronged her. She demanded he make reparation by giving her a place to bring up the child that resulted from their union. Loctar agreed, though his council later tried to dissuade him. I lived with my mother in something like happiness for almost four years.

'Then a priest came to the village. He saw my mother for what she was. Once Loctar realised he had been enthralled by a sky-cursed woman, he wanted her out of his village. And me, in case I was also tainted – which I am not, else my life might have been very different.

'They came for her in the night. That was their mistake, because the darkness worked to her advantage. She befuddled them. I crouched low beside the loom while men jumped and slashed at shadows. Then one stabbed something that was not a shadow. Loctar died of his wounds before morning, finally paying the price for his crime. The man she had tricked into killing him was banished.

'The priest knew she would do something like this. He waited outside our hut, and when she grabbed my hand and we ran, he caught her. I escaped.

'Now our positions were reversed: my mother was in the village and I waited outside, unsure of her fate.

'At dawn the next day a procession left the village. The priest was at its head, dragging my mother, who was tied and blindfolded and staggered as though drunk. Everyone followed them up to the mere to witness his judgment.

'Though I was told of her fate by Arthen, no one knows that I saw what happened from my hiding place in the reeds. The priest said my mother was a servant of Melltith, but that was not so. She was not evil. She was my mother, who had been abused, and who had risked everything for me. But what could I do? If I had protested, then I would only have joined her. The priest said they would send her back to her master. They tied stones around her wrists and her neck. Then they pushed her into the silent pools and watched her sink. They expected her to keep falling until she reached the Abyss. She did not, I am sure of that. She lies there to this day, unshriven, her soul bound to the land below, a damned spirit that can never be reborn.

'That is why I have no regard for the words of priests.'

'That's awful, Kerin. I am so sorry.' He sounded appalled.

Kerin wondered if he would try to hold her, comfort her. Part of her wanted that more than anything … But not yet. He felt a compassion some would call weakness, and she would not take advantage of that. She said, 'Please, do not be. Tis not your fault.' She stood up.

They walked back to the farm in silence.

Though neither of them spoke of their conversation Kerin felt a weight lift, knowing he did not think less of her for her past.

For the next few nights they camped in fields, so Sais had no further chance to try Einon's trance healing, though he continued to spend time with the priest. One day, about a week out from the market, he said to Kerin, 'Einon says he can arrange for me to stay at the Reeve's manor at Plas Aethnen. That should put me in a more relaxed state, especially as there's a promise of a bath and a bed. Given the nightmares are still holding off, I'll probably try another session of this Cof Hlesmair then. The only thing is, it means I'll be abandoning you for part of star-season.'

'Please, do not concern yourself! You must do what you need

to do in order to get your past back.' She meant it, though she also felt a twinge of disappointment that he would not be with her for all of star-season, and another of guilt, for she hoped that his recovered past would not turn out to include a wife.

'Thanks. After that, I'm probably going to ask Einon if I can carry on to the City with him. Is that what you'll be doing too? Because,' and he laughed, in that self-mocking way of his, 'though I get on pretty well with Damaru, considering, I don't much fancy travelling with Fychan and Einon without you along as well.'

Kerin smiled. 'I would like nothing more.'

'That's settled then.'

Not that the decision was theirs to make. Kerin could do nothing to influence Einon, but she did her best to make friends with Fychan. She avoided antagonising him or making him look foolish, as she had over the bogwood root. One night she suggested a game of gem. Fychan looked surprised, then agreed. They soon reached a point where she could win at a stroke. She wondered why he had not seen it. Her hand hesitated over her black; then she moved a brown instead. The game ended in a draw.

The weather stayed dry and warm for the final days leading up to star-season, though mist cloaked the land in the mornings and the afternoon sky was often filled with racing grey-tinged clouds. Every clear night she would catch sight of the silver streaks of falling stars. Occasionally a larger flaming trail would hang overhead before fading.

Their track became a stone-paved road running through rolling chalk downs. Trees overhung the road, green with new leaves and sprinkled with pungent off-white flowers. Their route was busy and smaller parties often had to move aside to make way for the drove.

One day they passed a cart accompanied by men in smart blue coats carrying small, intricate-looking tools that Huw said were weapons – the men were monitors, the church's warrior-guards, and the strong-box on their cart likely contained money: tithes for the church.

The whole land was cultivated now, either given over to

fields of crops, or grazed by large brown cattle. ('They give good milk,' said Huw with a herdsman's eye, 'but their meat is tasteless and fatty.') Kerin marvelled at seeing nature so thoroughly tamed.

The drove usually arrived before star-season, but the delays meant the Sul service marking the start of the festival had to be held outside Plas Aethnen. The next day an air of anxious anticipation hung over the drovers: they had had a long, hard journey, and had lost friends to reivers and the falling fire. Now they wanted the reward at journey's end.

They reached Plas Aethnen late that afternoon, the first day of star-season itself. The great manor house looked out over a sprawl of buildings extending down to a meandering river. Kerin tried counting the buildings, then gave up. The stone-built houses had two storeys and high-peaked roofs of red tiles; even the lowliest dwelling in Plas Aethnen looked to be as large as the moot-hall back in Dangwern. Now she understood the lowlanders' contempt for uplanders who lived in huts of brushwood and mud – and yet she could not help being born in the mountains, and it had not made her less able to think, or learn, or be useful.

On this side of the river, a massive tree-edged meadow enclosed on three sides by one of the river's loops was covered in tents and awnings and animal pens: the star-season fair, a temporary village devoted to trade and pleasure. Kerin was torn: part of her was eager to sample the new experiences; the other part felt unsure, worried that the combination of the lawlessness of star-season and her own ignorance might get her into trouble.

While the drove leaders went in to find the stockmen to take charge of the beasts the carts were unloaded and people reclaimed their trade goods. Kerin had decided to keep back her favourite skirt to wear for the fair and in the City; she suspected she might get a better price for it in the City afterwards. She added the left-over scraps from Sais's shirt to her woven items.

Sais came up as she sat next to her pile of possessions. 'I'm going with Einon now,' he said.

'Aye,' she said, more curtly than she had intended.

'We're here for six days, so I should be free to join you in a couple of days, depending on how things go with Einon.'

'As you wish.'

'You make sure you have fun, all right?'

'I am sure I will. Good luck.' She made herself look away from his departing back.

With the sun long-set and fires and lanterns springing up around the meadow, word came that animal pens and camping space had been allocated. As the last to arrive they were relegated to the marshy ground near the river. The men were eager to finish pitching camp so they could get down to the serious business of partying, and Damaru caught their restless mood. She sat with him, talking to distract him from the hectic anticipation of the camp – and to distract herself. Before they left this place, she felt sure decisions would be taken that would set the course of the rest of her life.

CHAPTER SEVENTEEN

As he walked through the crowded streets of Plas Aethnen – the first place he'd seen deserving of the name 'town' – Sais couldn't help feeling he was abandoning Kerin. Not that she couldn't look after herself, of course – he was amazed at how well-balanced she was, given all the crap she'd been through. Still, she was his best friend; he felt like he'd known her all his life.

In some ways, he had. And that was the problem.

Though he was getting better at interacting with the world – or at least better at faking it well enough not to upset people – he still had no idea who he was, or where he'd come from, or how he'd ended up here. His decision to carry on to Dinas Emrys was mostly down to the nagging sense of familiarity about Einon's lantern, which came from the City of Light; it gave him hope that he might find some answers there.

When they reached the Reeve's manor Einon became almost embarrassingly solicitous, requesting rooms for 'my guest', and offering to lend Sais money. 'You will not need anything while we are under the Reeve's roof,' he said, 'but on the road to the City of Light we shall be staying at inns. You can pay me back later.'

Sais had been wondering about money, as presumably not everyone lived by trading cows and skirts. He had no choice but to accept Einon's offer of a loan, though it put him further in the priest's power – as would attempting the Cof Hlesmair technique again. The priestly ability to spot lies made him uncomfortable. He had an idea that kind of thing wasn't normal where he came from. And that belief was one more indication that his home was

132

nothing like this place. Even the sky was wrong here. And as for the Skymothers ... how would a priest react to finding that the gods he worshipped meant nothing to Sais? He might be able to choose his words carefully when they chatted together, but would he be able to edit his responses when he was in a trance?

He was introduced to the Reeve, the cleanest, fattest person he'd seen so far, then shown to a room containing the sort of soft furnishings he'd been fantasising about for the last few weeks. Before worrying about anything else, he would just spend a day or two enjoying being dry and well-fed and *clean*.

He rang for a servant and asked for a bath and hot water to be sent up. While he waited, he took off his socks for the first time in weeks. His blisters had hardened to black calluses, making his feet look unfamiliar. He felt giddy. What made these ugly, rough appendages his? What made the memories that assaulted him his? What made him the person he was, other than a desire to re-learn who he had once been?

A goblet of wine and a long soak in a wooden tub of warm, scented water put things into perspective. He got out of the bath to find clothes laid out on the cushion-covered bed. The tight-fitting russet-brown leggings and sleeveless top were a little small, unlike the voluminous cream shirt, which needed constant tucking and adjusting. But the clothes were clean and smart enough that he didn't look too out of place amongst the Reeve's other guests.

The price for the Reeve's hospitality was to add interest to the festivities. While Einon kept largely to his rooms, Sais was expected to attend all of the long formal meals and associated entertainments, and to mingle with the other guests, all over-fed, overdressed and over-full of their own importance. His initial concern about making mistakes proved unfounded: word of his situation had got around and they treated him as a novelty, laughing at his odd accent, and asking him – repeatedly – if he really could remember *nothing at all* before he woke up in what one jowly gent described as *that nameless little cluster of mud huts*. Though he did his best to be polite, he missed the earthy honesty of the drovers. Despite the material comforts of the manor, he was tempted to head back down into the market.

But then he'd be running away from a chance to get his past back. Though he was always on the look-out for clues, he was also in denial; most of the time he didn't let himself think about the terrifying possibility that he might never recover his memory. Einon's offer was risky, both because of the likelihood of stirring up his nightmares, and for the chance he might inadvertently tell Einon something the priest would find unacceptable. But the alternative was to spend the rest of his life in a world he knew he didn't belong in, reliant on others' charity.

Civilisation at last. Even more than the prospect of getting clean, eating properly and sleeping in a decent bed, the chance to resume his studies lifted Einon's heart. Walking past the cattle pens on his way to the manor, he saw the loops of tally ropes and felt a tingle of anticipation. The hollow circles, meaning nothing and everything, recalled the entrancing possibilities for counting and calculation opened up by his discoveries.

His rooms were well-appointed and the Reeve, honoured at having a Tyr priest staying at his manor, was happy to supply him with parchment and ink.

Only one thing was missing. Einon had expected to find a letter from his Escori waiting at Plas Aethnen, instructing him, he hoped, to return to Dinas Emrys now he had brought the drove safely in. Though it mattered less now – the skyfool gave him reason enough to travel to the City of Light – Einon was desperate to know what was going on in the Tyr, and how it might affect him and his Escori. That Urien had failed to send word implied the situation – whatever it was – had worsened.

Two other matters further distracted him from his work. One was Sais. The man was a puzzle he felt compelled to solve, but he sensed a deep reticence in him. The other problem reared its head when, after dinner on the first night, Einon watched Sais politely but firmly refuse an invitation to dance a galliard with a painted maiden. Sais seemed to hold a particular appeal for the women at the Reeve's court, something he appeared largely oblivious of.

As he watched the girl sway her way off to find a more receptive partner, Einon felt the unexpected warmth of bodily desire. Such base distractions were an annoyance, easily solved in the Tyr by a visit to the *Putain Glan.* Here they were a complication he did not have time for.

He had his chance to address one of his problems the next day. A knock at the door made him jump and smudge his workings. The continued lack of any message from Urien was telling on his nerves.

'Who is it?' he called.

'It's me, Sais.'

Einon got up and went through to the reception room. He opened the door. 'What can I do for you?' He would happily put his work aside for a while if the amnesiac had finally decided to accept the offer of another Cof Hlesmair session.

'I was wondering about the arrangements for travelling on to the City of Light,' said Sais.

'As I said, we will, ah, be staying in inns.' Why was Sais asking him this now?

'All of us? Kerin too?'

'Kerin?'

'I'd assumed she would come with us. To look after Damaru.'

Einon had assumed no such thing. 'Fychan is the boy's appointed guardian.'

'Of course. It's just Damaru is so much calmer when she's around. And,' Sais smiled, 'I feel a lot more relaxed when I've got her to look after me.'

The woman showed an alarming lack of respect, but the men she travelled with appeared to value her company. In truth Einon had given very little thought to her fate once the skyfool's party left the drove behind. 'I suppose she *could* come with us,' he said grudgingly. 'She will, ah, have to make her own arrangements, of course.'

'I'm sure she's expecting to.'

When Sais did not immediately turn to go, Einon said, 'Was there something else, Chilwar?'

Sais considered for a moment, then said, 'I was thinking I might be ready to give your trance technique another go.'

'Excellent! Come through and sit down.'

They sat as they had before, though this time far more comfortably. Sais's eyes had already begun to close by the time Einon reached a count of four. He paused after reaching ten, praying silently that Sais's eyes would remain shut. They did.

Einon said, 'The door is opening before you, and you are going inside.' He saw Sais's eyelids flicker: a result! He had achieved the state of Cof Hlesmair.

'You are somewhere safe now,' he said gently, 'somewhere you know well. It is the first place you remember feeling comfortable and at home. Have a good look around. This place is known to you; you merely need to re-acquaint yourself with it.' He could see by Sais's face that it was working; that he was walking through old, perhaps lost, memories. He wondered what Sais saw. He carried on talking in a low, calm voice, telling him to touch things, pick them up, examine them in his mind's eye. He would have liked to expand the memory, maybe move it on, but he could feel the damage in Sais's mind; they must take it slowly.

He counted down to bring Sais back and waited while he reoriented himself. Finally his impatience overcame him and he asked, 'So, what do you recall?'

'I – I'm not sure,' Sais said, uncertainly.

'But it worked?'

'I think so. I just feel … a bit odd.'

Cof Hlesmair sometimes left the subject a little confused. Einon put out a hand, not wanting him to leave without revealing something of what he had seen. 'You should rest a while. I will fetch you a drink.'

Einon had wine left from lunch. He went into the reception room, where he had put the tray, and had just picked up the flagon when someone knocked on the door. He walked over and opened it, ready to tell the man to return for the tray later, but rather than a servant in the Reeve's red and green livery, the person on the threshold wore travel-stained midnight blue, and he had one arm in a makeshift sling. He gave a small bow, then said, 'Would you be Einon am Plas Rhydau?'

'Aye, that is me.'

'I have a message for you from Escori Urien. May I come in?'

Einon stepped back to let the monitor enter, closing the door behind him.

The man reached inside his jacket. 'I must apologise for the delay: I had some trouble on the road.' He proffered a letter, and Einon took it eagerly.

'I was instructed to await your reply.'

'Ah, I see.' So it *was* urgent news. Einon broke the seal, which showed the pinnacle and five stars of the Tyr. He recognised Urien's neat, precise handwriting and began to read.

Far from being clear orders on what Einon was to do next, the letter was full of trivial news: accounts of the preparations for Sul Esgyniad, observations on new acolytes, even comments on the weather. Confused, he raised his head from what appeared at first sight to be a shocking waste of both paper and the monitor's time.

A line of pain clamped itself across his throat, cutting off his breath. He tried to cry out, but managed only a faint burble. Even as he raised his hands to claw at his throat, he wondered why the monitor was not rushing to save him.

The constriction tightened as his attacker pulled him closer, into a lethal embrace. He smelled dust and sweat. He stopped trying to get his fingers under the cord across his throat and instead elbowed his assailant as hard as he could. He was rewarded with a faint 'whoomph' of surprise, but the grip did not slacken.

A deep hum grew to fill his head and darkness began to creep in at the edges of his vision—

Suddenly he was shoved forward into the table. The carved edge caught him on the hip, momentarily distracting him from the pain around his throat. He staggered back, aware that – thank the Mothers! – he was no longer being strangled. He took a deep, rasping breath and put a hand to his neck, where he felt a thin line imprinted across it, but no blood.

As sense returned he realised he was hearing sounds of a struggle. Someone grunted near his feet. When he looked down he saw Sais and the monitor fighting on the floor; it looked like the monitor had got the upper hand, for he was pinning Sais down with his body.

Einon's mind tried to make sense of what he was seeing. One of these two men had just tried to kill him—

The monitor got a hand free and reached for his belt. Einon saw the knotted thong still wound round his fist: a garrotte, the ultimate solution to the more extreme disputes in the Tyr.

Einon looked round for a weapon. The heavy earthenware flagon had fallen over and spilled wine across the table, but it had not broken. Einon snatched it up as the monitor drew his dagger and with the unnatural strength of the deeply terrified he smashed the flagon over the monitor's head.

The man paused for a heartbeat, then slumped over Sais.

Sais struggled out from under the monitor, onto all fours, then into a sitting position. He looked up at Einon. 'I was wondering what happened to that drink,' he said breathlessly. 'Are you all right?'

Einon, not trusting himself to speak yet, nodded. Then he staggered over and yanked the bell-rope.

This place was full of surprises, Sais decided, and most of them were nasty. Within moments of Einon calling for help, the priest's rooms were swarming with servants and guards. Sais, his limbs quivering and his temples throbbing, took the opportunity to slip away and wobbled his way back to his own rooms.

He lay on his bed, willing himself calm, trying to drive the madness of the fight from his head. He had no idea who the attacker was or why he had tried to kill Einon, and right now, he didn't care.

That unpleasant little interlude had interrupted him as he'd been coming to terms with the first real clue to his past. The therapy had been a success, with both his fears – of nightmares, and of saying the wrong thing to Einon – happily proving to be unfounded.

He'd done as Einon instructed: he'd visualised a room he'd slept in as a child. Even as he'd reached backwards under Einon's gentle guidance, part of him felt uneasy, aware that he was venturing beyond the veil of his amnesia – but the main part of his mind, relaxed in the trance, just did as the priest asked. The recollection had the garish clarity of a child's memory: a bright, spacious room full of unknown items, nothing he'd yet come across here. The quality of light was similar to that given off by Einon's lantern. He couldn't pin down details like the name or function of the items, only a feel for what they had meant to him: how he enjoyed playing with this toy, his preference for that item of clothing, the physical sensation of sitting in this particular chair. He did recall a window; unlike the narrow unglazed windows with their wooden shutters he'd seen so far here, this was a huge, single piece of glass, keeping out the pounding rain. Though whatever lay on the other side held little interest for his childhood self, he thought it might be significant to him now.

When night fell, he rang for a servant and gave his apologies for not attending dinner. Word of the incident in Einon's room must have spread, as his excuse of a bad headache was accepted without question. He was too unsettled to eat the food that was sent up, but he drank the wine gratefully.

Einon visited him shortly afterwards to thank him for his timely intervention. The priest still looked shaken.

Sais asked if he had any idea of the reason for the attack.

'Politics,' said Einon grimly. 'Matters I try to steer clear of, and which you, ah, would be wise to avoid altogether, Chilwar.'

That night the nightmares returned with renewed force. Time after time Sais woke sweating and gasping from dreams of pursuit, violation, suffocation. When he recovered enough to remember where he was he found himself torn between dread of returning to the dark chaos of the dream-world, and hope that his dreams might finally start to unlock his past, now the initial step had been taken.

He was awakened midmorning by a knock at the door: a servant, sent to check he was all right as he had missed breakfast. Sais sent his apologies to the Reeve and said he was still indisposed. As the door closed behind the servant it came to him: the window looked out over the *sea*. His room, the place where he had grown up, was near the sea – a word he hadn't heard here, but which he knew meant a great body of open water.

Wherever that room with its huge window was, it was nowhere on Einon's map.

CHAPTER EIGHTEEN

Waking up at the star-season fair that first morning, Kerin felt joyous anticipation, tempered with apprehension and an ache of desire as yet unfulfilled.

She followed some of the others through trees laden with pink blossom down to the river to get clean. Damaru could not be persuaded to do more than wash his face and hands, after which he sat on a flat rock, watching the water. As she reached inside her shirt to scrub herself, Kerin decided her best course of action was to let Damaru wander wherever he wanted – once she'd made sure the mark of his status was clear – and she would follow him. That way he would be happy, and she could view the fair safely under the protection of her sky-touched son.

Back at the camp she changed into her skirt and re-drew the circle on Damaru's forehead. Then they set off into the fair, Damaru in the lead.

She followed him out between animal pens where sellers and buyers haggled over the beasts until they emerged in front of a row of coloured tents with no fronts to them – stalls, Huw had called them. He had advised her against carrying her money, because she would either find herself spending it on things she did not need, or worse, have it stolen. She regretted her decision when she saw the tables laden with bread, honeyed fruits, fine cloth, wooden trinkets, scented unguents, leather shoes, fine-woven belts, glazed pottery … Everything she had ever dreamed could be sold or traded was here, and more besides.

Everyone they saw greeted Damaru with inclined heads and

smiles of indulgence. As usual he gave little sign of noticing. Instead he wandered between stalls, picking up items to get a closer look, or re-arranging displays in a way that fitted in with his idea of the correct pattern. Kerin doubted such behaviour would be tolerated from anyone else, but everyone considered it lucky to gain the attention of a skyfool ... although the man on the stall selling glass goblets was visibly relieved when Damaru moved on! They followed their noses to a griddle where festival cakes were being cooked. The stall-holder, seeing the now-smudged symbol on Damaru's forehead, offered him a round golden cake and then, after a moment's hesitation, gave one to Kerin too. The cake was made with a finer flour than Kerin was used to, giving a lighter texture, though the flavour was not as rich.

At first Kerin was uneasy at being amongst so many strangers, even with Damaru, who evoked universal goodwill in those they encountered. But most people ignored her and after a few awkward moments, she learnt not to look anyone in the eye, nor expect them to speak to her.

They passed a wooden stage where gaily dressed men and women were acting out the story of Carunwyd's Harper: she recognised the witch by her mask, and the skyfool bard who defeated her by the symbols painted on his face. The players broke off their performance to pay their respects to Damaru.

When he grew overwhelmed with the new sensations, they made their way back to the camp. A bullock had been butchered and was cooking in the fire-pit, filling the air with the delicious smell of roasting meat. Some of the drovers returning from the fair to share the feast already smelled of ale. Fychan had replaced his old scarf with a new eye-patch of fine leather. Free of the dirt of the road and wearing his best shirt, he looked as fine as any of the young men about the place. Cadmael wore a bright sash of what Kerin recognised as more of Sais's fabric – he must have found it up at the mere before the drove left.

Most of the men returned to the fair after the evening meal to dance, and maybe find themselves some company for the night. Kerin would have liked to dance herself, but Damaru was tired.

She stayed with him by the fire, watching the falling stars trace their paths in the dusk and wondering what Sais was doing.

The next day they visited the roped-off area at the edge of the meadow where drovers and townsmen were competing in games of skill and strength: running foot-races, demonstrating their accuracy with a slingshot or thrown spear or lifting yokes of weighted barrels. Kerin cheered on those Dangwern men who were competing. She was starting to become accustomed to the passing attention of strangers; the trick was to smile at people without looking straight at them.

When Damaru grew bored, they moved on to the stock-pit, where the audience watched showmen displaying their skills. They saw a man in motley being chased by a fully grown bull and cheered madly with everyone else when he got behind it, grabbed one horn and put the animal down with a deft twist of his wrist.

Mindful of Sais's promise to come and see her in 'a couple of days', she left early to head back to the camp. Though anyone who saw the symbol would treat him with respect, Damaru sometimes wiped it off by accident, and a lone, guileless boy without the protection of Heaven might come to harm in the wild star-season evenings – but this meant nothing to him and he was petulant when she insisted he go back with her. But Sais did not come, though she stayed up late, listening to the faint sounds of merriment drifting across the torch-lit expanse of the fair.

The next day cloud covered the sky and the smell of rain hung on the air. Kerin decided to stay in the camp to wait for Sais; Damaru wanted to go back to the fair, and threatened to throw a tantrum when she said he must stay with her. She was wondering if she should let him go alone when Fychan strolled back into the camp. The chieftain's son had not returned last night; the beribboned girl on his arm explained his absence. Fychan spotted Damaru and led his companion over. Damaru ignored them both. Kerin nodded a greeting at the girl and said, 'Fychan, I have chores around the camp. Please, would you accompany Damaru today?'

She saw his expression flicker: he was tired from an evening's enjoyment and none too pleased at Kerin's request – yet what reason would he have to bring the girl back other than to prove his claim to be guardian to a skyfool? He straightened and looked at his companion. 'Aye, I think we could do that,' he said after a moment.

Kerin finished Sais's shirt: the fabric had been so hard to work that it had taken far longer than she had expected. Then she cleaned some clothes and mended holes in their travelling gear. When the rain came on in the afternoon, she sat miserably in the shelter of a tree and wondered why Sais had not yet kept his promise to visit her.

The weather cleared in the evening, and the sun went down in a glory of gold. They were now halfway through star-season, and she had yet to dance. If Sais did come from the manor, he would have to pass the riverside arena where the dancing was held; she could keep an eye out for him. In the meantime, pining was doing her no good.

A little guiltily, she gave Damaru some bogwood with his evening meal; his attempts to join in the star-season dancing could be disruptive, and for once she wanted to enjoy herself. Once he was safely asleep, she accompanied the drovers to the meadow.

She could hear the music long before she saw the torches in their tall holders; heavy drum-beats and skirling pipes merged in the star-lit darkness.

Four separate parties had been set up, all with barrels and sweet-meat sellers off to one side. The men were heading for one hosted by a local vineyard. Kerin spent more money than she should have on a token that allowed refills from the barrel for as long as the music continued. From the edge of the crowd she could see the stone bridge that linked the fair with the town, though the figures who crossed were no more than shadowy shapes. Heaven's sake! She must stop thinking about Sais and instead do as he said and enjoy herself.

The first sip of wine surprised her. After Huw's description she had expected it to be sweet, and the way it ran along her tongue, sucking out the moisture, disconcerted her. The second sip went down more easily.

Walking back to refill her beaker she moved in time to the music, skipping to the fast-tripping beat. The next dance began slowly, and the floor initially emptied. Kerin's heart fluttered as she recognised the opening of the Morwynaith, the Maids' Dance. For this, any single woman could go out onto the floor alone. Though she had not danced it for years, she still remembered how. Before she could lose her nerve she put down her drink.

The heavy swish of her skirt round her ankles carried her out of the anonymity of the crowd onto the centre of the floor. She began with her eyes cast down, her movements slow and languorous, her mind empty of everything except the music. As the beat picked up, so her movements matched the increased tempo. The music sang through her and she found herself beginning to smile. She felt free, light as a feather, yet sure and steady as a river. All eyes were on her, and that was no cause for shame or embarrassment. The music quickened and she threw her head back, grinning wildly as she stepped and kicked and twirled. Above her, the sky was a rain of silver stars. Her spirit soared and she could have almost shouted out loud at the perfection of the moment. As the last notes faded into the night she stood, rigid with joy, arms wide and head held high.

The next dance started and she walked, a little unsteadily, off the floor to reclaim her drink. She stood to one side, watching Fychan dancing arm-in-arm with his new lady-friend, smiling to herself. A few men had already cast glances her way, and perhaps if one asked her—

'I wasn't sure it was you, until I saw the skirt.'

She turned to see a gentleman in a fine doublet. Then her wine-and-music-fuddled mind caught up. She resisted the urge to throw her arms around him and instead took another calming sip of wine. 'And you look quite the nobleman,' she said.

He looked down at himself. 'The Reeve's gift,' he said. 'The Reeve also insisted on sending a guard with me – he's in the crowd somewhere.'

So he had found his true place. Before she could stop herself Kerin said acidly, 'Perhaps you should not have come, and put your host to such inconvenience.'

'Kerin,' he said, spreading his hands, and she wondered if he, too, had been drinking, 'I've had enough of them, with their "wit" and their "banter" and their "snobbery". I wanted some real people.'

'So then, shall we dance?'

He hesitated. 'I don't know the steps.'

Kerin felt suddenly contrite. 'Oh— Of course. How did…? How is your memory?'

He pulled a wry face. 'I think Einon *can* help me get it back, but it's not going to be easy.' He frowned. 'I have got some good news,' he said, though his expression belied it. 'I've persuaded Einon to let you come to the City with us.'

Kerin tried not to let her elation show – but Sais still looked uneasy. 'Is something wrong?' she asked.

'Last night someone tried to kill Einon.'

'No! Who would attack a priest?' She felt faint at the very thought of such impiety.

'No idea yet. They're questioning the man as we speak.' He grimaced. 'But that can wait – for now, I just want to have some fun with my friends.'

Kerin wished she had known he would come, so she could have given him the shirt she had made. She said instead, 'Can I get you some wine?'

Her token was good for only one cup, so she filled hers and brought it back to where he waited, smiling and tapping his foot to the music. She gave him the drink and he took a swig, then looked at her.

'Aren't you having any?'

'I – I thought we could share it.'

'Sure.' He gave it back.

'Are you sure you do not want to dance?'

'I'd like to, if I thought I wasn't going to trip everyone else up. So best not, I think.'

'Then' – she took a gulp of wine to get her nerve up – 'then maybe we could go for a walk?'

Behind them the party continued, the dancing getting wilder, the laughter louder. Kerin heard occasional giggles and groans from the darkness and wondered if he heard them too, and thought as she did. Or perhaps he heard only her heart, banging like the stones on a loom. When they passed a closed-up stall with no one in sight she said, 'Shall we sit?' Her voice sounded shrill in her ears.

'Good idea,' Sais said easily. 'I'm exhausted.'

She sat first and he passed the beaker down to her and sat next to her. She moved up against him and he hesitated, then put an arm around her.

'You're a good person, Kerin,' Sais started. 'Your life ... the things you've endured' – she felt him shrug – 'I don't know – I can't remember what I've experienced, but if it's half as grim as your life—'

'Hush,' she said, 'none of that is important now. Tis star-season, and only the moment matters.'

She pulled back a little, turning to look at him. Though the sky was bright with stars, they were in shadow and she could not see his face clearly. She put the wine down and reached up, her hand brushing his hair. He turned to her and she felt a sudden tension go through him.

She waited for him to kiss her. When he did not, she turned her head, eyes half-closed. Her lips brushed his cheek, then found his lips. She kissed him, tilting her head back, dizzy with the moment.

After a slight hesitation, he returned the kiss. She felt his lips part.

How odd, to lead the way like this, she thought. *How wonderful; how wicked.*

Abruptly, he pulled away.

She leaned back towards him, but he shook his head.

'Tis all right,' she whispered, against a chill that had nothing to do with the night air. 'I know you may have a wife somewhere, and I know that my dead husband's soul may stir at this, but tonight, now, in star-season, to love like this is the will of Heaven.'

'It's just—' He shifted awkwardly. 'This is wrong.'

'No, tis right, as right as anything in Creation! Please ...' All or nothing. 'I love you.'

'What?' He jerked backwards.

'I said, I love you.' She began to wish she had not said it.

'Kerin— I— I had no idea!' He sounded genuinely shocked.

'What do you mean, *you had no idea*?'

'I'm not— Kerin, I like you a lot, but—'

'No!' She scrambled to her feet, kicking over the wine. 'Do not say another word!' She turned and ran. She heard him start after her, and some part still hoped that he would stop her and tell her he cared after all. But she knew the truth now. She had been a blind, wanton fool, seeing love where it did not exist.

She ran blindingly, ducking under ropes and past stalls, aware only of the need to get away from her bitter embarrassment and disappointment. Revellers pointed and laughed, but she ignored them.

When she finally slowed down and looked around she found herself near the show-pens. There was no sign of Sais. She took a deep sobbing breath and started back towards the camp.

She jumped as a man lurched out of the shadows.

'Who'zere?' he slurred.

'No one, I am no one,' she murmured, surprise turning her tongue to nonsense.

'No, someone,' said the man unevenly. 'Someone pretty, mebbe, who wants company?'

'No. Not pretty at all.' She looked around. They were in a passage between two tents – she either had to push past the man, or turn her back on him.

''m sure y'are. Tis star-season. Our sacr'd dooty.'

'No!' Kerin had twice taken advantage of star-season to bed men other than Neithion; both had been men she had liked, and neither experience had been particularly special. A drunken stranger propositioning her when she had just been spurned by the only man she wanted was a cruel joke.

He did not take the hint. 'C'mon, mistress! Have some fun!' He lunged forward – surprisingly quickly for one so drunk – and grabbed her arm.

Kerin tried to shake him off, but he held tight, his fingers digging into her flesh. He got his other arm round her. Kerin's attempt to break free threw his balance and the two of them fell back into the side of the tent, which bowed, then began to rip.

Suddenly her wounded heart mattered not a jot. She cried out and tried to hit the man. Her blow went wide and her scream died in surprise as they fell through the fabric.

He landed half on top of her and clamped a hand over her mouth. 'Shhh, shh,' he said, almost tenderly. 'I won'nurt you. Stay quiet now.'

He took his hand off slowly. He reeked of ale and sex and his cock pressed against her flank. She drew breath to scream.

He cuffed the side of her face, just hard enough to shut her up. 'No!' he barked, 'no screamin', or else. Hear me?'

Kerin blinked back tears. Had Sais been following close enough to hear her shriek when she fell? Even if he had, how would he know it was her? She was on her own, and this drunken brute was too strong for her.

She nodded slowly.

'Tha's good,' he said. 'Jus' a bit of fun. An' our sacr'd dooty.' He began fumbling with his breeches with his free hand.

'Aye,' she whispered, 'our sacred duty.'

She saw the flash of his smile.

'Let me help,' she said. She made herself reach into his breeches. His cock was hot and sticky. The smell of him almost made her gag.

'Tha's good,' he said again, though this time it was more like a sigh.

She moved her hand further down, trying to ignore the stuff that crusted under her nails as she ran her hands over his balls, stroking that place that should ensure the complete attention of any man.

As he moaned happily she brought her free knee up and across into his belly, at the same time squeezing her hand as hard as she could.

She had never heard a man make a noise quite like that before.

CHAPTER NINETEEN

Why hadn't he seen the signs? He'd shown respect to Kerin, something men rarely did to women around here, and she'd obviously misinterpreted it – perhaps he should just have treated her like dirt from the start, and saved them both a lot of grief! No, that wasn't the answer. He wasn't sure what was, but he couldn't let her go off like that.

The guard, who'd hung back at a tactful distance while he was with Kerin, soon caught up as he ran after her. When it became obvious that he'd lost her he asked the guard to show him where the upland drovers' camp was, but when they got there she still hadn't returned. Sais wondered for a moment if she'd gone back into the fair to dance and drink her sorrows away, but as he turned around she stumbled into the camp, distraught, her face red and tear-stained.

He ran up to her. 'Shit, Kerin, are you all right?'

She raised her chin and looked over his shoulder. 'I am fine,' she said quietly.

'I was worried about you,' he said. 'It's not safe out there.'

'You should not concern yourself.'

'I am concerned! Listen, I just want to say that I—'

'No!' Her voice, which had been a whisper, was suddenly an angry shout. 'I do not want to hear it. Go away!'

'This is my fault. I didn't realise you felt that way. I care for you, but—'

'I said, leave me alone!' She looked him in the eye, and the pain he saw there made him flinch. Then she took a step back, raised her hand to hold it in front of her eyes, her thumb straight across her open palm, and screamed, 'I do not see you! You are nothing to me!' She turned and strode away.

The guard put a hand on Sais's elbow. 'Master, she will not return. She has declared you am-annwn.'

That must be the personal version of the council's ruling back in Dangwern, he thought. Until Kerin changed her mind, he didn't exist for her.

Finally she felt able to look back. Sais was gone and the few people around were carefully ignoring her. When she had arrived in the camp her heart had still been pounding from the terror of her near-rape, and the success of her desperate ploy which had left her attacker writhing in agony in the ruins of someone's tent. Seeing Sais calmed her, as though she had gone so far that nothing could affect her any more.

Her outburst had woken Damaru. When she staggered over to him he stood up, rubbing his eyes. He put his arms around her, comforting her as she had so often comforted him. Her eyes began to water and she was suddenly heavy with unshed tears. She sank to the ground, slipping free of his grasp. Hugging herself, she cried as she had never cried before, letting out a lifetime of hurt, her mind blank and her pain raw, under the cold gaze of the Skymothers.

Her first thought when the tears finally spent themselves was that she and Damaru should gather their gear and leave before dawn. She began to stuff clothes into packs, but her hand brushed sheer fabric and she recoiled, then pulled out the shirt she had made for Sais. She tugged at it viciously, trying to rip it, and when it would not tear, she flung it away as hard as she could.

The act brought her to her senses. They could not just leave: Damaru's destiny was to travel to the City of Light, and she must go with him. She had been neglecting her son. Now she must live for him again, as she had before Sais had come into her life. She would have to travel with the man who had broken her heart, and though she would rather walk on knives, that was what she would do.

Belatedly, she tried to pray, but no words came: Carunwyd, who had dominion over matters of love, had not granted her wish. Medelwyr would weave the future as she saw fit.

Too upset to sleep, and with dawn still far off, she lay in the dark and considered what she would do once Damaru was gone. Though her foolish dream of a future with Sais was shattered, life must go on.

Her skills were such as any woman of her background might have: cooking, crafts, keeping house. It was possible she might find a single man who valued her experience enough to marry her – aye, as likely as being able to step up into the sky and eat honeycomb with the Skymothers.

Neithion had told her that rich lowlanders lived in big households served by others who were not bonded to them. And even if she could not find a place as a paid servant, would being a bondswoman be so bad? She would lose her freedom, but she would have bed and board and purpose, however menial.

Then there was that other servitude to which women are said – by men – to be suited, the one her mother had endured. Sais had awoken physical desire in her, and though she doubted women who made their living selling themselves enjoyed the acts they performed, these were desires men would pay to have fulfilled ... though maybe not by an ageing and less-than-comely widow. And this path assumed she could bring herself to become an object for strangers to use. Her experience with the drunken oaf implied she might not be able to.

It looked as though she might have to return to Dangwern after all.

Finally the sky lightened and the men began to wake up. Kerin was searching for scraps for Damaru's breakfast when Fychan returned, looking happy and walking unsteadily. He was certainly making the most of the season. As he walked past, he noticed the abandoned shirt and picked it up. Before he could say anything she said, 'You like it? Then have it. Tis yours. I wish you joy of it.'

He took the shirt and nodded his thanks, looking confused.

Shortly afterwards she saw the other men talking to him, no doubt recounting the drama he had missed.

She spent the day listlessly following Damaru round the fair, barely seeing the entertainments and spectacles.

The men still treated her warily that night, looking away when she met their eyes. Huw brought her some food, saying she should eat. She muttered thanks and managed a few mouthfuls. After the meal Fychan came over. She was prepared for mockery or censure, but he held out a small pot. 'For Damaru,' he said. 'He keeps rubbing the charcoal off, and he can hardly be seen like that in the City.'

Kerin took the pot. It contained paint, such as women used to adorn themselves. It was orange, the colour of Medelwyr. Kerin was not sure which surprised her most: that Fychan should give Damaru a gift, or that he remembered which Mother ruled over her son's birth.

With the assassin safely in the care of those members of the Reeve's staff experienced in extracting answers from uncooperative subjects, Einon re-read Urien's letter, a task made more difficult by the wine stains it had acquired in the fight. But the only useful piece of information amidst the unimportant chatter was the observation that Idwal, the Escori of Carunwyd, was still missing.

Einon tried to return to his studies, but his concentration kept wandering. Even keeping his door locked and with a guard outside, he found himself jumping at every noise. Perhaps in response to his brush with death, his lustful thoughts returned with renewed vigour. The evening after the attack, the Reeve sent him a woman to alleviate the problem. She had some skill, but Einon still felt uncomfortable bedding a wench not conditioned to the task.

The next morning the Reeve's Rhethor came to tell him what his attacker had revealed. The assassin, a Tyr monitor, had been corrupted to serve Sefion, Escori of Mantoliawn. This did not surprise Einon, as Sefion was the most expedient of the five Escorai. The monitor's orders had been to intercept the letter despatched by Urien. If the letter was for Einon am Plas Rhydau, then the monitor was meant to find and kill the recipient, then bring back the letter. Because Urien's man was also a Tyr monitor, it had taken the assassin some time to persuade him to reveal Einon's current location, and the questioning had left the messenger dead.

Sefion's man was made of stronger stuff, and had survived the Reeve's enquirers. The Rhethor asked if Einon wished to publicly pass judgment on him – a formality, given the penalty for attempting to kill a priest was death. Einon declined: he felt no personal enmity to the man who was, after all, merely a tool of higher powers; plus he wanted to avoid attracting attention to himself.

He wondered what he should do now. To return to the Tyr openly would obviously be suicidal. Perhaps he should remain here: only Urien and the soon-to-be-dead assassin knew he had come this way ...

After some thought and much prayer, he decided to look at the letter once more. He could not believe Urien had gone to so much effort just to pass on gossip. As he unfolded the paper again, he realised the apparently meaningless words might not be the message, merely the carrier. Urien must have known there was a risk of the letter falling into the wrong hands, so he might have disguised its content. However, he would expect Einon to be able to find the real message. The letter must contain a cipher! When Einon had shown him his discoveries, Urien had commented on the possibility of using the new numbers for such tasks.

Einon set to work.

Finally, on the last morning of star-season, he uncovered the hidden words:

Corruption in the heart. Return at once. Take great care.

The short message raised more questions than it answered, and given the means by which Einon had come by the letter, the third part was redundant.

But his Escori had summoned him. He must obey.

Without Kerin or Einon for company, Sais threw himself into expanding the memory Einon had unlocked. After the first night, the nature of his dreams changed to include details stolen from his life here: one night he dreamed he was wading through a bog; when he finally managed to haul himself out he found he was trailing mud across the floor of the half-familiar childhood room. The next night he was being chased by unseen enemies in a house his dream-self knew well, and then up onto the moors where he found himself pursued by the villagers of Dangwern. Though less unpleasant than the recurring nightmares, they were no more helpful to his recovery.

He had more luck when he was awake. His mind began free-wheeling, chasing associations. Breakthroughs came at unexpected times: seeing a brother and sister talking at the Reeve's table he felt sure he had a sister who'd sometimes come to the room he remembered; watching a chandelier in the main hall being lit one evening made him remember that the lights where he came from were operated by switches and buttons. Nothing as concrete as names or images accompanied these flashes, and he wished he had some objective evidence for what he was remembering – he was worried his imagination might be filling in details he was desperate to recover.

The other guests began to avoid him, which suited him fine.

He hardly saw Einon; when they did meet the priest was friendly, but distracted. Though he asked whether Sais had remembered anything of interest from their Cof Hlesmair session he obviously had other things on his mind – understandably enough – and accepted Sais's vague answer. When Sais mentioned the upcoming journey to Dinas Emrys, Einon was equally vague in response.

Then, on the last evening of the festival, Einon came to his room and explained what they must do.

For the remainder of star-season, Kerin kept company with Damaru and tried to take what pleasure she could in the festivities. She considered trying to find herself a man, one she had chosen herself, before deciding she could not face a stranger's touch.

On the last afternoon, a messenger from the manor brought unexpected news: Einon had been called away to deal with a family crisis, and would not be accompanying them to Dinas Emrys after all. Though Kerin did not mind being spared the priest's company, she had hoped to benefit from his knowledge, not to mention relying on him to occupy Sais. Cadmael commented that Fychan should be able to enjoy his trip to the full now there was no priest to keep an eye on him; like most of the men, the bard envied Fychan his chance to see the City of Light.

When the time came to leave her people behind and accompany her son to the Cariad, Kerin said farewell to everyone from the three villages, even those who had shown her no consideration. To Huw, she said, 'I wish I could repay you for your kindness, and I pray we have not put you to undue trouble.'

He looked away, embarrassed, then said, 'T'was no trouble. I wish you and your boy the blessings of Heaven.' As she turned to go, he added, 'You are a powerful sharp woman, Kerin, sharp and strong. If you had been born a man you could have gone far.'

Kerin did not know whether to be flattered or furious.

CHAPTER TWENTY

The day after the star-season celebrations ended, Sais thanked the Reeve, then went down to the drovers' camp to say his goodbyes. Huw was genuinely sorry to see him go. When Sais said he wished he had some practical way to express his gratitude, the villager grasped his arm and said with a smile, 'You have given me quite a tale to tell my boy when he grows up. That is payment enough.'

Kerin stood off to one side, looking ready to take on any part of the world that didn't include Sais.

Once they'd left Plas Aethnen Sais explained Einon's ruse, saying that the priest had enemies who he wanted to mislead. The others were understandably disturbed by this turn of events, but Sais couldn't tell them much more; Einon hadn't confided in him exactly who his enemies were, saying he would be safer not knowing.

When they reached the inn Einon had told Sais about, they waited. Einon arrived a little after sunset and led them in prayers for a safe journey which, whilst they meant nothing to Sais, went some way to cementing their little group

Though Sais was glad of Einon's growing trust and friendship, he was still wary around the priest. Everything he'd got back so far implied he came from somewhere well outside Einon's experience; the priest operated from a position of self-assurance that occasionally bordered on arrogance, and Sais suspected it would be a mistake to challenge his worldview. A religious culture that executed people for attempted murder probably did something unpleasant and terminal to heretics. So when Einon asked what he had remembered so far Sais kept his answers unspecific, telling the priest that he'd had a safe and luxurious childhood with plenty of toys and comforts – and a sister. He didn't mention growing up near the sea.

Now they were on the road again, Sais no longer felt half-drunk on memory. On the drove he'd discovered that the best way to survive walking eight to ten hours a day was to let your body get into its own rhythm while your mind went off by itself. Walking allowed the strangeness from his subconscious to surface safely.

Though they mainly travelled in silence, Einon occasionally took it upon himself to explain the wonders of lowland life in his patriarchal-verging-on-patronising way. Two days out from Plas Aethnen they spotted a stone tower with wood and linen sails. Einon told them this was a windmill, a device that harnessed the wind's power to grind corn. Kerin took quite an interest, and this got Sais thinking about how few such things he'd seen here. Later, watching labourers engaged in the unpleasant task of crumbling clods of manure over a field of green shoots, he asked Einon why they didn't use technology to help with jobs like that too.

'Technology?' said Einon. 'That is, ah, not a word I know. Did you mean devices to help with the growing of crops?'

'Er, yes,' said Sais cautiously, cursing his carelessness.

'The Traditions have it that our food must be tended by man's hand from planting to harvest. As I am sure you will remember soon.'

'I'm sure I will,' said Sais. He doubted he would.

They spent the night at a large inn which had private rooms for rent as well as a shared dormitory, and he agreed to another Cof Hlesmair session. The inn also provided a bath, though they ran to only one lot of hot water, and Einon's status meant he got to go first. Sais waited in the inn's common-room while the priest got clean. He returned to their room as Einon was getting out of the bath. The candlelight glistened on the priest's body, picking out the taut skin across his shoulders, the flat planes of his back and the swell of his buttocks. Sais suddenly, unexpectedly, felt a hot flush of pure lust. Shock killed the desire at once – he felt no particular attraction to Einon; the response had been purely physical. But now he knew why he'd reacted to Kerin the way he had. She could have been the most beautiful woman in the world, but she'd never be more than a friend.

Though the incident didn't improve his state of mind, Sais still went ahead with the memory session: assuming Einon would go back to the Tyr when they reached Dinas Emrys, he only had just over three weeks with the priest to get his memory back.

He slipped into the trance-state easily this time and Einon told him to picture his sister. He saw a stern, aristocratic face in his mind's eye. The priest said he should visualise her at important times in their life together. Most of the memories were in the house, a bright, spacious place high on a cliff. These felt like childish memories. But he also felt an overlay of discomfort: after they grew up, his relationship with her had broken down.

When Einon brought him back and looked at him expectantly he said, 'That was much clearer.'

'And you remembered your sister?'

'I did,' he said.

'Can you tell me anything?'

'I think she's older than me. She bosses – bossed – me around. We're not close now.'

Sais's mind extracted its price in dreams that night, though at least they drew on images from his lost past: his sister as an adult, sitting in a luxurious bedroom, a look of horror on her face; the two of them standing by an open grave, his arm around her; sitting beside her watching a dramatic sunset over water fade into darkness.

Soon after they set off the next morning it started raining and the physical discomfort drove Sais further inside himself. When, tired and bedraggled near the end of the day, he heard a woman's nagging voice, he cried out, without thinking, 'God's sake, stop fussing, Elarn!'

As soon as the words left his lips the world crashed back in on him. On the road ahead, Damaru had picked up something (he later found out it was a dead crow), and Kerin (it was her he had snapped at) was trying to get him to put it down. Or rather, she had been. Now she was staring at Sais, as were Fychan and Einon.

Somewhere in his head the connection had been made between two forceful women in his life and he'd called one by the name of the other. He'd also used an oath that came from a religion other than that of the Skymothers, something he hoped Einon wouldn't pick up on. But he had his first concrete piece of information: he had a sister called Elarn.

He told the others not to worry, that he was fine. He didn't feel it. He felt torn between the vivid, mundane, alien present and his hidden, painful past.

He started to have sessions with Einon every third night, even when they were in dormitories – now he was used to it, he could fall into the trance easily. The couple of days' gap allowed the uncovered memories to expand and be absorbed. He put up with the unpleasant dreams and daily fugue states and slowly rebuilt his early life: he remembered his parents, his few childhood friends and more about the house where he'd grown up. He knew what it felt like to be held by his mother, the safe, milky softness of her. He recalled the less luxurious places where they'd stayed in his early childhood, and smelled the new furniture smell of the house. He heard the sea through an open window as it beat at the cliff below his room. He rediscovered names and functions for items unknown here. The level of detail, and the contrast to his current, primitive surroundings, confirmed that he was remembering, not inventing.

He walked a fine line with Einon, translating what he remembered into terms the priest could relate to whilst avoiding details obviously outside the other man's experience. Neither of them mentioned the weird oath Sais had come out with.

Fychan was enjoying his once-in-a-lifetime trip to the full, and Damaru was less trouble than Sais had expected, possibly due to his mother's careful and unwavering attention. Kerin still wasn't talking to him, though he'd seen the way she looked at him when she thought he wasn't looking. Perhaps she was thinking he was driving himself too hard. Maybe she had a point.

One day, about a week out from the City, they took their lunch sitting on the grass verge by the side of the road as usual. It was pleasantly warm and Sais lay back and flung his arms over his head. His hand brushed something damp and a moment later he felt a sharp pain in his right thumb. He snatched his hand back and sat up. Specks of white froth covered the side of his hand and on closer examination he found a tiny scratch at the base of his thumb. He wiped his hand on his clothes.

During the afternoon, the pain in his thumb got worse until his whole hand started throbbing. The redness spread and the skin soon felt taut and hot to the touch. By the evening the red scratch had developed a head of pus with a tiny black point in the centre, and he felt light-headed and queasy.

This damned place seemed determined to do him in.

Though the injury might be enough to convince Kerin to speak to him again, he decided to try and deal with it himself.

They were in a dormitory of eight beds, and he hung back when the others went down to the common-room, saying he was going to rest for a while before coming down to eat. He had to open Einon's pack one-handed; any pressure on his wounded hand resulted in distant waves of pain and nausea. Though that wasn't what he was looking for, when he found the flameless lantern he got it out and examined it. There was a small switch on the base. He flicked the switch. As he expected, cold white radiance filled the room. He put the lantern on the floor. He'd need good light.

Finally he found the razor and managed to get it out of its leather sheath. He had an idea he needed to clean – no, *sterilise* – it, and he went over to the oil-lamp on its shelf by the door, and reached up to run the blade through the flame. Then he sat back against the bed and grasped the blade's handle with his good hand. The wounded hand almost seemed to pulse.

Before he could lose his nerve he sliced across the swelling.

But he was using his off hand, and even as he felt the rush of hot pain he knew he'd screwed up. He'd cut too low, going deep into the flesh at the heel of his thumb, but missing the infected area.

Blood started to pump from the wound with terrifying speed. He dropped the razor and grabbed his wrist.

Leaning against the bed he tried to lever himself up, but all the strength had gone out of his legs.

'Mothers preserve us!'

He looked up to see Einon in the doorway, staring at him in horror.

How cruel of the Weaver to test her so! One day she might be able to look on Sais and not wish the Abyss would swallow her up. One day her pierced heart would heal. One day ... but not yet.

And now he was hurt and Einon had *ordered* her to go to him, to touch him, to heal him.

She obeyed the priest. It was her duty to the Mother of Mercy – and for all she wanted to hate Sais, she could not.

When she reached the dormitory, she found Sais sitting on the floor by Einon's bed, his face pinched and white. His right hand, which he held in his left, was covered in blood. A blood-stained blade of what looked like skymetal lay at his feet. As she approached he gave her the foolish, pained smile of a man who knows he has made an idiot of himself.

Einon picked up the flameless lamp from the floor and reached under it. The light went off at once, leaving the room full of shadows.

Kerin said, 'Gwas, would it be possible to light your lantern again please, so I can see to tend my patient?'

'Ah, aye, Chilwar. A good idea.' Another touch, and the light returned. Einon reached for the skymetal blade, then thought better of it and went to stand near the door. Kerin had seen that reaction before: he had a problem with blood.

Kerin asked Fychan to fetch clean water and linen. When he left she wiped the worst of the blood from Sais's hand. He had a nasty-looking bite, though the blood came from a fresh cut just below it.

'What happened?' she asked brusquely.

162

'Something on the roadside bit me. It was living in some sort of white froth.' He was careful not to look at her.

'Spit-weevil. We have them in the mountains.' She looked over at Einon. 'Gwas, may I ask a favour?'

'What is it, Chilwar?'

'Sais has an infected bite, which must be cut to release the poison. Your skymetal blade would make a far cleaner cut than my knife. Would you consider helping me by lancing the wound?'

'I— I am not sure I could.' Einon frowned. Then he said, 'But in this case I am sure the Mothers would allow you to wield sky-metal, Chilwar. You may use my razor to help Sais.'

That was what she had hoped he would say. 'Thank you, Gwas.'

Finally Fychan returned. She had him tear the linen into bandages while she washed Sais's hand. Sais tensed, but did not cry out.

Then she took his hand in hers and murmured, 'Look away, and do not move your hand, no matter how much it hurts.'

He gave a tiny nod and turned his head to the side.

She drew the blade across the bite.

Blood and pus spurted from the wound. She squeezed the skin on either side to get more pus out. Sais made a rasping noise deep in his throat, but kept his mouth shut and his hand still.

Causing him pain gave her no pleasure at all.

When she was sure she had purged him of all infection, she bound his hand. As she tied the dressing in place, he murmured, 'Thank you.'

She pretended not to hear him.

His hand bleed freely in the night and she rebound it the next morning. There were no signs of further infection, and the slight fever she had felt on him had receded. She told Einon that Sais was fit to travel.

As she had managed to talk to Sais and not die from the pain of it, she wondered if she should lift the am-annwn. No: she needed more time to heal her own unseen wounds. She knew Sais had done nothing to deserve her ire: he had treated her well, according to his own code. The problem was that he had done nothing to deserve her love either. It was natural for him to show her care and consideration such as a woman would only expect from a good husband. She had been a fool to see compassion resulting from his upbringing as love for her. Her pride, as well as her heart, had been hurt, and she could blame no one save herself.

They came off the downlands that evening, walking down a tongue of high land that sloped onto the plains. The flat open expanse looked odd to Kerin's eyes. They now shared the road with better-dressed travellers who often rode in covered carts, sometimes attended by servants. Damaru was always treated with respect, while she, Sais and Fychan, in their drab upland clothes, were objects of curiosity.

Although Fychan flirted outrageously at the inns, he behaved better around her, deferring to her in matters of Damaru's care, and no longer putting her down in front of others. In return she found herself growing almost fond of the lad who, after all, was her nephew. He even paid for Damaru's lodgings with money given to him by his father.

Einon grew more apprehensive the closer they came to the City of Light. He kept his head bowed when they passed people on the road, and no longer joined them in the common-room in the evenings. He instructed them to tell him at once if anyone asked about him, though no one did. Kerin wondered what was going on, but knew better than to ask.

Einon's attitude to her improved after she treated Sais, as though demonstrating a useful skill had allowed the priest to see her as a person for the first time.

She decided to take advantage of this when they were still a few days out from the City. When she took his meal up to his room, she said, 'Gwas, may I ask you something?'

'What is it, Chilwar?'

'I wish my son to be as well-prepared as he can be for the upcoming testing. So I wondered, how many skyfools will there be?'

'The most I have ever known is six. The least, two.'

'And how many are chosen?'

'Of the six, two were chosen. Last year, ah, three candidates were presented, but none were found worthy.'

As she had feared: Damaru's chances were not good. 'And what tests will my son undergo?'

'The day after his presentation to the Cariad he will be called on to, ah, to demonstrate his command over the pattern in the public testing. The boys' guardians must convince them to affect matter without touching it.'

'And if they fail?'

'Then the boys' claims will be seen as an offence against the Mothers. They will be put to death, and their guardians sent away in disgrace.'

The smashed bodies of the reivers back at Maen Bulch were testament to her son's ability to affect the world without touch; he could pass such a test, she knew he could. 'So those who succeed, they ascend at the festival of Sul Esgyniad?'

'No, those who succeed go into the Tyr for the final test.'

'And if they fail this final test?'

'Then, ah, then they die.'

Kerin swallowed painfully; her mouth was suddenly horribly dry. 'And what is the nature of the final test, Gwas?'

'That is between the Cariad and the candidate. Such matters are not, ah, not for anyone else to know.' He spoke firmly, but without anger.

She thanked him and left.

CHAPTER TWENTY-ONE

Day by day, Sais was building up a picture of his past. On the first session after he injured his hand, they worked through later memories of his parents. The next day he pieced together his family history. His parents had had a business together; his father had located mineral deposits, largely at sea, while his mother sold the exploration rights and handled the other business aspects of their partnership. The rig-accident that killed them had almost certainly been sabotage by a rival company. He still felt anger over that, even though it had happened years ago. He had an idea that their parents' deaths had begun the rift between his sister and him. He felt sure Elarn was his only living relative.

The next evening he gave Einon an edited version of his family history, telling him his father had traded in rare minerals, and both parents were dead, killed in an accident that might have been the action of a business rival.

After digesting this, Einon said, 'I have been thinking that you may come from a land unknown to even the most learned men. There is nothing in the Traditions to say that other lands do not exist beyond the realms shown on our maps.'

'Would that be a problem, if I did come from off the map?' asked Sais carefully.

'Not at all,' said the priest with a smile. 'I think it is fascinating.'

Sais tried not to let his relief show.

At the next session he asked Einon to help him find out what he did for a living. He got the concept of an enclosed, bright, yet cluttered place with connotations of 'home', along with memories of negotiating and socialising with people in strange places, including other enclosed spaces. He told Einon he suspected he was some sort of trader who travelled widely, which was how he came to be so far from home. Einon accepted his explanation.

The priest said he would be staying with them until Damaru's testing, which would give them another week together in the City. Given Einon's increasing paranoia, it was obvious he was walking into something potentially dangerous in Dinas Emrys, but he still refused to discuss it.

Sais considered getting Einon to help him relive the weird experience he'd had when Damaru had saved the drove from the reivers. He knew this feeling was important, but it was also vague, more a sensation than a memory, and it had been pretty disturbing. He decided to leave this avenue of investigation until he ran out of other options.

Instead, he used the last memory session before they reached Dinas Emrys to ask who mattered most in his life now, and whether they were looking for him.

His mental view flashed on images of his sister, and of several men he knew had been more than friends. Einon asked if any of those close to him knew he was here. Suddenly he saw the nightmare eyes, and felt a sharp pain in his head. Einon brought him out of the trance at once. He was panting, and sweat filmed his palms. Apparently he wasn't ready for that knowledge yet.

As they neared the City, settlements became more frequent. Sais didn't ask why some of the houses they passed had shuttered windows with blue circles painted over them – the frequent pyres told him all he needed to know. He was sure the falling fire was no visitation of divine will. Diseases were spread by physical contact, or in water or food. Even if the only cure was this red rain that miraculously fell at the end of the winnowing times, simple precautions could prevent the spread of the disease and ease the suffering. But he suspected the Traditions might say otherwise, so he kept quiet.

They saw Dinas Emrys the day after the road began to parallel a slow, wide river that Einon called the Afon Mawr. A steep-sided mountain – the Tyr itself – emerged from the distant mists. It squatted on the plain, dark against the green-tinged fields and the bright expanse of water on the far horizon. Those must be the fenlands the Afon Mawr emptied into, Sais thought, one of the boundaries of the known lands, according to Einon's map.

At dusk twinkling lights appeared around the base of the mountain and part-way up its sides.

That evening Kerin spoke to him for the first time since she'd had to treat his hand. He suspected she had been waiting for a moment when they could be alone, and it came in the unromantic setting of the inn's latrines. She walked in as he walked out. He was about to pass her when she put out her hand.

He stopped and looked at her. The decision had to be hers.

'I release you from am-annwn,' she blurted.

'Good,' he said, 'because having to get Fychan to repeat every-thing so we can communicate is really beginning to piss me off!' It came out bitter, when he had intended it as a joke.

They stood there in silence, neither of them willing to concede more for the moment. Then he took a step towards her. Words had got them into too much trouble; he wondered if she'd let him hug her.

She backed away and he cursed his assumptions. 'Sorry,' he said, feeling foolish. 'Where I come from, friends make up by embracing.'

She raised her chin. 'Outside of star-season tis not permitted for a man to act so with a woman who is not his wife.'

He was heartily sick of what was and wasn't permitted around here. 'So, would all your problems be solved if I married you then?'

To his surprise, she took his comment at face value. 'Are you offering to? Have you changed your mind and want me now?'

'Another thing about where I come from: I'm pretty sure we marry for love. I don't love you, Kerin. To marry you would be dishonest.'

'T'would be an act of compassion to marry me, Sais, and I know you are not short of that. But I would not ask you to sacrifice your valued principles of honesty for me.'

'Christos, Kerin, you are one prideful woman!'

She stared at him and he realised he'd let another of his unacceptable oaths slip out.

Into her silence he said, 'I like you and I respect you. You're brave and you care for a world that doesn't care for you. You want me to be the person who saves you from all the shit this uncaring world's thrown at you. I'm not going to, and it's not just because I don't feel that way about you. It's also because I know you're strong enough to save yourself.'

'Sais, look at me! I am an ugly widow with no property, no skills, no money, and once my son has gone to the sky, nothing to live for. Perhaps where you come from having a hard will and a soft heart would be enough to overcome these disadvantages. Here, it is not. I must accept that, and so must you.' She walked off.

But the am-annwn was broken and the following day she was willing to speak to him, though only so far as it made their journey easier.

By noon they could clearly see the buildings of the City itself, like a multi-coloured fuzz infesting the lower part of the Tyr. Curls of smoke came from off to one side of the main settlement; with so many people living in one place, the pyres must burn constantly, Sais thought. As the view grew clearer, they caught sight of a large structure, one of the highest up the slope, built into the side of the Tyr itself: Einon told them that this was the Senneth building, where nobles and leaders of the City's guilds met to decide matters of law and administration, overseen by the five Escorai of the Tyr or their representatives.

There was no wall delineating the start of the City, just a point where more land was given over to buildings than farming. As the sun set behind them, a silver line flashed into life overhead. It ran from the top of the Tyr up into the sky, like a ribbon of white light. Everyone stopped and looked at Einon, who pointed unnecessarily and said, 'Behold, the Edefyn Arian, our link to the Heavenly realm.'

Sais saw Kerin circle her breast. Fychan did the same, his mouth open in awe.

Then memory engulfed him.

The reason everything here kept confounding his expectations was that he came from another *world*. That slender, impossible, silver thread was a *beanstalk*, a link between the surface of this world and an orbital platform. Everything he had seen, everything on Einon's map, was a small part of *one planet*, and this planet was just one of hundreds in human-settled space.

The sky wasn't where God – or the Skymothers – lived. It was where he came from. It was his home.

As he stood gawking at the beanstalk he felt the universe balloon out towards infinity, the boundaries of possibility expanding in a vertiginous wave. The certainties he'd built up over the weeks were blown away in a moment by the sight of something from his own world, his own life. Here was evidence of the truth – a truth it appeared that only he knew.

A truth that went against everything those around him believed.

Out of the corner of her eye, Kerin saw Sais take a step backwards, still staring at the Edefyn Arian. She went over to him and whispered, 'What is it? Are you ill?'

He shook his head. 'I'll be all right, really. I'm just tired.'

Though she suspected he was lying, she nodded and moved away. She had to wean herself back into his presence slowly. If he was unwell she would help; if not, she would leave him be.

Smaller paths joined theirs as they continued, and the last fields gave way to houses. The ground began to slope upwards and soon they were close enough to the Tyr that Kerin had to crane her head back to see the top, where the Edefyn Arian emerged.

The houses had two or more storeys and were built of red brick, their steep roofs tiled in blue-grey slate. The only growing things here were flowers in carved wooden boxes under the windows of some of the larger houses. When the lanes between houses – Einon called them streets – began to close in Kerin felt like she was walking through dim, man-made chasms. Though most windows were shuttered for the night, some houses had wide front openings that reminded her of the stalls at the star-season fair. When she saw one whose shutters were still propped open, Kerin realised this was exactly what it was: a giant, permanent stall built into a house. This one was serving food. Her stomach grumbled at the scent of meat sizzling on a griddle. The smell was soon lost in a dozen others: ordure, incense, rotting vegetables and many she had no name for.

Even in the City, where there were so many people, they attracted plenty of attention. Though interest focused on Damaru, Kerin had changed into her skirt and it drew admiring glances from some of the women. Perhaps she did have something to trade. But a number of men and older women frowned at her uncovered head; she had considered buying a scarf at the fair before deciding that any problem people had with her appearance was down to them, not her.

She turned her attention to her surroundings, trying to work out the function of the new things they came across. The narrow ditches running at the side of the sloping streets carried away filth. Symbols painted on the walls of some houses indicated what went on within – loaves of bread, piles of coins, scissors and thread, a joint of meat. Other, more complex symbols were painted on the houses at the ends of streets.

At first she was perplexed by the poles made of a dark substance, neither wood nor metal, that stood along the sides of the streets at regular intervals. Then, as the daylight failed, small white globes at the top of the poles began to glow like tiny full moons.

'How do they shine like that, Gwas?' said Fychan, gawping up at one of the lights like the ignorant clansman Einon probably thought he was. Kerin had seen that cold glow before: these devices were cousins to Einon's flameless lantern.

The priest indicated the light-dimpled mass of the Tyr looming over them. 'Through the beneficence of the Beloved Daughter, Chilwar. This is why she named this place the City of Light, because her radiance permeates it.'

Fychan circled himself, though Einon hadn't exactly answered his question.

Einon had told them he knew a place to stay, but from the way he kept stopping to peer at the street-corner symbols, Kerin wondered if he really knew where he was going. Now that darkness had fallen, the streets had emptied. A group of men came marching down the street towards them, moving so quickly and purposefully that Kerin half expected them to walk straight over her. Instead they halted, and the one in front said, 'Badges please.' Kerin had seen enough monitors on the road to recognise the uniform, but she had no idea what they were asking for.

Einon pulled off his broad-brimmed travelling hat. His shaved, tattooed head shone in the unearthly light from the poles. The monitors' demeanour shifted from hostility to respect. Einon indicated Damaru, who stood behind Kerin, holding onto her arm. 'I am accompanying this skyfool and his people to his presentation. We have only just arrived; I shall ensure they register as soon as we are settled.'

'Of course, Gwas. Good evening to you.' The men traced the circle and left.

She knew about registering with the authorities from Neithion: it was something drovers did to record their cattle and the money they made from selling them, making them accountable for taxes and tithes. Why people might need to do it she did not know. Sais, speaking for the first time since he had seen the silver thread, voiced her concern for her. 'What did you mean about registering us?'

'Nothing to worry about. You just need a visitor's badge.' Einon spoke with forced levity.

Soon after that they turned down a street whose corner displayed a shallow bowl painted in faded pink below a tall brown triangle. Kerin later found that what she had taken to be a bowl represented an open hand, and the triangle was the Tyr.

'This is Stryd Dechreur, the Street of the Acolytes,' said Einon. 'Youths wishing to enter the priesthood stay here while undergoing their initial training and preparation for the acolytes' examinations. Companions of priests who come to the City on official business may also stay here at a reduced cost.' Einon spoke as though he was doing them a favour, though the house he stopped outside was the smallest and shabbiest on the street, next to a close-shuttered house whose blue-painted lintels spoke of the passage of the winnowing times.

Kerin asked innocently, 'And is this the house where you stayed when you were an acolyte, Gwas?'

Einon said, 'No,' and for once, did not elaborate.

CHAPTER TWENTY-TWO

Einon had found his travelling companions did not vex him as much as he had feared on the journey to the City of Light. Fychan was growing into the responsibility laid on him, and the woman – Kerin – showed commendable solicitude towards her son. Einon had no idea what had caused her and Sais to fall out, nor to make up again; he might be a priest, but the depths of human emotion remained a closed book to him. He was aware Sais was not fully disclosing his recollections. Einon was concerned, for there was a faint whiff of blasphemy about Sais – the odd oaths he used; his lack of piety towards the sacred blade ... and yet he had risked his own life to save Einon's. He did not want to believe the worst of him, nor embroil him further in priestly politics.

It hurt to sneak back to the City of Light like some miscreant. He longed to return to the sacred precincts of the Tyr and lose himself in the cold, safe beauty of numbers. But until he knew why Sefion had sent an assassin after him he would follow his Escori's orders and remain in hiding. He chose the guest house with care: it was cheap – a necessity, given the dent paying for Sais had made in his funds – and it was anonymous. At least he reclaimed his privacy, for Sais was happy to share a room with Fychan.

He had four full days before Fychan was to present Damaru to the Cariad: four days to find out what was going on. Given the way power ebbed and flowed in the Tyr it might be that his death was no longer desirable, and he would be safe to throw his lot in with the skyfool and declare his presence. He prayed that this was so, but needed to rely on more than prayer to make his final judgment. He must gather rumours. There were so many Tyr priests throughout the City that one could be virtually anonymous, so he should not attract undue attention.

He must also get a coded message to Urien. After some thought, he hit upon an idea: he would hide his words in a poem about pastries. Urien patronised a particular baker in the upper City, and received a weekly bill for his costly delicacies – pastries that he had introduced Einon to. If the bill arrived with an innocuous note extolling the virtues of their favourite pastries, then Urien would, Einon devoutly hoped, be able to decode the hidden message within – his address.

Einon had to admit his plan was not entirely sound, but cast adrift without the resources of the Tyr and unsure what perils awaited him, it was the best he could do. Sais agreed to take the note for him after Einon admitted, 'I may have enemies in the Tyr, but I also have friends.'

The lodging house was run by a spry old widow named Ebrilla, who shared her home with a cat called Palfau. Kerin thought the cat a good substitute for a husband: more useful around the house and unlikely to answer back. The only other guests were Gorran, a sallow lad with a harelip, and his father Meilyg, who had travelled to the City from the Eastern Marches so Gorran could take the acolytes' examinations.

Ebrilla was delighted to have a skyfool grace her house, and insisted on moving Meilyg and Gorran to a back room so the priest and the skyfool could have the two larger rooms facing the street. The easterners complied without complaint. Though Gorran and Meilyg had already eaten, she cooked a fresh meal for her new guests, and when Damaru picked up a handful of rice grains and squashed them into Ebrilla's well-scrubbed wooden table, she just smiled indulgently and made the circle. Kerin wondered if their hostess would be quite as happy if Damaru failed to find the latrine, as had happened a couple of times on the journey.

The next day they went out early to register as visitors, a process which, Kerin was unsurprised to find, cost money. Einon pointed out the imposing building, but stayed well away from the stern-faced monitors who stood guard on either side of the door. Sais gave his name as Sais am Dangwern, which caused raised eyebrows all round, but they had no problems getting their official badges.

Then, it being Sul, they went to the local capel, where Einon joined them, somewhat to Kerin's surprise. She had assumed he would go up to the Tyr to worship with his fellow priests, but when she mentioned this, he said he didn't wish to leave Damaru alone in a strange place. His reason seemed odd, and she wondered if Sais knew more of his true motivations, but she did not ask. Sais had been very quiet since arriving in the City, more distracted than ever.

After capel, Kerin offered to help Ebrilla, who was more than happy to talk about the City and the skyfools' presentation and public testing. Kerin was dismayed to find that only the appointed guardians could accompany the boys at these events, but Ebrilla patted her hand solicitously and said, 'Do not fear, your boy is bound to triumph. Tis a special year, for when she accompanies the Consorts on Sul Esgyniad, the Cariad will also petition Heaven to send the red rain – the end of the winnowing times are in sight, praise be the Five!'

Kerin spent all her free time with Damaru, who had started acting up – maybe because there were so many strangers, or perhaps because he sensed the impending separation. He rearranged objects in the house, much to everyone's annoyance, and refused to eat at mealtimes, instead demanding food at odd hours. In a bid to distract him, Kerin encouraged him to wander the City with her. She tried to fix the memory of him in the places they went together, so that when he was gone and she remained, she would be able to look back on this time.

But City life would take some getting used to: the very air was different – hotter, drier, smellier. Neither of them was used to the huge crowds of strangers, and Kerin wondered how she would ever understand the complex divisions between guildsmen and nobles, craftsmen and priestly servants.

Damaru led her along wide bustling thoroughfares and into pokey back streets where rats scrabbled through piles of refuse. In the great square in front of the Tyr's main entrance they watched acolytes chanting the Traditions from memory. They saw the painted women of the Stryd Putain, and Kerin shuddered at the maimed and deformed men sitting listlessly before wooden begging bowls in the lower City. The wind often brought the stench of smoke and they frequently passed carts taking bodies to the pyres that burned night and day.

Yet as well as poverty and suffering, they also saw great affluence: markets and shops with wares that put the star-season fair to shame, and individuals flaunting their wealth, bedecked in finery and travelling in miniature carriages pulled by burly bondsmen. Even the moderately wealthy displayed extravagant fashions: many men's shirts had far more buttons than were needed just to keep them fastened, and women often wore several layered skirts, each in contrasting colours, with the outer ones pinned up to show off those below. If the panelled jackets of the young people were anything to go by, then embroidery was prized. She discussed with Ebrilla the possibility of setting herself up as a needlewoman once Damaru had gone to his fate; it would not be such a bad life.

They saw little of their travelling companions. Einon and Sais were either closeted in their rooms, or off on unknown errands in the City, and Fychan was spending much of his time in the local hostelries, returning late every night stinking of ale and cheap scent. He did offer to take a turn looking after Damaru, but Kerin declined, suspecting it had nothing to do with consideration and everything to do with having it known he was a skyfool's guardian.

When Fychan first wore the shirt Kerin had made, Sais went deathly white. Kerin would have been pleased to see him so upset a few weeks ago, but no more. His reaction had nothing of envy and everything of shock, as though the shirt were a thing of the Abyss. But he remained quiet and withdrawn, and as the time for Damaru's presentation approached, Kerin's mind was filled with the upcoming sorrow of bidding goodbye to her son forever.

His name was Jarek Reen. It came to him that first morning in Dinas Emrys. He woke up and he knew who he was – or rather, he knew who he had been before he came to this world. He had already adjusted his worldview in the face of his new knowledge. He was taller and weaker than the people here because he came from a world with lower gravity. The night sky was probably so bright because this world was near the galactic core, and the falling stars of star-season weren't divine semen, they were meteors burning up in the atmosphere as the planet moved through a patch of space debris. The miraculous lights that gave the City its name, and Einon's lantern, were rare examples of technology on an otherwise lo-tech world.

Rediscovering his name should have been the final piece of the puzzle, but despite his initial excitement, the memories still felt patchy and distant, as though they belonged to someone else. Though he knew he was Jarek, he still thought of himself as Sais.

When he saw Fychan wearing the shirt Kerin had made, it triggered another revelation: it was made of *smartchute fabric* – and that meant he had come down in some sort of emergency escape vehicle; the 'chute had somehow failed and he'd crash-landed in the mere above Dangwern.

But why had he abandoned his ship?

He had no idea … There was still so much missing. He knew *what* he had been before he came to this planet – a freetrader, transporting specialist items between star-systems – but he had no idea *how* he ended up in this particular system. That memory didn't exist, almost as though it had been excised.

He worked alone, so it was unlikely anyone knew he was here. He might have managed to send off a distress call, so perhaps someone was on their way. Or, he thought wryly, perhaps they'd already turned up at Dangwern – that would give the villagers something to talk about! But he'd seen no sign of offworld influence at all. People here thought they were alone in the cosmos. This place was a real backwater.

Sais wondered if he had abandoned his ship in orbit – if so, it might still be up there. Certainly there must be *something* up there, given the Consorts apparently ascended the 'silver thread'. Not many planets still had beanstalks; advances in grav-tech had made them pretty much obsolete, but that didn't mean they didn't work: he could use this one to get up to orbit and off this planet himself. Well, in theory – two obvious problems sprang to mind: he had no idea what he'd find at the top, and there was a rock fortress full of hostile priests at the bottom.

Sais was desperate for someone to talk to, but even if Kerin had managed to forgive him for breaking her heart, he couldn't begin to imagine her reaction to discovering her world wasn't what she thought it was.

He spent a couple of days walking the hot, reeking streets of the City, checking out ways into the Tyr. There were five main doors, and a number of smaller service entrances, and he investigated all of them, from the wide processional avenue in the main square to a small wooden door set into the rock wall at the end of a dead-end street. Every entrance was either locked, guarded, or both.

There were plenty of windows, many with balconies, higher up the slope, presumably belonging to priests whose status got them a room with a view, but the near-vertical rock face made them a non-starter.

As well as checking out his options, Sais also tried to put together the pieces of his old life. Sitting in his room that evening, the shutters thrown wide against the muggy night air, he remembered the name he'd called out in his delirium: Nual. He still had no idea who Nual was. Was this person the key to what had happened to him?

The bruised sky darkened into night and lights came on outside. As the first fat drops of rain began to fall, he decided to ask for Einon's help one last time. The priest had suggested another Cof Hlesmair session several times since they'd arrived in the City. Now fully aware of how far outside Einon's idea of normality he fell, Sais had fobbed him off – but if he wanted to get back the parts of his past still lost to him, Einon might be his only hope.

He found the priest in his room, poring over his papers. At first he looked flustered, but he was quick to agree.

They sat opposite each other as they had before, and this time Sais took the lead. Rain hissed on the shutters, and the flame of the lamp between them danced in a sudden draft. 'I'd like you to try and find out about somebody called Nual,' he said.

Einon frowned. 'Nual? I think, ah, I think you said that name during one of your bad dreams.'

'Really? Can you remember when?'

'Sorry, no. Those inns have rather blurred into one. Do you think this individual was, ah, important to you?'

'I do.' Sais was apprehensive about focusing on something from one of his nightmares, especially given the unpleasant reaction they'd got when they'd tried to find out who mattered to him now, but he had to complete the picture, to find out who he really was.

'Then we must ask, and see what comes of it,' said Einon firmly.

Sais slipped into the trance easily, his mind now attuned to Einon's voice—

Running down red-lit corridors, your hand in mine ...

Standing side-by-side on the top of the cliff, laughing into the wind ...

Elarn, screaming, 'How dare you bring that abomination into my house?' ...

As I kissed your forehead, you said, 'This is my final gift' ...

<Do not resist: it will only make the pain worse>

Every image, every thought, was blotted out by the vision of void-dark eyes boring into his mind, stripping his soul bare. He wanted to fight, but he was too weak.

Some part of him was aware of someone calling out, 'Return! Return!'

He tried to open his eyes, to focus on the voice.

Failed.

<Do not attempt to resist>

'This is my final gift ...'

Oblivion.

CHAPTER TWENTY-THREE

Kerin had left the shutters in their room open so Damaru could watch the patterns the falling rain made in front of the light-globe across the street. She was sitting with one of his hands clasped in both of hers, heedless of the splashes coming over the sill onto her lap, when a scream pierced the night. She had not believed a human voice could hold so much horror and madness—

Damaru started as she jumped up. She grasped his shoulders, looked into his eyes and said, 'Damaru, you *must* stay here until I come back. Do you understand? Stay here!'

When she was sure that he did understand, she ran across the hall to the priest's room, where the terrible sound had come from.

Einon stood against the far wall, shaking. Sais lay on the floor, thrashing about, his heels banging the wooden boards, his head whipping from side to side. Kerin recognised this as a fit, such as Damaru sometimes suffered, and rushed over to him.

Sais's teeth were clenched, his eyes rolled up, and shivers ran up and down his body in waves.

She called out, 'Einon! Pass me the pillow from your bed – *now*, please! We need to stop him hurting himself.'

The priest grabbed the pillow and thrust it towards her and Kerin slipped it under Sais's head. Pink-tinged foam bubbled out of his mouth where he'd bitten his tongue. Kerin checked, relieved to find he had not swallowed it and could still breathe freely.

'What happened?' she asked Einon.

'I do not know! I was, ah, I was trying to help him get his

memory back.' He shook his head in disbelief. 'The technique is harmless – we have used it many times.'

Deciding Einon knew nothing of use, she turned back to Sais. As he exhausted himself, so the shudders became less intense.

The doorway was full of people, all watching in silence as the fit finally subsided. Sais gave a great heaving sigh, his breathing grew even and his body relaxed. His eyes remained closed.

Ebrilla spoke from the hall. 'I know a good physic, though he will want paying.'

Kerin was not sure what a physic was, but she trusted Ebrilla's judgment. 'Please, fetch him. I will pay.'

'No, ah, I must pay,' said Einon, looking embarrassed.

'I must see to Damaru,' Kerin said. 'We need to make Sais comfortable while we wait for this physic to arrive. Will someone lift him to the bed?'

Sais didn't stir as Meilyg and his son moved his limp body.

The physic, a tired-looking young man with a crooked back and delicate fingers, turned out to be a healer. He examined Sais, said his condition was not due to fever or injury – something Kerin could have told him – and announced that he might wake up as normal the next day – or he might not. They should be prepared for him to awake changed, or even to remain in this state for some time.

'There is little you can do for him save prayer, though a watch should be kept in case his condition changes,' the physic said. 'You could try and drip water into his mouth, but do not attempt to move him.'

Einon offered to sit beside Sais in case he awakened in the night, but the next morning he lay as they had left him, still as death, barely breathing.

At the end of the morning meal Einon took Fychan aside. They spoke in Ebrilla's parlour, after which Einon returned to his room while Fychan remained in the parlour with the door closed. A little later a sharp knock sounded on the lodging-house door. Kerin rushed out from her room in time to see a priest disappearing into the parlour.

Ebrilla came upstairs and found her. 'The priest wants to meet the sky-blessed boy,' she said. 'He will take Damaru to his presentation tomorrow.'

Kerin wondered where Einon fitted into all this.

The priest, a balding man with a tendency to twitch his head when he spoke, introduced himself as Rhidian, a second-tier priest of Medelwyr. He managed to capture Damaru's attention briefly, as Einon had, before her son decided he was more interested in looking out the window.

As soon as Rhidian had gone, Kerin said to Fychan, 'Can I ask you something, please?'

'Aye,' he said cautiously.

'I just wondered why Einon is not accompanying Damaru. Did he confide in you?'

Fychan looked uncomfortable. 'He said it was better that he remain in the background.'

'Did he tell you not to mention him?'

'Kerin, we should not question the will of priests!'

So Einon did not want the Tyr priests to know he was here. Interesting, Kerin thought.

She asked Ebrilla where the best place to watch the presentation was, and the housekeeper said sympathetically, 'Do not worry. After lunch tomorrow I will show you just the spot. Your boy will have a good view of you, too.'

Kerin smiled at the older woman; in truth, being where Damaru could see her was her main concern.

When Kerin offered to take a turn watching Sais, Einon refused, politely but tersely. 'I am quite capable of keeping an eye on him while I am working,' he explained, indicating his pile of papers.

Sais's condition remained unchanged and Kerin remembered the first time she had waited like this, praying he would open his eyes. So much had happened since then – and though much of what she had experienced these last weeks had come with a burden of suffering, and the future was haunted by uncertainty, she did not regret leaving Dangwern.

The day of the presentation dawned bright and hot. Though Kerin would not have to bid farewell to her son for another two and a half days, today marked the point of no return. Once the Cariad had looked on the candidates and accepted them for testing, they were committed. She wondered what would happen if she took her son's hand, gathered their few possessions and walked out of the City now. Nothing good, she suspected, given their presence was known and registered.

That morning Kerin took Damaru and Fychan to what Ebrilla described as 'a respectable bath-house' – one where men and women were segregated. Afterwards Kerin felt cleaner than she ever had in her life.

In order to get a good vantage point, she and Ebrilla had to leave before the priest came to fetch Damaru and Fychan. After some thought, Kerin gave Damaru a little bogwood root with his lunch. She had already told him that he must go with Fychan later, but he had paid little attention. She left him in Fychan's care, both of them sitting on the padded bench in the parlour, Damaru dozing and Fychan looking nervous.

When she followed Ebrilla out of the house, Kerin glanced up at the window where Einon sat with Sais. If – *when* – Damaru ascended, the first prayer she would offer to the Mothers who had taken him to their breasts would be to let Sais awaken unharmed.

Ebrilla led her to the great square in front of the main entrance of the Tyr. The crowd was already gathering behind the coloured ropes around the edge. A tent had been set up near the entrance, its sides painted with pictures of the Skymothers. Five great skymetal bowls stood in the centre of the square, and the cobbles between them were covered in a bright patchwork of woven rugs, such as the townsfolk knelt on when they prayed. Ebrilla told her, 'Tis good luck to have a rug from your house chosen to cushion the knees of the candidates.' The end of the square under the shadow of the Tyr had wooden seats laid out on a low platform. The entrance to the stand was guarded by monitors. 'For the Senneth members,' said Ebrilla. 'But we shall have just as good a view standing here.' She led Kerin to a point far enough forward that they could look back at the carpeted centre of the square.

As the afternoon wore on, more people entered the square. Ebrilla pointed out the Oriel Glan, the sacred balcony high up on the Tyr where the Cariad would make her appearance. Kerin tried not to fret.

Finally, with the sun sinking towards the horizon, the great wooden doors set into the base of the Tyr opened and a procession of youths in coloured robes emerged. Some, mainly those wearing Carunwyd's red, carried instruments. They ranged themselves to either side of the entrance. Others applied torches to the sky-metal bowls and great gouts of pungent smoke started to belch upwards.

More priests filed out, each successive group older and wearing more ornate costumes, until the part of the square directly under the Tyr was full. The townsfolk, who now crammed every bit of available space around the edge, fell silent as four figures stepped forward from the press of priests, old men in metal-encrusted robes and high headdresses. They must be the Escorai – but only four? Where was the Escori of Carunwyd?

Music began, starting at the edge of hearing, then growing to fill the square, an exquisite blend of pipes and high voices. The last rays of the sun glinted on the Edefyn Arian. The silvery link to the sky looked almost close enough to touch.

Kerin, busy watching the Tyr, did not notice what was happening at the other end of the square until Ebrilla tugged at her arm. She turned in time to see the front of the painted tent being raised. Several figures stood on the threshold and with a rush she recognised her son, flanked by Rhidian and Fychan. There were five candidates in all, each with a priest and a guardian. One of the other groups stepped forward and a boy started hesitantly into the square. Then another. Kerin squinted, trying to see Damaru's face in the failing light; he stared fixedly at the cobbles in front of him.

The music swelled and the fourth boy stepped forward, cocking an ear to hear better. Now only Damaru remained in the tent.

'T'will be all right,' whispered Ebrilla. 'The boys are often unsure, poor mites. The music usually calms them. That and the presence of their guardians.'

Except when the guardian was not the person they wanted with them, thought Kerin, her throat tight.

Though the priests were trying to get their charges to approach the presentation area at a slow walk, the boys moved in that random way she knew so well: a few quick steps, then stop, look around, sometimes head off in another direction altogether, only to be guided back on course by their guardian.

The first boy reached the rugs. Damaru still had not moved. Fychan took his arm and pulled him forward. As though only now noticing his surroundings, Damaru raised his head and shook Fychan off, then darted forward. She saw Fychan's mouth open to call out, though she could hear nothing above the music. Damaru must have heard him though, as he turned back to face the tent, almost slipping on the cobbles. He put his hands out, as though for balance, then turned again, towards the crowd. Suddenly he put his head down and ran straight towards Kerin.

She rushed forward, pulling the rope barrier over, ignoring the man in uniform heading her way. She stepped out into the square and ran to Damaru, who raised his head at the last moment, careening into her arms. 'I am here now, tis all right!' she said. 'I am sorry I left you alone.'

She felt a hand on her shoulder and looked into the stern face of a monitor.

'I am his mother,' she said sharply.

The monitor hesitated. All but one of the other skyfools had been led to the centre of the square; the last had stopped halfway to look at them. As she watched he was persuaded to move on. Rhidian and the monitor had a brief conversation while Fychan stood to one side, looking awkward. Kerin felt sure everyone in the square must be looking at them.

Rhidian came over. 'Mistress Kerin, would you be so kind as to accompany your boy?'

'Of course, Gwas,' she said, then to Damaru, 'Will you come along with me now, please? We are not going far, then we can go back to our room.'

Damaru kept hold of her hand and she led him to the presentation area where the other skyfools waited with varying degrees of patience. As they came to a halt on the rugs, the beat of drums grew over the melody of voices, built to a climax, then stopped abruptly.

Like everyone else, Kerin found herself staring up at the darkened balcony above the entrance to the Tyr. Between one heartbeat and the next, the darkness was dispelled and the Oriel Glan became a beacon of silver light. A lone figure stood in the centre. Belatedly Kerin realised she should be kneeling, as everyone else – Escorai, Senneth members, townsfolk, monitors, priests – had dropped to their knees. Only the candidate skyfools remained standing. She knelt and bowed her head and for a while there was the silence of true awe. She was in the presence of the Daughter of Heaven.

The Cariad spoke. Her voice was low and sweet, yet it carried to everyone in the square. It was almost as though she whispered in Kerin's ear, tender as a lover, comforting as a parent. 'Blessings, children of the sky. The year turns, and I look upon you with the joy of one who loves you all. I stand ready to receive the petitions of those who would enter the Heavenly realm whilst still clothed in flesh, to take their place with the Skymothers.'

Kerin circled herself repeatedly during the speech, as did everyone else she could see, save the skyfools themselves.

'I wish first to view the skyfool from Plas Derwen Mawr,' the Cariad announced.

Ebrilla had told her that the order of presentation was something the Cariad decided on the day, and as such was subject to Heavenly will. It should not be taken to signify any order of precedence or merit, though the old widow claimed there were some Abyss-touched men who laid wagers on which skyfools would succeed based on such things. Kerin suspected the Cariad's reasoning was simple enough: she would not want to choose the most awkward candidate first.

She heard the first skyfool and his retinue stand and walk to the centre of the presentation area, heard the guardian declaim the boy's lineage and history and petition the Cariad for the chance to prove his worth.

'Your claim is true,' the Cariad said in response, 'and the candidate will be tested. Take light, that your child may become the light.'

Each guardian carried a torch made of a material similar to the light-globe poles, and as the Cariad spoke, the torch in the guardian's hand burst into flames.

By the time the fourth skyfool had been called up, Kerin's knees were beginning to ache.

Finally it was their turn.

Kerin could not resist glancing up at the Oriel Glan. The Cariad stood in the only light in the square, a distant figure swathed in black and spangled in silver, a mirror of the stars lacing the deepening darkness above her.

In reciting his lineage Fychan stumbled over the name of Damaru's grandfather. Kerin understood why: quite aside from nervousness, he was speaking of the family's, of the village's, shame, even if none here but the three of them knew it.

Unless the Cariad knew too, of course.

Kerin felt the same disorientation she had felt at Piper's Steps. She was kneeling before the Beloved Daughter of Heaven! Did the Cariad know their very thoughts? Could she sense the hearts of everyone here?

Fychan completed the rest of his recitation without incident, and visibly sagged with relief as the Cariad spoke: 'Your claim is true, the candidate will be tested. Take light, that your child may become the light.'

The Cariad raised an arm from which stars appeared to drip and gestured towards Fychan's torch. Flames leapt from the wick.

Kerin waited for them to be dismissed, but then the Cariad spoke again. 'I wish a private audience with the guardian from Dangwern.'

Despite the clarity of the Cariad's speech, Kerin was not sure she had heard correctly – and she was not the only one, to judge from the reactions around the square.

When no one acknowledged her request, the Cariad said, 'Fychan am Dangwern, you will come to me now. All others, go with my blessing.'

Fychan did not move. 'You must go,' whispered Kerin, 'you cannot refuse her.'

Fychan nodded and stumbled forward. The priests, in some disarray, parted to let him through.

The light on the balcony faded and the Cariad disappeared into darkness. The skyfools left the square to the beat of solemnly banging drums.

As soon as they entered the tent and the flap was lowered, Kerin turned to Rhidian. 'Gwas, please, what just happened?'

He looked as stunned as anyone, but replied quickly, 'The Cariad has the right to invoke Gras Cenadol.'

'You mean she wants to—' Kerin paused, searching for an appropriate word and settled on, 'she wants to have congress with Fychan?'

Rhidian nodded, surprise stealing his dignity. 'Her Divinity has not taken this right since before I came to the Tyr.'

'And what will happen?'

'What do you mean?'

'What will happen to Fychan?' Kerin could not imagine what it must be like for a mere man to take pleasure with a goddess.

'I do not know.'

So much for priestly wisdom. 'What happened last time? Surely you have records?'

'Aye, aye we do, though this is not a matter of official record. The last time this happened, the man was never seen again.'

CHAPTER TWENTY-FOUR

If only he had come up with a reason to deny Sais's request, this might never have happened – whatever 'this' was. Einon had gone over the trance session repeatedly, but he still had no idea why asking about someone called Nual should have provoked such an extreme reaction. Einon looked at the unconscious man. If not for him, Einon would be dead: he must do everything in his power to ensure Sais recovered.

Perhaps someone in the Tyr might know better what ailed him – not that he could ask them ... He had visited some of the establishments that serviced the priesthood, but though rumours about Idwal's disappearance abounded, no one knew anything. He had taken a chance and asked about the recent exile of a certain Einon am Plas Rhydau, third-tier priest of Frythil. A porter at the Papermakers' Guild had heard that a priest of that name had committed some sort of offence and a clerk at the dairy that provided the Tyr's butter said he'd heard the priest in question had badly beaten an acolyte; 'They say he has quite a temper on him,' the man whispered. It was true Einon's temper had got him into trouble before, but he had better things to do than beat – or even teach – acolytes. Such tittle-tattle left him no wiser.

He consoled himself by spending his evenings working on his numbers, investing money he could ill afford in writing materials and paper.

The original idea that had begun his intellectual investigations was elegantly simple: what if one were to replace the holding dot in large numbers with a symbol? He had been working on the

Tyr's accounts and had looked by chance into a goblet on his desk that had held water, and was now empty: lacking content, but not substance – and suddenly he saw that it was possible to represent nothing!

What if this 'empty' symbol were used instead of the holding dot in a large number, such as three hundreds, five single? Rather than representing it as 3♦5, what if he wrote it as 3O5? That felt like a different sort of number. He had worked through the night, transforming the accounts by use of this new symbol, which he called heb – 'without'.

The final revelation had come a few days later: using the heb symbol, it was possible, in theory, to count *downwards* from one, to have numbers that were *a mirror image of normal ones*. It was a fascinating idea – and an alarming one, recalling as it did the relationship between Heaven and the Abyss. When he went to Urien, fearful of such potentially heretical investigations, far from warning him that this strange concept went against the will of the Mothers, his Escori was delighted with Einon's discovery. As well as its potential use in ciphers, Urien said this knowledge made sense of certain symbols found in the Sanctaith Glan, the inner sanctum of the Tyr, which only the Cariad and her Escorai could enter freely. Two days later, he had asked to see Einon's notes, and Einon had handed them over.

Three days after that, the rumours about Idwal's disappearance had begun.

And the very next week Einon had been sent away. He had no idea what had become of his notes.

Some part of him still wondered if, despite what his Escori had said, heb went against the will of the Mothers. But he could not unlearn what he had discovered. And it had such potential—

He jumped at the sound of a knock on the front door. It was probably just some delivery for Ebrilla, but he peered cautiously out of the window, ready to run at the sight of monitors. A single figure waited below, a skinny youth in tattered clothes: an odd choice for an assassin. Besides, assassins rarely knocked.

However, such a beggar-boy would make a good anonymous messenger – and with everyone at the presentation, this was the ideal time for Urien to get word to him.

He called out, 'What do you want?' The boy looked up. Old scars, white and pale pink, marked the bottom of the boy's grubby face. He held up a folded piece of paper and pointed to Einon.

'I will be right down,' said Einon, nearly tripping on the stairs in his haste. When he accepted the paper the boy bowed, then turned and left without a word.

Rather than the Tyr's tower, the letter had the quill and flower-bud motif of Frythil on the seal. Einon returned to his room and shut the door before opening the letter. He recognised the hand-writing covering the paper, and was not surprised to find neither salutation nor signature. At first sight the note was gibberish, random words strung together, but Einon soon realised that Urien had employed the code that Einon had already worked out at Plas Aethnen, though the first line indicated that in this case he should use every third, rather than every ninth, letter to decipher the true message. He had just managed to get the first line:

You were driven out by a plausible lie

– when he heard the front door open. He froze, then relaxed, as Ebrilla started to fuss downstairs. More arrivals were announced by slamming doors and voices. He turned his attention back to the note:

Your safe return brings joy to me.

It was as he hoped, as he feared: his Escori had not forsaken him, but had tried to save him from danger because he had an important role to play.

Remain hidden for now. Continue your work. Seek allies without the Tyr. When I call, be ready to obey without question.

From his reaction, Rhidian was as disconcerted by the Cariad's behaviour as Kerin was – as *everyone* was: on the walk back the reverent looks Damaru got were tinged with unease.

When they returned Ebrilla was already preparing the evening meal. Einon did not come down. Damaru was restless, so Kerin asked Ebrilla for a pot of uncooked rice and another of dried peas and tipped both out on the table, stirring the two piles together. Then she brought Damaru in and sat him down and asked if he would separate the patterns for her, an old trick she had used since he was a child.

Thinking of the upcoming tests, she considered asking him to move the rice and peas without touching them, but he was upset enough already.

She wondered what would happen if Fychan did not return from the Tyr. Would she be the one to take Damaru to his testing?

She left Damaru teasing the grains apart with one finger, a look of happy concentration on his face. Ebrilla brought Kerin a herbal tea and made her sit down.

'Well, tis a turn-up and no mistake,' she started.

Kerin did not have to ask what she meant. 'The priest who accompanied us has never witnessed the Cariad make such a request.'

'No. Tis her right, of course, but even so—'

'He told me that the last time she invoked Gras Cenadol the man she chose disappeared.' When Ebrilla shrugged, Kerin said, 'And I counted only four Escorai. Surely there should be five, one for each Mother?'

'Ah, of course, you not being of the City, you would not know!' Ebrilla said importantly. 'The rumours started a while back – now let me see: I first heard tell that the Escori of Carunwyd had disappeared, oh, way back in late winter. Then people started saying he was ill, though he is a young man, not like the other Escorai. I did hear there had been an accident, and the priests were covering it up. Mind, that came from a woman whose cousin delivers meat to the Tyr, and he is a rough sort so I would not credit his word too much. One of the other housekeepers here has a nephew who works at the quillmakers, so he is likely to be more reliable. He reckoned the Escori had eloped with one of the Putain Glan, of all things!'

When Einon did not come down for the evening meal, Kerin took some bread and cheese up to him. The priest sounded nervous when he answered her knock. Kerin put the tray on the floor just inside the door rather than disturb his papers.

'Is there any change, Gwas?' she asked.

Einon looked confused for a moment, until his gaze fell on Sais. 'No. As you see, he, ah, he remains as he was. For now, all we can do is pray.' When Kerin did not leave Einon added, 'Was there something else?'

Kerin turned and closed the door. 'Gwas, I am worried.'

'About what, Chilwar?'

'I want nothing more than for my son to take his place as a Consort, and I accept that he will soon go into the Tyr and not return. Yet – forgive me, Gwas – I see that things are not right in the Tyr, and I fear for him.'

'What do you mean, ah, about things being amiss in the Tyr? What have you heard?' asked Einon.

'After the presentation, the Cariad invoked Gras Cenadol. With Fychan.'

'She did *what*?' Einon looked stricken.

'She called him up, in front of everyone. And there were only four Escorai there. I have heard that the Escori of Carunwyd has been missing for some time. Is this true?'

'Aye, it is,' whispered the priest.

'Forgive me, I know I have no right to question what goes on in the Tyr, but I must know, for Damaru's sake: Is something wrong?'

Einon stared at nothing for a while, then he whispered, 'Aye. I believe something is most grievously wrong. I have, ah, been praying the Mothers may show me what.'

'So that is why you have not been to the Tyr yourself?'

He nodded, then remembered his dignity and said, 'But, ah, whatever is happening is priestly business, and has nothing to do with you, Chilwar.'

'Aye, Gwas, you are right, it has not – but it has everything to do with my son.'

For a while the only sounds were the background noises of the City: voices in the street and the distant clatter of carts. Then

Einon said, 'I do not know for certain what the problem is, but I may, ah, need help from those I can trust.'

A priest asking her for help? Mothers forefend! She squashed her pride and whispered, 'Of course, Gwas – whatever I can do.' As her mother used to say, *Hard times make strange allies*.

Run! Ignore the pounding in my head and run ... Got to get back to my ship before *they* find I'm free – before my mind unravels totally ...

Through the 'lock, off *their* ship, onto mine. Bang the *door close* panel with my palm. Nothing. Try again, tears flowing, hand stinging. *Close, damn you, close!*

Was the ship attacked? It's powered down, but I can't see any damage. Hell and damnation: *why can't I remember?*

Every moment counts: every second more of *me* goes and soon there'll be nothing left. Wish I could forget the eyes, but they're still clear as a penitent's soul, watching me, mocking.

Perhaps this is all a trick, one of *their* illusions— What if this isn't real, what if the mute only let me out on *their* orders? Or maybe she didn't let me go at all and I'm still in the cell? *What if all this is only happening in my head?*

I spin away from the door, down the familiar corridor. My home, my ship: I have to believe this is real. I have to believe I'll survive, take what's left of my mind and get as far away as possible, and ... and warn them. I have to warn them – Elarn, Nual ... Except I can't remember who they are. I'm not sure who I am any more ...

Onto the bridge; my command couch, something familiar. Yes, I know this place: the controls – need to unlock them, but I can't remember how. It's a sequence, a goddamn simple sequence. Ah, got it.

Nothing.

Is something broken? Or have *they* locked the controls so my codes don't work any more? My random twiddling starts something: an upside-down window on the universe opens up in front of me. Below is a dark planet. Wonder if I should know its name –

maybe I did once, but not now. I know less every second.

The planet's not entirely dark. Faint lights appear, a scattering near the equator: lights mean people – people, as opposed to the monsters who captured me.

Some other systems are working. I recognise one of the lit telltales: the evac-pod. The lights below are sliding past. Got to hurry.

Down off the bridge, through the rec-room, into the cargo-hold. One of these service-panels isn't really a panel. Which one? Here. Lift the flap, press the button.

The panel opens to reveal a tiny red-lit cave. I climb in.

I have to turn my back on the hold to sit down. My shoulder blades prickle. This is where *they* pull me out and make me walk back to my cell, laughing as I dance like a puppet for *them* . . .

I hit the door-panel: no complicated instructions or security codes here, everything simple as possible for emergency use, thank Christos. Behind my head, the door hisses shut.

Space Recovery or *Planetfall*? I'm as sure as I can be, which isn't very, that the only ships in orbit are mine and *theirs*, currently docked. I select *Planetfall*.

And *Go*.

I'm slammed back into the seat as the pod bursts free of the ship. On the instrument panel in front of me a blue light winks comfortingly. The text beside it says *Transponder activated*.

Oh no. *No, no, no*. We don't want that. I reach out, fighting the gees from the pod's ejection. I hold one elbow locked with my other hand. My outstretched fingers brush the light. Is it just an indicator or a switch? Let it be a switch, please let it be a switch. I press the light, my fingertip numb, my arm twitching from hold-ing out against the pod's thrust. My straight arm folds, flies back to bounce off the wall behind me. My other hand hits me in the mouth and I feel a burst of pain as my lip splits against a tooth.

The blue light is gone.

Then the acceleration's gone too, and I'm lifting off the seat, in freefall. A larger impossible-to-miss sign lights up, flashing red. *Gel imminent: Brace and exhale*

Gel? I should know what that means.

Then I find out.

Everything goes white and I'm engulfed in freezing goo. I remember, almost too late, to breathe out. The gel presses on my eyes, forces itself down my nose and throat, into my lungs.

I'm drowning, oh God I'm drowning—

No I'm not. Relax, let it in. No need to breathe. Just stay still and let it happen.

Not breathing, not moving, not panicking. In limbo. I feel movement again, in the distance. The pod lurches. Suspended in the gel, I don't panic at first. Another lurch – an impact? Have I landed already? Too soon, surely. Or have *they* come after me, caught me and reeled me in? I'm in *their* cargo-bay now, and soon *they*'ll crack the pod and I'll be back where I started ... Except my gut tells me I'm still in zero-gee.

A third lurch. Now my body tells me I'm falling.

The pressure on my ears and eyes increases. The gel's not cold any more. It's warm, getting hot. I'm in atmosphere, but I'm not slowing down. Air too thin? No, people live here. Anyway, the 'chute should compensate. Something's gone wrong—

Darkness presses on me, rises up inside me. Cold, comforting, safe darkness— No! Got to stay conscious, not give into the darkness. If I pass out now, then I'll lose everything, the last of my memories, the last of me. Perhaps I won't even—

—wake up.

Wooden beams, lit by a guttering flame. He was lying in a hard bed, under a ceiling made of wood, in a room where the only light came from an oil-lamp.

His name was Jarek Reen, but everyone here called him Sais. He was in a lodging house in the City of Light, and he had walked here from where his evac-pod had crash-landed.

His head hurt, though not so much that he couldn't move it. He looked around the room. Someone was asleep in the other bed – Einon, the priest.

The last thing he remembered was Einon putting him under, hypnotising him to get his memory back – and it had worked, sort of. His past – Jarek Reen's past – was all there. He had access to everything, though it didn't feel quite real, not in the same way Kerin and Damaru and all the other people he'd met here felt real. He viewed his old life as if from a distance – hardly surprising, given how the memories of that life had been wrenched from him.

He knew now why he had come to this system, and what had happened to him when he got here. He knew how he had come to be on this planet.

Far from reassuring him, the knowledge terrified him.

CHAPTER TWENTY-FIVE

Kerin was in the kitchen, kneading bread for Ebrilla, when Einon came in and announced that Sais had woken up and needed a drink. She wiped her hands and said, 'I will take it to him, Gwas.' Without waiting for a reply, she poured a mug of water from the jug.

'He is still weak,' said Einon anxiously, 'and I believe his spirit is troubled. Do not vex him, woman!'

Kerin ignored him and ran up the stairs to find Sais sitting up in bed, staring into space.

'I brought you a drink,' she said redundantly.

He drained the mug and murmured, 'Thank you.' After a moment's silence he added, 'I'm sorry I worried everyone.'

'Do not be; it is not your fault,' said Kerin firmly. 'But I must apologise to you. I am sorry for mistaking your intentions and making you the vessel for my hope. It was not your fault that I – I came to feel the way I did. And I was too proud to acknowledge that.'

Sais shook his head slowly. 'It's not your fault – I hated that I hurt you, Kerin. You've been through so much already.'

'I am fine. Really, I am. And I forgive you. Do you forgive me?'

'Oh, come here,' he said, and held out his arms. She leaned down and let him hold her. It felt good: not a touch of passion, but of companionship.

She turned at the sound of a throat being cleared. Einon stood in the doorway, looking confused.

'I should give you your room back,' said Sais. 'I'm sure you have work to do.' He got up carefully. Kerin stood by, ready to assist. Einon waited by his desk like a monitor guarding treasure while they made their way out.

When Einon closed the door behind them Kerin said, 'We left you in there because that is where you became ill. Do you remember?'

'Oh yes, I remember.'

Something in Sais's tone chilled her. 'What is wrong?'

He shook his head. 'Nothing.'

Kerin *hurrumphed*. 'Do not tell me "nothing" when you have spent the last two days asleep and several weeks before that walking around in a daze!'

He looked at her with haunted eyes. 'Oh, Kerin, part of me wishes I could— No, just— No. I think I should go back to my room.'

'As you wish.' Perhaps he would tell her later, when he had recovered fully. She shadowed him, ready to help. When he got back to the room he shared with Fychan he said, 'I assume Fychan is still out enjoying the delights of City life?'

Kerin frowned. 'No, he – the Cariad invoked Gras Cenadol with him at the presentation.'

'What? You mean she – she wanted to sleep with him?'

'I assume so. He has not come back yet.'

'Oh shit.' Sais sat down heavily on his bed. He muttered something under his breath that sounded like, 'But she's ...' Suddenly he punched his hands down hard. 'I have to go,' he announced, no longer sounding vague with worry, but driven by fear.

'Go where?'

'Anywhere – I'm putting you in danger by being here. It'll be better for you, and for me, if I walk out and keep walking. I've caused you enough trouble already.' He stood up shakily.

'You are leaving? Now?' She strode over to the door, slammed it shut and stood in front of it. 'I think not.'

'Kerin, what the—?'

'Get back into bed.' She uncrossed her arms long enough to

200

point at the bed, in case he failed to understand. 'Lie down. I will bring food, and send for a healer. Unless you would prefer Einon examine you? Perhaps not, given t'was his meddling that caused the problem.'

He did not move. 'What problem?'

'When you first awakened in my hut, you had the power of speech and you had sense, but you had no recollection of your past. Now it seems you have lost your senses as well!'

'You don't give up, do you? The problem isn't that I've lost my senses. The problem is I've got them back – and my memory.'

'You have? This is good news, surely?'

'Not as good as you think.'

'Why not? Tell me – are we not friends?'

'Yes, we are. And that's why I can't explain. I'm trying to protect you!'

'From what?'

'Not what, who,' he muttered. 'Please don't ask, Kerin. You really, really don't want to know.'

'You are the one who insisted I am so strong! Strong enough to save myself, you said – but not strong enough for the truth? Or were you lying when you talked about respect and admiration and all those feelings men never have for women?'

'I've never lied to you, Kerin.'

'No, you have not. So why will you not tell me this great and terrible secret you have suddenly discovered?'

'Because you'll be happier not knowing,' he whispered. 'Please, don't ask me to explain. Just let me go.'

'If you think the purpose of my life is to be happy, then you do not understand me as well as you think. And I will *not* let you just walk out without a word.' She had never stood up to any man like this. Some of her defiance came from the knowledge that he would not raise a hand to her, but she also felt a passion of the spirit that she had no name for. 'Tell me why you are so afraid. And if your fear makes sense to me, then go with my blessing.'

'No, you— What can I say to convince you that you don't want to know this?'

'Nothing! You claim to respect me – so give me the truth!'

'You'll think I'm mad.'

'Let me be the judge of that,' she said more gently.

His shoulders sagged. 'All right, but you're either not going to believe me, or you'll hate me forever.'

'So be it.'

He sat down again and moved along the bed to make room for her. 'You'll need to sit down for this. Alcohol would help, but we don't have any.'

She sat next to him, suddenly afraid. Perhaps he was right, perhaps she should let him keep his terrible secret.

He took a deep breath. 'First off, I don't come from this world.'

'What you do you mean, "this world"? The world is the world – Heaven, Creation and the Abyss. If you mean you come from a distant land, somewhere beyond the mountains where life is very different, then that I can well believe.'

'No, I mean another *world*.' He looked apologetic. 'I'll understand if you say I'm damned, or mad, but you asked for the truth.'

'Aye, I did. So what is *this* world then? I might wish the Abyss did not exist, though the priests tell us otherwise. But we can see the Mothers in the sky, every night!'

'The stars aren't goddesses, Kerin. They're suns, like—'

'No! This is blasphemy!' She turned to go, rather than hear any more unthinkable, impossible words – but his expression, sad, almost pitying, stopped her. 'How can you believe such things?' she whispered, in no doubt that he truly did.

'I believe in what I've seen.' He sighed. 'But I'll understand if you don't want to know.'

'No,' she said. 'I have to know.' She focused on the lesser heresy. 'You say there is more than one world. Please, explain how that can be.'

'For a start, this world isn't a flat plain, it's a globe, like – like an apple. Imagine we live on the outside of a massive apple, so big we don't know we're on it.'

'We would fall off.'

'You'd think so, but there's a force that keeps us, well, stuck to the surface.'

What a bizarre idea. 'And what about Heaven? Is it all around this apple that we are somehow stuck to?'

'Yes, it is – and the sun is a far bigger globe, and it shines like the light-globes outside. Our globe – our apple – goes around it.'

If this was sense, then she was a skyfool. 'And where are the moons in this strange world of yours?'

They're smaller than the world, your globe, but closer, and they go round it.'

'And the globe we live on goes around the sun? How can that be when we see the moons and the sun travel across the sky?'

'They just *seem* to, from the globe's surface. It's an illusion, like – like when you look down the street at night and the light-globe on the corner appears tiny compared to the one outside. And if you walk past the window with the shutters open at night and look out at the globe across the street it looks like it's moving across the open window, doesn't it?'

'I suppose it does.' Though Kerin could not imagine how these globes moved, when he described it that way it sounded plausible. And intriguing.

'It's a bit more complicated than that, but that's the theory. Now here's the difficult bit.'

Despite herself Kerin laughed. 'Oh good, it gets hard now, does it?'

'Yes, and I'm impressed you've managed to keep up this far. Right. This world – this ... apple and its light globe and its moons, all that stuff, it's just one world. And there are many, many worlds like – like embers swirling up from a fire.'

Kerin tried to picture every ember as a tiny glowing land – no, a round world with its own sun and moons. The thought made her dizzy. Every answer prompted more questions. But he had not yet answered the most obvious one. 'Sais, even if it is true – and I am not saying I believe you – why should remembering that the world is this way suddenly make you want to flee for your life?'

'Because there are people out there in the sky, people from another globe, another light in the darkness, and they're my enemies. They're called the Sidhe. If they find I'm here, they'll come after me.'

'Then why have these Sidhe not found you yet? You have been here the best part of a season, and you have hardly been hiding! On the contrary, we have told people about you everywhere we have been!'

'Perhaps they thought I was dead. The way I escaped from them was pretty risky. And once I was down here, on your world, they had no easy way to find me. Only now—'

'Only now *what*? What has changed?' He had merely been preoccupied and subdued until she told him about Fychan being called into the Tyr. You said "who" earlier – do you mean the Cariad? Is this about the Daughter of Heaven?' Kerin raised her arm to trace the circle, then stopped with her hand halfway to her breast, suddenly self-conscious.

In the silence that followed, Kerin heard a door bang downstairs. Finally Sais said, 'Kerin, I'm sorry, she's not the "Beloved Daughter of Heaven", or whatever title she uses.'

'Are you saying the Cariad is not divine?'

'That's exactly what I'm saying.'

'You did not see her at the presentation, Sais! She was clothed in light, and she called forth flame with her hand.'

He looked a little taken aback, then he laughed and said, 'That's nothing divine – it's technology, like … like the windmills on the way here. You'd never seen them before, you had no idea how they worked, but when Einon explained them, you understood. It's like the light-globes, or Einon's lantern.'

'This is more than a new means to grind flour or banish darkness! Are you saying the Beloved is just an ordinary woman who uses this "technology" to *appear* divine?' She could accept, even welcome, the idea of new and marvellous devices; claiming the Cariad was a trickster was quite another thing.

'She's not a goddess, Kerin – but I don't think she's exactly ordinary either, and that's the problem.'

'Then what—?'

The door flew open. Fychan stood on the threshold, looking pale and exhausted and insufferably pleased with himself.

Sais sprang to his feet. 'Are you alone?'

'Aye,' said Fychan, 'who would be with me? The Cariad herself?'

'You weren't followed here? I mean, you've just come from the Tyr, haven't you?'

'Aye, I have just come from the Tyr.' Fychan's tone implied he thought this might be more important than Sais's ravings.

Kerin raised a calming hand. 'Sais is awake, as you see, but he is still not himself.' She caught Sais's eye.

He sat down again. 'Kerin's right. I'm sorry, I just … Fychan, your shirt – did the Cariad say anything about it?'

Sounding smug, Fychan said, 'No Sais, she did not. Most of our business was conducted with me out of my clothes.'

Sais said, 'She didn't ask where you got it?'

'No, of course not. Why should she?'

Kerin answered that question for herself: because it came from the sky, with Sais, and if Fychan had told the Cariad about that, then she would know Sais was here— Mothers' sakes, she was starting to think like Sais!

Sais shook his head. 'No reason.'

'Good,' said Fychan. 'Now I need to get changed and go out again.'

'Go out?' said Kerin. 'But Damaru's testing is this afternoon.'

'Aye, so I cannot waste time.'

'Where are you going, Fychan?' asked Sais.

'That is between me and the Cariad, and t'would not be any of your business.'

'But perhaps, ah, it is mine, Chilwrau.' The three of them looked up to see Einon standing in the doorway.

Kerin and Sais exchanged looks. *What if he had heard them talking before Fychan burst in?*

'Aye, Gwas, of course,' said Fychan, 'but I did not want to disturb you.'

Einon said, 'It might be best if I, ah, speak with Fychan alone.'

In her most demure voice Kerin said, 'Gwas, we would be deeply honoured to hear the words of the Beloved, if you permit us.'

The priest looked uncomfortable. He could hardly refuse such a humble and devoutly phrased request. 'I suppose that could be allowed. Kindly do not interrupt, though.' He closed the door. The room felt very crowded now.

Einon started, 'You have been truly blessed, have you not, Chilwar?'

'Aye,' said Fychan, a little uneasily. He had just had the most amazing sex of his life, and he was not sure he should be bragging about it to a priest.

Kerin stifled a smile.

'To say you have, ah, experienced joy such as most men dream of would sum it up, I think.' Einon nodded to himself. 'But her Divinity also made a request of you. What is the, ah, the nature of this request?'

'It might be best if I showed you, Gwas.' Fychan reached inside his shirt.

Sais tensed, then when the lad produced a bundle of papers, relaxed. Fychan handed the bundle to Einon, who whispered, 'Mothers preserve us! Do you know what you have here? These, ah, these are promissory notes. Each one, ah, of these pieces of paper could be taken to the mint and exchanged for a hundred marks. Why would her Divinity give you a fortune?'

'Tis not for me,' said Fychan, though he kept his hand on the notes. 'The Cariad wishes this to go to a young woman called Anona. She says this girl must be given the money and instructed to leave the City at once.'

Kerin guessed everyone else was as confused by this request as she was. In the stunned silence, Fychan unrolled the notes. Inside the bundle was a small, crudely made child's poppet. 'Her Divinity said that this doll would convince Anona to do as she was told.'

Einon said, 'Fychan, you are, ah, are you saying that the Cariad, the Beloved Daughter of Heaven, wishes you to find a girl, show her a child's toy, then, ah, give her money to leave Dinas Emrys?'

'Aye, Gwas.'

'Did she, ah, inform you of this in the presence of any priest?'

'No, I met no one else in my night in the Tyr. The Cariad herself escorted me at all times.'

'And you, ah, agreed to her request, of course.'

'Of course. But I am not sure where to go. She gave me an address and directions, and I was going to ask Ebrilla—'

'I will find this girl for you,' said Einon. 'You must, ah, conserve your strength for your duties as Damaru's guardian.'

'Are you sure, Gwas?' asked Fychan. 'She gave the task to me—'

'I know the City, and it would be my honour to do the Cariad's will.'

Fychan still looked unsure, but Kerin understood at once: Einon suspected this girl might be the key to whatever was going on in the Tyr.

Einon clapped his hands. 'Good, then, it is, ah, it is decided. Fychan, where is this Anona to be found?'

'She is the daughter of Dilwyn the clerk, whose house is on the upslope corner of the Street of Lesser Reckoners.'

'Excellent. Then I shall leave as soon as I have broken my fast. We must not, ah, keep her Divinity waiting.'

Kerin wondered why a goddess needed to send people from outside the Tyr on such a strange errand ... unless she was not a goddess at all.

CHAPTER TWENTY-SIX

Einon left as soon as they'd eaten. Even if he had overheard Sais's conversation with Kerin, he obviously had other priorities.

Fychan, who looked exactly like a man who'd gone ten rounds in the bedroom with a goddess, went to lie down.

Kerin took Damaru to their room. Quite aside from her desire to spend what time was left with her child, she had a lot to think about. After all, someone she trusted had just told her she was living a lie.

Sais shouldn't have admitted the truth, no matter how she pestered him. But if anyone here could handle it, Kerin could. He'd had faith once too, in a male duality of loving father and self-sacrificing son. And he'd grown up somewhere where belief was the norm, though he didn't remember it being as all-pervasive as it was here. He had lost his faith and survived.

He went and sat in the parlour, where Ebrilla's cat immediately colonised his lap. He stroked the animal and listened to the comfortable chaos of the household. It looked like his initial panic about the Cariad had been unfounded. If she were Sidhe, she wouldn't have *asked* Fychan to find the girl – she would have *compelled* him. Though he no longer felt the immediate need to run, he had no intention of attending the testing, just in case he was wrong about the Cariad. He eased the cat off his lap and slipped out into the anonymity of the streets.

He had assumed the Cariad was the Sidhe representative on the planet, in which case she should have recognised the smartchute fabric. Of course, if she was Sidhe, the fact that she hadn't asked

Fychan about the shirt didn't mean she hadn't found out through more arcane means. Or she might have asked, then removed the memory from Fychan's mind. The Sidhe were good at that. Then again, given the Sidhe left the Cariad to rule alone for years at a time, she might not have any technical knowledge beyond that necessary to keep the 'divine magic' of the City of Light ticking over. She might just have thought the shirt was unusually fine, not an offworld product.

As ever with the damn Sidhe, he had no way of knowing. Perhaps he'd have been safer if he'd stayed in Dangwern. The Sidhe probably assumed he'd been killed when his evac-pod got shot down by the planetary defences – he probably would have been if he hadn't been cushioned in gel and crashed into a bog. Even if they thought he'd survived, with the pod at the bottom of the mere and any celestial visitations likely to cause widespread panic, trying to find him would have been more trouble than it was worth – assuming they even cared: he'd been seriously messed up when he escaped, and they had no reason to think he'd recover from their *ministrations*.

Now he thought about it, they probably weren't that bothered about him. If he kept his head down, he should be safe enough. Given how detached he felt from his old life, perhaps he could even make a new life here in the City, though he'd have to accept the lo-tech living conditions, not to mention celibacy.

Only, this wasn't just about him.

He'd been a freetrader for most of his adult life, but for the last seven years he'd had a secondary mission: to find out what he could about the Sidhe, the apparently lost race that had once dominated human-space. He was one of a tiny handful of humans who believed the Sidhe weren't dead after all; and most of those who thought that way had little evidence, and even less influence.

For years he had chased rumours and legends, only to have most of them vanish like mist. When he'd heard about a large, unaffiliated, freetrader ship called the *Setting Sun* that journeyed out into uncharted space every twenty-five years or so, he'd half assumed the story was just deep-black chit-chat, despite the data's usually reliable source – just like he'd once dismissed stories of Sidhe lurking in the voids between the stars. He'd got himself into the right place at the right time and managed to slipstream the *Setting Sun* when it left the shipping-lanes – a risk, but life was boring without the odd risk, and even if the transit failed he would probably just find himself back where he started. When he followed the ship he'd been thinking less about the Sidhe than about the delicious possibility of picking up a lost transit-path the traders were keeping to themselves – an extremely lucrative find.

Instead, he'd found an entire lost colony, defended from intruders by orbital weaponry and kept in lo-tech ignorance by theocratic rule, the whole place apparently set up to provide the Sidhe with a crop of uniquely talented adolescent boys: if one or more Consorts got chosen each year, then there must be several dozen waiting for the pick-up, presumably held in stasis somewhere in the Tyr. And he'd found the ship that had come for them: not a freetrader at all, but actually crewed by Sidhe and their slaves. Or rather, they'd found him.

He'd bet the *Setting Sun* was docked at the top of the beanstalk right now, ready to collect its strange harvest. He had no idea what the Sidhe wanted the Consorts for, but he doubted it was to make the lives of the poor bastards down here any better, whatever the 'Traditions' might say.

He finally had the lead he'd been looking for: proof that the Sidhe weren't just lurking in a few deep-space colony ships, but that they controlled at least one settled planet. And they were up to something big. This vital information would never leave this world if he spent the rest of his life here.

As well as his idealistic hopes of saving humanity from a threat they refused to believe in, two people he cared about were in danger because of his carelessness: his sister, Elarn, and Nual, the Sidhe child – by now a grown woman – who'd rejected her heritage and started him on this crazy path.

Nual was well hidden. They'd both known the risks he ran in attempting to uncover Sidhe influence, so before they'd parted company on a distant world, he'd let her into his head so she could hide any knowledge that could lead the Sidhe to her. When they'd captured him, they'd broken down the walls she had put in his mind, nearly destroying his psyche in the process. He wasn't sure how he'd managed to reconstruct himself: perhaps some combination of the priest's delving, his own resilience and Nual's lasting influence. It could even be partly down to the skyfool: Kerin had told him that when Damaru first played music to him, the boy said he'd been trying to heal Sais's mind. Whatever the cause, he remembered everything now. And he had to assume that his Sidhe interrogators knew it all too.

Which meant they knew about Elarn. His greatest regret, in a life which included some spectacular mistakes, was introducing Nual to his sister. Elarn had never forgiven him for drawing her into the conspiracy, for bringing the fascinating alien child into her peaceful, lonely life.

Seven years ago, when he left his sister in the magnificent cliff-house that had once been their home, she'd told him she never wanted to see him again – but he'd left her with the knowledge that the Sidhe were not dead. She'd never use that knowledge, but that might not stop the Sidhe wanting this threat to their secret eliminated.

He had to warn her that the Sidhe might come for her, and Nual too, if she was still in the system where he'd left her. Assuming he wasn't already too late: the *Setting Sun* could have broadcast the results of his interrogation by beamed virtual – but to whom, though? Despite years of research, he still had only the sketchiest idea of how many Sidhe remained at large, how widespread their influence was, and most importantly, what they were up to.

On the other hand, if the Cariad had a beevee unit in her rocky fortress and he could get access to it, then he could contact Elarn and maybe Nual. The Sidhe had several months' lead on him, but they also had limited resources and no reason to hurry.

He couldn't just live out his life pretending to belong here. He had to try to get word out about what he'd found. And that brought him back to the inescapable conclusion that he had to get into the Tyr.

Einon had never actually been to the Street of Lesser Reckoners, and he got lost several times, perhaps because he found his mind wandering. Given how cold they had been towards each other up until recently, Einon had been surprised at Kerin's eagerness to see Sais when he awoke. Though he trusted each of them – to an extent – he was wary of them together, and he had considered eavesdropping when he heard them talking in Sais's room – but the Mothers had spared him that temptation; Einon had ducked back into his own room when Fychan ran upstairs, ready to just happen to walk past the boy's room as he spoke with Sais and Kerin.

He too had been relieved to hear that Fychan had had contact only with the Cariad herself, but he was puzzled at the Beloved Daughter of Heaven's mundane request. Perhaps it was a test ... he only wished he could work out what or who was being tested.

When he finally found the clerk's house it was grander than he had expected: three storeys high with a small portico. He asked the servant who answered the door if Anona was in. The girl blanched and told him to wait. He stepped back to check if the falling fire had beaten him here, but the lintels were unpainted.

After a while the door was re-opened by a well-dressed man with thinning hair, obviously the master of the house, who neither invited him in, nor introduced himself, but said only, 'I am sorry, Gwas. Anona is gone.'

'Gone? Gone where?'

'We do not know.'

'But you are her, ah, father, presumably? How can you not know?'

The man hesitated, looked around, then at last said, 'Please, step inside.' He led the way to a finely appointed parlour, but did not offer refreshments. After they were seated he said, 'She has run away from home. My wife and I are most upset.'

'When did this happen?'

'Two weeks back. We think she may have left with her beau, a mason – not the sort of suitor we encouraged.'

'I see,' said Einon, who did not. 'And do you know why? Had she, ah, got herself into trouble with this boy?'

'Oh no, I am sure tis nothing like that – and if it were, we would forgive her. We disapproved of the relationship, but we would never do anything to drive away our little girl.'

'So why did she leave?'

The man hesitated, then said, 'I wish I knew.'

Einon sensed a lie – not a big one, but enough to worry him. He considered showing the man the doll, then decided against it – he knew too little to give away information.

Once he had been shown out, he went to the vegetable market at the end of the street, found an eating-house with a view of Anona's house and waited. After a while a servant emerged from the house with a basket. He intercepted the girl at the edge of the market; in return for one of the Cariad's promissory notes, she was happy to talk and then swear secrecy.

She confirmed that Anona had left home suddenly in the company of an apprentice mason, but only after monitors in Tyr livery had called demanding to see the daughter of the house. The family had been out visiting a relative sick with the falling fire, and when the housekeeper told them of the visit the parents had hustled Anona away. She had left later that day. That explained the father's reticence.

For the Cariad to ask Fychan to get the girl out the City was strange enough. To find the task already complete piled confusion upon conundrum.

CHAPTER TWENTY-SEVEN

Though Kerin tried to pray for guidance, the words would not come. Instead, she sat in the sunshine by the window, listening to Damaru picking at his harp and thinking about what Sais had told her. He believed he spoke the truth, but that did not make what he said true. A priest would immediately brand him as Abyss-touched and call for his death for such talk – just as a priest had called for, and got, the death of Kerin's own mother.

The concepts Sais described – a world of many worlds, the sun and moons as globes – were hard, but not impossible, even if she remained somewhat hazy on the reasons why people did not fall off their globes. If this great world of worlds allowed a place for the Skymothers, she would have tried to embrace it, but the revelations he had reluctantly shared had been prompted by fears about the Cariad – ridiculous, blasphemous, unthinkable fears.

Yet when Fychan spoke of her odd request Kerin had to at least consider the possibility that the Daughter of Heaven was not divine perfection made flesh. And if she was not what she claimed to be, was anything Kerin believed really true?

She shook her head. She could not afford such uncertainty, not with Damaru's testing fast approaching. Ebrilla and the other guests had already gone out in search of good vantage points, so she got her son some food and sat with him to wait for the priest.

When Rhidian arrived, both Einon and Sais were still out and Fychan was still asleep. Kerin went up to wake him. From the way he smelled, Kerin had no doubt he had enjoyed his night.

She suspected that Rhidian wanted to ask Fychan about his

encounter with the Cariad, but by the time the lad had made himself presentable, it was time to leave.

Rhidian repainted the circle on Damaru's forehead with his own paint, in 'a more suitable colour'. The particular shade of dark orange reminded Kerin of a fungus that grew on dead bogwood trees back in Dangwern, and the act of painting the circle recalled again Sais's words about the many worlds. If he was right, a single circle was wholly inadequate.

Though Rhidian did not mention her place in the upcoming test, he did not stop her attending Damaru. It was as though he viewed her as an appendage of the skyfool. When they left the house he said only, 'Kindly remain a step behind us, unless your boy needs you.'

Damaru attracted more attention than usual on the streets. As the four of them passed, people stopped what they were doing and stood with heads bowed, some murmuring prayers or circling their breast repeatedly.

In the upper City people lined the streets to watch them. Kerin gave no mind to the curious looks and muttered comments her presence drew and held her head high. The mood of the crowd changed as they neared the square. Kerin recalled star-season in Dangwern, when the villages played each other at games; she felt the same charge, the same anticipation of sport. When she glimpsed tokens changing hands in the crowd, she remembered Ebrilla's words about those who placed wagers on the candidates.

Over the heads of the crowd Kerin glimpsed the empty balcony of the Oriel Glan. Monitors cleared a way through the crowd for them and they entered the painted tent.

Inside, refreshments had been set up, and seats put in five groups. Servants waited to attend the skyfools and their guardians. The skyfools were uneasy, staring hard at each other, then looking away, twitching and flapping their hands. Kerin recognised the reaction; they must see other skyfools as aberrations in the pattern, and they were searching for a way to make the world right. Only the oldest boy appeared unconcerned.

Functionaries and guards fussed in the background and the air of anticipation grew. Rhidian told them that rather then entering the square together as they had for the presentation, each candidate group would wait in the tent to be called forward. The test would be conducted and overseen by a group of priests. Kerin found herself relieved that the Cariad would not be watching them. Various tests had been used at different times: this year Rhidian said the skyfools would be asked to exert their will over water; Kerin thought this sounded more like a showman's trick than proof of divine ability.

The skyfools would be tested in the same order they had been presented in, so Damaru would go last. Despite Kerin's confidence in her son, she was not looking forward to the wait.

The first skyfool was called forward, and the rumble of the crowd died away as the front of the tent was raised. Kerin glimpsed the square, with the wooden frame of the test in the middle, before the tent flap was lowered again. A priest announced the skyfool and requested that the test begin. The crowd murmured as the preparations were made.

Silence fell. Then the murmurs began; low voices encouraged the boy. The murmurs grew into cheers. When the crowd grew quiet again the priest announced that the boy was worthy to face the final test in the presence of the Cariad and should take his rest until he entered the Tyr the following evening.

The tent flap was raised, and the boy and his companions returned. Kerin watched the skyfool, trying to assess how the test had affected him. He looked mildly bemused and a little tired, but not too upset, which was good. The monitors escorted the successful group out the back of the tent and the next candidate was brought forward.

This time the murmurs grew in volume as the test proceeded, and a few lone voices shouted out 'Unworthy', only to be shushed, then overtaken by cheers. When this group returned, the guardian had splashes of red on his shoulders and face. For a moment Kerin thought it was blood. Then she remembered what Rhidian had said: the water whose course the skyfools had to divert was coloured, the better to be seen – by the crowd, as well as the skyfools, Kerin presumed.

The third candidate passed with only the faintest murmur before the cheering began.

The fourth boy, the oldest candidate, did not fare so well. The muttering grew and swelled. She heard a man, presumably the boy's guardian, shout something, possibly to encourage his son, then the cries of 'Unworthy!' drowned him out. The cries became a chant, hundreds of voices, shouting, baying, some screaming. Fychan looked ashen, and Kerin swallowed and put her hand on Damaru's arm. Her son shivered under her touch, his eyes distant and uncertain.

Finally the voices fell away.

A few moments later the flap was raised to admit the priest and the failed boy's guardian, drenched in red dye and openly crying. The priest took the man's arm and steered him out the back of the tent. Several of those inside made the gesture of am-annwn as he passed, and when he left he was greeted with jeers and catcalls. He would return to his home in disgrace. His fate would be better than that of his boy, who would be held by the monitors at the edge of the square until the testing was complete, then stoned to death by those same people who had earlier urged him on.

On Rhidian's signal, Kerin stood, her legs shaking.

The four of them walked to the front of the tent. 'Medelwyr be with us,' murmured Rhidian. The flap was raised.

As they crossed the square Kerin found herself staring at the strange contraption at the far end. A chair stood in front of a high wooden wall. A copper spout peeped over the top of the wall. Water from earlier tests had splashed over the chair and up the wall and pooled on the ground like wine, or blood.

Rhidian murmured for them to stop about twenty paces away. A priest walked out from behind the wall and announced Damaru. Two less overdressed priests approached and led Fychan to the chair. Kerin saw his lips moving in prayer.

She stepped forward to stand beside Damaru. Rhidian did not stop her. 'You remember what you have to do, Damaru?' she whispered. 'Stop the water falling and wetting Fychan.'

Damaru gave no sign of having heard her.

The priests strapped Fychan to the chair to avoid his movements influencing the test.

Kerin resisted the temptation to touch or talk to Damaru. She prayed that his apparent indifference indicated he was gathering his strength.

As the crowd grew quiet, a faint but peculiar noise began behind the wall: *squeak-thump, squeak-thump* – a pump, Kerin realised, like the ones at inns and street-corners that raised water.

A red drip fell from the lip of the spout onto Fychan's head. Then another. Kerin held her breath, willing Damaru to show his talent.

All around, people began to murmur.

The drips became a trickle. Kerin stared at the spout as though she, not her son, were the one with the power to influence the flow. The trickle became a stream. She waited for the first cry from the crowd, but they had fallen silent.

She blinked and looked down, expecting Fychan to be wet with dye. He was not. A hand's-breadth above Fychan's head the flow of water stopped. It was not being diverted to splash onto the wall. The water was being taken out of existence and then – yes, she saw it now! – returned in another place. The pool around the chair was growing. Not a drop touched Fychan. Nerves gave way to a stranger feeling, a sudden unease of the soul, as though something indefinable had changed when her back had been turned.

She felt the sensation of the world bending to her boy's will.

The crowd began to cheer.

CHAPTER TWENTY-EIGHT

As he turned back into Stryd Dechreur, Sais heard distant cheering from the direction of the Tyr. He found the door locked, and wondered if Einon had joined Ebrilla at the testing, but knocked anyway. He saw movement at the window, and a moment later Einon stuck out his head.

'Ah, tis you,' he said.

Sais wondered who he'd been expecting.

When Einon let him in, Sais asked, 'How did your errand go?'

'All is well. The girl is safely out of the City. I, ah, need to get back to my work now. You should, ah, eat – regain your strength,' he suggested.

Sais had had only one meal in the last three days and now Einon mentioned it, he realised he was ravenous. He was just cleaning his plate when the front door opened and he came out of the kitchen to see Damaru trudging up the hall, followed by Kerin. He'd been so wrapped up in his own problems he'd hardly spared a thought for the boy. Damaru looked drained but unharmed.

Sais smiled at Kerin. 'He did it then?'

'Aye. He will want to rest now.' She looked tired herself. 'Did Einon succeed in carrying out the Cariad's request?' she added.

'He says so. He wasn't particularly informative.'

'No, I think he has his own problems.' Kerin closed the front door.

'Isn't Fychan with you?' asked Sais.

Kerin sighed. 'He has decided to celebrate. As the guardian of a successful skyfool, I expect he will not need to buy his own drinks all evening.' As she passed him she said, 'I will get Damaru settled, then can we talk?'

'Of course. I'll be in the parlour.'

When Kerin came back downstairs, Sais was still trying to work out what to say. For all Kerin's open and enquiring mind, he was basically telling her that she had spent her life worshipping false gods. Though he'd got over losing his religion, that had been a gradual process; and he came from a culture where, whatever the authorities on his homeworld might wish, there was no universal faith followed unquestioningly by everyone. Here, there was, and it would be hard to overthrow a lifetime's conditioning.

Kerin sat on the other end of the bench. 'Sais, I am worried for Damaru. He has proved his worth this afternoon, and tomorrow he must go to the Tyr. I believe he will succeed there too. But if what you told me this morning is true – and I am not saying I believe you – then I fear Damaru may not go to Heaven when he ascends.'

He wasn't going to lie to her. 'I'm afraid you may be right.'

She digested this, then said, 'His next test is with the Cariad. How does she fit into all this? You were so scared of her earlier – did you think she was one of these, what did you call them?'

'Sidhe.'

'Sidhe, aye. But now you are not so sure, are you? Because she did not ask Fychan about your shirt and a Sidhe would know it to be an unearthly object.'

An unearthly object – an odd phrase, but accurate. 'That's right. And her request was a bit odd.'

'I agree.' Kerin paused. 'Tis not a request I would expect a divine being to make. But if she is not the Beloved Daughter of Heaven, who is she?'

'I don't know. I assumed she was Sidhe, but I wasn't really thinking straight.'

'You were scared. We do foolish things when fear takes us.' Kerin's gaze had been focused on her lap. Now she lifted her eyes. 'You fear the Sidhe greatly. Are they the ones who stole your memories?'

He nodded. 'That's right.'

'How? And why?'

He thought for a moment. The less she knew the safer she was, but she needed some explanation. 'Most people don't know the Sidhe still exist. They used to rule over everyone, a long time ago.' He didn't add, *like they still do here*. 'Humanity – people – overthrew their rule, and thought they'd wiped them out. They nearly did – and now the Sidhe need people to believe that they're dead. Anyone who knows otherwise is a threat to them. In trying to find out how much I knew about them, they damaged my mind.'

'But you escaped.'

'Yes. I had help. They have servants – bondsmen – who work for them, and one of them helped me.' He wondered what had happened to the poor bitch who'd unlocked his cell. Something unpleasant, probably.

'And then you fell from the sky?' Kerin's tone made it obvious how absurd this sounded.

'Yes, I was on a ship. A ship is like … a closed box that travels through the sky. I came down in a far smaller ship that got damaged and crashed. The fabric you found was meant to slow it down, but it got ripped. When you found me I was probably suffering from exposure, and maybe in shock – there's stuff in the ship that cushioned me and it slows your body down. I must have opened my little ship and crawled free before it sank into the mere, but I don't remember.'

Kerin's expression showed how hard she was finding it to get her head round all this. Finally she said, 'And people in the sky have no clothes?'

'Sorry?'

'You were naked when I found you.'

'I'd forgotten that. No, we have clothes. The Sidhe took mine away, to make me feel more vulnerable.'

The front door opened and they heard Ebrilla come in, humming cheerfully to herself. They shut up.

They heard her grunt as she bent down to stroke the cat, who'd streaked out of the parlour when the door opened. 'All alone,

Palfau?' she said. 'Tis quiet as a winnowed house in here! Ah well, best get supper started anyway.' Clattering sounds came from the kitchen.

Suddenly Sais had a new thought: the falling fire. That came from the sky – as did the cure. And the winnowing times happened approximately every twenty-five years – *the same as the interval between visits from the* Setting Sun. The falling fire was brought by the Sidhe! These people were regularly culled by a divine pestilence they were conditioned to accept: it kept the population size limited, manageable and in constant fear – perfect for a single autocratic ruler to control.

More than that: Kerin had told him priests, with their empathic abilities, rarely caught the falling fire; skyfools, with their more extreme talents, never did. Which meant it was a tailored pathogen, designed not just to keep the population down but to select for certain genetic traits. Add in the divinely sponsored sex-fest at star-season to give the genes a good mix-up, and what did you have?

A millennia-long, planet-wide, selective-breeding programme.

'Sais? What is it?'

He looked up to see Kerin staring at him. What could he say? *Your entire world is a sick experiment administered by malicious aliens for an unknown purpose?* He felt his scalp crawl. 'I'm just – I'm fine,' he murmured.

'Are you sure?'

'Yes, really. What else did you want to know?'

Kerin gave a tiny, stressed laugh. 'I am not sure I *want* to know any of this. But I must. I cannot stop now, or I will spend the rest of my life wondering. So: if what you say is correct, and the world is just one of many, why has no one else come here in these sky-travelling boxes?'

A good question. 'You're a long way off the beaten track. Most people have no idea there's anything out here. Also, you've got orbital defences up in the sky. Weapons, like the monitor's crossbows, only larger. They shoot down anyone who comes too close.'

'Are they what damaged your ... little ship?'

'Yes. They shot at my big ship too, but they missed. I'm not sure whether they're programmed to fire warning shots or whether they're not as efficient as they used to be. The Sidhe claimed their ship had been badly damaged before they could move it away, and the people on board were in danger. Idiot that I was, I went in to help. That's how they caught me.'

'I think I understand, though I cannot picture these ships and weapons. This all seems like a lot of trouble for them to go to. Why do they hide our world?'

'I'm not sure yet.'

'Might these Sidhe not be sky-people like yourself who have discovered our faith, which is true, and corrupted it for their own ends?'

How Kerin must want to believe that. 'It's possible,' he conceded.

Kerin nodded to herself. 'Aye, I think it must be so. Unless these Sidhe are powerful enough to have made our world, in which case they would be divine and hence worthy of our worship!'

Sais had met plenty of people who believed the universe had been created by a divine force, and though he didn't share their belief, that didn't mean it hadn't been. But he had a good idea how this particular world had come to be the way it was. 'I'm pretty certain the Sidhe did set this place up, but it was nothing divine.'

'What do you mean?'

'You're not going to like this.'

'I imagine not. Go on.'

'What almost certainly happened is that the Sidhe brought settlers out here a long time ago, when they were at the height of their power. Your ancestors would have come from another world, along with some of the plants and animals you need.' Though not *everything* – he'd never seen bogwood before; and the Sidhe didn't appear to have brought horses – presumably because that would have made travel too easy. 'They probably made the first colonists forget they came from somewhere else. They gave them a book of rules – the Traditions – which told them what they mustn't do, building in stuff to keep you primitive, like saying iron – *skymetal* –

could only be used by the church, and that plants had to be cultivated by hand. They put in place a priesthood to control the people, and set up the Cariad in her miraculous City of Light as a reminder of their divine rule.'

'I find this ... hard to believe.'

Before he could work out what to say next, the door opened and Ebrilla came in. Her hand jumped to her throat when she saw the room was occupied. 'Mother of Mercy, what are you two doing in here? 'Tis nearly dark. I will light the lamps.'

They sat silently until she had gone, then continued their conversation sitting in the golden glow. Kerin wanted to know more about his old life and how things worked in the universe beyond her world. She asked perceptive questions and once Sais had hit on a suitable analogy, her keen mind digested the information and moved on.

Sais suspected she was glad to be called to dinner. They were joined by the other two lodgers, who had also stopped off for a post-test celebratory drink. Meilyg reckoned Fychan was set for the night, for not only could he regale the tavern patrons with stories about Damaru, he also had his amazing night with the Beloved Daughter of Heaven to boast about.

After dinner, Kerin went up to her room. Sais joined Gorran and Meilyg, who were playing gem in the parlour. He even joined in, and was beaten soundly by the son, though he managed a draw with Meilyg. Einon sat with them for a while too, though he refused all invitations to join in the game.

Having spent so much time unconscious recently, Sais had trouble getting to sleep that night. Fychan's late return from the tavern, announced by drunken stumbling and muted swearing, didn't help. Eventually he fell into a dream in which he was having some sort of theological argument with Kerin, or it might have been Elarn; the argument was taking place on the barren surface of a tiny, rocky planetoid in deep space. He felt a vague yet persistent anxiety: if he did persuade his companion that science was the truth and religion a comforting illusion, then she might realise they were sitting in a vacuum, and they'd both die horrible deaths.

In his dream, he thought the sharp bang must be the air, rushing out. They were going to die!

Then he heard someone say, '—am Dangwern?'

The dream collapsed and he opened his eyes. In the grey pre-dawn light, he made out several figures blocking the open doorway to his room.

He heard a familiar voice, bleary with sleep and drink, say, 'Hoo's askin'?'

One of the figures in the doorway turned to him. He thought there was something wrong with the man's body. 'Are you Fychan am Dangwern?' he asked Sais.

Sais levered himself up onto his elbows, fear rising in him. 'No,' he croaked.

'Look, iv iz 'bout the girl—' Fychan was saying from the other side of the room.

'So, you are Fychan then?' said the man, now ignoring Sais. There was nothing wrong with the man's body – he was wearing armour. These were monitors – church police. What the hell was going on?

Sais heard Fychan reply, 'Aye,' his voice suddenly small and serious.

'Come with us, please,' said the monitor.

Sais tried to keep his breathing under control. He heard Fychan getting up. When the monitors shifted impatiently, he heard the creak of their leather armour and once, the jingle of metal. 'Quickly, now,' said one of them.

Fychan didn't speak again and a few moments later everyone trooped out.

Sais waited until he heard the front door close behind them, then jumped out of bed.

CHAPTER TWENTY-NINE

Kerin was not sure what awakened her. She thought she heard a step on the stair, then decided she must have imagined it. Unable to get back to sleep, her mind returned yet again to her conversations with Sais, trying to find some inconsistency in his views, some contradiction or error in his answers. Yet she could not, no matter how many times she went over what he had said.

At least he could present no evidence to *disprove* the existence of the Skymothers. Beyond that, all was uncertain.

As dawn approached she concluded that she had two choices. Though he believed he was right, Sais might still be misguided, or insane, or Abyss-touched. If so, she should pity and help him, and pray for the forgiveness of the Mothers, because she had let doubt infect her spirit.

Or, he was correct, and everything she believed was a lie and her life was all but meaningless. She might as well give up – and yet even if he spoke the truth, her love for Damaru, and the need to survive once he was gone, remained unchanged.

All she could do was focus on the things that mattered and continue the observances that defined her life – whilst allowing for the terrible possibility that her faith was false.

She started at the sound of someone on the landing, then got up quietly, and opened the door.

Sais stood at the head of the stairs. He looked over at her, then down the stairs again. She heard the front door being re-barred and Ebrilla's steps returning to her room.

Sais gestured for her to come over, and Kerin crept along the landing. He held the door to his room open. As he closed it behind her she saw Fychan's bed was empty.

'Monitors took him!' whispered Sais urgently.

'What did they say?'

'Nothing! They just asked who he was and told him to come with them.'

'Did they speak to you?'

'No.' He sat down on his bed. 'But … once they've spoken to him, I reckon they'll want to.'

Kerin's mind raced. 'I am not so sure. This must be about the Cariad – remember how Meilyg said he was boasting in the tavern? Word must have got back to the Tyr.'

'Yes, but why the hell did they let him go and then recapture him – no wait, he said the Cariad was with him all the time, didn't he? There must be another faction in the Tyr, opposed to her. God, I wish I knew what was going on in there!'

'There is something else you might not know – one of the Escorai has disappeared. There are all sorts of rumours – that he's ill, or dead, even that he has run off with one of the Putain Glan.'

'The what?'

'The sacred harlots who serve the physical needs of the priests.'

'Another quaint local custom! I wonder where Einon fits into all this? I didn't think he was anyone's first choice to lead the drove, then someone tried to kill him, and now he's staying clear of the Tyr.'

'I think we need to talk to him,' said Kerin. 'He has already said he may enlist my help.'

'That's good. I saved him from the assassin at Plas Aethnen, so he owes me.'

'I did not know that.' Kerin thought for a moment. 'We should wake him up, now. We should ask him for his help, and see how he reacts. I suspect he will be even more worried than you about the monitors coming here, and the combination of begging for his help and his own fear might just convince him to confide in us, or at least make him careless enough to let information slip.'

'Kerin, you have a surprisingly devious mind.'

'Thank you. I think.'

Sais knocked on Einon's door. Kerin stood at his shoulder. On the third knock, a sleepy voice said, 'Who is it?'

'It's me, Sais. We need to talk. It's urgent.'

'Ah, wait a moment.' Einon opened the door with an expression between annoyance and apprehension. His bleary gaze flicked over Kerin. 'What is it, Chilwrau?'

'Monitors came, just now,' said Sais, 'and took Fychan. Can we come in, please?'

Einon whispered, 'Aye, quickly!' He closed the door behind them, then ordered, 'Tell me what happened!'

Sais recounted his rude awakening while Einon paced. When they were done he said, 'Thank you, you may go. I need to, ah, to—' He looked over at his paper-strewn table.

Kerin and Sais exchanged glances. Kerin said, 'Gwas, please, can you tell us anything of what is happening? We are afraid, and we know nothing.'

Einon pulled at his lip with long, ink-stained fingers, then sighed. 'I, ah, I am not sure myself.'

To Sais, Kerin said, ''Tis as we feared.' Then to Einon, with a desperation only partly feigned, 'Gwas, what should we do? I fear for my son if he goes into the Tyr when all is in turmoil.'

'Take heart: there are those who remain true. But—' He stopped and looked at the table again. 'You may, ah, you may help me greatly.' He strode over and began to gather his papers. 'Kerin, will you take these and keep them safe? The monitors would not, ah, disturb a skyfool's room.'

Kerin saw the look Sais was giving her – here was Einon's secret. He moved forward and said, 'Let me help you, Gwas.' He picked up a piece of paper, then stopped, peering at the squiggles covering it.

Einon looked at him. 'What is it?'

Sais shook his head. 'Nothing, probably.'

'Chilwar, do you – are those, ah, are these symbols known to you?'

Sais pursed his lips. 'Perhaps ... but then, writing's only for priests, isn't it?'

'Aye. It is, here, but I already know that you, ah, come from a far land.'

'And the idea of people being able to read and write there, that's one you could handle?'

'I – perhaps I could. This is, ah, a time of great change.'

'What are these papers anyway?'

'I am not sure I should, ah, tell you.'

'And I'm not sure I really do recognise this.'

For several heartbeats the two men stared at each other.

Then Einon's shoulders sagged. 'I doubt it will mean much to you anyway. I have devised a symbol I call heb. It allows, ah, it allows new ways of counting.'

'But now you want us to hide your work,' said Sais. 'Why is that, Gwas?'

'I – I think there may be those, ah, those in the Tyr who would misuse it.'

'Misuse it? How?'

'It—' Einon grabbed the table for support. 'This discovery is related to the Cariad's most sacred place, the Sanctaith Glan, but in what way, ah, I do not yet know.' He blinked rapidly, getting control of himself again. 'So have you, ah, seen these symbols before?'

In response, Sais reached across the table and pointed to a particular mark. 'Is this your "heb" symbol?'

'Aye, it is.'

'Where I come from, we call it zero. And those numbers with the dashes? They're negative numbers.'

'Negative numbers,' echoed Einon, his expression unreadable. 'Mothers preserve us.'

When the priest said nothing more, Sais asked, 'What'll happen if Fychan isn't back in time for Damaru to go into the Tyr?'

'I, ah, I am not sure. The Traditions state that the boy's nearest male relative must stand guardian.'

'His nearest male relative is several weeks' walk away. But his mother is here. In a situation like this, can't Kerin go in with him?'

'It would not be right,' he said with a frown.

'Does it explicitly say so anywhere?'

Einon hesitated, no doubt running through the Traditions. Finally he said, 'There is nothing to forbid a woman accompanying a male guardian to the tests, though it is most irregular. But she can only go as well as a man, not instead. The Traditions are clear that the boy must have a male relative with him at all times.'

'Does it have to be a blood relative?' asked Sais.

Kerin suddenly saw where this was going. Her heart jumped into her mouth.

'What do you, ah, mean?'

'What if she was married? Could she go in with her husband? He would be the boy's father, legally speaking.'

'In the eyes of the Mothers a man is responsible for his woman and any children she has borne, aye,' Einon said.

'Thank you, Einon. We'll keep these papers safe for you.'

Carrying the stack back to her room, Kerin asked, 'Did you really recognise what Einon has written here?'

'Yes, though he's a messy worker. Comes of using a quill and having to pay a fortune for your paper, I suppose. Forbidding zero – and advanced maths – would be another way of keeping your people primitive. I'd imagine it is forbidden knowledge, even if someone in the Tyr wants it.' Then, almost to himself, he added, 'Though if there're examples in the Tyr, that also implies there's Sidhe technology in there.'

'Is that bad?'

'Yes and no. It means my chance of finding a communication device is higher, but it also implies the Sidhe have been in this Sanctaith Glan place Einon mentioned.'

'But you will be going into the Tyr anyway?'

'I have to.'

'So … you will be marrying me after all?'

'Yes, I will.' He looked at her with frank admiration. 'If that's all right with you.'

Not so long ago, this would have been the fulfilment of a dream. But the woman whose greatest hope was for a kind and caring husband had been left behind on the road. This was the only way to get them both into the Tyr. She had to find the truth and, if it was as Sais said, save Damaru from falling into the hands of the Sidhe.

'Aye,' she said. 'It is. Shall we ask Einon now, then?'

They returned to Einon's room to find him stuffing clothes into his pack.

'Are you leaving?' asked Sais.

'I hope not. But I must, ah, be prepared.'

'Then we'll ask another priest.'

'Ask them what?'

'To marry us.'

Einon looked between the two of them, his eyebrows almost comically high.

'We need to get married today,' Sais said, 'to provide Damaru with a male guardian.'

'Ah, of course. I – I will do it, but it cannot be in capel. We can use Ebrilla's yard.'

Ebrilla swept into action as soon as Sais announced their intentions, and would not be gainsaid. 'You must both go to the bathhouse – you have time if you are quick. And I must go out too! We need more than small-beer in the wedding cup, and I have no oil in the house save that for cooking and the lamps!'

Walking back from the baths under a lowering sky, Sais turned to Kerin, a strange, sad expression on his face. 'Kerin,' he said, 'if we both get out of this in one piece, you should divorce me.'

'Divorce you?' Even though her passion had matured into friendship, to have him state such intentions before they were even married bruised her heart.

'Yes, assuming that's possible. Or I can divorce you, if it's easier.'

'A man can unbind himself from a willing woman by a public declaration of his reasons in capel.' Perhaps he might not divorce her, but would choose to live with her ... if he did not leave. If they both survived.

They found Gorran loitering outside the house when they got back. 'Mothers' blessings!' he said brightly as they went in.

'Are you not coming to the ceremony?' asked Kerin.

The boy shook his head. 'The Gwas asked that I wait here, and tell him if anyone approaches the house.' His tone made it obvious that he thought the request odd, but would not consider disobeying a priest.

Ebrilla had bought flowers and woven a chaplet for the bride. Wearing the skirt that was her last link to Dangwern, and with a strand of blossom hanging over one eye, Kerin walked into the tiny yard to be married to Sais.

Einon spoke the words of joining with an officiousness better suited to a great capel than a cramped yard. The ceremony was witnessed by her son, two relative strangers and an indifferent cat. Sais, of course, had to be prompted, both to speak his vows and to anoint Kerin's forehead. Then they were sharing the wedding cup, and Kerin had wine for the second time in her life and, for the second time in her life, became a man's wife.

Afterwards, when Kerin went to take Damaru back up to their room, Ebrilla chided her, 'Tis your wedding day! I am sure your blessed child can amuse himself for a while with peas and rice in the dining room; I will keep an eye on him while I cook.'

Kerin, her head in a whirl, said, 'You have done so much for us already. Please do not trouble yourself further – we are not required at the Tyr until later this evening.'

Ebrilla lowered her voice and said, 'Precisely. And it would not be fitting to enter the Cariad's presence without consummating your union. Now go you to your husband, woman.'

She did as Ebrilla said. When the door closed on his room, she and Sais looked at each other, then spoke at the same time.

'Did you wish—?' she began.

'I think we—' he started.

They both stopped, and burst out laughing. Finally Sais said, 'God, Kerin, come here.' He held out his arms.

She came over and let him hold her. Part of her, a low part, wanted more.

He pulled away and said, 'I think we need to prepare ourselves for the Tyr.'

'How? We have no way of knowing what we will find.'

'Which is why we need these.' He pulled out a cloth-wrapped bundle from under the bed. 'I'm sorry, this isn't exactly a romantic wedding gift,' he added. Inside were two knives, one short, one long.

'Where did you get these?'

'The short one is Fychan's – hopefully I'll be able to give it back to him some time – and the long one belonged to one of the reivers. I'd recommend you take the smaller one – unless you know how to use a knife?'

'Only to prepare food or cut cloth.' She laughed uncertainly. Kerin would never have imagined herself spending her wedding night – well, afternoon – this way: being taught how to knife-fight by a stranger from a different world.

The clouds outside lifted at sunset and as darkness fell they did lie together for a while, though chastely, giving comfort rather than spending passion. Kerin cried a little, and he stroked her hair.

She trusted Sais as she trusted no other living man. She loved him too, and always would, but it was not the love of man and wife. It was a strange kind of friendship, born of adversity and misunderstanding, built on trust and the knowledge that they were both outsiders.

Despite the short notice, Ebrilla had prepared an impressive wedding feast: smoked river-fish, seared meats in spicy sauce, rice fried with vegetables and fresh herbs, a long plait of wheat-bread, and afterwards, fruit chopped into cream with sweet pastries still hot from the oven. They also drank the rest of the wine. Kerin, too nervous to eat much, was tempted to drink to give herself courage, but limited herself to one cup. From the laughter and shouts outside, not everyone was being so restrained this evening.

She took Ebrilla aside after the meal and thanked her for all she had done. The old widow brushed off her thanks, saying. 'A prayer to the Mothers when your boy ascends to take his place in the sky will be reward enough.' Kerin hoped she would be granted that wish.

When Rhidian arrived to accompany them for the last time, Sais met him in the parlour with Kerin, who sat demure and silent. Sais introduced himself as Kerin's husband, and said that Fychan was indisposed. No lies, merely incomplete truths. As they had hoped, Rhidian was pleased that a man had finally come forward who Kerin would defer too, even if that man insisted she attend the final test. Sais's argument was that though she was a woman, she was Damaru's relative by blood, which Sais was not – and Rhidian already knew how difficult Damaru could be without his mother.

Finally, Kerin prepared Damaru for their departure, explaining again what was to happen, how he must obey the Cariad and be prepared to go with her if she demanded it. He put his hands over his ears, not wanting to listen, then stamped round the room, shaking off Kerin's attempts to calm him. The outburst left him sulky, but compliant.

CHAPTER THIRTY

That afternoon, Einon visited the Stonemasons' Guild, leaving Gorran to watch for visitors at Ebrilla's. There was little more to be gleaned about Anona's disappearance there. The boy had been seeing her for a couple of seasons, but the other apprentices had been surprised when they eloped together. Einon had expected something like that. The trail was cold.

In truth he had gone out mainly because he did not want to sit alone with his fears in his room, without even the comfort of his papers. He had been surprised at the request to marry Sais and Kerin, though it made sense. Hopefully Sais would keep her in hand. He had been more surprised, and not a little put out, to have spent so much time and effort – not to mention paper and ink – and suffered temporary exile and assault, all in the cause of exploring the new numbers, only to have Sais casually flaunt his own knowledge of them.

None of which mattered as much as his concern at what Fychan might be saying to his questioners in the Tyr. Of course, the Escorai did not know that Einon had travelled with the boy, but those in the tender care of the enquirers were apt to give away information as a boatman might bail a leaky boat, throwing out whatever was needed to save his skin.

He considered not returning to Ebrilla's – but where would he go, what would he do? The Tyr was his life, and Urien was his master.

Rhidian led them through streets thronged with people in party clothes, many of them masked, some dressed as animals or fools or monsters. They passed dancers and acrobats, men juggling fire-sticks or walking on stilts. People broke off just long enough to make the circle at Damaru. Sais made himself return the gesture, empty though it was. They were sent on their way with drunken cheers, though they also got themselves a following of more sober celebrants carrying lanterns and torches, singing what sounded like a hymn.

The square was one huge party. Booze and food sellers were doing a roaring trade, and music came from several competing bands. Dancers whooped and spun and couples embraced in the twilight, laughing and groping. A pair of monitors carrying flaming torches came up to them, made the circle, then began to clear their path of any revellers partying too hard to notice the approach of a sacred procession. Sais glimpsed more torches at the maw of the Tyr's entrance: presumably another skyfool, going in ahead of them.

The Tyr loomed over them, a great menacing mass. As he watched, the sun sent out a last flash of light from the beanstalk. He shivered for a moment and looked past Damaru to Kerin. Her lips were pressed into a thin line, her eyes bright. He felt nervous; she must be shit-scared. Sais again felt a warm flush of admiration for her; he doubted he'd be as calm in her situation. He'd like to have admitted his reason for not wanting her physically, but he'd encountered prejudice before, not least on the world where he grew up, and he was damn sure his sexuality was unacceptable here. He'd subjected the poor woman to enough culture shock already.

As they neared the Tyr the party-goers ebbed away and they were escorted by priests and soberly attired townsmen. Brightly dressed children threw cut flowers under their feet, filling the air with the smell of bruised petals. Monitors with more hi-tech torches stood to attention along the wide walkway cut into the mountain. They passed into the shadow of the Tyr to shouted blessings from the followers left outside. The cobbles of the street gave way to stone, and the walls closed in.

Damaru came to an abrupt halt. Kerin stopped at once, Sais a step further on. He looked over to see the boy whimpering and hugging himself, while Kerin comforted him. Rhidian, walking a few paces ahead, finally noticed and turned around.

Sais caught Damaru's eye and said quietly, 'It's going to be all right. Your mother won't let anything happen to you.'

Damaru stared at him reproachfully, but carried on, though he continued to eye the stone ceiling dubiously.

Rhidian whispered, 'Did you not give him something to calm him?'

Kerin shook her head, as though daring the priest to tell her off.

The tunnels were machine-cut and lit by light-globes, though the doors set into the walls were wooden. They saw priests, monitors and uniformed servants. Some of the priests were on their way to join the party outside, and were already a little tipsy. Everyone stopped and circled their breasts as Damaru passed. Most of them stared at Kerin, and Sais had to resist the temptation to say, 'What's the matter, never seen a woman you haven't broken before?'

They went deeper into the mountain, turning down smaller passages, emerging into larger ones, going up steps hewn into the rock. Sais tried to remember which way they'd come, but he didn't reckon much to his chances of finding their way back out by themselves. Finally Rhidian led them to one of several similar doors in a long straight corridor. Their escort peeled off. Sais hoped they'd leave, but the two guards just marched a little way up the corridor, then stopped.

The priest turned to them. 'You will be called to the testing chamber when the Cariad is ready to receive you. As your test is the last, this may be a while. I will have refreshments sent to you.'

Her voice strained, Kerin asked 'Gwas, please, can you tell us anything about what will happen?'

Rhidian's face assumed the affronted expression of a proud man forced to expose his ignorance. 'I cannot. You are in the hands of the Mothers now. Your escort will accompany you to the Divine presence and guide you out. Did you wish me to return with you to your lodgings once the test is done, to provide spiritual guidance when your child has gone to his fate?'

'We'll be fine, thank you,' said Sais stiffly.

Rhidian opened the door to reveal a small room with no other exits. It contained a padded bench and a table. After showing them in he circled his breast. 'Mothers bless you all,' he said. Then he closed the door. Sais waited a while, then tried the handle. As he had expected, they were locked in.

Damaru began to pace. Sais and Kerin sat down on the bench to get out of his way.

A few minutes later the door opened and a servant came in carrying a tray of cakes. Sais tensed, wondering if it was worth going for the man, but decided to wait and see what happened.

Damaru was distracted by the cakes, which smelled fresh-baked. Kerin picked one up and offered it to him, but changed her mind just as Sais shouted, 'No!' She snatched the cake out of Damaru's grasp.

'I think it's drugged,' said Sais.

Kerin nodded. 'Aye, the same thought just occurred to me – they did not mention food until they knew I had not given my boy anything.'

Damaru didn't understand why he couldn't have a cake. He made a dive for the table, then, when Kerin blocked him, squealed in frustration. He sat down and began slapping the floor with his open hands. Kerin, who'd obviously dealt with this particular flavour of tantrum before, watched but didn't approach.

Sais was tempted to suggest that maybe giving him just one drugged cake might not be such a bad idea.

After a while Damaru's rage blew itself out. He gave a dramatic sulky lift of his shoulders, then lay down on his side, hugging his knees. Kerin went over and put a hand on his shoulder, but he shrugged her off.

The three of them sat in uneasy silence.

Sais tried to formulate a plan, but he didn't have enough to go on yet. He needed to somehow lose the guards, and find the coms system, which would most likely be in the inner sanctum. For now, all he could do was watch, wait, and keep up the pretence.

As they walked through the Tyr, Kerin kept reminding herself that this place was designed to inspire reverence and wonder. She must not let herself be overawed; the priests were just people, and the cold, fireless lamps merely clever devices, not miracles.

Yet still she felt terror such as she had never known, not for her life, nor even for the life of her son or her new husband, but for her very soul. She had entered the holiest place in the land, prepared to believe it was founded on a lie and willing to disobey the authority it represented. She wanted nothing more than for her boy to assume his rightful place in Heaven, but she could not take the risk that Sais was right. She would not allow Damaru to be used as part of some great and terrible deception – but nor would she stand against the will of the Skymothers, unless she discovered for herself that the deception was real.

When Damaru's petulance exploded into anger after she refused him the cake, she felt a different set of emotions: that strange heated mix of irritation, guilt and love for her ungrateful child, who took and never gave, who might not even love her as other children loved their mothers, but who relied on her utterly, and who she would not, *could not*, let come to harm. Soon he would be gone, and she would be free of the constant worry over him. And she would bear that alone, for even if Sais had loved her as she had hoped, the bond to her child was a unique one, and the hole his loss would tear in her heart would never heal.

Finally the door opened and the same pair of guards returned. Sais took that to mean there would only be these two for the duration of their stay. Good.

Kerin crouched down and took Damaru's hands in hers. 'Please,' she whispered, 'you have to come with us now. I promise I will not let anyone hurt you.' He let her drag him to his feet. She kept hold of one of his hands and led him out. Sais caught Kerin's free hand. From the look she gave him she was glad of the support.

Without Rhidian in front of him, he got a better look at the guards. They wore the standard monitor's armour: midnight-blue hardened leather strips, more ceremonial than practical, but probably enough to stop a bronze knife. They had short blades on their belts and small, intricately crafted crossbows on straps across their backs.

Their escort led them to a tall double-door made of what looked like bronze banded with iron, although a closer look revealed that the bronze was a beaten sheet, no doubt covering ordinary wood. The guards pushed the doors open and indicated that the three of them should enter.

They walked into a huge circular cavern, lit on their side by light-globes around the wall that left the high ceiling and the far side in darkness. What Sais initially took to be a shadow on the floor turned out, on a second look, to be a chasm, a straight-cut pit four metres wide that stretched across the centre of the room from wall to wall, dividing the light and dark sides. The gap was bridged by a flat, rail-less bridge wide enough for two people to cross comfortably.

Their escort peeled off to stand on either side, about four or five steps away. He checked over his shoulder and saw another two guards closing the door. Four in all. Not good odds. As the guards by the door took their places in front of it, he noticed what looked like a primitive neural-interface helmet on a stand beside them.

The light level increased abruptly as a golden glow bathed the far side of the room, illuminating a dais in the centre of which, sitting on a high-backed throne, was a woman dressed in heavy black robes encrusted with sparkling white gems. She wore a high, horned headdress with a black veil hanging from it that obscured her face. She was flanked by two men in almost equally ornate metal-encrusted robes, one in orange, one in yellow. Sais barely registered them, for the Cariad's presence dominated the room. Her eyes were invisible behind the veil but she would be looking at him, maybe picking up his mood, his surface thoughts, ready to dive deeper if she suspected he was anything other than the guardian of a candidate skyfool.

Sais tried to fill his head with memories of Dangwern, of Kerin's hut, of mud and ordinariness and things entirely of this world. He hoped she would read his fear as religious awe.

The worst of it was that he might not even know she was reading him; Sidhe could be subtle as well as brutal. Hell, he had *thought* that, thought the word 'Sidhe'. *Idiot, idiot, idiot.* Sweat prickled his skin and his heart caught in his chest.

The Cariad shifted slightly in her seat, sending dazzling reflections dancing round the room.

Sais braced himself for pain.

CHAPTER THIRTY-ONE

Despite Kerin's resolve not to be taken in by the Tyr, the testing chamber still amazed her: you could fit Ebrilla's entire house in here! Then, in a wondrous, instant transformation, the darkness was banished, and there, before her, was the Beloved Daughter of Heaven. And only two Escorai – those of Medelwyr and Mantoliawn. She knew of the missing Escori of Carunwyd, but what of the other two, who served Frythil and Turiach?

Even as she thought this, she dropped to her knees. Sais still stood, his face full of fear. 'You must kneel,' she whispered self-consciously.

He looked over to her, his expression relaxing a little, then fell forward onto his knees.

For a while there was silence, save the thudding of her heart. Then the Cariad spoke, her voice soft yet penetrating.

'Arise, Chilwrau.'

Kerin climbed to her feet. Out of the corner of her eye she saw Sais stand. Damaru was staring at the Cariad, his head on one side.

'Approach the bridge.'

Kerin led Damaru forward. Sais followed. When they got about half way the Cariad raised a hand. They stopped. She pointed to Sais, who flinched.

'Who is this man?' asked the Cariad.

Kerin answered, her voice quavering, 'He is my husband, Divinity. He stands in the place of Fychan am Dangwern.'

'So be it.'

Kerin could have sworn the Cariad sounded *upset*. Surely that could not be. And what need would a goddess have to ask such a question? Surely she would know?

The Cariad continued, 'The test requires that the child be blindfolded. It is the responsibility of the guardians to ensure that the skyfool accepts this, and all other requests that are made of him. Do you understand?'

'Aye, Divinity,' said Kerin.

Sais cleared his throat. 'We do,' he said.

Guards approached, one of them carrying a helmet like a larger version of those worn by some of the monitors, with a shining plate over the eyes.

Kerin turned Damaru to face her. 'Damaru, you must let this man put this ... special hat on your head. You will not be able to see, but I will still be here beside you.'

Damaru looked unhappy.

'He will show it to you first.' Kerin nodded to the guard who obliged by holding the helmet up so Damaru could see it.

'He is going behind you now, and he will put it on you.'

The guard lifted the helmet over Damaru's head. As he began to lower it Damaru twitched his head out of the way.

Kerin felt her composure slip. She must keep her boy calm, allow things to take their course and hope all would be well. Aye, hope – when not so long ago she would have prayed, trusting to the Mothers. She swallowed hard, striving to keep her voice even. 'Damaru, please. You have to let him do this. All will be well.'

Damaru squirmed, but he kept his head still enough for the guard to put the helmet on him.

For a moment, he stood unmoving. Then he reached up, trying to pull the thing off. When it would not move he started to keen.

'Calm him!' muttered the guard.

Damaru fell to his knees and Kerin threw her arms around him, holding him to her breast.

The Cariad said, 'Do not worry, he will adjust soon.'

Damaru's keens subsided into whimpers, then died away. Kerin helped him to his feet.

When he was standing up again, the Cariad said, 'Now lead the boy to the bridge. When he reaches it he must cross alone.'

This was the moment he had been born for. Yet Kerin could not move. She looked at her hands, holding onto her son's.

Almost gently, the Cariad said, 'This is the final test. It cannot be refused. He must come to me.'

Kerin raised her head. 'Damaru,' she murmured, 'I love you. I will never stop loving you. But you must go. You have to obey her. We have no option.' How she wished she were wrong, how she wished she had taken any one of those paths in the last weeks that would not have brought them to this point!

A guard had come to stand next to her: if she did not accompany Damaru, the guard would. She dropped one of Damaru's hands. Compliant under the shiny helmet he shuffled forward beside her as they walked up to the chasm. The guard shadowed them.

Her steps faltered before they reached the bridge. Though she knew she must do this, she could not make him go through with it.

To her surprise, Damaru did not stop. Kerin, still holding onto him, tried to follow. The guard put a restraining hand on her arm. Damaru took a second step. His hand pulled free of Kerin's. The loss of his touch felt keen as a blow. She covered her mouth with her hand, rather than cry out.

Damaru took another step. He was on the bridge now. He walked slowly, as though in a daze. In another couple of steps he reached the centre of the span.

With a barely audible hiss, the bridge disappeared.

So did Damaru.

Shock grabbed Kerin by the throat. Then everything twisted.

In that moment Kerin knew that Damaru had succeeded, and where he was now. She spun round in time to see him collapse to the ground behind her. She shook off the dazed guard and ran to her boy. She felt like she was sinking into the mere, though by the time she reached him everything had begun to settle back into place.

She crouched next to him, calling his name. He made no

response, just kept shaking his head. When a shadow fell across her, Kerin looked up to see the guard. 'Get this thing off him!' she hissed.

The guard nodded and bent down, fumbling with the helmet. Another guard held out a beaker to her, but she waved it away.

The Cariad spoke, her voice distant and unreal. 'The boy is found worthy.'

Sais knew what the Sidhe wanted the skyfools for.

The first time he'd felt reality take that crazy sideways step, back during the reivers' attack, he hadn't been able to pin down the feeling. The second time, he'd been about to come down with the falling fire, and hadn't even realised what had happened until much later. Now, with his memory back, he recognised the sensation – as well he should. It was one he'd experienced a lot.

Shiftspace.

Damaru could create shiftspace portals, to bypass normal space-time, moving himself – or others – instantaneously between two points.

Just as Sais did in the *Judas Kiss* when he travelled between the stars.

Everyone – everyone who didn't live on an isolated world like this, anyway – knew that the engines that allowed interstellar travel were stolen Sidhe technology. It was part of the legend of humanity's fight-back against the Sidhe Protectorate: humans taking control of the stars for themselves. Or so people thought. But what if the transit-kernel at the heart of every shiftship wasn't just black-box technology the average spacer knew better than to tamper with? What if the power to move ships across space without obeying the usual laws of physics came from minds like Damaru's?

He remembered the first time Nual had experienced a shiftspace transit. She had descended into a temporary insanity far worse than the usual hallucinatory weirdness anyone who stayed conscious for a transit had to endure. When he'd tried to help her, one of the things she'd ranted about was *darkness in the heart*. At the time he'd put the comment down to her disturbed state of mind – he'd just saved her life, and she was in shock. Now he saw how her reaction could have been due to her mind touching the mind hidden aboard his ship, the one he had known nothing about, the one imprisoned in the ship's drive.

This whole culture had been created and maintained in order to breed minds capable of entering shiftspace.

He had to get the news out.

The guard finally got the helmet off Damaru's head and Kerin bent over him. His eyelids fluttered and he began to stir. She pulled him close. She heard someone speaking nearby, but she ignored them. Damaru was quivering like a wild creature, breathing harsh and fast. She helped him sit up, supporting him in her arms.

Above her she heard Sais say, 'She is very upset, but I will persuade her.'

He bent down next to her. 'Kerin my love, the guard says Damaru must drink this.'

Sais was pressing a beaker into her hand; drugged, no doubt. Sais positioned himself so he blocked the guard's view. Kerin murmured, 'Of course, husband.'

She took the beaker and pressed it to Damaru's lips. He drank a little, but then, after checking the guard could not see, she pulled the drink away, letting the rest trickle over her skirt where the liquid would not show against the dark fabric.

The Cariad said, 'You must say your last farewell now.' She did not sound imperious so much as regretful.

Damaru's eyes opened. Kerin looked up at Sais. Seeing his expression, she whispered, 'This is wrong, is it not?'

Sais murmured, 'As wrong as it gets.'

She put her arms around Damaru and buried her face in his neck.

'Do not be concerned, mistress,' said the Cariad. 'Your child will ascend to Heaven to take his place amongst the stars. All will be well.'

Despite the Cariad's gentle tone, and Kerin's desperate desire to believe, she knew she could not trust the Beloved's words. She tightened her grip on Damaru. He wriggled in her grasp – even now, he disliked feeling smothered by her love.

From above her she heard a guard say, 'You must persuade your wife to release the boy.'

Sais said evenly, 'You have to let him go, Kerin.' Then, in a whisper, he added, 'If we fight now, we'll lose. But we'll get him back, I promise.'

Kerin shook her head, not sure what she was denying.

Someone took her arm, and a moment later Damaru was pulled out of her grasp. 'No!' she shouted, trying to break free. The guard got his other arm round her shoulders. He pulled her against his chest and pinioned her arms.

Damaru struggled in the other guard's grasp, his vague gaze searching for reassurance. A third guard came up to help and two of them began to half-drag, half-carry Damaru towards the bridge which, Kerin noted dully, was back in place. She glanced at Sais, who was looking round in desperation. *Do something!* she thought. *Stop them!* But what could they do?

She had no choice but to watch her child being taken from her. Nothing else in the world mattered, save the growing distance between them.

Damaru's struggles became more frantic when the guards stepped onto the bridge. The guards lifted him off his feet and crossed the bridge with a careful sideways shuffle.

As soon as they reached the far side, the bridge disappeared again.

The Cariad stood and said, 'Blessings of Heaven upon you all.'

With the bridge gone and Damaru out of reach, Kerin felt something, hope perhaps, drain out of her. Her eyes did not leave her son as the guards carried him after the Cariad. The two silent Escorai brought up the rear.

Finally, when the procession had disappeared into the darkness behind the dais, she dropped her head. The worst had happened. She cursed the Mothers, naming them in her head, demanding that if they existed, they should strike her dead now, as then she would at least know the truth as she died.

The guard holding her loosened his grip and turned her round. She did not resist. He began to steer her out, one arm around her shoulders.

Sais walked beside her. She realised, as she stumbled along, that he was trying to attract her attention. She blinked back tears and looked over at him. He gave a tiny nod, as though asking her something. Or ... *telling her something*. Telling her it was time to fight. She was as good as dead already – what did she have to lose?

Keeping her head down, she nodded in response. Looking over at Sais from under her hair she saw him check round, then look back at her and mouth one word:

Now.

With a groan worthy of a star-season actor, Kerin collapsed to the floor. Out of the corner of her eye, she saw Sais charge the other guard.

Kerin's guard grabbed for her with a curse. She ducked, and he missed. She wanted to fight, to tear into the guard with her bare hands, putting all the fury and frustration of her loss into the attack, but she was on the floor, and he was standing up.

The guard grabbed her hair. She screamed – and, ignoring the pain, turned in his grasp, surprising him into dropping her. She lashed out and up. Her hand hit hard leather. The guard caught hold of her arm and jerked upwards and she found herself suspended painfully by one wrist. The guard shifted his grip, pulling her round until—

'Let her go or I'll cut your friend's throat.' Sais had his knife pressed against the other guard's neck.

Her guard paused. If she could use her free hand to get to her own knife, she might even the odds. She began to fumble at her waist.

Sais's guard said, 'What do you hope to achieve by this sacrilege?' He did not sound afraid or angry.

Kerin managed to get a hand inside her skirt, where the knife was hidden. Before she could get it out, the guard pulled her to her feet. As she straightened she felt a sharp point prick her ribs. She froze.

Sais's guard said, 'Now let me go, you foolish peasant. Unless you wish my corporal to gut your wife, after which time he will be free to help me.'

They had lost everything: Damaru was gone and their ill-conceived ploy had failed.

The door flew open, knocking Sais and his guard to the floor. In the doorway stood a tall man in brocaded robes of green and white. He spoke with an easy authority. 'What in the name of Heaven is going on here?'

He must be the Escori of Frythil, thought Kerin. Not only had she failed to guard her son, but now they had attracted the attention of an Escori. She wondered, absently, if he would have them put to death.

The guard who stood over Sais said, 'Gwas, these people attacked us.'

'So I see,' said the Escori. 'You may let the woman go.'

Her guard pulled the knife away, but kept hold of her.

'She is no threat,' said the Escori. Kerin spotted another priest in the corridor behind him. 'The man too. Let him stand.'

Sais got up. His guard walked over to his crossbow, which he had dropped in the fight.

'Leave that.'

The guard stopped in the act of reaching down. Kerin's guard released her, a little reluctantly. 'Good,' said the Escori, as though praising the work of a backward child. As he came in from the corridor, Kerin realised who the other priest was: Einon. 'Now, men, you may go.'

What was Einon doing here? More importantly, why was the Escori dismissing the guards?

The guards were obviously as confused as her. 'But these peasants—' began the one beside Sais.

'Are not your concern, Captain. I have business with them. But since you feel they may be a threat, perhaps you should give your crossbow and quarrels to my assistant here.' He nodded to Einon, who had followed him in. His face blank, the guard handed his crossbow over, along with a small case from his belt. 'Thank you,' said the Escori by way of dismissal. The guards left, pulling the door closed behind them.

Sais asked, 'Who are you?'

Einon winced at the disrespectful tone; Kerin found herself amused at the priest's discomfort. Though both her hands were now free, she made no move to circle her breast.

Without taking obvious offence the man replied, 'I am Urien, Escori of Frythil. And you must be Sais.'

Ignoring the question, Sais asked, 'Where are the other two Escorai?'

'The Escorai of Carunwyd and Turiach are dead,' said Urien, then added, 'As would you most likely be, had I not intervened.'

To be told that two Escorai were dead confirmed that chaos had entered the Tyr. Knowing this, Kerin found the strength to speak. 'Escori, I thank you for saving us, but my son has been taken from me wrongly.' Einon swung the crossbow in her direction as she spoke.

'Has he?' asked Urien. As he looked at her, Kerin realised she was talking to one of the five – no, *three* now – most powerful men in the land. But she had lost all she had to lose, and felt no fear. Urien put a hand up to stop Einon doing anything rash and waited to see what she had to say.

Amazed at how calm her voice sounded, she said, 'Aye. And I believe we have been lied to. All of us.'

CHAPTER THIRTY-TWO

Sais had a crazy urge to smile. Even without understanding the full truth, Kerin trusted him enough to stand up to an Escori and deny everything she'd once held dear. She was quite a woman.

Urien turned to Sais, as though questioning how a man could allow his wife to say such a thing. Damn this sexist world. 'She's not wrong,' he said.

Urien's gaze flicked over Kerin and back to him. 'Why do you say that?' he asked with the air of a man interested in hearing an argument so he can blow it away.

The Escori wouldn't have dismissed the guards if he wasn't interested in what Sais had to say, and the fact that he'd arrived with only Einon in tow implied he had no other allies. Time to shake the tree and see what fell out. 'For a start,' said Sais, 'the Cariad is an impostor.'

Urien blinked, then said, 'We must find somewhere to talk.'

Kerin, her eyes bright, said, 'But my son—'

'—is currently being accompanied to the Sanctaith Glan by two guards,' said Urien. 'When he is within, and prepared for his ascension, they will return. At which point there will be no guards beyond the bridge, and our chances of getting to your boy will be much improved. We have a while before the ascension begins; waiting here would be … counterproductive.'

'Lead on,' said Sais.

They left the testing hall and walked down the corridor. A couple of priests crossed the junction at the far end, but didn't look their way. From her expression, Kerin was desperate to ask

Sais what he'd realised in the testing. He wasn't sure quite how he would explain that her son was due to have his flesh stripped away so he could become the living engine that would power a ship between the stars.

Urien opened the door to one of the candidates' waiting rooms and gestured for them to enter. He came in last and left the door ajar. Einon put his crossbow down on the table. Everyone remained standing.

'So,' said Urien, 'what makes you say that the Beloved Daughter of Heaven is not what she claims to be?'

Sais hesitated. Even if his influence was on the wane, Urien must be a skilled politician, not to mention one of the highest spiritual authorities on this world. He could hardly say that he'd concluded the woman on the throne wasn't an alien because she hadn't picked up on his stupid mental panic and because she'd had to resort to a neural-interface helmet to force Damaru to take the final test. But Urien expected an answer. Remembering the priestly ability to spot lies, Sais went for an edited version of the truth. 'If she was,' he said, 'she wouldn't have to rely on tricks and gadgets to impress people.'

Urien looked at him and said nothing. He remained silent, his eyes unreadable, for some time. Sais barely resisted the urge to say something – *anything* – just to break that cold, appraising gaze.

Finally Urien said, 'Where are you really from, Sais am Dangwern?'

'A long way from here.'

'That much Einon has told me. And he says you know the lore of numbers. Is this true?'

Sais was beginning to feel like a witness at his own trial. 'What if I do?'

Unexpectedly, Urien sighed and sat down. 'We are not enemies,' he said.

Sais had no idea if the change of tack was a ploy, or an indication that Urien wasn't as confident as he looked. Either way, he'd take the opening. 'I hope not – because I think we can help each other.'

'You are a most unusual man, Master Sais.'

With more confidence than he felt, Sais said, 'You're right. You won't have met anyone like me before.' Out of the corner of his eye, he saw Kerin fidgeting, no doubt worrying what was happening to her son.

'Indeed,' said Urien. 'And I would very much like the chance to discuss the differences between us at length some time.'

'That might be interesting.' *If we're still alive.* 'But I've promised I'll help Kerin get her son back, and I intend to do just that.'

'Do not worry. When the time comes we will act.'

When Urien didn't immediately add anything Sais said, 'So, I'm right then? The woman who's running the show isn't the real Cariad?'

'She does not, as you put it, run the show,' said Urien. 'She is one of the Putain Glan.'

'A holy prostitute?'

Urien said, 'That is so, specifically, a woman called Lillwen.'

'So how did this Lillwen come to take the place of the Cariad?' asked Sais. 'What happened to the real Cariad?'

'I do not know – most probably, some unforeseen accident took her life.'

'Isn't that unlikely for a goddess?' he said.

'It would be impossible, if she were one ... which implies she was not.' Urien paused. 'I see from your face that this thought does not appal you, Master Sais.'

Sais said nothing.

A tiny smile flitted across Urien's lips. He carried on, 'Lillwen was selected to take her place by the other Escorai, probably because of a physical similarity to the real Cariad, and because her talents were strong.'

For the first time Kerin spoke, her voice uncertain. 'Her talents?'

Urien said, 'For sky-cursed women born in or near the City of Light, becoming one of the Putain Glan is an alternative to the usual fate.'

Kerin went a shade paler, but said nothing.

Trying not to let his disgust show, Sais asked, 'Aren't you worried these women will use their "talents" on you priests?'

'I believe that the Cariad – the real Cariad – would condition those joining the Putain Glan to be obedient to any desire expressed by a priest.'

Typical of the Sidhe, to turn women into mind-neutered whores. 'Is this just personal experience?' he asked acidly.

'No, it is logic,' said Urien, apparently unoffended. 'The older Putain Glan live only to please men; this is not true of those few who have been accepted into the service in recent years.'

'I see.'

'And I believe the old Cariad also conditioned her Escorai.'

'But not you,' said Sais.

'No. As I say, I suspect the Cariad has been dead for some time – long enough for two of her conditioned Escorai to go to the sky themselves. Idwal became the Escori of Carunwyd five years ago. I had the honour to take up the highest service to Frythil just over two years ago. The other Escorai – Prysor, Sefion and Alden – accompanied the Cariad in all rites, whilst Idwal and I were excluded from the private ceremonies and have never been permitted access to the Sanctaith Glan.'

'You said there were three Escorai loyal to this Lillwen. There were only two at the test.'

'Alden, the Escori of Turiach, took his own life last night. I believe he was no longer able to reconcile his calling with the demands made on him by the Cariad's conditioning.'

'What about the other Escori? Is he dead too?'

'I believe Idwal is dead, though I have no evidence save logic and a sense of the lies of my fellow Escorai.'

'You think they killed him.'

'I believe their conditioning will not permit them to harm other Escorai, even those not so conditioned. This measure would avoid further chaos in an already uncertain time. It may be the reason no attempts have been made on my life, only on those of my loyal servants. But they know how Idwal died. Alden admitted as much to me some weeks ago.'

'So now I guess the two surviving Escorai are trying to hold things together. Were they the ones who had our friend arrested? A young lad by the name of Fychan.'

'I imagine—'

He stopped, and Sais too heard footsteps approaching down the corridor. Everyone froze. The footsteps passed.

When they were gone Kerin whispered, 'Was that the guards, leaving after taking my son to the Sanctaith Glan?'

'That is so.'

'Then we should go.' She started towards the door.

Urien held up a hand. 'Do you decide for Sais then, Mistress Kerin?'

She stopped, looking confused and chastened.

Sais flashed her an encouraging smile. 'No,' he said, 'but she decides for herself.'

'And what do *you* decide, then?'

'That depends on what will happen next. Presumably we're going to the Sanctaith Glan?'

'That is so.'

'I thought you said the Cariad wouldn't let you in there.'

'What I actually said was that I was not permitted access. The secret of entry is known only to the loyal Escorai. And presumably to the Cariad who has now gone to the sky. Lillwen does not know it, as she is the puppet of the conditioned Escorai. Or rather, of her own conditioning.'

'So how am I going to be able to help?'

'The key is a puzzle, a puzzle of numbers such as I have not seen before, though Einon has conjectured their existence. The precise form of the puzzle changes each time anyone attempts to enter the Sanctaith Glan.'

'And what happens if you fail to solve the puzzle?'

'Nothing. The puzzle is presented to any who approach the door. If the correct answer is not provided, it fades and nothing further occurs.'

As far as you know, thought Sais. He'd bet that the real Cariad – the now-dead Sidhe who'd been left to rule here – had something set up to notify her of anyone poking around her inner sanctum. 'Have you tried to solve the puzzle yourself?'

'I have not.'

'How about you, Einon?'

Einon, who had been listening intently, started and said in a mildly affronted tone, 'I would never venture into the sacred precincts of the Cariad without permission!'

I'll bet you wouldn't. Sais looked back at Urien. 'So how do you know about this puzzle?'

'Idwal told me.'

'How come he got to enter the Cariad's "sacred precincts"?'

Urien looked a little uncomfortable. 'He was Lillwen's lover.'

'Really? I bet the other Escorai weren't too happy about that.'

'No, but, as I say, their conditioning would not let them harm him. And to kill the false Cariad would present its own problems. They did not like it, but there was nothing they could do.'

'Are the two remaining Escorai in the Sanctaith Glan now, with the Cariad and the Consorts?'

'That is so.'

'Presumably they're waiting for the ascension. How soon will that be?'

'Soon enough that I need your answer now. Einon has an intellect suited to these new numbers but lacks the experience of using them. You would be my first choice to open the way.'

What with me being expendable. 'And if I refuse?'

Urien just smiled.

'Yeah, that's what I thought,' said Sais. 'Well then, I'm ready when you are.'

Einon was outraged. Sais and Kerin should be obeying Urien without question, not negotiating with him as though this were some street-market!

When the beggar-boy had returned shortly after Sais and Kerin left, he had led Einon to a rarely used entrance to the Tyr where Urien met him in person. His Escori listened to his report, then had Einon swear his loyalty and willingness to do whatever was asked of him. Only then did Urien explain the situation. To Einon's shame, his first thought on hearing that the Daughter of Heaven had been replaced by a Putain Glan was to wonder if the woman was one of those he had taken his pleasure with before the substitution had been made. The thought both excited and disgusted him.

But apparently Sais already knew this awful secret. What else did he know? What other truths had he hidden?

Einon hoped his Escori would not regret taking Kerin and Sais into his confidence. Urien would wish as few people as possible to know what went on here today. Such dangerous knowledge must be contained.

As they set off back to the testing chamber, Einon decided to view the alarming events unfolding around him as a game of gem: his Escori was the black; Einon was a red; Sais and Kerin, mere browns. They were the least of the players in this game, there to be used.

The fact that Urien appeared to trust Sais indicated that, no matter what else occurred on this holiest of nights, Sais and Kerin would not be leaving the Tyr again.

CHAPTER THIRTY-THREE

If so great a lie as a false Cariad could pass unnoticed, what else might be deception? Could Sais be right? Tomorrow, if she lived that long, Kerin must find time to consider what had been said here, and to work out what it meant for her, and for the world.

For now, she was glad to leave the waiting room and set off to rescue her son. When Sais and Einon pushed open the doors to the testing hall, she held her breath, half expecting to find the Cariad or her guards here, despite Urien's assurances.

The room was empty, the far side in darkness. And, she saw with a sinking heart, the bridge over the chasm was gone.

Urien said, 'Wait here. Idwal told me what must be done.' He strode up to the chasm.

Sais stooped to pick up the guard's discarded crossbow. Kerin took the chance to move up to him and whispered, 'Tell me, what is Damaru's fate if we do not save him?'

Sais looked up at her, his expression dark, and said, 'They'll use his mind to move ships between worlds, and drive him mad in the process.'

Not while there was breath in her body to oppose them they wouldn't.

'Put that down!'

They turned to see Einon pointing his own crossbow at them. He indicated the crossbow Sais was in the process of reloading.

Urien, kneeling beside the chasm, called back, 'Let him be, Einon. We may need another weapon before this night is through.' He reached below the lip of the chasm. Suddenly the bridge was back in place. The speed of it reminded Kerin of the way a simple touch instantly lit or darkened Einon's lantern. The Escori stood and waited for the others to join him, then led them across.

As they stepped onto the dais, a formless radiance grew around them. Einon hesitated, no doubt captivated by the divine light. Kerin suspected it was more of Sais's technology. Urien walked up to the Cariad's high-backed chair and reached under the armrest. As quickly as it had appeared, the bridge was gone; this time Kerin was watching, and she saw it slide into a recess under the lip of the chasm.

They followed Urien past the chair and through an opening directly behind it, which brought them out into the middle of a short passage. To the left, the passage ended in a wooden door. To the right was what appeared to be the ghost of a door: a rectangle the same size as an ordinary door, but dark grey, with no handle or markings. A paler grey rectangle was set into the rock wall beside it. The rectangle had some sort of pattern along the right-hand side. Urien turned this way.

'What's back there?' asked Sais, jerking a thumb behind them to the other door.

'The Cariad's personal chambers,' replied Urien.

'And this is the only way into the Sanctaith Glan?'

'That is so.'

So it was a door, and beyond it she would find her son, who, unless she saved him, would suffer a strange and terrible fate. Kerin darted past the others and ran up to the grey door.

'Wait!' called Sais.

It was too late. The smaller rectangle began to glow, as though a cold fire had sprung to life behind it, and more markings appeared across it. They were symbols of some sort – numbers, perhaps?

She looked over her shoulder to see Sais approaching. The two priests waited back down the corridor, looking uncertain. Kerin took half a step back – her thoughtless concern for Damaru may have put them all in danger. Sais brushed past her and stared at the marks on the screen. He made a quiet 'hah!' sound, and gave a small shake of his head.

'What are you doing?' called Urien.

'What you asked me to do,' he replied. 'There's a good chance they know we're coming, so you might want to bring that cross-bow up here, Einon.'

He turned back to Kerin. 'I'd stand to the side if I were you,' he muttered. 'That way they'll shoot Einon first.'

Kerin pressed herself against the wall. Sais touched some of the symbols on the right-hand side of the rectangle. The pattern changed, with more symbols appearing at the end of the currently displayed ones. The pattern became brighter. Then it disappeared.

The door slid to one side.

For a moment, everyone stood still. Kerin heard a strange sound, a faint *peep-peep-peep*, and smelled something sweet and rotten on the air.

Sais ran into the chamber, brandishing his crossbow. Einon and Urien did not move.

She could not leave Sais to face the threat alone. After a moment's hesitation she charged in after him.

She found herself in another large, round room. But unlike the testing chamber, the ceiling here was not much higher than in a normal room, giving the place an oppressive air. The room was dominated by a half-circle of odd-looking black objects, like great boxes with bulging tops and glowing lights on the end, large enough for a person to lie in. These strange boxes were arranged on a circular platform in the middle of the room. From the very centre, a thin column of silver disappeared into darkness – the Edefyn Arian. The boxes must go all the way around the base of the Silver Thread. There had to be fifty of them on the platform in all.

Sais was chasing an orange-robed figure round the far side of the ring of boxes.

Kerin skidded to a halt, and looked around for the remaining Escori. He stood further round the wall, beside a panel like the one outside the door. The section of wall above it was smooth and covered in a complex pattern of lights of many colours. He had one hand raised to touch the lights, though he was looking at her. A moment later Einon and Urien ran through the door. Urien looked grave, Einon wild-eyed.

As soon as they had entered the chamber, the door slid shut again. Kerin thought of a hunter's trap, catching a fox.

The Escori by the wall drew back his hand at the same time as Einon raised his crossbow.

Urien's shout – 'No!' – rung out as the Escori slammed his fist into the lights.

A moment later, he screamed and fell over.

'Einon!' bellowed Urien.

'I'm, ah, I'm sorry, Escori! I panicked!'

Kerin ran over to the fallen man. The hand he had smashed the lights with had tiny pieces of coloured glass embedded in it, and bled freely. His other hand was wrapped around the crossbow bolt sticking out of his thigh. From the look of the blood pumping through his clenched fingers, this was a far more serious wound. Kerin knelt next to him. He blinked up at her, confused. 'Who?' he muttered.

'Lie still. I can help you.' She got her knife out and started ripping into the hem of her skirt. She had to slow the blood-flow or the man would die.

'What have you done, Sefion?'

Kerin looked up to see Urien standing over them, his face showing a mixture of pity and horror.

Her patient blinked and focused on the standing Escori. 'Made sure you receive Her judgment,' he whispered hoarsely.

Kerin managed to tear a strip from her skirt. Coloured threads, the remains of her embroidery, hung from the fabric. It would have to do. She started to ease it under Escori Sefion's leg. 'Who—?' he murmured again, staring at her.

'Let her tend you,' said Urien softly. Kerin suspected he knew, as she did, that this man was most likely doomed. She began to form a prayer to Turiach, then stopped. Somewhere in all the wild talk and the ritual and the fear, she had lost her faith. Maybe it was when Sais confirmed that her son was being taken from her to serve others' terrible schemes, or the way she saw apparent miracles controlled by a mortal's touch; perhaps the last straw was seeing Sais's easy mastery of the door puzzle. Whatever the cause, at some point, she had changed. She no longer believed her prayers would be answered.

Sefion looked back at Urien, though the fallen Escori's gaze had already clouded. He gave a laugh that turned into a cough. 'I have been true to the Skymothers,' he croaked. 'I do not fear death.'

Kerin tied the fabric off. The pool of red had already seeped out to wet her knees. The flow was slowing, though she suspected that had more to do with the Escori's failing heart than with her skill.

She looked up to see Sais approaching, preceded by the Escori of Medelwyr. Sais had his crossbow pointed at the other man. Einon had lowered his own weapon and stood, his face stricken, staring at Urien's back, as though waiting for his Escori to turn round and tell him what to do.

Kerin looked back at Sefion, whose eyes had closed. She had done all she could. She stood up and wiped off the worst of the blood on her tattered skirt. Urien, his lips pressed tight, made the circle over Sefion, then turned away. He strode towards Prysor, who looked less confident than his dying companion.

Sais, keeping an eye on the pair of them, began to move round towards Kerin.

His voice harsh, Urien asked, 'Where is Idwal?'

The other Escori flinched, then raised his chin. 'He is dead. As will you be when the Cariad returns.'

'Where is She now, then?'

Prysor looked away. 'Her Divinity awaits rebirth,' he said. 'She will return in glory, bringing the red rain, and all will be well.'

Kerin very much doubted that.

'Then why the deception?' asked Urien. 'Why have we been bowing down to a mortal woman for all these years? Why has the Beloved Daughter of Heaven not been reborn already?'

Sais reached Kerin. 'I need to look at those controls on the wall behind you,' he whispered.

She stood aside so he could get to the smashed lights and now-dim panel.

'You should not question her will,' said Prysor. He sounded like he was on the verge of questioning it himself.

'I do not want too, but your actions – the three of you – have forced me to do so!' said Urien. 'Tell me what is really going on.'

'I – all right. The time is near: you can do nothing to change what happens now, so you may as well know the truth,' said Prysor. 'It happened nearly six years ago. We had not seen her Divinity for some days. Eventually we crossed the chasm in the testing hall. We had to get guards to bring planks, as we knew nothing of how the Cariad had made the bridge appear. We found her in her bed, as though she slept. But we could not wake her. She was dead. At that moment I felt – I felt as though Creation had been swallowed by the Abyss. For the Escori of Carunwyd, that was the end. His heart had always been weak and it gave out, then and there.'

'Why did you not tell us this, me and Idwal!' said Urien.

Above her, Sais was muttering to himself. Suddenly he darted away, towards the door.

'Because she forbade it – even in death her will lives on. When we saw her lying there, we felt the world change around us, like a door opening in our minds. We knew this was not the end, merely part of the cycle of the Cariad's existence. Knowledge only she had held before flooded into us, as though part of her entered our souls, to be kept until her rebirth; which, we now knew, would come when the winnowing times returned. It was our sacred duty to keep the secret until then. We selected a woman we thought would be a good substitute until her Divinity's rebirth. We did not choose wisely, as she has been … difficult. No matter, all will be well when the Cariad returns.'

'So we must hope,' murmured Urien.

Sais, over at the door, suddenly said, 'Shit!'

Everyone turned to look at him.

'I think we're locked in,' he announced. He nodded at Prysor. 'Unless you're registered on this palmlock.'

Prysor looked down his nose at Sais then turned and addressed

Urien. 'I have no idea what this peasant is talking about,' he said.

Urien said, '*Are* we locked in? Did Sefion somehow stop the operation of the door?'

Prysor looked uncomfortable. 'The means to open the door from inside is somewhat more complicated than the simple puzzle that allows entry. Sefion has destroyed that mechanism.'

'This can unlock it too.' Sais pointed at another panel, small and plain, about the size of a hand. 'For the right person.'

'Can it?' Urien asked Prysor.

'Touch it and see!' said Prysor.

Sais shook his head. 'Don't think so. I've seen these before. If there's no cell-match, then depending on how the security's set ... well, on the highest setting you only get one try.'

'Who is this madman, and what gibberish is he spouting?' muttered Prysor.

Sais said, 'So, Prysor, are you on the guest list?'

'I think,' said Urien, 'that my rather strange companion is asking whether your touch will open this door.'

Prysor shook his head. 'Only the hand of Heaven can open the way. And though I expect to be rewarded when the Cariad is reborn, your fates will not be so good.'

'Oh, great,' said Sais. 'Well, Prysor here already admitted to me that the carousel goes up automatically. He was expecting to hang around here for the day, praying and meditating while he waited for it to come back. Except now we're all locked in with him, and when the carousel comes back, it'll have the Cariad in it, and while she might want to reward him for his faithful service, I suspect he's right about her not being so pleased to see the rest of us.'

'Master Sais,' said Urien, 'though I find your speech most interesting, I am having some trouble working out what you mean. I do not know the word *automatically*. And what is this *carousel*?'

'Sorry, yeah, I was just— well, panicking, actually. "Automatically" means there's nothing any of us can do to stop it. And the "carousel" is that.' He pointed at the strange circle of boxes. 'The sacred ring that goes up the Silver Thread carrying all the Consorts.'

Kerin had not grasped all the conversation, though she knew that they were trapped and in trouble. But when Sais indicated the boxes, she remembered in a guilty rush why she was here. 'Is my son over there?' she said, speaking to Prysor, and pointing at the thing Sais had called the 'carousel'.

'Your son – the Consort? Aye.'

Kerin started to run towards the boxes. 'Which one is he in?' she shouted. Though they may be doomed, she would not let Damaru be used by their enemies. She would fight them with her son by her side.

'The two Consorts who were found worthy have only just entered the sacred sleep,' said Prysor stiffly.

'Where is he?' She was almost at the ring of boxes now. They were larger than she had thought. She could see no way of opening them.

'One of the chambers with amber lights. He will be in there.' Then she heard him add more quietly, 'Urien, can you not stop this woman?'

Behind her, the Escori of Frythil muttered, 'Prysor, I suspect very few forces in Creation can stop this woman.' She might have laughed, had she not been so worried.

Each box had a panel of clear glass set in the top. To see inside she had to climb on the box itself. A step had been provided for this very purpose. She looked in through the window, straining to see the figure within. The light was bad; she found herself squinting to make out details – and saw skin stretched tight over bones, wide-open eyes rotted in their sockets. The box contained a corpse.

She screamed.

CHAPTER THIRTY-FOUR

Sais looked up at Kerin's scream. 'What's wrong?' he called.

'I – there is a dead body in here!' said Kerin, backing away.

He went over to Kerin, watched by the three priests. He shouldn't have started using jargon with them, but after weeks of mud and wood and stone, the bright, clean lines of inset screens and comaboxes suddenly reminded him of the world he belonged in.

The puzzle to open the door to the Sanctaith Glan had been pathetically simple: a ten-digit keypad with a minus sign above it, and next to it a child's sum:

19 – 30 =

Even as he'd typed out '–11', he wondered at how easy this was. He should have known getting out would be harder – perhaps, now Sefion had smashed the lock, impossible. The idea of being locked in here when a vengeful Sidhe came down from orbit made his balls shrivel.

There was an alternative. It wasn't a full harvest – several of the comaboxes had dark telltales. But given the carousel would be unloaded into the hold of a Sidhe ship, hitching a ride in an empty box wouldn't be his first choice.

The comabox Kerin had looked into showed green telltales. The occupant was on ice until the Sidhe picked them up. The next three along had amber lights, indicating that the stasis cycle was underway. The boxes were an odd design, but used standard principles. He just needed to work out how to reverse the process.

'It's all right, Kerin,' he said, 'that's not Damaru. He's in one of the ones with the amber lights. I can get him out.'

'Of course, the Escori did say!' She checked the control panel on the end of the next box round, then stepped up to look in the observation window. ''Tis too dim! I cannot see who this is.'

The trio of priests had approached the carousel and now watched with a mixture of alarm and interest.

Sais called over to them, 'Prysor, which one of these boxes is the Consort from Dangwern in?'

'You must not ... you must not profane the sacred sleeping chambers!'

Sais resisted the temptation to retort *Or what?* Einon still held a loaded crossbow, even if he seemed to have forgotten it. He had no intention of letting any more innocents than necessary go up to the *Setting Sun*. He looked at Kerin and whispered, 'I'll wake them all.'

She nodded, though her gaze kept going back to the box with the body in.

Sais called, 'Prysor, did you know that one of the Consorts is dead?'

'That is not a Consort,' said Prysor defiantly.

'Then who is it?'

Prysor said nothing.

Beside him, Urien asked, 'Prysor, is that Idwal?'

Sais turned back to the control panel; as long as the priests were talking they wouldn't be shooting him in the back.

Prysor said, 'Idwal does not rest in sacred slumber! He defiled this place by his presence – as do these peasants!'

'So Idwal got in here?' asked Urien. 'He solved the puzzle, did he not?'

'Aye, though we later destroyed the blasphemous scribblings that gave him the knowledge to so do!' Prysor said, then added nastily, 'And I believe Sefion tried to cut off the forbidden knowledge at its source.'

Sais glanced over his shoulder to see Einon looking nauseous.

A soft ping made him turn back to the comabox. Assuming these boxes worked like those he was used to, he had just halted the stasis cycle. Next, he needed to reverse it. If he screwed up now, he could kill the box's occupant. Despite the need to concentrate, he found himself listening to the priests.

'But what happened to Idwal?' asked Urien.

Prysor said, 'When we could not find him, we realised that he had managed to enter the Sanctaith Glan. We found him lying dead by the door, struck down by the vengeance of the Cariad.'

Sais was glad he hadn't tried to test the door security. Looked like he'd guessed right: having the wrong DNA was enough to fry you if you tried the palmlock. Idwal's body must have been in here a while: the place still smelled of death. He wondered in passing why the chamber had two independent unlocking mechanisms – a palmlock and the panel that Sefion had destroyed.

Behind him Prysor was saying '— burnt his body in the testing hall where no one would disturb the ceremony. Alden wanted to take him outside so his soul might be freed under the sky, but then we would have had to declare the death. Sefion said that was too much of a risk. The Cariad needs us to keep the Tyr stable until she returns, reborn.'

If only you knew, thought Sais. Under his nimble fingers, the amber light went off. *Got it.* Now the system should start bringing the occupant round.

'Then we return to the original question,' said Urien. From his tone it sounded like Urien's respect for his fellow Escori was long gone. 'Who is the dead body?'

Sais didn't hear the answer; Prysor pitched his voice too low. He stood up, ready to move onto the next box.

'Can I help?' whispered Kerin.

'I don't think so. Just stay close.'

He heard Einon exclaim, 'That cannot be!'

Before he started on the second box Sais called out, 'What can't be?'

The priests looked up at him. He didn't expect an answer, but Urien, looking startled, said, 'Prysor says that is the Cariad. The real one.' He turned to the other Escori. Sais bent down and got to work, keeping half an ear on the conversation.

Prysor sounded halfway between defiance and panic. 'Idwal had a light with him; he must have checked the sleeping chambers. On finding one contained the Cariad, he attempted to wake her, but he lacked our holy knowledge. He disrupted the processes that kept her uncorrupted. When we found what he had done we tried to undo the damage, but it was too late. She had – she had already begun to decay.'

'Like an earthly mortal,' said Urien, his voice thoughtful. 'I wonder: how will the Skymothers react to finding their Beloved child returned as a rotten corpse?'

'That thought has never left my mind!' Prysor wailed. 'Every prayer I have uttered since we found Idwal in here has begged for their forgiveness and understanding.'

Now Sais knew what he was doing, reversing the stasis was a lot easier. He moved round to the third and final box.

Prysor continued, 'We argued how this could be, the three of us. I think that was when Alden began to lose his hold on sense.'

'He had words with me, and though he did not lie, I knew much remained unsaid,' said Urien. 'So much pain could have been averted had you only confided in me!'

'We could not!'

'Sais?' whispered Kerin as he bent down.

'What is it?'

'The Escori said only two Consorts passed the final test. Why are there three boxes with amber lights?'

'Good point,' he said. 'Let's ask.' He finished the reset first. The Escorai traded criticisms and accusations while Einon looked on. Sais stood up and called out, 'Who's in the third box?'

The priests stopped arguing and looked over at him.

'You said only two Consorts passed the final test. So why three boxes?'

Urien stared at Prysor. 'It is Lillwen, is it not?'

Prysor nodded.

Poor cow: exploited for sex all her life, then forced to take part in the priest's deception, and now sent up to orbit to have her mind emptied by the Sidhe who was due to take over as Cariad.

He looked at Kerin. From her expression, she was thinking the same thing. Then her gaze sharpened, and she said quietly, 'I want to know it all. No matter how bad, I must know the full truth.'

Taken aback, Sais said, 'You mean – about the Sidhe?'

She nodded.

'You believe me then?'

Kerin gave a tight, mirthless smile. ''Tis as they say: Season a lie with the truth and t'will go down easier. These Sidhe told us lies with the truth in, and like cattle being driven to the slaughter, we believed them. They' – she nodded at the bickering priests – 'still do. I do not. Tell me everything.'

Where to start? 'Shit, Kerin, it's a long and twisted story. They've been around for thousands of years. And though they aren't divine they have got a bit of a god-complex. Goddess-complex rather. They're all female – that's one thing your religion has got right. I reckon there really were five of them originally, when they set themselves up as your gods.'

'And does Melltith exist?'

'Melltith? That's … the Adversary, isn't it? No, that's just … that's part of the lie: something to be frightened of so you'll love the Skymothers more.' Sais heard a faint noise. The alarm on the door had stopped when Sefion smashed the panel, so it couldn't be that.

'So, the Cursed One is no more than a story … Sais, can you hear something?'

'Yes, I can.' A deep thrumming was rising through the floor. Sais looked around and, for the first time, up. A circle the size of the carousel had been cut out of the ceiling and replaced with the heavily shielded cover the carousel slotted into for its journey up into orbit.

'It is time!' said Prysor. Sais looked over to see the priest drop to his knees.

'What is happening?' asked Kerin. 'What is that sound?'

Prysor had closed his eyes. Urien answered for him, 'The ascension is announced by a Heavenly song that grows to fill the Tyr.' Einon made to kneel too, until Urien put out a hand to stop him.

Sais said, 'I was afraid of that. How long do we have?'

'Less than the embrace of love, more than a dying breath.' Prysor spoke with fearful ecstasy.

'Very helpful,' muttered Sais.

Kerin turned to him. 'We must make them tell us which box Damaru is in. We have to get him out!'

'We can't. The boxes won't open until the process has been reversed.' He'd been assuming they had time to get Damaru, Lillwen and the other Consort out. He'd been assuming a lot of things. He realised he couldn't do it. He couldn't let Damaru go up to the Sidhe ship, and he couldn't just wait here until the Sidhe came for him. He stepped off the carousel.

Prysor began to pray. 'Blessed Mothers, search our hearts, and find us not wanting ...'

Urien started towards the carousel, calling Einon after him.

Kerin followed Sais around the outside of the array.

He found an unlit box and bent down. With the box powered down, it was just a matter of pressing a button. The lid clicked. He stood, and lifted the bottom of the lid. It rose easily, opening up towards the beanstalk like the petal of a flower.

'What are you doing?' asked Kerin.

'The only tech in here was that control panel Sefion smashed, so I'm not going to be able to send my message from here. Plus, I don't fancy hanging round waiting for the Sidhe to come down. So I'm going up.'

'You're *ascending*? But – you can't.'

'The empty box will just carry me up, it won't put me to sleep. When I get to the top I'll let myself out, try to find Damaru and – wait, Kerin!'

'If Damaru is going up, then so am I.' She ran to the next box and started to batter at the control panel with her palms.

'No! I'm likely to find a bunch of Sidhe up there. You've no idea what they're like—'

'Aye, so you will need help. Open this box for me. Please.' His own box shuddered under his hands.

'God's sake, woman! All right.' He came over and touched a button. The lid clicked and she pushed it up.

Sais went back to his box. He glimpsed Urien examining the panel on the box beyond Kerin's, Einon at his shoulder. The whole carousel began to shake. Sais called out to Kerin as they climbed in, 'Pull the lid down and make sure it clicks shut. You'll be in there for a while, probably a couple of hours. It'll get cold, and it'll be pitch dark, but you'll be fine. These things are designed to keep you safe. Just stay calm.'

'I will try.' She grasped the edge of the box.

'You won't feel like you're moving, but you'll know when we reach the top, because it'll get light again. At that point, you have to fill your mind with nonsense. Think of nursery rhymes, or stuff from the village. Don't think of me, or what's happened today. The Sidhe could pick up what you're thinking, and we mustn't let them know there're two of us.'

He heard Urien say, 'You swore you would obey without question: now keep your promise!'

Einon stood on the step of the open box, looking in. Urien stood behind him. As he watched, Einon half-climbed, half-fell in. Urien slammed the lid down and stepped back.

With a final shudder, the carousel started to lift.

'Close the lid now, Kerin!' called Sais.

He closed his own box, then flopped back on the pillow, dry-mouthed and sweat-moistened. He felt the initial motion of the lifting mechanism – then the cover clicked into place, everything went dark and all sensation of movement ceased as the drive cut in.

Well, he was committed now.

They both – all – were.

He drew a long slow breath. He needed a plan, ideally an exceptionally smart one. He reviewed what he knew. The *Setting Sun* was a large cargo-hauler with passenger capacity. It would dock with a transfer-station at the geo-sync point along the beanstalk. Given they left this place alone for decades, the Sidhe would want the set-up as low-maintenance as possible, so most likely the transfer-station was just a big pressurised room clamped around the beanstalk, with an irised airlock in the floor to admit the lifting carousel.

When he'd first spotted the *Setting Sun*, back before he knew it was a Sidhe ship, he'd estimated it would have a crew of six to ten, most likely an extended family, with additional space for up to a dozen passengers. The initial request for aid had come from a male pilot. The appearance of the nondescript, rather scruffy man had driven any thoughts of Sidhe influence out of Sais's mind, and the man's convincing air of panic had reeled him right in.

Even now the details of his imprisonment and interrogation remained mercifully vague. He was fairly sure he'd met two different Sidhe – he remembered how his main interrogator had summoned help to batter down the defences Nual had left in his head.

He'd seen a female mute – a wretched-looking creature minimally dressed in drab grey – in the distance when he'd first been led, his will slaved to his captor, through the ship to the holding cell. And – he cringed at the memory – one of the methods the Sidhe had tried to break his mind had been to fill him with lust until he had sex with a mute they'd pushed into his cell. They made him do this twice: the first time they had used a woman; later, when they had a handle on his sexuality, a man. He was pretty sure the female mute was the one who'd later freed him, and it occurred to him that his hesitant treatment of her under the Sidhe's compulsion might be one reason she'd let him out. Perhaps other Sidhe-glamoured men had used her less gently in the past.

The old myths claimed mutes were human slaves who'd had their voices, their minds and, some said, their souls stolen by the Sidhe. Certainly the two mutes he'd encountered hadn't spoken, and had reacted more like animals than people. In some ways they reminded him of Damaru. At that thought he felt an elusive idea flit through his subconscious. Something about the Consorts, the way the Cariad dealt with them. Then it was gone. He was too hyped up to chase it.

He had to hand it to the Sidhe; they had a clever set-up here on ... whatever the hell this world was called. Assuming it even had a name. They kept the population limited, and afraid, with a balance of promised reward and tangible threat. Periodically dumping a tailored retrovirus into the population didn't just sift the genetics of their subjects, it allowed the Sidhe to keep the Cariad under their thumb. Being marooned from your people and worshipped as a goddess could go to your head, and there must be a risk that the Sidhe who took on the role of Cariad might decide her personal cult mattered more than the Sidhe's grand plan. The Cariad had to ascend for the cure to the falling fire. In other words, each time they seeded the atmosphere with the pathogen, the returning Sidhe ship used a slightly different strain, so the current planetary ruler had to go up and get the cure. That would ensure she gave her report and handed over the latest batch of Consorts. If she didn't, the disease was probably programmed to mutate, maybe even keep infecting people until she didn't have any worshippers left. On the years when the Sidhe didn't visit, no doubt the carousel just went up and came down again. After all, the only people who knew whether the Consorts had been unloaded were the Cariad, or her conditioned Escorai.

Sidhe paranoia also explained why the door to the Sanctaith Glan had two locks. The key to the puzzle that opened the door was implanted in the Escorai's heads by the Cariad. The knowledge would be kept locked away unless she died in office, as had happened this time. In that case the Escorai were programmed to keep things ticking along down here until the replacement arrived. If the conditioned Escorai all died too, or if the Cariad disobeyed her sisters and went her own way, then they had an override. They could probably summon the carousel from orbit then come down via the Sanctaith Glan, descending like goddesses from Heaven without having to land a shuttle and panic the locals. The door was a failsafe: he'd bet it took the DNA of a living Sidhe to open it.

The bitches were certainly thorough. Cold as vacuum, but thorough. They planned carefully and they planned long-term.

His plan, such as it was, was to get himself unloaded onto the *Setting Sun* with all the other Consorts, then wait until things were quiet, spring the lid on his comabox, let Kerin out – he still wasn't sure about Einon – and sneak back to the *Judas Kiss*. Hopefully, now he had his mind back, he could unlock the controls – but even if he just managed to get the coms working, he could get a message out, which was the most important thing.

He'd probably had worse plans in his life. He just couldn't think of any right now.

CHAPTER THIRTY-FIVE

As Einon lay in the darkness, Urien's frantic words echoed around his head: *You must discover what lies at the top of the Edefyn Arian. I have to know the truth!*

But Einon already knew the answer: the Edefyn Arian led to Heaven, a route permitted only to Consorts – and apparently, the reborn Cariad. Urien must know that a mere priest could not make this journey – yet his Escori doubted, and had sent Einon like some messenger-boy to question the will of Heaven!

Already this day he had witnessed divine miracles: the bridge that sprang from the air to give passage over the chasm, the numbers that manifested upon the wall, this strange box that transported him to the sky. And already this day he had committed a mortal sin. He had shot Sefion, not in panic, but because that Escori had ordered his death. Einon shuddered at the memory of Sefion lying in a pool of blood, his life oozing out of him.

Surely the perpetrator of such an act should be damned to the Abyss ...

He shoved the crossbow to one side and raised his hands, pressing them against the lid of his prison. He found a recessed handle and tugged it, but nothing happened. Horror rose within him. What if he were in the Abyss now, a plaything for the Accursed One? What if he were already dead, forever separated from the grace of the Mothers by that one fatal mistake? This was unfair – he had done his best! Until his last foolish act of vengeance he had honoured the Skymothers and their precepts in all he did.

And his final choice – to disobey his Escori, or to follow him into blasphemy – had been an impossible one.

He hit the cold, hard barrier with his hands, once, twice, thrice, his blows reverberating around the tiny chamber.

'I tried,' he cried. 'I tried to do right. Have mercy on me: I served you as best I could!'

No answer came and he banged harder, the violent action becoming a compulsion, almost an act of devotion in itself. He shouted into the darkness, beseeching the Mothers to hear his prayer, to give him some sign, to show him he was not truly damned.

None came.

Eventually his arms grew tired and he dropped his hands onto his chest. His hoarse shouts subsided.

Kerin made herself breath slowly, taking comfort in the rhythm of the air rushing into and out of her body. She ran her hands over herself in the darkness, flinching when she felt the damp spots on her skirt – Sefion's blood. But it was still her body, even if it was confined in this strange box and on the way up to Heaven—

But there was no Heaven. Her breathing sped up. *If I die today, this is the end. There is nothing beyond death.*

Perhaps not – but even if that was true, Sais had survived this truth. And anyway, she had no intention of dying in this box, or up amongst the Sidhe. She had to save Damaru.

Though she knew in her soul it was futile, she tried to pray, but the words were meaningless sounds in the confining darkness. Sais had told her to use nursery rhymes to stop the Sidhe sensing the truth – but that was all her petitions to Heaven had ever been. Prayers she had spoken more times than she could remember, believing they would be heard – they were just empty words.

She had been deceived. Everyone she knew, save Sais himself, had been deceived. Their whole lives were lies, manipulated by heartless outsiders who cared nothing for the people they kept in ignorance, who stole their children for their own vile purposes—

She lost the last of her fear and found anger.

*

277

Sais didn't mean to fall asleep, but he'd had very little rest in the last two days, and he was in no immediate danger. His body over-rode his brain.

He awoke confused, in semi-darkness. His hand touched wood. Crossbow. As memory came crashing back he realised light was trickling through the observation window over his head. They must have reached the top of the beanstalk.

No need to panic: he would just lie here until the coast was clear, with his mind blank, not putting out any sort of mental signature. Just wait, thinking of nothing, until his chance came to get out. Stay calm. *Remember to breathe.*

He found himself squinting out of the observation window. He couldn't see much; this place wasn't very well-lit for a cargo-hold – but he wasn't in the ship's hold yet; he was still in the transfer-station, which probably didn't have its own lights. He needed to wait for them to unload the box onto the *Setting Sun*.

Except they wouldn't unload his box, would they?

Fuck it! His plan was a dud – he, Kerin and Einon were in *inactive* boxes. Why would the Sidhe bother to remove them from the carousel when they thought they were empty? On top of that – and this was ironic! – Kerin needn't have come at all; the journey up the beanstalk would have taken long enough that the boxes belonging to Damaru, Lillwen and the other Consort would be inactive as well!

Sais decided his only chance was to make his move after the Sidhe had replaced the full boxes with empty ones for the next crop, and before the carousel headed back down, ready to return to the Tyr at sunset on Sul Esgyniad.

He listened for external sounds, but these comaboxes would probably survive being dumped into vacuum; he wasn't surprised he couldn't hear anything outside. There was no reason for anyone to come close, so perhaps he could risk popping the lid. He pulled the emergency release, wincing at the deafening *click*. He kept hold of the handle, not letting the box open more than a crack. His ears popped as fresh, warm air flowed in through the gap round the lid. He tensed, murmuring nonsense, waiting for a Sidhe to wrench up the lid.

No one did. He heard noises, hard to identify at first: a clunk and a bang, then what might be footsteps. After a while the sounds died away.

Sais pushed the lid open. As he sat up he thought he heard the sound of running feet.

He was looking from the unlit transfer-station through open cargo-doors into a large and well-lit ship's hold. Comaboxes – presumably those with Consorts in – were laid out in a line across the centre of the hold. There were more stacked against the far wall.

Suddenly a figure darted into the light. Sais recognised that silhouette: Damaru. He must have opened his box at the top and freaked out. As Sais watched, the boy reached the line of unloaded comaboxes, hesitated for a moment, then broke to the left.

Sais jumped out of his box and ran forward on a surge of adrenalin. He skidded to a halt as another figure, a man in a short grey tunic, ran across the hold: one of the Sidhe's mutes, chasing Damaru. When Damaru reached the far end of the comabox wall he pelted round the corner, further into the cargo-hold, with the mute close on his heels.

Sais ran to the doors that separated the transfer-station from the hold. A moment later he heard a familiar screech; it looked like the mute had caught Damaru.

This wasn't how it was supposed to go! Sais estimated the wall of boxes was at least thirty metres long. He needed to sneak up and take out the mute, then somehow get Damaru under control and back to his box. Assuming there was only one mute—

'Do not damage the boy!'

Sais felt his heart jump and his bowels loosen. The voice came from directly in front of him. Though all he wanted to do was run and hide, he made himself look at the Sidhe. She was standing on the other side of the unloaded comaboxes, at the end nearest him. All he could see from here was the top of her head, dark hair drawn up in a high ponytail. She was walking slowly towards Damaru and the mute; it looked like she had no idea he was here.

Fear had conveniently emptied Sais's mind, and he held onto that void whilst willing his body to move. He dodged into the cargo-hold, then ran up to the end of the comabox wall and looked along it. The boxes were laid out in a double row, as he'd expected. He edged along the side of the first one, back pressed into it. There was a small gap, then he felt the second one. The pressure of the boxes on his back grounded him, became his reality. Somewhere in the back of his mind he was terrified, but that was a long way away, and he used every grain of willpower to keep that distance.

When he reached the end of the box he pivoted round the corner, crossbow raised, before he could think better of it.

The Sidhe was about ten metres away with her back to him.

Sais took aim on her head. He'd only get one chance—

The Sidhe turned, faster than anyone should be able to—

He fired—

Her hands flew up to her face and she fell over—

Out of the corner of his eye he saw two mutes, frozen in the act of moving a box from the row by the wall onto a grav-trolley. At the far end of the room, Damaru struggled with two more. He ignored them all and started towards the fallen Sidhe. If he hadn't killed her outright and she managed to summon her sister mentally, they were in deep shit.

She sprawled on the floor, one hand out-flung, the other splayed against her cheek. She wore a long-sleeved top and trousers, practical spacer clothes, but they didn't detract from her elegant, unearthly beauty. While he was still several paces away, she shuddered, then lay still again.

Was that a trick, to get him to approach close enough to catch him? Sais wondered. *Would she look up and – blam! – that was him screwed? Again ...*

She didn't move.

He crept closer.

His crossbow bolt had gone in just below her eye, shattering her cheekbone. The eye bulged obscenely, and her mouth was open in a silent scream. *Not so beautiful now, bitch.* Hopefully, she'd died at once and the shudder had just been a final spasm.

He looked up at sudden movement. Damaru had managed to shake off the male mute who'd been chasing him, though a female was still hanging onto his arm. The male looked at the Sidhe, at Sais, at the Sidhe again. Then he began to run towards the closed door next to the stacked boxes.

Sais yelled, 'Don't move! Everyone stay where you are!'

Mutes were said to be conditioned to obey; somewhat to Sais's surprise, they did. The one sprinting for the door slowed then stopped and all four of them looked at Sais expectantly. He brandished the unloaded crossbow at them, at a loss what to do next. Damaru scuttled away, back towards the darkened transfer-station.

Looking at the empty boxes gave Sais an idea and he said firmly, 'All of you: go over there and climb into those comaboxes.' He pointed to the boxes by the wall with his free hand. 'Quickly, now!'

They turned their calm, incurious faces in the direction Sais had pointed and walked towards the boxes.

Sais didn't think there was much Damaru could damage himself on in the transfer-station. As soon as he'd got the mutes safely locked away he'd let Kerin out to help the boy.

The first mute reached a box and stood at the foot of it. They probably had no more idea how to open them than Kerin had.

Sais ran over and bent down to open the box. He set it to put the occupant under as soon as the lid closed. He moved on to the next one, glancing over his shoulder at the closed door connecting the cargo-hold with the rest of the ship, expecting the other Sidhe to storm in at any moment and trash him with a thought.

Third box. He wished he had some way of knowing if the Sidhe had sent out a silent alarm before she died.

Fourth and last box. Actually, he did know: she hadn't. He could tell that because he was still alive.

He addressed the mutes: 'Now get in your boxes and pull the lids closed!' In other circumstances it might have been funny.

As soon as the last lid clicked shut he looked around for a light. The grav-trolley had a detachable torch. He grabbed it and ran back into the transfer-station. Good job he'd trained for all this running about with a couple of months' hard walking!

A snuffly whimper came from the floor: Damaru was huddled at the foot of an open box.

'Damaru, I'm going to get your mother, all right?' he said as calmly as he could manage. His voice echoed hollowly.

Kerin was in the box beside his. The next one along, Einon's, was ajar, the lid undone but still down. He could hear harsh breathing coming from it.

Kerin sat up as soon as he opened the lid. She was pale but lucid. 'Where is my son?' she asked immediately.

'He's fine, he's over there.' Sais shone the torch beam just above the boy's head. 'I don't think he's hurt, just scared.' He helped her out of her box.

Kerin smiled shakily at him before running over to comfort Damaru.

Sais was tempted to slam the lid back down on Einon's box and go check on Lillwen and the other Consort, who would both have woken up halfway to Heaven with no idea what was going on, but Einon still had the spare crossbow bolts, and Sais's only bolt was embedded in the head of the Sidhe on the floor. Which reminded him – it would be a bad idea if anyone came in and saw her lying there. He checked the door, but found no obvious lock. He fetched the grav-trolley and loaded the dead Sidhe onto it. Even as he cursed at the difficulty of manoeuvring the unwieldy body onto the trolley he felt a little embarrassed at the soul-shrivelling fear this inert lump of meat had once inspired in him. He steered the trolley round to their side of the full boxes, so that anyone coming through the door wouldn't immediately be confronted with the sight of a body.

Time to deal with Einon.

The noises from the priest's comabox sounded more urgent. 'Einon?' Sais called. 'I'm going to let you out. Everything's fine. There's no threat here. I'm opening the lid now.'

There was no answer, other than a catch in Einon's breath. Sais stood to one side, just in case, but as he opened the lid he could see

Einon lying quietly in the comabox, crossbow by his side. He had a fearful, haunted expression on his face.

'I heard voices,' he said shakily, 'and I saw a grey light, like the dawn. I found a mechanism, but I was unsure if I should come out.' He pointed upwards with a shaking, bloodied hand to indicate the emergency release. 'See? Tis quite ingenious, the way it opens. Such clever contraptions, these.'

'Yes,' said Sais carefully, 'yes they are.' Looked like something in Einon's head had snapped on the way up. Sais decided against asking him for the bolts. Now might not be the best time to remind the priest that he had a weapon close at hand. 'Einon, why don't you stay there? I'll be back in a minute.'

'I think I will. I have a great deal to think about. A very great deal,' he said.

Sais thought he could hear banging from one of the other closed boxes. Though he understood why the occupant might be hysterical, he wasn't sure he could deal with any more crazies right now. He shone the torch over at Kerin. She was crouching in front of Damaru, holding his hands in hers, talking to him.

'Kerin,' he called softly, 'is Damaru all right? Can you leave him for a moment and give me a hand here?'

'Aye,' she said. After murmuring something to Damaru, she came over. She gasped, noticing the dead Sidhe on the trolley for the first time, then looked at the box next to Sais. 'Is that Lillwen in there?' she asked.

'Either her or the other Consort. Will you try and calm whoever it is when I open the lid?' He popped the catch, and waited. There was another thud, then silence. He raised the lid fully and shone the torch inside. A woman in a black robe was lying with her hands wrapped around her head. She was muttering to herself.

'Lillwen?' said Kerin gently.

Lillwen started. From the look on her face, she was expecting something terrible; when she saw Kerin, her expression changed to one of uncertainty.

'Tis all right,' said Kerin. 'You are safe now.'

Well, not exactly, thought Sais. He watched Kerin help Lillwen sit up. The other woman was whispering, 'I am cold ... it was so dark, like the Abyss ... where is this place?' Kerin shushed her and stroked her hair.

No sound came from the box with the last Consort in. Sais shone the torch through the observation window. The boy looked half-asleep, blinking and struggling to focus; whether it was shock or the after-effects of the drugged drink Sais had no idea, but he set the box to cycle the lad back into stasis. He had enough screwed-up people to look after right now.

'Who is *that*?'

Sais turned to see Einon sitting up in his box, pointing at the dead Sidhe.

'She's—' He broke off when the torch beam caught Damaru fiddling with the controls at the foot of his comabox. 'I'll explain in a minute, all right?' he said hurriedly and went over to Damaru. 'Damaru, don't touch anything, *please*.' The boy was fascinated with the controls, and he gave no sign of having heard Sais. Still, provided he didn't climb inside, there wasn't much harm he could do – actually, Sais thought, climbing into a box and letting Sais put him to sleep again might not be such a bad idea. As soon as he had a moment he might see if he could persuade Damaru to do just that.

'Did you, ah, kill her?' Einon was still staring at the dead Sidhe, his head on one side.

He wondered how well Einon's priestly lie-detector was working right now. He'd better give him something like the truth. 'Yes, I did. She was going to kill us otherwise.'

'Because we should not be here,' whispered Einon.

'You're right, but not in the way you think. That woman is ... she's from the sky, but she isn't a goddess.'

'How do you, ah, how do you know that?'

'I know because I've met people like her before.'

'You are not from over the mountains, are you? You are from the sky, like her.'

'I'm from the sky, yes, but I'm not like her. Let's just say her people have a ... less friendly attitude to those below. If it helps,

think of it as a war in Heaven. She's on the side of, well, evil.'
Sais knew this was a pretty limp explanation, but he wasn't up to
anything more complex at the moment.

'Did her people build this place, and the Edefyn Arian?'

'Yep.'

'I, ah, I see.'

Sais wasn't sure he liked the priest's tone. 'Einon, they are *not*
people we want to meet. They will *kill* us if they find us here.'

From the stricken look on the priest's face that probably wasn't
the best thing to say either. Oh, to hell with it. 'Einon, just … just
stay in the box and chill out. Please.'

CHAPTER THIRTY-SIX

When Lillwen had calmed down a little, she asked, 'Are you the skyfool's mother?'

'Aye, my name is Kerin.'

Lillwen's eyes glittered in the twilight of the great room. 'Fychan – did he save her?' she asked urgently.

It took Kerin a moment to work out who Lillwen was talking about. 'You mean Anona?'

'Aye. Is she all right? Sefion told me Fychan had been arrested, but he would not tell me why, or what had become of him. Did he get her away first? '

'I believe so,' said Kerin, then added gently, 'Anona is your daughter, is she not?'

Lillwen nodded. 'They would not let me see my little girl after they made me take her Divinity's place. I had to stay in the Cariad's rooms, only go out for official functions. I thought about Anona all the time. Idwal managed to get some news, but we had to be careful. Every day I wondered what she was doing, how she was, whether she still hated me.'

'I am sure she did not,' murmured Kerin, appalled.

'She told me she did. It was bad enough that they would not let us keep our children, the ones the priests got on us. But while I was just a servant of the Tyr, I could see her sometimes – during star-season, at Sul Esgyniad, on her naming day. The family who adopted her let us have time together. But when the Escorai made me take the place of the Cariad, Sefion ordered me to go and tell her myself that it was the will of the Mothers that I never see her again. And I could not tell her why. She was so angry. She threw her favourite doll at me. I used to sleep with it under my pillow.'

Kerin remembered the poppet Fychan had said would convince Anona to leave. Through a tightness in her throat she said, 'She was a child then; she is a young woman now. She will have forgiven you.'

'I pray she has. But at least she is safe. They never said anything directly, the other Escorai, but I knew, I knew if I disobeyed them, then soldiers would come for her, hurt her, maybe … my life has not been good. I want hers to be better.'

Kerin put her arms around the other woman and embraced her. Into her shoulder Lillwen said, 'It is so good to be able to talk to someone. Since Idwal disappeared there has been no one, no one to talk to at all. The Escorai hate me. I sense it. They hate me because I am a fraud. But that is what they made me!' She pulled back. 'I am so scared.'

So am I, thought Kerin, but she said, 'All will be well. Sais – my husband – will save us.' *I hope.*

'No, no, there is nothing he can do. Nothing anyone can do. It is up to the Skymothers now. You see, I have ascended to get my reward for serving them. Only I have not served them well. Idwal, he was … the others had to honour my decision, because I announced it publicly, but his faith was weak. Not like an Escori should be. He questioned. And I kept things from the others. There was this wall, in my – in the Cariad's – rooms. Sometimes it lit up or made noises. One day, just before the winnowing times returned, I saw writing on it. I said nothing to them, because I wanted to have something only I knew.' Her voice dropped to a whisper. 'And Fychan … I needed a man. She made us that way, you know. The Cariad. After Idwal, once he was gone, the need burned inside me. Fychan looked so fine in that shirt. And I saw you there, so I knew the boy still had his mother, if it came to it. They could not refuse me, not when I asked in front of everyone. I have been so worried about Anona since Idwal disappeared. So I asked Fychan to help her. I am so glad she will be all right.' Something in her voice reminded Kerin of a cloth unravelling.

'You know, sometimes I think – I think if the Cariad can die, and a silly Putain like me can pretend to be her, then what if it is all lies, what if there is no reward, only darkness and death? What if everything we believe is an illusion …'

Kerin wished she had some word of reassurance for Lillwen, but all she could do was hold and comfort her.

Suddenly Lillwen's head lifted. 'Who is that?' she said, looking over Kerin's shoulder. 'And where are the rest of her clothes?'

Kerin whirled. A woman wearing a sleeveless grey top and no skirt stood at the end of the boxes in the lighted room, staring at the body that Kerin had been trying hard not to look at. No one else had noticed her. Kerin called, 'Sais!'

As Sais stood up, the woman turned and fled.

Sais swore and strode up to Einon. 'I'm sorry, but I need those crossbow bolts!'

'Why?' Einon sounded curious, a little affronted.

'Because if whoever that was raises the alarm, we're all going to die.'

Einon reached down and gave Sais the case of bolts. Sais thrust the light he was holding towards Einon. 'It's a torch, a bit like your flameless lantern. Take it. You'll feel better if you've got some light.'

He started towards the room beyond the great doors, calling back to Kerin, 'Stay here. Try to get everyone back in the boxes—'

'No.' The word left Kerin's lips before she could catch it. 'I am coming with you.'

'That's not a good idea.'

Damaru had always been her first priority, but she had to fight those who would hurt him – the evil ones who had been hurting generations of children. 'I have to,' she said. Then to Damaru, 'Damaru, love, stay here. I must go with Sais.' He looked up at his name, then went back to studying the box.

Sais waited for her at the entrance to the lighted room. There was an open door in the far wall and together they ran over to it. Once through, Sais pressed part of the wall and the door slid shut with a faint hiss, just as the one in the Sanctaith Glan had.

288

They found themselves halfway along a passage. The walls, floor and ceiling were all made of the same smooth grey stuff, and it was lit by a harsh white light, though Kerin could see no torches or globe-lamps. A faint, persistent hum hung on the edge of hearing. Though the air was warm enough, the bleak nature of the place made Kerin feel cold.

The doors along the passage were all closed. There was nothing to show where the naked woman had gone. Kerin looked to Sais.

'She's probably heading for the bridge – the ship's control room,' he said quietly. 'The quickest route there should be this way.' He turned right.

Kerin followed. 'Is she a Sidhe?' she whispered.

'No,' said Sais, cocking his crossbow and slotting in a bolt. 'She's a mute, one of their servants.'

'But we need to stop her before she reports us?' *Stop and kill her, though she is innocent.*

'Ideally.' Despite the urgency he did not run, but set off at a fast creep. 'But we don't want to run into a Sidhe unexpectedly.'

The corridor turned left. While Sais peered round the corner, Kerin got her knife out. 'All clear,' he whispered, then added, 'this might sound odd, but if we do meet a Sidhe we'll stand a better chance if we're not together.'

'You think we should split up?' As though she was not scared enough, sneaking through these stark, shining passages where every door might hide an enemy – now he was suggesting that she should do it alone!

'Not exactly, just leave a gap between us. That way the Sidhe won't be able to attack us both immediately: if she goes for one of us, it might give the other one a chance to fight back.'

'So you will go first?'

He grimaced at her. 'Only if you know how to use a crossbow.'

'Ah.' He was asking her to be the bait in his trap. 'If you think that is for the best …'

'Forget it. You're right. It's a stupid idea.'

'No, Sais, it makes sense. If having me walk ahead to attract our enemy's attention is necessary, I will do that.'

'No one can accuse you of not having balls – figuratively speaking,' he said with a faint laugh. 'All right. Off you go. I think we need to take the next left.'

Kerin crept up to the turning, breathing hard, and peered round. Nothing. She walked round the corner. There was a right turn off the passage up ahead. She looked back, waiting for Sais to tell her what to do now.

He did not come round the corner.

She thought she heard a faint sound, a sort of fast swish, like an expelled breath. She had heard a sound like that recently.

Then she heard another noise, this one louder. It sounded like a body hitting the floor.

She froze, her thoughts caught in terror like a fly in honey. She turned around. Not daring to breathe, willing her heart to be silent, she peered back round the corner.

The first sound had been a door, of course. It was still open, and a woman was standing next to it, her back to Kerin. She was dressed in a shirt and breeches. The shirt was half tucked in and her hair was messy, as though she had dressed hurriedly. Even so, Kerin felt the force of her presence. *Here was someone of importance.* Beyond her a scantily dressed woman – the mute – was bending over something on the floor.

Sais.

At once, Kerin's instinctive reverence for the clothed woman dissolved into anger, the same hot passion she had felt as she ascended. This was a Sidhe, and she had hurt her husband. More, she meant to hurt her son. More still: her people had been hurting Kerin's people for generations.

She wrapped both hands round the hilt of her knife, raised the blade above her head, then stepped forward, ready to plunge it into the Sidhe's back.

The Sidhe turned.

Kerin felt something try to pierce her mind, like an invisible blow behind the eyes. At the same moment her knife connected with the Sidhe's arm. Cloth ripped and Kerin felt the blade tear flesh.

Though she knew this creature could destroy her, Kerin was in the grip of righteous fury. They fell, the Sidhe toppling backwards, Kerin on top of her. By the time they hit the floor, the only thing Kerin was aware of was that this was an enemy she must destroy.

For my son. For my world.

She drew her arm back, stabbed again, and again. She felt the blade go deep into the Sidhe's chest and warmth erupted over her hands. She watched herself lift the bloody blade free one more time, saw it come down into the hollow of the Sidhe's neck, and as it did, so the life went out of those wondrous dark eyes.

Her breath coming in frantic gasps, Kerin half-crawled, half-fell off the Sidhe's body. She looked at Sais, who was kneeling up. He had twisted the arm of the mute behind her and pinned her to the floor.

He looked back at Kerin, then beyond her to what she had just done. 'What I said about the divorce?' he said. 'I'm not going to ask you do to *anything* you don't want to do – not ever!'

Kerin started to laugh, until she saw how her hands were red with blood, then the laugh cracked and before she could catch herself she spewed what little there had been in her stomach across the floor. She began to tremble.

She had just killed someone. *How could she have done that?*

Sais gave her a look of silent sympathy. He pulled the mute to her feet. The woman acted pliable, witless. Kerin watched her rather than look at the body.

Suddenly Kerin wanted to run back to the big room and just shut herself in the box that had brought her here, hide away, let someone else deal with these impossible horrors that looked like beautiful women.

But it was too late to go back now. She must finish what she came here to do. Sais wanted to escape and warn his friends, but she needed to save her world. She had to see this through.

Sais helped her stand. He pushed the mute through the door the Sidhe had emerged from, into what looked like a private room. The Sidhe must have been asleep when the servant found her. Though clean and large and luxurious, the room looked lived-in. The bed was unmade, clothes were thrown over a chair, and a dressing table displayed a mess of pots and coloured bottles, with a filmy green and silver scarf discarded over the stool. This was a normal place where someone lived, dressed, slept ... and would never sleep again, *because Kerin had killed her*. She pressed the back of her hand against her mouth and swallowed convulsively, then pulled her hand away again as the smell of blood filled her nostrils.

The mute watched silently as Sais swept the clothes off the chair. She let him tie her to it with the scarf. Her gaze was dull, uninterested.

Then Sais fetched Kerin some water. He made her drink it, and helped her to wash the worst of the blood off. Kerin found herself desperate to remember the Sidhe's face, because to have killed and be unable to recall her victim made the awful act even worse.

Sais's expression said that he understood Kerin did not want to talk about what she had done, that perhaps she never would.

'The Sidhe was sleeping, not on this "bridge",' she said when she had calmed down enough to consider what they should do next. 'Do we still need to go there?'

'Don't you want the cure for the falling fire?'

She had been wrong about Sais. He *did* want to help her. 'Aye. I do.'

'Then let's go get it.'

Finally, he understood: it all made sense! He had thought through everything, examining the facts as a seeker of knowledge should, and despite the distracting whimpers from the false Cariad, he had found the answer. His final sin had not damned him after all.

The Traditions did not lie: the Edefyn Arian *was* the path to Heaven. Yet the way was not just open to Consorts, and Heaven was not what he had thought.

Purged of all past illusions, and privileged above all other priests in having been granted the grace to enter this place, Einon saw the truth.

Heaven was not a place of omniscient, incomprehensible beings, merely – hah! *merely!* – a place of glorious wonders. Those who created these wonders were not divine, though they were as far above the priests who served them as priests were above dumb beasts. Miracles occurred here, yet they were miracles an intelligent man could comprehend.

Much of the creed Einon had lived his life by still remained true. Below, men ruled women: above, women had dominion over men. T'was ever so, and finding the true nature of Heaven did nothing to change the natural order.

Sais had admitted he came from the sky, and he had said his people opposed those who had built this place. Finally the man was honest with him – but only because he had no choice. Despite his one brave and noble act in saving Einon at Plas Aethnen, Sais was not the man Einon had hoped he was. He had withheld truths, spoken strange oaths and used forbidden metal. He called the sky-women evil; in truth, Sais was the evil one.

If only Einon had seen these things earlier! He should never have given Sais the crossbow bolts, but he had still been confused then, lost in fear and uncertainty. He felt stronger now.

He decided to climb out of his box. He was thirsty; perhaps there was something to drink here. He used the torch Sais had left him to shine a beam of pure white light around the dark room. This was a strange, barren place. Despite the room's great size there were no supports holding up the high roof. Once he was out of the box, he pointed the torch at the body he had seen earlier, the sky-woman Sais had murdered.

Someone screamed.

The false Cariad must have been watching him, and had seen the body when he illuminated it. He turned to shine the light in her face and in the moment before she threw her hands up, he knew her. He felt sure he had taken his pleasure of this one, back before she took the Cariad's place. The thought repelled him.

'Ah, shut up, you stupid whore!' he shouted.

The woman kept her hands in front of her face and wailed loudly. Her pathetic cries reverberated around the room.

Suddenly furious, Einon strode over to her and without pausing, hit her with the torch.

She fell back into the box.

In the sudden silence, Einon heard a gasp and shone the torch towards the sound. The skyfool had stood up and was backing away from him.

Einon grabbed the edge of Lillwen's box, feeling sick, but the moment passed and he pushed himself away from the ominously silent woman. He had been right to hit Lillwen. Rather than the helpless tool she appeared to be, might she not be a schemer who had colluded in this terrible deception? Had she not come to a position of great power while men stood by? For all he knew, *she* had been the one who had killed the true Cariad, then used her sky-cursed wiles on the Escorai. Certainly her influence had made the Escorai foolish. She had even taken one as a lover, the better to ensure her hold over him.

If he *had* killed her, it was no bad thing. She deserved it. But he could not bring himself to check, fearful of blood, and certainty.

And what of the real Cariad? He had to know the truth. He took the torch and looked in the few remaining boxes on the sacred ring. All save one were empty, and that contained a sleeping Consort. The true Cariad must be in one of the boxes in the lighted room beyond.

Einon did not let himself look at the body of the sky-woman on her strange floating bier as he passed.

The first five boxes Einon looked in contained sleeping boys. In the sixth, he found a decayed body dressed in black and silver finery. His eyes filled with tears and he looked up, trying to blink them clear. He had hoped – believed, *prayed* – that whatever else might be disproved this day, the Cariad – the real one – would be reborn as Escori Prysor had claimed. All these miracles were as nothing without this one hope.

His knees gave way and he fell to the floor. He tried to pray, but the words would not come. He pulled himself into a tight ball; his mind hung suspended between enlightenment and madness.

When he looked up next he thought Lillwen was not lying in her box after all.

The woman standing before him wore a black robe, as Lillwen had. Her hair was long and dark, like the deceiver's. But he realised there was nothing else in common between the two: this woman was the most beautiful, most perfect, most noble being he had ever seen.

He sat up.

His prayers had been answered after all. This was a true Daughter of Heaven, a magnificent, divine creature.

He looked into her eyes; they were a colour he had no name for. He felt a strange sensation tickling the back of his mind, and after an initial moment of disorientation the feeling spread and warmed, opening out like an arousal of the spirit. It was as though he had finally found the missing piece of his soul.

He let out a long, even sigh. Then he leaned forward, brought his hands in front of him and prostrated himself before her. Pressing his face into the chill, smooth floor, he breathed, 'I am yours.'

<I know.>

CHAPTER THIRTY-SEVEN

When they reached the junction for the command corridor Sais paused and looked around the corner. The airlocks at either end of the corridor both showed green telltales. The *Setting Sun* had little internal security – what need, on a ship run by telepathic domin-atrixes and staffed by mind-controlled slaves? One of the docked ships was his, so the other must be an atmosphere-capable shuttle.

'What is it?' asked Kerin. She'd been silent since leaving the Sidhe's bedroom.

Sais wondered how she was dealing with having just murdered a complete stranger. He wasn't sure how he felt about it himself, though he understood her anger.

'I'm just thinking,' he said. 'The Sidhe will have a smaller ship, which will have the cure for the falling fire on board. Someone needs to take the small ship down to your world and … let the cure out. Maybe I could do that, leaving you to get Damaru and the others back into the comaboxes before they go back down.'

'A good plan.' Kerin sounded relieved. Sais didn't blame her: in her position he'd want to be safely locked up in a nice secure box waiting to go home too.

'In theory, yes. Except, there's a couple of problems. Firstly, I don't know whether or not the process that sends the boxes back down is automated.'

'Automated?'

'Whether it happens by itself, rather than because the Sidhe make it happen. If they usually send it back, I'll need to work out how.'

'I am sure you will be able to do that.'

He admired her optimism, but he wasn't so sure. 'The other problem is the pilot – the man who controls this ship. He's probably on the bridge – that's behind the door in the next corridor – but he may come out when he realises something's wrong. Even if he stays put, he's likely to stop any ship that tries to leave – and that includes the one with the cure on board.' *Or mine.*

'Then we will have to deal with him.' Kerin made it sound so simple.

Leaving Kerin at the junction, Sais crept up towards the bridge door. He was surprised to find it had a lock. It looked like an iris-scanner: always a spacer's favourite, as they were designed to work with a suit on. He motioned for Kerin to stay back while he went in for a closer look.

As Sais sidled up, the door opened. He froze. It was possible it was set to open automatically when someone approached, but then, why the lock? No, someone had opened it – the pilot, presumably.

Staying to the side of the door, Sais pulled out a crossbow bolt and tossed it through.

The soft and deadly *phhhhssst* of a needle-pistol confirmed his suspicions.

From inside, a contemptuous male voice said, 'Gone native, Sirrah Reen?'

The pilot must have a camera covering the corridor. 'I've made the best of my situation, as you'll no doubt know if you're monitoring the ship,' he said. The pilot didn't rise to the bait and Sais continued, 'I don't think we were ever introduced.'

Laughter, almost a snigger. 'Oh, I know all about you. They share *everything* with me.'

Sais didn't have to ask who he meant by *they*. 'Lucky you. No, I meant I don't know your name.'

'You're assuming I have one.' That threw Sais, and the pilot, apparently beginning to enjoy himself, continued, 'I've used a few for convenience, but I don't need a name with my sweethearts. They know me and love me, and I provide indispensable services

297

for them. I have the life I want. How many men can say that, Sirrah Reen? Or do you mind if I call you Jarek? I feel I know you so well.'

Sais knew he was being wound up, but he still found himself considering the *indispensable services* this man provided to his Sidhe *sweethearts*. 'Call me whatever you want; I'll just call you pilot. Well, pilot, I've got some bad news for you. Your services are no longer required.'

The sound of an indrawn breath told Sais that the pilot didn't know his Sidhe *sweethearts* were dead.

'You're lying,' he said flatly. 'There's no way one man could defeat a Sidhe.'

Kerin was where he'd left her – outside the range of the camera – watching him carefully. 'You're right,' he said, 'I had help. Your surveillance isn't up to much, is it? You don't know your girl-friends are dead and you haven't spotted my friends.'

If the man did have cameras, he might check them now, but Sais heard no movement. When the pilot answered he sounded uncertain. 'Friends? I'd say that's extremely unlikely. I've no idea how you got up the beanstalk, but I do know you'd have no chance of persuading any of those pious pricks down there to come up with you.'

So he couldn't see Kerin. Good. 'Then you really should be a lot more frightened of me than you appear to be, given I just took out two Sidhe by myself.'

No reply. Sais wished he could see the man's face. Then he heard a sigh. *A relieved sigh*.

He'd been wrong in assuming there were only two Sidhe. Trying to keep his voice casual, he said, 'You still in there, pilot?'

'Yep, and I'll stay in here and you can stay out there, and we'll see how long your luck holds.'

Sais said evenly, 'Is there anything you'd like to share at this point?'

The pilot snorted a laugh. 'There is, actually: a bit of advice. Rather than staying out there, why don't you come in here, and

I'll do you the favour of killing you cleanly. Or you can turn that wooden toy weapon round and shoot yourself in the head.'

'And why would I want to do that?'

'Because if you've really killed two of the sisters, then when the third one finds you, she'll take your fucking mind apart – and this time she won't leave anything behind except the pain.'

Sais pushed himself off from the wall and sprinted back down the corridor. The pilot shouted after him, 'Or you can run, for all the good it'll do you.'

When he reached Kerin he motioned her to go back down the corridor ahead of him until they were out of earshot.

'So there is another one?' whispered Kerin, her face pale.

'Looks like it.'

'What is your plan?'

Good question. 'We still have to take out the pilot and get control of the bridge. We got lucky with the first two Sidhe, largely because we surprised them. We have to assume the third one knows there's a problem, even if she doesn't know the extent of it. Once we're on the bridge, we can lock her out and keep watch using the cameras – Sidhe powers are limited without line-of-sight. And the pilot's got a weapon that's way more effective than a crossbow or knife.'

'Is he alone on the bridge?'

'Reckon so. I suspect he doesn't play well with others. So at least we outnumber him.'

Sais had meant it as a joke, but Kerin took him seriously. 'Then I could act as a diversion!'

'What?'

'I could rush in there to distract him, then you come in with the crossbow and ... *incapacitate* him.'

'Kerin, this weapon I referred to, it's called a needle-pistol, and it fires a stream of metal slivers extremely fast. You won't have seen anything like it. It slices people up.'

'Then I must try not to get hit,' she said simply. 'What is the alternative? You said it yourself: we have been lucky; the only chance we have of killing the third Sidhe is to be in a position of strength, with a closed door and the best weapon. Either that or we keep skulking around until she finds us.'

'When you put it like that – all right. Let's do it.'

'Can I have one of your spare crossbow bolts?'

Sais handed a bolt over. Kerin took it, grasped her knife firmly, then nodded to show she was ready.

'I'll be right behind you,' he said.

Kerin turned and ran back round the corner into the command corridor. When she reached the door she flung the crossbow bolt in, then charged through after it, head down. Sais followed hard on her heels.

The pilot was standing to the side of the door, just as Sais expected. He was swivelling round, his gun tracking Kerin. Before Sais could react, Kerin cried out.

Sais made himself focus on his target. He fired.

The pilot looked surprised, and dropped his weapon. His mouth opened, but any sound he might have made was drowned out by Kerin's scream. He pressed his hands to his side and fell over.

Sais, still standing in the doorway, punched the door closed. He passed the pilot, writhing on the floor, kicked the needle-pistol out of reach, then carried on to Kerin. She was down too, and she wasn't screaming any more.

She held her arms tight across her chest. There was a lot of blood, but her eyes were open and they tracked him as he approached.

He crouched next to her. 'Kerin, Kerin, can you hear me?'

She nodded, her eyes wide, her lips pressed into a hard line.

'I need to see – where did he hit you?'

'Arm,' she croaked.

A survivable wound, thank God. 'Hold on there, Kerin. I'm going to get something to deal with it.'

'Help me … up,' she whispered

Sais hesitated, but she was the healer, even if she was the patient too. 'Are you sure?'

'Raise the wound … Need to slow the blood.'

As he lifted her into a sitting position he could see the extent of the wound. She had taken the flechette round in her right arm, and the needles had sliced the flesh to the bone along most of the length of the forearm. Though the wound was nasty and was bleeding freely, the damage was limited to that one area. Her face was pale and waxy-looking, but her eyes were bright. She cupped her elbow in her other hand and looked at him, around the room; anywhere except at the meaty mess of her arm.

Sais straightened and looked up. The place was more like the den of an oversexed adolescent than the bridge of a ship. Two or more cabins had been knocked into one, and the long room was softly lit. Space art, holos of glam-models and music posters covered most of the walls. The sleeping area sported an enormous round bed piled with black satin-covered pillows. There were stacks of entertainment and game units, and luxury foodstuffs were piled on a sideboard, some of them open and partially eaten. A drinks cabinet sat next to a sumptuous massage chair. One corner was more brightly lit and relatively free of decadence: the chair there faced screens and instruments, with the largest viewscreen showing an uninteresting if familiar stretch of corridor. Sais got Kerin to her feet and half-guided, half-carried her to the seat in front of the pilot's control console. The pilot watched them from the floor, breathing heavily through his mouth.

'Where's your med-kit?' Sais asked him.

For a moment he thought the man wouldn't answer, but he needed patching up as much as Kerin did, from the look of the blood seeping through his fingers. 'Under the console,' he muttered.

By the time Sais had found it Kerin's eyes were closed to slits and she had given up trying to support her wounded arm.

Sais gave her a shot to kill the shock and mask the pain. After a few seconds, her eyes opened.

'Are we safe?' she asked, looking around her.

'For now,' he said, rooting through the med-kit. 'But if you see anything change on that screen overhead you just let me know.'

'Screen? I am sorry, I do not know what you mean.'

'No, of course you wouldn't. It's— Do you see that picture there, of the corridor? It's showing what's outside the door here.'

301

'A picture?' Kerin frowned. 'Why would a picture change?'

'It's not so much a picture, more like a window – except it doesn't show what's directly behind it, but a scene from elsewhere; in this case, the corridor outside.'

'Aha! Is that how the man knew you were there?'

'Got it. I'm going to do something about your arm now. The wound's messy but you haven't lost too much blood.'

Kerin nodded, her eyes focused on the screen.

'Right, this, well, bag, goes over your arm. It's meant for fractures but it'll keep everything in place. Your arm will go numb once I pull the tab, so we'll need to rig up a sling. How are you feeling?'

'A little odd, but my arm no longer hurts.'

'Welcome to the miracle of modern medicine.'

'When you've finished there ...' the pilot sounded uncertain. And in pain.

'I'll get to you when I'm ready,' said Sais unsympathetically.

First, he needed to get the bridge locked down. Though they had nominal control of the ship now, there was still another Sidhe on the loose. They'd been lucky twice but he'd be willing to bet the last one – presumably the one scheduled to become the next Cariad and carry on centuries of corrupt theocracy – wouldn't be so easy to deal with.

CHAPTER THIRTY-EIGHT

While Sais worked at the panel in front of her chair, Kerin made herself watch the screen as he had asked. Now he had explained it, the idea of a window to elsewhere made sense, even if she had no idea how it worked. If anything, the chair was more disconcerting: it swivelled and, if she leant back too far, tipped. Damaru would love it, she thought.

Sais finished making his adjustments and went over to the pilot. Kerin heard the man mutter, 'Even if you somehow manage to kill her, you're still fucked, you know.'

'How so?' said Sais.

'The *Setting Sun* won't work without their touch.'

Kerin thought the medicine must have addled her mind, as this made no sense. Sais said, 'What are you talking about?'

'It's their ship. To start the engines, to shift, for any major function, it needs one of them.'

'You're joking.'

'I'm not.' The pilot shrugged. He sounded as though he did not care whether Sais believed him or not.

Sais swore under his breath, then said bitterly, 'So what do they let you do? Or are you just a driver and sex-toy?'

'Wouldn't expect you to understand ...' he muttered.

'No, because you know me so well, don't you? You know I'm not the most patient person, and you know I can be expedient.'

The pilot laughed. 'And I know you wouldn't torture a wounded man.'

Movement on the screen – had she imagined it? Best be sure. Kerin called out, 'Sais!'

He looked over and she pointed to the screen. 'I think I saw something, just there.'

As they watched, a figure appeared in the picture: Einon. He looked puzzled.

So was Kerin – what was he doing here? They had left him in the cargo-bay with Damaru. *Damaru.* Was there a problem?

'We have to let him in,' Kerin said urgently.

Sais said, 'I'm not so sure.'

'Something must have happened in the cargo-bay – Damaru was there!'

'All right. I'll open the door, but be careful.'

Einon had apparently given up; he walked out of the picture again.

Sais snatched up the pilot's weapon and came over to stand by Kerin. He pressed a button on the panel, then stood facing the door, needle-pistol in hand.

What little of the corridor they could see was empty. Then Einon peered round the door. When he saw them he said, 'Ah, there you are.'

Sais said, 'You were meant to stay in the cargo-bay.'

'Aye, but Damaru—'

She was right, Damaru was in trouble! 'What is it?' Kerin used her good arm to lever herself out of the seat and managed to stand. Her legs felt too long for her body, though the prospect of falling over did not worry her as much as it should.

'Kerin, wait—'

Einon was saying '—some sort of fit. He is shouting, asking for you.'

Out of the corner of her eye she saw the pilot getting up. 'Don't you move!' bellowed Sais, swinging the little silver weapon towards the other man.

Kerin started to stagger across the room. If Damaru was in trouble, she had to go to him.

Einon withdrew his head. She bounced off the doorframe and

followed him out. Sais was calling out to her again, something about not knowing how Einon had found them, but she wasn't paying attention.

Einon stood a little way up the corridor, beckoning to her. Kerin registered a dark shape near him, but all that mattered was staying upright long enough to follow the priest back to her son. She should not have let the desire for vengeance and foolish heroics get in the way of caring for Damaru. He had to be her first priority.

The change came without warning, swift and violent as lightning.

One moment, she was heading unsteadily after Einon, her head full of concern for her boy.

The next, she saw only the figure who stepped out into the centre of the corridor. The woman wore a long black robe. She had a cold, immortal beauty, with eyes as old as Creation. All thoughts left Kerin's head save awe and wonder at being in what must surely be a divine presence.

Beside the figure, she was vaguely aware of Einon dropping to his knees, his face twisted in rapture. The woman strode up and looked her full in the face.

Kerin felt, at that moment, the comfort her mother had given, the love she had herself given to the Skymothers, and the surety of knowing that all would be well, provided she obey without question.

At the same time, deep in her soul, far from the world-filling wonder of the radiant gaze, horror grew. The small part of her mind still her own screamed that this was a Sidhe, and she had been caught.

The Sidhe put a finger to Kerin's lips, a half-smile growing on her face. Behind the apparent humour Kerin sensed a deep, burning malice. The Sidhe broke eye contact and stepped back; Kerin found herself turning to face the open door to the bridge. Out of the corner of her eye she saw the Sidhe move behind her, hiding.

Sais ran through the door, crouched low, the pilot's weapon at the ready. Though Kerin already knew she would not be permitted to shout a warning, she still tried. Her throat was locked tight.

Sais stopped when he saw Kerin, started to open his mouth to speak—

—then jerked upright, a look of shock on his face.

The pilot ran unsteadily through the door and stumbled into him. Sais sprawled forward.

The pilot looked grey-faced, but despite this, he attacked with an animal ferocity; when Sais started to get up he brought both fists down onto his back. Sais collapsed.

The pilot looked up, past Kerin, and his face erupted into a huge smile. He stepped back from Sais and bent down to pick up the weapon Sais had dropped.

Sais rolled onto his side and got an elbow under him, then stopped as he realised the pilot was pointing the needle-pistol at him.

'Look at her,' said the pilot, his voice slurred yet full of suppressed anger. 'Look at her or I'll blow your fucking head off.'

Sais raised his head and turned it towards Kerin.

'No, not her,' the pilot said angrily.

Moving like a man who knows he is doomed, Sais let his gaze slide on to the Sidhe, who had moved out to stand next to Kerin. She could tell the moment he truly saw their adversary; he went rigid, his body frozen in place, his face slack as death.

The pilot glanced down at Sais, gave a quiet '*hhhmmph*', then kicked him hard in the ribs. Sais quivered at the impact, but made no other response. The pilot stepped over him, then walked slowly back up the passage towards Kerin and the Sidhe, who were standing side-by-side. He was obviously in some discomfort, yet he smiled so hard Kerin thought his face might crack.

He stopped in front of the Sidhe, head bowed, still smiling. Kerin found she could now turn enough to see them clearly: it was as though the Sidhe had become the centre of her world. The Sidhe reached out and touched the pilot's cheek. It was a gentle, sensuous touch. He raised his head and closed his eyes, leaning into her hand as though his very life flowed from her. Then he opened his eyes and looked up at his lover. Kerin could almost sense the silent communication passing between the two of them.

Finally the Sidhe nodded and the pilot dipped his head, stepped back, then walked up the corridor to where Einon knelt. Kerin tried to watch him, but she could turn her head so far and no more: she had to keep the Sidhe in the centre of her vision.

She saw the pilot extend an arm – the one holding his weapon – and heard a whistling hiss, short and sharp, followed at once by a thin spatter, as of someone throwing a beaker of water onto a stone floor. She did not recognise the strange strangled gurgle, but the damp thud that followed told her enough to fill in the details.

She heard the pilot mutter, 'That position was already taken, arsehole.'

Despite knowing that what she saw would be terrible, she tried once more to turn her head to look down the passage.

<You certainly are persistent. If it matters to you that much, then you may as well see what becomes of those we have no further use for.>

The gentle, commanding voice filled her mind, its presence a terrible intimacy. A moment later Kerin found her head turning fast enough to crick her neck.

The pilot stood over Einon's body. He must have shot the priest in the face: the front of Einon's head was a bloody mess, and much of the floor behind him was covered in blood.

Kerin had a sudden urge to vomit. The Sidhe must have stifled the reflex, as all that happened was a small dry retch. Even as the burning stench of her stomach juices rushed up the back of her nose Kerin found her head turning back, more slowly this time.

The Sidhe turned to face her, then stepped back against the opposite wall: from there she had a clear view of both Kerin and Sais. Kerin could now see Sais where he lay, though it was an uncomfortable stretch. The pilot walked in front of her on his way to stand beside his mistress.

Had she imagined it, or was there a momentary lessening of control when the pilot passed between her and the Sidhe? Could the medicine in her system be cushioning her against the horror? Maybe it would allow her to fight the Sidhe? Or was it something else?

Looking back at the Sidhe now, Kerin saw that she had turned to look at the pilot – for more silent words, no doubt. But it did seem that, for whatever reason, the Sidhe's control over Kerin lapsed a little when she concentrated on someone else. Perhaps she could use that in some way.

The Sidhe looked at her again. *<My servant asks that I give you to him – both of you, though I think he has different uses for you.>*

So, thought Kerin, is she talking in Sais's head too? Does that put a strain on her, to speak to us both?

<For myself, I want nothing more than to crush your soul. You have murdered my sisters, you who are not fit even to serve them.>

Suddenly Kerin wanted to flee and hide, anything to escape this hatred that burned colder than the sky in winter – but she could not even move.

The voice in Kerin's head softened; no longer the embodiment of unearthly vengeance, it was more like a song she was desperate to catch the melody of.

<But first we have work to do. I am sorry to say that you have caused me considerable inconvenience and pain.>

Even as, deep within herself, she looked for ways to escape, Kerin felt contrite and ashamed to have caused this amazing being any trouble.

<Just how much harm you have done remains to be ascertained. Naturally, you will tell me everything I wish to know.>

She was right, of course. This sky-woman was so majestic, her might assured ... and yet she was arrogant – there must be a weakness somewhere they could use!

The Sidhe cocked her head to look directly at Kerin.

<I think I already know the answer to one minor query. I believe your mother was – what do the peasants call it? – sky-cursed. You certainly have a strong will, to even consider you might have some way of defeating me.>

The fragment of Kerin's mind that remained free froze.

<No, you should try. Go on.>

Kerin felt the presence in her head uncoil and begin to withdraw.

As soon as the pressure was released she tried to assert her will. Maybe she could raise her hands, or look away—

Searing pain exploded throughout her body; every part of her burned in cold fire. The sensation was unbearable. If she could only concentrate enough to speak, she would beg for an end to the pain, even if that meant her death—

The agony was gone as quickly as it had come and she found herself held rigid. The very act of breathing was granted as a boon. The Sidhe was right. She was a goddess who must not – could not – be opposed.

<*I hope I will not have to teach that lesson twice.*>

'Maman?'

Kerin felt her head whip round. The Sidhe and the pilot looked towards the voice with the same unnatural speed.

Damaru walked into the corridor, just beyond Einon's body. He looked distraught.

Kerin felt her heart tear. She and Sais were lost, but her boy – surely not him too!

He took a step towards her and she strained to speak, to warn him, though she knew it was futile. Any moment now he would fall to the ground, or freeze, another victim of the Sidhe.

But he did not.

Kerin realised she could move her head again. When she looked at the Sidhe, the sky-woman was looking around, an expression of panic on her face. The Sidhe's gaze fell on the pilot, standing beside her, his smile gone in a look of confusion. For the first time the Sidhe spoke out loud, a far harsher and more uncertain sound than the voice in Kerin's head.

'Shoot it! Shoot it now!'

The pilot appeared to come to his senses. He took a step away from the wall and started to raise his weapon—

Everything stopped.

A heartbeat, drawn out to a lifetime ...

A flame flaring, then dying ...

The heart restarts, the fire is rekindled.

Kerin knew who she was, and a fraction of a thought later, where she was.

Everything was as it had been, except for the Sidhe. She was gone.

Kerin found she could move freely. She staggered up the corridor to Damaru, who was sitting on the floor, shaking and keening. There was something on the wall of the corridor beyond him, but that did not matter now. He had exercised his power and saved them.

She embraced Damaru with her good arm, laughing and crying all at once, and murmuring, 'My son, my child.'

Behind her, she could hear Sais shouting at the pilot. As she calmed down in the aftermath of Damaru's miracle, she wondered what it was that she had glimpsed up the corridor. She looked over Damaru's shoulder.

The wall had an imprint on it, a human figure in profile, arms outstretched. The imprint dripped red, and at the base of the wall was a pile of shattered bones, shredded flesh and mangled organs covered in streamers of black fabric.

With nothing left in her stomach, she was reduced to dry heaves of revulsion.

CHAPTER THIRTY-NINE

Ignoring the combined after-effects of the Sidhe's mental lock and the unreality of close contact with shiftspace, Sais made himself stand. The pilot was still facing away from him. The corridor swayed and dipped, and there was a roaring like the sea in his ears. His current state didn't allow for any clever attacks. He put both arms round the pilot's shoulders and pulled him backwards.

The pilot crumpled and Sais stepped back to let him fall. Then he bent down and swiped the gun from the man's limp hand, narrowly avoiding joining him on the floor as a wave of dizziness hit. 'Don't move,' he grunted.

The other man stared up at him blankly. Sais kicked him – gently, compared to the kicking the pilot had given him, which had bruised, if not broken, a rib – and said, 'On your front, hands behind your head.'

The pilot showed no sign of having heard him.

Further along the corridor, Kerin gasped, then gave a rasping retch. Sais looked up to see her on her hands and knees next to Damaru, who was sitting on the floor looking dazed. Although she was retching violently, neither of them appeared to be hurt. When he looked beyond her, he could see the reason for her reaction. So that was what had happened to the Sidhe. *Nice one, Damaru.*

'Are you all right?' he called.

She waved a hand to show she would be.

He turned his attention back to the pilot, who hadn't moved. 'Listen, you prick, I really don't have time for this,' he said.

'Then kill me,' murmured the pilot. With the last Sidhe gone, he'd lost the meaning of his life.

It was tempting, but he was too useful.

'No. Stand up,' said Sais. He took a deep breath and hauled the pilot to his feet, trying not to stagger. The pilot leaned against the wall.

'Kerin,' he called down the corridor, 'can you two walk?'

'Aye,' she called back shakily.

'Then we should get out of here.'

Kerin and Damaru stood, leaning on each other for support. The pilot started to slide down the wall. Sais rammed the needle-pistol into his guts, just below the crossbow wound. The man squealed and his vague gaze sharpened. 'We're leaving now,' said Sais. 'And you're coming with us.'

The pilot looked at Sais's feet and muttered, 'No.'

'The alternative is that I cause you a lot more pain, trash this place, then leave you locked in the cell they put me in.'

Though Sais wasn't sure he was capable of carrying out his threat, either emotionally or physically, the pilot must have thought he was. He levered himself away from the wall. Sais grabbed him by the scruff of the neck and pressed the gun into the small of his back.

The four of them limped back to the cargo-bay. Sais led them the long way round, to avoid the bodies.

Kerin went back into the transfer-station to check on Lillwen while Sais dragged the pilot up to the control panel and sat him on the floor at his feet, the needle-pistol against his neck. According to the countdown flashing on the screen they had just over an hour before the carousel was due to start its descent. And the pilot hadn't lied: the controls were locked out.

'Is this automated?' he asked the pilot.

'No. Why would it need to be? It's not like the set-up on the planet, with all those ignorant priests. We knew what we were doing.' He spoke with an odd mixture of disdain and despair.

'I suppose there's no point asking you whether there's a work-around on these controls?'

'Even if there was, I wouldn't tell you, you bastard.'

'Thought not.' Sais pulled the pilot upright. 'Then you're no further use to me.'

He felt the pilot tense – however upset the man might be about the death of his mistresses, he wanted to live. Good. Sais had no intention of killing him, but neither did he want him hanging around, potentially making trouble. He marched the pilot over to one of the empty comaboxes by the wall and shoved him in. As soon as the lid clicked shut, he started the stasis-cycle. That was one problem solved for the moment.

Kerin's cry was magnified by the transit-station acoustics. Sais ran towards the cargo-doors and called, 'Kerin? Are you all right?'

She had picked up the torch and was shining it into Lillwen's box. 'I am fine, but Lillwen is hurt.' Sais came over to find Lillwen lying unconscious in the box. There was blood on the headrest behind her and a large bruise was coming up on her forehead. 'I think – I think she banged her head,' said Kerin to Sais as he peered in. 'I am not sure what to do.'

'Me neither, but you're in no state to be treating anyone.' He had an idea. 'Listen, Kerin, we passed the med-bay on the way back here. I'm going to see if I can't do something more permanent about your arm, and maybe find something for Lillwen too.' And me, he thought. A numbing exhaustion had begun to creep up on him, and he knew he didn't dare give in to it. The Sidhe might be dead, but they weren't out of the woods yet.

The med-bay held good and bad news. The good news was that it was a top-of-the-range set-up, able to do pretty much anything short of resurrecting the long dead. The bad news was that, as the pilot has promised, it was control-locked, though he managed to make some of the minor functions work: he got all of them energy replacement drinks, and found Kerin another analgesic patch for when the meds wore off.

'You two should rest here – these beds are as comfortable as any,' he told her. *And they don't belong to people we've killed or incapacitated.* 'They've got condition-monitors on them, so if there's a problem they'll start beeping at you. If that happens, you need to ask Damaru to come and find me.' *Not that I can do much about it ...*

Kerin nodded and climbed gratefully onto one of the couches. Sais would have liked to do the same, but he still had work to do. Some serious stim would have helped, but that was also off-limits, thanks to the Sidhe's gene-lock.

Instead he explored the ship, finding out whether things really were as bad as he feared.

They were. Though he could dim lights, fire up the pilot's entertainments centre and fix himself a meal in the galley – which he did – every critical system was locked, including the docking clamps on the *Judas Kiss*, and on the Sidhe shuttle.

So, they had the cure – but he couldn't deploy it. They had the carousel – but he couldn't send it down. He had his ship – but he couldn't leave. He could enable local coms – the pilot would need free access to them to do his job – but there was no one within light-years, and the beevee system was locked down.

While he thought about where that left them now, he disposed of the bodies. He ended up losing his meal while trying to get the Cariad's remains out of the airlock, but he didn't want Kerin or Damaru to have to see that again.

It looked like the three of them would be spending the foreseeable future up here.

Parked and running on minimal power, the *Setting Sun* was more-or-less self-sufficient, so they'd have enough air, water and food to survive for years. Long before their supplies ran out, the Sidhe would wonder why their latest shipment of adolescent shift-space savants hadn't checked in. If they sent a ship, then the three of them were screwed. Most likely they'd call first – so would an incoming call unlock the beevee system? If so, perhaps he could get a message out—

Idiot! He was tired, not thinking straight. The *Judas Kiss*'s coms weren't gene-locked; even if he couldn't use his ship to leave, he could use its beevee, and once he'd got his message out to Elarn and Nual, he could maybe call for help. He had a few favours

314

owing, though unless he could find the beacon ID of this system, a physical rescue would not be an option.

He ran back to the *Judas Kiss* and sat at the console, working the familiar controls without thought—

—and without result. The manual lock-down was still in effect. That might be the pilot's doing, in which case the pilot would know how to take it off. He could wake him up and ask. At the thought of sleep, sweet sleep, he found himself yawning.

Before he did anything else, he needed to rest, but he'd better check on Kerin first.

When he got back to the med-bay he found Kerin sitting up, the couch locked into a semi-upright position. Damaru was standing at a monitor station, his hands splayed over the panel, a look of happy concentration on his face.

'You got the bed to work, at least.'

Kerin said, 'Aye. Damaru says there are devices here that can help me, but he does not know which ones I need. Do you?'

'Devices that can help ...' echoed Sais dumbly. 'I – well, yes, there's everything here from regeneration baths to a bone-moulding vat. But none of it's working.'

'Damaru says it is now.'

'What? Let me have a look.' He went over to Damaru and said, 'I need to get in here, please.' The boy looked up, a bright, faraway expression on his face. 'Damaru? I know how to use the devices that can help your mother, all right? But you need to let me find out what we've got.' The skyfool nodded and moved off, though he continued to watch Sais as he worked.

Sais ran a basic inventory and analysis program. Kerin was right: they had full control. 'This is amazing. What did you do, Damaru?'

The boy shrugged.

'Right. Never mind. It's working now, so let's make the most of it.'

He got Kerin over to the smaller gel-bath and took the dressing off. The bleeding had stopped, though the flesh hung in pale tatters around the open wound. Kerin stared at the ceiling and sucked air in sharply, but she didn't complain. He programmed the bath for a basic cleanse and stimulate; he didn't have the knowledge or time to set up a full muscular rebuild, but he could at least guarantee the wound would heal cleanly.

'You need to stay here with your arm in this tank of goo for at least four hours, ideally six or eight. The longer we give it the better chance it'll have of mending itself.'

'But the Edefyn Arian! It was due to return to the Tyr.'

'Shit, I forgot about that. It should have gone by now.' He had a sudden thought. 'I'll be back in a moment.'

He stumbled to the cargo-hold as fast as he could. What if, once the countdown completed, some systems came online again? He wasn't sure why that would happen, but he couldn't think of any other reason why the med-bay had suddenly started to co-operate.

When he reached the cargo-bay he found everything as he had left it, with the exception of the countdown, which was flashing on zero. He tried the carousel controls, but he was still locked out. It looked like they'd had their luck for the day. But why would the med-bay start working by itself?

He went back to see if they still had control there. Kerin and Damaru hadn't moved: she was reclining with her arm in the gel while he fiddled with a console. She raised herself on her good arm and asked, 'Has it gone?'

'The carousel? No. If was it was going to go by itself, it would have done so.'

Kerin fell back. 'When it does not return at sunset, people will panic, wondering if Heaven has abandoned them.'

'There's not much we can do about that.'

Sais took advantage of the med-bay's sudden unexplained co-operation and ran a portable diagnosis unit over his ribs. They were just bruised. Then he sorted himself something to keep him going for a bit longer.

As the stims cut in he felt the fog lift and found himself thinking clearly for the first time in hours. 'Kerin, when did it start working?'

'When did what start working?'

'Everything in here.'

'I – I am not sure. Damaru woke me up and said he had found devices that might make me better.'

'Found, how?'

'While he was playing with the buttons and switches here some of the lights came on.'

'He was *what*?'

'Playing. With the devices.'

'Holy shit. Kerin, can I borrow Damaru?'

'Borrow him?'

'I need him to try some of the other controls for me.'

'Feel free to ask him. He seems fascinated by this stuff.'

He certainly was. When Sais managed to get the boy's attention, he suggested that they go and find some other devices to play with. Damaru looked over at his mother, then at Sais. 'Other devices,' he said slowly. Then he grinned. 'Aye.'

Sais led him to the bridge first. Damaru took about twenty minutes to get everything working, from full coms to the docking overrides. It was all Sais could do to stop him from firing up the engines.

While he watched the boy's hands fly over the console, his vision blurred as exhaustion fought the wake-up shot he'd given himself. He wondered if he was imagining this. No, he wasn't.

Damaru only agreed to leave the bridge controls alone when Sais promised he would find him more devices he could investigate after they'd been back to see his mother.

'Is everything all right?' asked Kerin when he returned. The colour was already coming back into her cheeks.

'I think it will be. Your son, he's – well, the technical term is "machine empath".'

'What does that mean?'

'It means he's a genius with technology.'

'Technology, like the devices in this place?'

'That's exactly right.'

'But I thought the pilot said only a Sidhe could make everything here work. Or did I remember that wrongly?'

'No, you remembered right, and that implies Damaru is Sidhe.'

'Do not be ridiculous! He is my son.'

'The lock on the controls is to do with what race you are. It takes either knowledge like mine or a talent like his to understand how the tech works, but the machines won't actually respond unless the person touching them is Sidhe.'

'You must be mistaken.'

'I don't think so. It makes sense: according to legend, the male Sidhe were machine empaths, but they had a monumental battle of the sexes with the females. As far as anyone knew, the women wiped them out. But it wasn't easy because Sidhe are meant to be partially immune to each others' powers; that's why the Cariad – the one Damaru killed – told the pilot to shoot him, rather than just turning him into a puppet like she did with you and me. She couldn't affect his mind. And that explains why the Cariad needs the guardians to come to the final test to look after the boys, and why she uses that helmet to get them onto the bridge; she can't control skyfools like she can everyone else.'

He could see Kerin was having problems with this, and he didn't blame her. Damaru had gone back to examining the med-bay tech. 'Damaru?' she said softly. He looked up again, mildly annoyed to be distracted, then seeing who it was, spared a smile for her. 'Damaru, do you remember the woman who you put in the wall?'

He frowned, then said, 'I wanted to make her leave. The wall got in the way.'

'Aye, so it did. Did she – did she try and hurt you?'

'She tried to grasp my pattern. I did not let her. She was hurting you. So I made her go away.' He stated it like it was the most obvious thing in the world. Kerin still looked unconvinced.

'Kerin, it makes sense,' said Sais. 'Sky-cursed women, like your mother, they have Sidhe-type powers – nothing so extreme, but the same sort of thing. Even the priests, the way they can spot lies: that's a Sidhe trait.'

'You are saying that I am Sidhe? That all of my people are?'

'There's a hell of a lot of misinformation out there about the Sidhe — dozens of theories, hundreds of stories. Some people believe the Sidhe weren't a different race at all, that they were humans who were changed somehow, and that they didn't always breed true — Sidhe sometimes had human children. In theory, I suppose it could happen the other way around. In some ways it's a bit like the upland cattle and the dales ones: they're very different animals, but they're all cows.'

'Cattle do not build devices they alone can use. Or steal the will of other cattle!'

'That's very true. Listen, Kerin, if it makes you feel any better, this is pretty hard for me too. Where I come from, people see the Sidhe as wicked alien monsters, so to find they're most probably mutated humans is a bit of a shock.'

'Not as much of a shock as finding your son is one! I am sorry, Sais, but this is too much.'

'No shit! I'm amazed you're coping as well as you are. Maybe there's another explanation, but I can't think of one right now. Whatever the reason, the important thing is that we've got control of the ship.'

'Does that mean we can cure the falling fire?'

'Yep, just as soon as your arm's sorted. And when we've both had some sleep.'

'What about the carousel?'

'We'll send it back for dusk, just a day late. The truth has to come out eventually. This can be the first sign from Heaven.'

Kerin nodded slowly. 'Aye. And I need to think about what will happen when we go back down.'

I'll bet you do, thought Sais. He wondered whether he should remind her that the 'we' didn't include him. No, she knew that.

Kerin looked up at him, bright-eyed. 'Can we wake up the other Consorts?'

Sais hesitated. 'In theory, yes — but what would we do with them? You can hardly re-unite them with their families.'

'We cannot just leave them here!'

Sais felt a strange mixture of guilt and hope. 'They'll be fine,

Kerin, really. For now, leaving them asleep up here is the best plan. You can stay safely in stasis for years.'

'If you are sure ...'

'I think people back down below are going to have enough to deal with without a load of unexpected skyfools running around.'

'All right,' she said, though she still didn't sound entirely convinced.

He took the portable diagnosis unit out to Lillwen and found she had a serious concussion. Putting her back into stasis like that would be too risky, so he administered the drugs the unit recommended, enough to keep her out cold for the next day or so.

He also untied the mute they'd caught earlier and got her to help him load the empty boxes back onto the carousel, along with the four boxes with mutes in. He took the sleeping Consort off the carousel. That gave him thirty-seven in all. He had the mute get into an empty box.

He prepared a meal for them all in the ship's galley, then the three of them grabbed a few hours' much-needed sleep in the med-bay. Damaru would have preferred to keep playing with the tech, but Kerin, still immobilised in the gel-bath, persuaded him to rest for a while, and at last he curled up next to her bed.

When they awoke, Sais eased her arm out of the gel and put a light dressing on it. He found a bag and packed it with spare dressings and drugs.

As he handed it over, she nodded solemnly, and looked up at him. 'When the time comes for my people to rejoin the community of the sky, medicines such as this will be one of the first things we would wish to get.'

In that moment, Sais knew that all the shit they'd been through might be worth it; despite the mess they'd made just trying to survive, this could work.

CHAPTER FORTY

Kerin felt better for a few hours' sleep, and the pain in her arm had been reduced to a dull throb. But her mind was reeling: Sais was asking her to collude in manipulating the beliefs of everyone in the world ... but their beliefs were lies, and they deserved the truth. Whether they could handle it was another matter.

She accompanied Sais and Damaru back through the eerie humming corridors. When they passed the bridge there was no sign of yesterday's carnage, save perhaps a faint unpleasant smell in the air. She had to ask, 'What happened to Einon? To his body, I mean.'

'I put it outside the ship. The poor bastard wanted to see Heaven, and now he'll spend the rest of eternity floating round in it.'

Kerin nodded. For all his flaws, and despite his betrayal, she could not hate the priest.

Sais took them through a short passage to a long room with seats along the side and at the front. He told her this was another ship, though she was not sure how that could be.

Damaru rushed up to the controls at the front, but Kerin only had eyes for the view. The huge window – or was it a screen? – before them showed the top half of a great glowing globe, set against a dark background. The upper area was white, and froths and specs of white covered the lower part too. And there were so many other colours down there! Greens, yellows and a hundred shades of brown, forming random, intricate patterns.

'What is that?' breathed Kerin.

'That,' said Sais, 'is your world.'

'My ... world?' He had told her the world was a globe, but she had not imagined it could be so big, so bright, so full of detail. 'Tis beautiful.'

'Most places are, from space. Damaru, could you move over please? I think I'd better drive.'

She and Damaru sat on the seats at the side while Sais took control. Though she felt no movement, the picture changed. They seemed to be falling into it, and for a moment panic thrummed through her. But Sais remained calm, so all must be well. Kerin watched in wonder as the glowing land rose to fill the view and the darkness around it disappeared. Trying to make sense of what she saw, she asked, 'What are the white things?'

'Ice. Only the equatorial region – the bit in the middle of the globe – is warm enough to live in.'

'No, the little ones. They almost look like they are moving.'

'They are. They're clouds.'

'But they're so small!'

'We're still a long way up. We need to get down to just above them, then we can start spraying.'

'Spraying the red rain?' Kerin was unsure how big this ship was, but she doubted it was large enough to make rain over the whole land.

'We spray a substance that reacts with the water in the air and makes the red rain. You see those dark curving lines cutting through the land? They're rivers – the Glaslyn and the Afon Mawr. We need to concentrate near them.'

Sais pointed out other features – the bleached yellow-brown drylands, the watery fens that patterned the south like broken veins, the rich green lowlands and then, further west, the high-lands, which looked like crumpled cloth from up here. Kerin tried to work out where Dangwern was. She spotted a tawny circle that could be the grass plain, then all at once the view began to shimmer as though in a heat haze. Again, Sais appeared unconcerned, and a few minutes later the view cleared. They were now so low that the land appeared to roll out under them.

Sais said, 'We'll work our way west to east, to make sure we spray as much of the sky as possible, especially the uplands where the clouds form.'

'Did the Sidhe spray the falling fire over the land like this?'

'Yeah, they did. It was a good way of keeping your people scared and obedient.' He went on to explain the intricate, careful, vicious details of the Sidhe's scheme: how they created diseases and their cures; the way they replaced the Cariad when she aged or if she died in office: all this care, this *planning*, all this deliberate suffering, in order to breed people they could use – people who, if Sais was right, were of the same race as they were. Kerin felt an echo of the hot hatred that had driven her to kill the Sidhe on the ship. She did not fight it.

Watching the unreal view of the world seen from above, she asked, 'Will the Sidhe come back for the Consorts?'

'Eventually, yes, so you'll need to be ready. That reminds me, I've put the five mutes to sleep in the carousel, ready to go back down. Damaru knows how to work the boxes; when you get back you should maybe wake the mutes up. They're a bit like skyfools, though without the scary powers. They'll need looking after. You're good at that. There're a lot of people who are going to need looking after.'

Something in the way he spoke made her look over at him. Suddenly she knew, as surely as if she had her mother's abilities – the abilities of a Sidhe – what he meant.

They were flying over cloud now, and the land below was hidden in white. Kerin felt light-headed, as though she might float away. 'I ... Are you suggesting what I think you are?'

He gave her a lopsided smile, and nodded.

They came out of the cloud and the view jumped into focus. Here was a sight of wonder, a sight no one else had ever seen. *Her world.* 'Then you had better show me how this Sidhe technology works.'

'I'm not sure how much I can tell you in the time we've got, but we can cover the basics.'

The idea that pressing a button, touching a panel, or sliding a lever could have such a great effect – a single switch controlled the distribution of the spray that would cause the red rain, and so cure the falling fire – made her head spin at first, but once she accepted the idea, the apparently delicate devices made more sense, even if the full details were currently beyond her comprehension.

Finally, when she had taken in as much as she could, Sais took the flying ship higher so they could see more of the land. She was shocked to see part of the globe of the world sliced away by darkness. 'What is that?' she gasped.

'The terminator: the point where the globe turns away from the sun, so it gets dark.'

'So that is the shadow of night, advancing over the world?'

'Yep, and it's nothing to worry about – it happens every day. But it's probably our cue to get you and Damaru back to the carousel if you want to arrive at Dinas Emrys for nightfall.'

They persuaded Damaru into his box with relative ease, as he was as tired as either of them. Then it was Kerin's turn.

'So this is goodbye,' she said. She wanted to say a lot more, but her feelings for Sais were a small matter compared to the task she now faced.

'Not exactly. You can call me.'

'Call you? Oh, the coms, aye.'

'Told you you'd get the hang of it. If I don't hear from you, I'll call you this time tomorrow – the middle of the afternoon, your time. And if I don't get an answer, then I'm coming down to check you're all right.'

'But the carousel—'

'No, I'll come down in my ship, maybe land on the Tyr. Let Urien explain that one away.'

Kerin laughed, and threw her arms around him. He winced when she squeezed his bruised ribs, then clasped her in return.

'Good luck,' he said.

'And you.'

He held her a moment longer, then let go.

She climbed into her box. The lid closed, and she was alone.

Cocooned in the box, she considered what might await her below. Perhaps the Escorai were all dead. Poor Sefion would be for sure. The other two would have been locked in with his corpse. Or maybe Urien had managed to open the door and had taken control. No, Sais said there was no chance of that; the priest was not truly Sidhe. He had explained how the potential to produce a Sidhe child – a potential that she, or the priests, or any of her people, had – was not the same as ... How had he put it? *Having the trait fully expressed*. He had said that in some ways this was like the difference between Einon's map, which was drawn on paper and represented the world, and the view of the world itself that she and Damaru had now seen, laid out like a map before them, but real, not just a representation of what *might* be.

She wondered what Urien must be thinking right now. He would know the truth soon enough. She hoped he could take it. If he did not believe her, or if he could not accept what she had to say, then all was lost. The lie would continue. Even if Sais did come down to save her, it might not be enough. Urien might have her and Damaru killed before he arrived—

Eventually her mind would let her worry no more and she fell into a fitful doze.

The slight jolt at the bottom awoke her at once. She panicked for a moment, then counted her breaths to calm herself. One – two – three ...

She opened her box as Sais had shown her and sat up. Prysor had abased himself on the floor before the carousel. Urien stood behind him. The Escori dropped to one knee as she emerged, though he looked uncertain. She climbed out. The next box along remained closed; Damaru, exhausted and with no worries to distract him, had almost certainly fallen into a deep sleep.

As she stepped off the carousel Urien's eyes widened. 'Kerin am Dangwern?' he croaked.

An understandable reaction. She must be an odd sight, in a black robe that Sais had found in one of the Sidhe's rooms, and with a bandaged arm. 'Aye,' she said, 'tis me.'

The Escori opened his mouth, then closed it. 'But ... what? How?' he said, his voice barely audible.

Kerin walked over to him. As she passed Prysor, the other Escori raised his head briefly, then lowered it again and began to mutter slurred prayers. She handed Urien a clear container made of a substance whose name Sais had probably told her.

To his credit Urien took the strange item without flinching, though he looked dumbstruck.

'It has water in it,' she said. 'You have been in here for almost two full days. You must be thirsty.'

He nodded, then uncapped the container and drank half of it. He put the rest down next to Prysor. 'His mind is broken,' he said, indicating the prostrate Escori. 'And Sefion is dead.' Then, his voice stronger, he added. 'What has happened that you return alone from Heaven?'

Kerin looked him in the eye. 'There is no Heaven. It is as I said: we have been lied to.'

Urien stared back, doubt and confusion in his eyes. Finally he nodded and said, 'Tell me. Tell me everything.'

Kerin did. She answered his many questions as honestly and fully as she could. She let him take the lead with his queries, as that seemed the best way to pass on this strange and terrible knowledge.

Finally he said, 'I think I understand, though tis hard medicine to swallow. I have always sought knowledge, but I never dreamed of this terrible truth.' He paused, then added, 'Surely these sky-people – either the Sidhe or Sais's own folk – will come here now the plan of the Sidhe is foiled?'

'Only if we let them.'

'*Only if we let them*? Kerin, you are a woman of rare perception, but have you forgotten that we are trapped within this strange room of Sais's 'technology'? We cannot save ourselves, let alone help our world!'

For the first time in some while, Kerin felt a smile tugging at her face. 'We are not as powerless as you think,' she said. 'Sais told me much of technology, and you yourself have used it, in controlling the bridge in the testing room.'

'That may be so, but we are still trapped!'

'No, we are not. Wait here.' She went back to the carousel. Urien, looking uncertain, stayed where he was. She went up to Damaru's box. 'The Sidhe have power over these devices, even those we cannot operate ourselves. And not only the Sidhe.' She was still not sure how she felt about Sais's claim that Damaru was Sidhe. For now, all that mattered was the result. She woke Damaru gently while Urien looked on. Despite her bold words, she was trembling. This was the true final test. She told Damaru what he must do, then led him past Urien and up to the door. Urien trailed after her. Prysor remained on the floor.

At the door, she whispered to Damaru, 'Will you let us out now?'

Damaru looked at the door, frowned, then reached for the palmlock.

Kerin held her breath. *If Sais was wrong—*

The door slid open.

She heard Urien's expelled breath behind her. Ahead, the corridor was as they had left it. She turned to Urien.

'Do you have people in the Tyr you trust?'

He raised an eyebrow. 'Some,' he said.

'Then I suggest you might want to get them to help. Prysor should be ministered too, and Lillwen is also returned and in need of aid. In addition there are five sleepers who Damaru will wake. They are innocents, used by the Sidhe. It may be fitting that each Escorai is assigned one to care for.'

Urien's dubious expression had matured into stark disbelief. 'What Escorai? There is only myself and Prysor, and he has all but lost his mind.'

'There must be changes. I will need your help. The first task is to appoint new Escorai. Do you have candidates in mind?'

Urien looked at Kerin in amazement. Then a cold, canny smile crept onto his face. 'Do I take it,' he said slowly, 'that you yourself are laying claim to a position you believe to be vacant?'

Though her innards twisted, Kerin kept her expression composed and her voice even. 'I cannot see any alternative. Lillwen was only ever an unwilling tool. Of course, the Sidhe will return one day, and they will wish nothing more than to put one of their own back in place, and return us to the servitude and ignorance in which they have held our people for untold generations. Is that truly what you wish for our world?'

Urien shook his head, his expression dark. 'Of course not, but this is … absurd. You are hardly qualified to rule!'

'I have some knowledge of the devices here, and I know how the world works. My son understands the devices better than I, and, more importantly, he has the ability to make them work for us. You need this. Our people need this.'

'It is unthinkable.'

She spread her hands. 'Urien, please. I am no politician. I do not crave power – but it has been given to me. I will need good advice. I wish only to find the path that will save those I care for from further harm.'

Urien narrowed his eyes and looked at her long and hard, a gaze nearly as sharp as the Sidhe's, though without the malice. Then he said, 'You brought water from Heaven to quench the thirst of a stranger who may have been your enemy.'

'But one whom I hoped would be my ally,' she whispered, her voice beginning to fail.

'Aye,' said Urien. 'So you did.'

Kerin said nothing. There was no other argument she could use.

Finally Urien said, 'We should go. I believe we have much work ahead of us.' He moved aside to let her through first. 'After you, Divinity.'

CHAPTER FORTY-ONE

With Kerin safely on her way home, Sais went back to his ship. As he stepped on board the *Judas Kiss* he said to himself, 'My name is Jarek Reen, and this is my home.' He almost believed it now.

He slaved his com to the ship's so he wouldn't miss Kerin's call, then tried to call out, but he couldn't connect. There was no beevee reception in this system, which meant no active beacon – which meant he'd been taking an even bigger chance than he'd thought when he slipstreamed the Sidhe ship here. And finding this place again would be a bastard. He wondered how the Sidhe managed to travel here regularly if there really was no beacon to guide them out of shiftspace.

He set to plundering the *Setting Sun*. Before Damaru left he'd convinced the boy to unlock everything that could be unlocked, from the physical clamps holding his ship, to the virtual access blocks on the computer. His attempts to scan the ship's files soon ran up against encrypted or inaccessible data. Rather than risk scrambling the data irrevocably by trying to read or copy the files when he didn't have full system access, he physically pulled the entire memory-core. He'd worry about what he'd got later.

He did some physical pillaging too, stocking up on spares and supplies. He also took the comabox containing the unconscious pilot. It might have been more merciful to kill the man, but the pilot knew more about the Sidhe than any human he'd ever met, or was likely to meet. He planned to have a long, frank talk with the man at some point in the near future.

He was on the bridge of the Sidhe ship, having a last look

around, when the com beeped. About time too: he was beginning to worry.

Kerin, standing in front of a hanging of heavy red fabric, looked flushed and excited. 'Sais? Oh, I see you!'

'How's the brave new world? Everything all right?'

'Aye. Though I look forward to finding time to rest soon.'

'So the Escorai have accepted you as the Cariad?'

'There is only Urien – Sefion is dead and Prysor is insane. Urien reminds me of Arthen, back in the village. He listens to everything and misses nothing, but he says only what needs to be said. And he puts the good of his people first. Given his position, that means the good of all our people.'

'How about you? How're you dealing with being a goddess?'

'I am not a goddess, you know that!' She laughed, and Sais knew that she'd never fall pray to the temptations felt by the Sidhe Cariads. Then she looked sombre. 'As for what I should believe now ... as Urien says, just because malevolent beings pretended to be goddesses, that does not mean there is no divine power beyond our comprehension. It merely makes the seeker's job far harder. Too hard for some.'

Like Einon, thought Sais. He said, 'Urien's giving you good advice, Kerin. There are plenty of people who believe in some form of god, though thanks to the Sidhe, goddesses have rather gone out of fashion.'

'Do you?' Trust her to call his bluff.

'Do I believe in a god?' *Not any more*. 'No, but that's just me. I don't claim any special knowledge on the matter.'

She nodded as though satisfied, though she must have been hit hard by having her religion yanked out from under her. Then she said, 'Did you manage to contact your friends?'

Typical Kerin: dealing with an enormous hole left by her loss of faith, faced with an uncertain and difficult future, and she still thought of others first. 'I've had some trouble with the local beevee – the network that sends information between the stars. I'll have to wait until I leave this system to get my messages out. Which reminds me: I've found out the name of your world.'

'The name? Oh, yes, of course – if everyone out there called the globe they live on "the world" things would get very confusing, would they not?'

'They certainly would. The people who first came here called this system "Serenein".'

'Serenein. That is a word meaning "our star" – not much more original than "the world", I suppose.'

He laughed. 'Maybe not. So, you reckon you'll be all right, then? You don't need me to come down and scare the priests into behaving?'

'They are quite scared enough. Urien is doing a good job of reassuring them, but I need to be seen to be around.'

'How about Lillwen and Fychan?'

'Urien ordered that Fychan be released from the Tyr's dungeons. He will be given money and told never to return to the City. Lillwen is recovering. I hope she will one day be able to rebuild her life and find her daughter.'

'I guess you're stuck in the Tyr for good now.'

'I am not! I may have to appear as the Cariad when required, but once things have settled down I will be going out – with enough paint and powder I could pass as a Putain Glan – though that is one tradition I intend to put a stop to – and Damaru has already found pictures showing ways out of this place into the City that no one else knows about.'

That's my Kerin. 'How's Damaru coping?'

'He is as happy as I have ever seen him. He is showing me how the technology works, though he keeps getting annoyed because I am too slow for him; a bit of a change from the normal way of things! He is staying with me here – I'm in the Car— in my sleeping chamber, in case you had not worked it out.'

Sais was going to say that the ruler of the world shouldn't have to share a room with her son, until he remembered that for much of her life Kerin had been content sharing a one-room hut with him. 'But you're getting the hang of the tech?'

Kerin pulled a face. 'Slowly. Damaru has no such problems. Except' – she looked down – 'he is having trouble with the weapons in the sky. As you said, we need to have control of them if the Sidhe come back.'

They both knew it was *when*, not *if*. Sais had been afraid that this particular bit of tech might be a problem: the Sidhe wouldn't want the Cariad controlling the orbital weaponry in case she went native. 'I'm sure he'll work it out,' he said with more confidence than he felt.

She looked away for a moment. 'Urien is at the door. He gives me little peace! I should not complain – that he includes me in so many decisions means he trusts me. But there is so much to do!'

'No shit. You should go.'

'I should, aye. And you must let people know what has happened here.'

'That's the plan.' Part of the plan, anyway.

She hesitated, then said, 'Will you come back?'

Sais thought of the thirty-seven Consorts in stasis in the cargo-bay of the *Setting Sun*, every one of them capable of taking out a Sidhe. 'Rely on it.'

'Though you will not be "Sais" then. I suppose you are not now. I mean, the pilot called you by your real name.'

'Yeah, he did. Right now I'm sort of between names.'

'Well, you will always be Sais to me. Until we met again, Sais – farewell.'

'Goodbye, Kerin.'

It was only after he'd signed off that he remembered she was still technically his wife. He locked down the bridge controls as far as his inadequate DNA would allow, then walked through the darkened corridors back to his own ship.

Turn the page for a sneak preview
of the new novel from Jaine Fenn

GUARDIANS
OF PARADISE

Coming soon from Gollancz

PROLOGUE:

NERVES SHEATHED
IN SILVER

Above, golden sunlight sparkles off an azure sea. Down here, white light shines on clean, cold surfaces. The green-and-orange robes of the woman walking between the sealed tanks, monitoring stations and interface consoles are a splash of colour in the otherwise antiseptic lab. The hem of her robe has a subtle batik pattern on it picked out in white and midnight blue: a breaking wave against a starfield.

The same design appears as a logo on the breast pocket of the older man who walks beside her, though he's dressed in a white shirt and grey slacks. His skin is several shades lighter than hers, and has an unhealthy pallor due in part to spending too much time under artificial light. She has listened to what he has to say, and now she responds, 'So this last one is definitely viable?'

He nods. 'The transference is almost complete; I'll be starting the first test runs today. We have a ninety-seven-point-five per cent chance of a completely successful encoding.'

'Good. That'll give us twenty-eight from the original thirty-five.' She smiles mirthlessly. 'Five fewer than last time; good job it's a seller's market.'

'Will the buyers want to come down here? Last time, one of them did.' He shivers at the memory, decades-old but still enough to thrill and chill him in equal parts.

'So Mother said. Frankly, I have no idea. It's not like we can tell them what to do.'

'How about the new batch? Any word yet?'

'No.' Her reply doesn't invite further conversation and he draws back, expecting her to leave. Then she says, 'I've seen your latest test results.'

'Which tests?' he asks warily.

'Yours. Not the project's.'

'Oh.'

'You should have told me yourself.'

'Yes, I ... I probably should.'

'I'm sorry,' she says, and makes to put a hand out to him, withdrawing it when he flinches away.

'I need to get on,' he says, not looking at her. 'If that's all right.'

'Of course.' She walks back towards the elevator, leaving him alone in the lab.

He returns to his workstation, the only one active. He spreads his hands over the console's tactile interfaces, then blinks to coordinate his optical displays with the tank readouts. He feels a momentary disorientation as his consciousness enters a limited unity with the machinery and what is held within – a state few human minds can achieve. The sensation passes and his view of the featureless black oblong in its nest of wires and cables is overlaid with a familiar pattern in glowing silver: a central column emerging from a rough-edged oval, and a tracery of fine lines branching out from the column. The dark patches in the cortex are in the usual areas: memory, sensation, emotion, all functions now surplus to requirements.

His hands dance over the controls, programming the test. After forty years' experience he can almost do this in his sleep, but he still barely catches a nutrient-feed imbalance which, left unchecked, could disrupt the final transition.

The irony that his own brain is degenerating beyond science's ability to heal is not lost on him. He is determined to complete this last encoding before he succumbs, just as he has said he would.

Finally the parameters for the current test are set. He applies the stimulus slowly, with an instinctive feel for how much is required when. How much what, he is careful not to consider. Not only because this is where science shades into more arcane disciplines, but because then he would have to think about the reactions he is producing in human terms, and that would mean using words like distress and pain.

He makes the final adjustments.

The tank shimmers, as though straining at the edge of reality, then flickers out of existence. Almost before his dual sight registers the disappearance, the tank is back in the real world. By the time he's dealt with the brief backwash of nausea, his overlays are back online too.

He calls up the results. The test was flawless. He was being pessimistic when he said ninety-seven-plus per cent: it will be more like ninety-nine-plus.

He smiles, though with his own mortality catching up on him, he finds himself briefly thinking about what he's doing, and who he is doing it to.

As he has hundreds of times before, he reminds himself to take the long view. In effect, they are already dead before they arrive at his lab.

And what he does here, though unseen and uncelebrated, is essential to the human race. It is vital work.

Holy work.

ACKNOWLEDGEMENTS

Firstly, gratitude and love to Dave Weddell, who never tires of letting me bounce ideas off his brain, and whose own brain I never tire of. My thanks to the Tripod crit group: Jim Anderson, Mike Lewis and Alex Bell; and to Milford class of '07. Thanks also to beta-readers Vaughan Stranger, Emma O'Connell and James Cooke, who all provided different perspectives, and helped me get the distance I needed in the limited time I had. Thanks to fellow author John Meaney who hypnotised me in the cause of research, and who resisted the temptation to make me think I was a chicken (as far as I remember). And thanks, finally, to my editor Jo Fletcher, and agent John Jarrold who will, between them, make a proper pro of me yet.